His lips were hot, and his arms crushed her against his strong chest.

She had forgotten the potency of passion, but it came swarming over her senses, inundating her in a wave of sweetly remembered desire. A low moan echoed from her throat. Suddenly his lips grazed with rough tenderness across her cheek and whispered in her ear. "God, I have been wanting to do that forever! You have been feeling it, too, Beatrice. I knew I could not be mistaken."

She pinched her lips to firm their trembling and took a deep breath. "How dare you!" she said in a menacing whisper.

Southam made the horrible error of laughing. "What is this, a Cheltenham tragedy? I prefer—"

She lifted her hand and struck him full on the cheek with such force that he fell back a step. "How dare you barge your way into my room and force yourself on me!" she demanded, her voice firming.

He rubbed his cheek in confusion. "I thought you wanted it!"

BATH SCANDAL

Joan Smith

FAWCETT CREST • NEW YORK

A Fawcett Crest Book
Published by Ballantine Books
Copyright © 1991 by Joan Smith

Library of Congress Catalog Card Number: 91-91981

ISBN 0-449-21948-8

Manufactured in the United States of America

First Edition: October 1991

Chapter One

"You were aiming too high, to think Stuyvesant might be interested in Lady Gillian," Deborah said bluntly. The Honorable Miss Deborah Swann always spoke bluntly to nonroyals. It was a residue of her three years as lady-in-waiting to the royal princesses. When you daily consort with royalty, something will inevitably rub off. In Deborah's case what had worn off was a great air of condescension. She had returned to Alderton a year before. The royal princesses had dispensed with her services the minute their dear brother, the Prince of Wales, arranged sufficient income for them to get out from under Queen Charlotte's iron fist and set up their own establishment.

Miss Swann's consolation was that she "corresponded regularly" with the dear ladies still. This was partly true. She certainly scribbled letters off to them with awful frequency. Occasionally a short reply was received in return.

"A baron too high for the daughter of an earl?" Lord Southam demanded. "Gillie has ten thousand a year. He would do well to get her."

1

Deborah knew the traces of anger that lingered about his haughty visage were not directed at her. Southam was distraught on his sister's behalf. Half sister really, as she had to remind him upon occasion. By dint of repetition, Deborah had convinced him that it was time Gillian found a mate. In the small provincial society of Alderton inhabited by them, eligible *partis* were rare. In fact, Lord Stuyvesant was the only gentleman of a suitable rank for Lady Gillian. That he was a dasher of the first stare who considered Gillie a child was a little obstacle that must be overcome.

"Unfortunately Gillie has not the accomplishments to match her dowry," Deborah said. "You ought not to let her loiter about the stable, Southam. A lady is known by the company she keeps."

"Damme, she's out of the schoolroom. What is she to do with herself all day? She likes horses. Better the stable than peeling off to the village."

"Is there no relative in London you could send her to, to rub off the rough edges? Oh, I don't mean a *Season*." This was said with contempt. Deborah held strong views on the corrupting power of a London Season. "It is only March. Send her to town to smarten up her toilet and her manners. I shall arrange an introduction to the royal princesses, of course. Stuyvesant will come around, you'll see."

As well as ex-lady-in-waiting to the royal princesses, Miss Swann also wore the mantle of prophetess, due to her links with the biblical Deborah. Throw in a papa who was in Lord Liverpool's cabinet, though without portfolio, and you will understand that she was no ordinary lady.

"Could *you* not do something with her, Deborah?" Southam asked. It seemed a fitting job for his fiancée. Soon Deborah would be his wife, the mistress of Elmland, and in loco parentis to the girls. Their mama, Southam's stepmother, had died in childbirth some years before.

Effie and Alice were still in the schoolroom. They would be no problem, but Gillie, at seventeen, promised to be a thorn in his beloved's side. Gillie had taken a dislike to Miss Swann on sight, and the feeling deepened with every encounter. Were it not for Miss Swann's breeding and Southam's temper, their meetings would end in a cat fight. The more usual termination was for Gillie to be told to apologize to Miss Swann and go to her room.

"You forget, Southam, I have to look after Mama. Dear Princess Augusta still depends a good deal on me as well. I must answer her latest letter. She wants to begin a little garden, as her dear father would wish if he were in any state to realize what is going on. Farmer George he is still called, despite his unfortunate malady. The princess has asked my advice. And then there is Papa. A member of the cabinet, you know ..." Just what chores Miss Swann, situated deep in the country in Hampshire, rendered to her papa in London were not specified. "It would be easier if I were here every day," she added pensively.

"You *are* here every day—nearly," Southam pointed out. "You mean, if we were married? Why don't we get on with it, then?" There was more impatience than ardor in the question.

"As soon as Gillie is taken care of," Miss Swann replied firmly. "You and Effie and Alice will be quite enough for me to handle, dear. We shall get Gillie bounced off first; then we shall marry. Now, where can we send her? There is your Cousin Germaine, in London."

"Cousin Germaine is seventy years old! She could not begin to handle Gillie."

"What of your mother's sister, in Cambridge?"

"Aunt Eleanor is a widgeon. Besides, the town is full of rambunctious male students. We'd have a runaway match on our hands."

"Mrs. Searle, then, who married your Cousin Leonard. She is of the proper age."

"Beatrice Searle?" he asked, surprised. "I hardly know her. I only met her twice. At her wedding and at Leonard's funeral."

"She was at Miss Slimmer's seminary with me. Much older than I, of course! A Miss Watkins, she was. Only genteel—there is no noble blood in the family. She did very well for herself to nab Leonard Searle."

"Do you know her well enough to impose in this way?"

"She would be in alt to strengthen her connection to the Southams. It would give her a leg up in society to have Lady Gillian staying with her. You would be doing her a favor. And she is a good, firm lady, as I recall. She would not let Gillian run wild. Well, *Bath!* How much mischief could anyone get into in Bath?" she asked, in a rhetorical spirit.

"Is that where she went after Leonard's death?"

"That is where she was from. She returned home to Bath."

"I cannot think a few months in Bath will smarten Gillie up much."

"Nonsense! It is the very thing. If you send her to London, she will want a Season. Beatrice Watkins was always an elegant creature, as much as her pockets would allow. She is refined and genteel. She won't take any nonsense from Gillian. We can invite Mrs. Searle for a visit after we are married, to repay her."

"I'll discuss it with Gillie," Lord Southam decided.

"Do it, Southam," Miss Swann said. She did not

4

raise her voice. It was understood, at least by herself, that an ex-lady-in-waiting to the royal princesses would be obeyed. She rose and wound her shawl about her narrow shoulders.

Miss Swann was not beautiful, but she was accustomed to hear herself called elegant. Both her face and her figure were on the long, lean side. Her ash-blond hair was neatly but unostentatiously arranged. Her blue eyes were pale but by no means vacant. Certainly she was the most elegant lady in the small parish of Alderton. She had been twenty-seven years old upon her sudden release from royal duties a year before. She had returned home to a sick mother and an aging aunt. Marriage was the obvious solution. Her choices were limited to two: Lord Stuyvesant or the Earl of Southam. Southam's title was higher and his estate larger. She had decided to marry Lord Southam. Within a day of making her decision, she went to call at Elmland, using the pretext of an interest in ancient sermons. Elmland held a famous collection of these boring articles. She soon made Southam realize that his motherless house was in a shambles. It needed a mistress, and his sisters needed a mother. Until she got her offer, she was all smiles and affability. With the offer now tucked in her pocket, she could be less devious.

The engagement was now of six months duration. Lord Southam was much of a mind to get on with the wedding, but he knew that he must first find a husband for Gillie. She and Deborah could not rub along. A man of plain speaking and little guile himself, he found nothing reprehensible in Deborah's behavior. He knew she wanted to help, and if she occasionally annoyed him—well, it was only to be expected. His whole family knew he was an irascible, impatient sort of man.

Deborah came to plant a dutiful kiss on his cheek

5

before parting. Southam pulled her into his arms for a more satisfactory kiss. He found nothing amiss with her lukewarm response. Deborah was too much of a lady to let passion enter their relationship before marriage. He could wait.

That night he wrote the letter to Mrs. Searle, not because Deborah had told him to, but because he was at his wit's end with Gillie. She had failed to appear for dinner that evening. He found her in the kitchen three hours later, covered with filth, just returning from the stable, where she had assisted the groom in the breech birth of a colt. She discussed this unappetizing affair with gusto while she gobbled down her dinner. Yes, certainly the girl needed training. No local lady had ever succeeded with her. The stables were too convenient.

He went immediately to his office and wrote the letter. Oddly he had no difficulty remembering Mrs. Searle, though he had met her only twice. Her mother, Leonard said, had been Black Irish, and Beatrice had what he thought of as an Irish face. It was pale and oval, rimmed in raven hair. Her eyes were deep green laughing eyes when he had first met her at Leonard's wedding. Perhaps she was not outstandingly beautiful, but she had such charm and liveliness that she seemed beautiful to him. At the funeral service she had been subdued, but even in her grief she was still beautiful. It was a tragic affair, Leonard's death, and with no glory to enhance it. He had been killed in a hunting accident, which was, one felt, the way that sportsman was destined to meet his end.

All that was long ago, of course. Leonard had been dead for five years, and they'd been married five years before that. The woman, Bea they called her, would be older than Deborah now. She must be thirty-something. Odd she had never remarried. His mind softened by these reflections, he wrote a

6

tender letter, just touching on their former meetings and inquiring for her well-being. He phrased his request as a suggestion, nothing more, and apologized for the imposition of the suggestion. Naturally he would understand if her style of living precluded the presence of a young lady in her household. He just wished they might be closer. Perhaps she would like to come to Elmland and meet Gillie before making her decision? Odd Deborah had not thought of that; she was usually so correct.

Mrs. Searle was handed the post with her coffee two mornings later. She flipped through the letters, recognizing many of the writers by their hand or their stationery. Southam's franked letter caught her eye, and she opened it first. As she read through, a gentle smile played about her lips. Lord Southam—Leonard's noble cousin from Hampshire! Oh, yes, she certainly remembered *him*! He had given her a pearl necklace as a wedding gift. The grandest gift she received, and one she still treasured.

He was rather like Leonard in appearance. Tall, with that crow-black hair and a somewhat forbidding countenance, all hawk nose and square chin, but with a spark of mischief lurking beneath the severity. He had flirted with her a little. "Lucky Leonard!" he had said as he bent over her fingers. "Where does one find such beautiful ladies? I don't suppose you have any sisters?"

Shy of the title, she had blushed. "I'm afraid not, Lord Southam."

"I might have known you were unique."

Had he been a little bosky? Very likely. The wine had been flowing freely.

She read with interest that he was still a bachelor. Might this request be a ruse to look her over

7

and judge her mothering potential? Southam had a houseful of young sisters, if memory served.

What had Leonard said? "Raoul—they pronounce it Rawl, as the second Lady Southam was a Somerset lady, and had that drawl—has three half sisters. His own mama died when he was young. The papa remarried after several years—trying for another son, but he got a nurseryful of daughters. Old Southam was too ancient for such carrying on as marrying a young wife. He soon stuck his fork in the wall. Then the second wife upped and died, leaving Southam with a houseful of kiddies and no mother or father. But he'll soon remedy that. Rich as Croesus. Every lady in the parish will be throwing her bonnet at him."

Yet, after all this time, he was still a bachelor. She studied the letter for some time—there was no mention of the Honorable Miss Swann—and soon took her decision. A trip to Hampshire in late March held no allure. Let Southam bring this Gillie to her, and if she cared for him, then she might return with them later. Mrs. Searle was not the lady to marry for a title and estate. It was the man she was interested in, and she did not have to go to Hampshire to look over the man.

She had her reply sent off immediately after breakfast, along with replies to various invitations she had received. Mrs. Searle led an active social life in Bath. The post was rife with missives from Elmland for a week. Should Gillie be accompanied by her old governess, Miss Pittfield? Southam would not want to tie Mrs. Searle down entirely. Was there space in the household for Miss Pittfield, or would Mrs. Searle prefer to let her own woman handle the girl? A respectable widow of thirty years did not feel it necessary to hire a companion. She wrote back that there was plenty of space for Miss

Pittfield, and Gillie might be more comfortable with someone from home.

A day was set on for Gillie's arrival, the spare room was duly turned out, and a suitable feast prepared. During all the preparations, it was Lord Southam and not Lady Gillian who was uppermost in Mrs. Searle's mind. How would he look after all these years? Would he still think she was beautiful? She dressed with care in a becoming gown of deep green, to match her eyes. Her ebony hair was lifted from her brow, and fell in a bundle of curls behind. As she primped in front of her mirror, she thought that Lord Southam would not be disappointed in her appearance. He knew time had passed.

As twilight fell, the clatter of a carriage drawing to a halt in front of Mrs. Searle's house told her the guests had arrived. She took one last look around her elegant saloon, patted her hair, and prepared a welcoming face. The butler appeared at the door and announced, "Lady Gillian Foster and Miss Pittfield."

Mrs. Searle looked to the doorway, glanced over the ladies' shoulder for a glimpse of Lord Southam, and saw only vacant space. Then she looked at the ladies. Miss Pittfield wore the impoverished gentlewoman's regulation costume: a round bonnet and plain pelisse. She was fiftyish, tall, thin, and cross from the strain of travel. Next Mrs. Searle examined Lady Gillian.

The young lady, girl really, looked like a boy dressed up in a bonnet and gown. She was disheveled from travel, but even if her bonnet had not been askew, and her gown unwrinkled, she would still have lacked style. She was a squab of a girl, with undistinguished brown curls, dark brown eyes, a pug nose, and a determined chin. After perform-

9

ing a graceless curtsy, she gave tongue to an obviously rehearsed and unfelt speech.

"Lord Southam sends his regards. It is very kind of you to have me, ma'am. I appreciate it, and I'll try not to be any trouble." Then her face, tense with the effort of reciting, gave way to a trembling smile of hope. "Do you have any mounts, ma'am?"

"Mounts?" Mrs. Searle said, casting one last still-hopeful look to the doorway.

"Horses, to ride. Or even to drive," Lady Gillian added with diminishing interest.

"I ride, but I have only one mount. . . ."

"That's all right, then." The round face eased into a not unattractive grin. "Rawl will forward Penny for me. He didn't like to do it till we found out whether you ride. He'll pay for her upkeep, of course. I'll write him tonight and tell him."

"Gillian!" Miss Pittfield's sharp voice rapped out. "Mind your manners. The girl is horse-crazy, Mrs. Searle. Always was, always will be." She turned a sorry eye on her charge. "You look as if you'd walked all the way to Bath, missie. Where can I take her to tidy her up, ma'am?"

"The servants will show you to your rooms. I hope you will both join me for sherry before dinner. We shall dine at seven."

Mrs. Searle saw them up the stairs before returning to her saloon alone. She looked at the expensive bouquets of flowers gracing the tables, at the fire glowing in the hearth; she thought of the elaborate dinner prepared for Lord Southam, and her heart hardened in anger. She had had Cook scour Bath for a turtle and ordered up a rack of lamb for this tomboy of a girl and her governess! This was *infamous*! Palming off an unwanted duty on her, whom he scarcely knew!

She poured herself a large glass of sherry and drank it quickly. She must not let her Irish temper

10

run away with her. There was—there *must be*—
some explanation. Lord Southam was held up at
the last moment on some estate business. He would
be joining them soon. A pity that tonight's preparations were wasted and must be redone another
time, but still, it was a good investment. It would
be a fine thing to be Lady Southam, wife of Lord
Southam, with the dark eyes and reckless smile.

Chapter Two

As Lady Gillian's toilet was in sore need of repair, Mrs. Searle did not expect to see her before seven. This suited the hostess. An hour should be sufficient to recover from her disappointment and meet her guest with composure. In approximately one quarter of that time, the clatter of unladylike steps galloping down the stairs announced the return of Lady Gillian.

"Oh, there you are!" she said in far from ladylike accents when she spotted Mrs. Searle on the sofa. "Have I got time to write to Rawl before dinner? Perhaps you would be kind enough to lend me some paper and a pen. Whoever thought I would be writing a letter the minute I arrived, for in the general way, I never write anything if I can help it."

"Is something the matter?" Mrs. Searle inquired politely. As her guest replied, the hostess scrutinized Lady Gillian's toilet. Hair an utter mess. Naturally curly? It looked as if it had been trimmed by a footman and combed with a pitchfork. Her citron gown was too highly garnished for a predeb.

That clutter of bows must go. Her manner was unpleasantly abrupt, and her voice was rough. Lemon juice and the constant use of a parasol might bleach those freckles. . . .

"No, what should be the matter? I want to ask Rawl to forward Penny immediately. I brought my riding habits with me, for I made sure I could borrow a mount from time to time if you did not ride. I must remember to ask him to send my tan gloves. I forgot them. What do you ride, ma'am?"

"Just an old gray hacker I've had forever."

Lady Gillian did not wait to be asked what she rode, but rushed on to volunteer the information. "My Penny is not a thoroughbred, either, though there's good blood in her. Some Welsh pony, with a strain of Arabian. She's only thirteen hands high, but she has the long, low, straight stride of a thoroughbred."

Mrs. Searle interrupted this spiel long enough to offer her guest a glass of sherry.

"Could I have an ale instead?" Lady Gillian replied.

"I'm afraid I don't have any."

"Perhaps the servants have some in the kitchen. I'll ask the butler," she said, and hopped up from her chair.

Since Mrs. Searle was in charge of smoothing out the lady's rough edges, she decided to begin her duties immediately. "Ale is not served to ladies in this house, Lady Gillian. Lord Southam sent you to me to polish your manners. Let us begin by taking the proper drink for a lady."

"But I hate sherry!"

"A lady does not hate what is offered in the way of refreshment when she is a guest. If she fears the refreshment will actually make her ill, then she declines politely. She does not suggest an alternative. That is the hostess's privilege."

13

Gillie listened patiently. "What do you suggest, then?"

Mrs. Searle took a sip from her glass unconcernedly and said, "I suggest you wait till dinner, when wine will be served."

Gillie frowned. She fidgeted a moment, glanced at the clock, and said, "We usually have dinner at six at home."

"So I would assume. In the country one usually keeps country hours. I shall be serving at seven—a little early tonight, as I thought you might be peckish after your trip."

"I am starved!"

"A lady is never starved. She is allowed to feel peckish—if she is asked."

"I expect you and Miss Swann were great friends," Gillie said with a scowl.

"Miss Swann? Who is that?"

"Did Rawl not tell you? It was Deborah's idea to send me to you."

"Deborah Swann! Good gracious, I haven't heard that name for over a decade. We were at school together. Do you know Deborah Swann?"

"Know her? She lives only a mile away. She is Rawl's fiancée. It was her idea to pack me off here, to get rid of me." Gillie failed to notice that her hostess's face had stiffened to stone. She rattled on, "They tried to match me up with Lord Stuyvesant, as if I'd marry that old rake. He's at least thirty!"

"That old!" Mrs. Searle said in a chilly tone.

"It seems ancient to me, for I am only seventeen."

"Time will rectify that. You are young to be looking about for a match yet," Mrs. Searle said, though her quick mind was canvassing more interesting matters.

"I don't want to get married. It is all Miss

14

Swann's idea. She won't have Rawl till I am out of the house, you see. We are forever coming to cuffs. It is her horrid way of calling me missie that gets my back up, and acting as if she were my mother, only my mama was never so horrid. I hate her."

"A young lady does not hate anyone, Lady Gillian," she replied. Yet, if there were to be an exception to that rule, she would not hesitate to nominate Deborah Swann for the role. What a managing creature Deborah had been. And now she had nabbed Lord Southam! How could such a thing have happened?

Gillian crossed her arms and glared. "Then I am not a lady, because I hate Deborah Swann."

"And she is actually engaged to your brother, you say. Formally engaged?" Mrs. Searle asked, wondering if it was only a straw in the wind.

"Yes, she has the ring and everything. She is forever at the house, poking about and complaining to the servants and Rawl, as if she were already married to him."

Mrs. Searle digested this with no visible trace of her rancor. "I read some time ago that she was lady-in-waiting to the royal princesses."

"When she is not complaining, she is boasting of that. And of course her father, who is a member of the cabinet, only they won't let him have a portfolio. I wonder he doesn't buy one, since he is supposed to be well greased."

Lady Searle found a sudden interest in Miss Swann and did not discourage this line of complaints as she knew she ought. "As she is a near neighbor, I expect this match has been in the air since Deborah and your brother were youngsters." It must have been arranged eons ago by the family. No sane man would willingly offer for Deborah Swann.

"Not at all. It only happened this past year, when the royal princesses sent her home. She is the bossy sort who must be ordering someone around, and since Effie and Alice and I were without a mother, she decided to take us in charge. She convinced Rawl that we had run wild, and now she is engaged to him, but she won't marry him till I am out of the house. And that is why she sent me to you, to smarten me up so Stuyvesant will have me."

"Why not London for a Season instead of here?"

"Miss Swann feels the moral climate there is not salubrious. I expect that means she's afraid Rawl will slip the leash."

Mrs. Searle realized she had been well and thoroughly taken in and was furious. That nice letter from Southam—probably dictated by Deborah Swann! They were *using* her, shoving this uncouth girl onto her, and she scarcely knew them. After all her plans and preparations, Lord Southam was not coming at all. An extremely troublesome and expensive dinner had been ordered—for this tomboy and her companion.

"Where is Miss Pittfield?" she asked. She determined on the spot that Miss Pittfield would take complete charge of Lady Gillian. As Southam and Deborah had pulled the wool over her eyes and got her agreement to the visit, she would make some nominal effort to smarten Lady Gillian up, but she would not have her whole life turned upside down to oblige Deborah Swann. Lord Southam was not the man she had taken him for if he had let himself be bullocked into an offer by that insufferable lady.

"She didn't know whether she was supposed to eat with us."

"Of course she will eat with us. She is your cousin, is she not?"

16

"A distant cousin. I'll tell her," Gillie said, and hopped up from her chair.

"We have servants in this house to perform errands, Lady Gillian. Pray sit down. And don't jump up again until dinner is announced, if you please." She took out all her annoyance on poor Gillie. "I can see why Deborah was displeased with your manners at any rate. You behave like a hoyden."

Mrs. Searle watched as her guest's boyish face tightened up like a fist. She held her breath, waiting for an outburst of stable language. "Yes, ma'am," Gillie said, and resumed her seat, where she sat without speaking for five minutes, while Mrs. Searle summoned a servant and sent the message off to Miss Pittfield.

That dame had been awaiting her summons and came below immediately. "Will you have a glass of sherry, Miss Pittfield?" Mrs. Searle said, and till dinner was announced, such conversation as occurred was between the two older ladies, while Gillie tapped her fingers, pulled at her curls, and glanced at regular intervals at the clock.

Miss Pittfield corroborated what Gillie had already said in blunter terms. Lord Southam had no intention of coming personally to Bath. Mrs. Searle swallowed this monstrous news and behaved like a lady for the remainder of the evening, but a lady with a grievance. She would brook no impertinence from Lady Gillian, nor would she curtail her own normal pursuits one iota. She had been taken in, but she would not allow anyone to know just how high her hopes had flown.

There followed a few days of curt civility between the hostess and her guests. The guests were presented to Mrs. Searle's callers. Gillie found very little amusement in doddering ladies and gentle-

17

men in their thirties and forties. They were also taken to the Pump Room, but as horses were not allowed, Gillie screwed up her nose at the water and asked how soon they could leave. At least on the street one could *see* horses, even if one could not ride them. The city offered challenging riding, with hills all around.

At the end of a week Mrs. Searle had assimilated her anger and adjusted to the situation. She was saddled with a country bumpkin for six weeks, which was the established duration of the visit. At the end of that time she would be going to London, where she would enjoy the Season with Leonard's aunt, Mrs. Louden. This annual visit was her major treat of the year and much anticipated. Meanwhile she decided to make the best of a bad situation and befriend Lady Gillian.

It was with this Christian thought in mind that she tapped at Gillie's door. She waited to be asked in, but no voice answered her knock. The girl couldn't be asleep. They had just returned from Milsom Street ten minutes before. She tapped again, more loudly. When still there was no reply, her vague worry escalated to fear. She turned the knob, fully expecting to see an empty clothespress and a note on the dresser.

To her astonishment she saw a small form crumpled on the bed, head buried in a pillow, sobbing. Her maternal instincts aroused, she hastened forward. "Gillie! What is the matter? Are you ill?" she asked anxiously.

The brown curls nestled on the pillow shook in a negative. "But what is it, my dear?" Without waiting for an answer, she knew. The child was homesick, and here she had been treating her roughly, never saying a kind word, doing nothing but nag. She felt like a monster. Her hand went out, and she began patting the silky curls, which had the effect

18

of deepening the sobs till the girl's shoulders shook.

"Come now, you can tell me," she said in a soft, motherly voice. "Is it my fault, Gillie? *It is!* I've been horrid, and it is only my own stupidity that caused this muddle."

Gillie lifted her head. Moist, red eyes looked a question at Mrs. Searle. "What muddle? What do you mean? It's not *your* fault."

Mrs. Searle extended her arms and pulled the girl against her breast. It felt good, to hold someone close, even if it was only this ramshackle child. This must be how a mother felt, all warm and soft and loving. "Tell me all about it, Gillie," she said in a cajoling way.

"I want to go home," she said. "I miss Penny and Abe and Elmer. I miss Effie and Alice and Rawl, too." Gillie began to rub her eyes with her knuckles.

"I know Penny is your mount, but who are Abe and Elmer?"

"The stablehands. They're my friends. I hoped Rawl would have sent Penny before now. I know something's happened to her. I *know* it."

"Nothing has happened. It would take a while for the letter to reach Elmland and for your brother to make the arrangements. You cannot send a mount through the post, you know. Very likely Penny will arrive tomorrow, and we shall go riding."

Hope blossomed through the tears. "Could we? The hills hereabouts are so lovely."

"Bath is considered pretty hard riding. I thought we might go west, along the Old Roman Road. I have been missing my rides, too. I have a friend on that road, Lord Horatio Evendon. We shall make him give us tea. Or perhaps ale," she added with

19

an arch smile. "Lord Horatio brews his own ale, excellent stuff. Would you like that, Lady Gillian?"

"I would like it of all things! You—you called me Gillie before," she said shyly.

Beatrice realized this forlorn waif wanted affection, friendship, and felt a sudden attraction to her. "That was previous of me. In the emotion of the moment—"

"I liked it!"

"Then you should have asked me to do so before. You are a lady. It is for you to confer that freedom, you must know."

"No, I didn't know. Please call me Gillie. It is friendlier. And may I call you Bea, as I hear your friends do?"

"I am so much older, I don't think . . . Perhaps you could call me Aunt Bea."

"But you're not my aunt."

"A sort of honorary title. Yes, that will do nicely." She smoothed the girl's hair back from her forehead. It was surprisingly soft and silky. "We should have something done to this hair. Shall we call in the coiffeur?"

"If you like."

"You will want a bit more style for the ball. There is a cotillion ball at the Upper Rooms tomorrow evening." She had been feeling guilty about Gillian and planned to take her on this outing. "I am a subscriber. We should put your name in Mr. King's book as well. It is kept at the Pump Room for people to peruse and see who is in town."

"I shouldn't think anyone would know me," Gillie replied.

Perhaps they would not, but a Lady Gillian, from Elmland, would excite some interest. People would be on the lookout for her and cause a little fluster of excitement. That might be good for Gillie's self-

20

confidence. "You are allowed to go to assemblies?" she asked.

"I go to the ones at home. Deborah says I need polish, and Rawl says he don't want me fired off from the schoolroom without meeting anyone."

"Yet he tried to set up a match with Lord Stuyvesant?"

"That was Deborah's idea."

"Then we shall begin attending the assemblies, and that will serve as your initiation. I don't see why you should not have a Season in London," she added pensively. If it was fast beaux Deborah feared, she would not have put that renowned dasher Stuyvesant forward. No, Gillie had hit it on the head. Deborah feared to take Southam there, but Southam's presence was not necessary for Gillie to have her Season.

"I'll never be allowed. Deborah has nowhere to stay," she replied. "Her papa is there, but he only has rooms somewhere."

The plan was forming for Beatrice to take Gillie herself, but until she had Southam's permission, she would not mention it. "I don't see why Southam doesn't marry his Deborah," she said with a *tsk* of disgust. "Then she would have somewhere to stay, and you would have a chaperon for your Season."

"Perhaps they didn't think of that."

"Then you should suggest it to them."

Gillie worried her lips. "I wouldn't want to rush Rawl into the marriage," she said. "Marry in haste, repent at leisure. I am hoping that he will get over her, you see. It must be only an infatuation, don't you think, Aunt Bea? I mean he cannot *love* her."

"There is no saying in these things," she said vaguely, though in her heart she agreed completely.

"That is true. He's changed since she took over."

"What do you mean, took over? She doesn't *live* at Elmland, surely?"

"She might as well. She is there every day, and she manages to keep other young ladies away. When the Lawsons called, she had the butler tell them she was busy with the painters. Miss Lawson is very pretty," she said knowingly. "Deborah *is* having the saloon painted blue, but the men hadn't even started yet. She and Rawl were just talking about their wedding. She wants to be married at Saint George's, in Hanover Square because of the royal princesses, you know, but Rawl wants to be married at home."

"They are actually making their wedding plans, are they?"

"She is making the plans. She says I can be her matron of honor if I marry Stuyvesant."

"He is too old and too fast for you, my child. I cannot think what Southam is about. You would have much better pickings in London. I shall suggest it to Southam myself."

Gillie expressed very little interest in this scheme. "I wonder if Penny will come tomorrow," she said.

"If not, I can borrow a hack for you. I have many friends. Someone will be happy to oblige us. And tomorrow evening, we shall go to the cotillion ball." She rose and tidied her gown before leaving.

When Beatrice was at the door, Gillie asked, "What did you mean, Aunt Bea, that your stupidity had caused a muddle? You said that earlier, when you first came in and started acting nice."

"Acting nice." The thoughtless phrase reminded Bea that she had been acting badly. "Nothing. It was just my confusion."

22

"But what muddle? You *said* I might come. Am I even worse than you expected?" she asked, a frown pleating her brow.

"Certainly not. You show great potential."

"You thought Rawl was coming with me. Is that it? You didn't know he was engaged to Deborah?"

"I had no idea Deborah lived anywhere near you. You'd best tidy yourself now, Gillie. You look a fright."

She got out without admitting the truth, but she had a sinking sensation at the pit of her stomach that Gillie had discerned her secret.

Chapter Three

A new closeness began to develop between Gillie and Beatrice Searle. Penny arrived the next day, and they had their initial ride out the Old Roman Road to the ramshackle estate of Lord Horatio Evendon, younger son of a duke, and uncle to the present Duke of Cleremont. In this unlikely gentleman Gillie found another friend. Lord Horatio was known to have little common sense and less money, but what little he had of both was devoted to the family failing: horseflesh. Though his house was crumbling to ruin, his stables were in excellent repair. Only six of the twenty stalls were full, but the animals were prime goers: a team of grays for his curricle, a team of bays for his city carriage, a hacker, and a hunter.

While Gillie examined the cattle, prying open mouths to look at teeth, bending to the ground to lift a hoof and feel an ankle, Bea talked to Lord Horatio. He had been a friend of her late father's, and was like an uncle to her. She had long since got over any surprise that the son and uncle of a duke should dress like a farmer and talk like a

24

groom. His full head of black hair was hardly touched by gray. He looked much as he had looked for as long as she could remember. His narrow face had always been the color and texture of leather, his eyes always a deep blue. Only his eyebrows had changed, sprouting long, wiry hairs over the years. He looked rather like an unkempt rustic satyr.

"Who is this young filly you're chaperoning, Bea?" he asked, drawing out a cigar to light.

"Lord Southam's half sister."

"Some kin to Leonard, then. Are you looking for a match for her?"

"She's too young to marry. I am looking for some safe beaux for her to cut her teeth on. Any ideas, Horatio?"

"Tannie's the one could set you in that line. You know my nevvie, Tannie, the duke?"

"Only by reputation. A duke in Suffolk, however, is no good to us."

"He's in Bath. He has an aunt and a million or so cousins here as well as myself. The boy is horse-mad. Comes by it honestly, what? I'll bring the young colt to call if you like."

"Please do, but do not speak of it as a match, or you will upset that million or so of relatives. Lady Gillian has only ten thousand dot."

"Money's no problem to that lot. Not to Tannie anyhow. Seeing how keen she is on horses, I wager they'd get along like roast beef and mustard."

"Who's he staying with in Bath?" Bea asked with rising interest.

"My sister, Mildred—old Lady Sappington. She is trying to bend Tannie in her niece's direction. It won't take. The girl is a bluestocking. Tannie prefers bay or gray. He'll soon be off to Newmarket. He has some nags entered in the races. I'll mention your gel to Tannie next time I see him."

"Are you entering the races this year?"

25

"My pockets are to let. I'll be only a spectator." He glanced toward the stable. "The gel has a way with nags. See how she is talking to Silver, and he acting as tame as a mouse. He won't usually let anyone but me near him."

Gillie placed a kiss on the horse's nose and came prancing forward. "What a perfectly-matched pair, Lord Horatio! Those grays must be sweet goers. Sixteen miles an hour, I wager."

"Sixteen and a half." He grinned. "Do ye drive, missie?"

"Only the gig at home. My brother won't let me have a carriage. He says hacking and hunting are enough. I have to ride an old worn-out hunter. I wish I were rich."

"So do I, too, and I'd marry you," he said, jiggling her cheeks between his fingers. "We'll begin our courtship with a driving lesson—if your chaperon permits?"

A beatific smile glowed on Gillie's face. "May I, Aunt Bea?" she asked.

"Quite cutting me out! I see no harm in your taking a spin with Lord Horatio. He is an excellent teacher. He taught me to drive."

"You didn't tell me you could drive!" Gillie exclaimed.

"I don't keep a phaeton since my husband's death. In my salad days, I was a notable whip, was I not, Horatio?"

"A regular Lettie Lade. The first lady in Bath to drive her own rig, if memory serves. Will you ladies come to the house for a glass of ale?"

"Could I have mine here?" Gillie asked. "I want to check out Silver's back. Did you know he has a little swelling on his muzzle, Lord Horatio? If it's a warble, you'll want to get a hot fomentation on it. I'll check his back and withers. Saddle warbles can be the very devil, and they come on so quickly."

"It's no warble, my dear. I accidentally hit him with the end of my crop. I don't have any warble flies. I keep the stable disinfected, but if you want your ale sent out, it's no problem."

"Yes, please."

"Watch for Lucifer. He'll get his tongue into your glass if you let him. He likes his ale."

"I am not a complete flat, Lord Horatio!"

"What a splendid day it has been!" Gillie exclaimed when they reached home.

Bea was coming to know her well enough to know it was not the coiffeur's successful morning visit, nor the prospect of the cotillion ball that evening that occasioned the remark. It was horses.

"I hope the evening will be equally splendid." As she had entered Lady Gillian's name in Mr. King's subscription book, she felt the ball would not be a fiasco at least.

That evening Bea arranged Gillie's hair herself and lent her a green shot silk scarf to enliven her white gown. The greatest improvement in her looks, however, was her smile. She was really rather sweet, now that she had got over her perpetual sulking.

"I hope they don't waltz," Gillie said as the carriage took them from Mrs. Searle's comfortable house on Saint Andrew's Terrace down busy Milson Street to the New Assembly Rooms.

"Waltz in Bath! My dear, only in the racier private homes, such as your aunt Bea's. The country dance is all that is usually permitted at the Assembly Rooms, but on Thursday we have the cotillion ball. Two cotillions are performed at the fancy ball as well. As this is Thursday, there will be cotillions but no waltzing."

"That's good, because I don't know how to do it. Deborah lets us have two waltzes at our local assemblies. She wouldn't let me waltz, because I am too young."

"Old enough to marry, but too young to waltz?" Bea exclaimed. "I should have thought marriage the more demanding chore. Is Deborah in charge of the local assemblies?"

"She is in charge of everything," Gillie said comprehensively.

Deborah obviously ruled the roost at Alderton, but her rule did not extend to Bath. With a real concern for Gillie growing stronger by the moment, Bea decided to make this holiday a time to remember. She was busy among her friends, and saw to it that Gillie never lacked for partners. There was no ignoring the fact that no gentleman lingered after a dance, nor did he request a second honor. It was not so much the girl's looks, for she turned out looking handsome enough, if a touch rustic. No, it was her harping on stable matters that cooled their ardor. The assembly closed at eleven sharp, and the ladies returned to Saint Andrew's Terrace.

"May we go riding again tomorrow, Aunt Bea?" was Gillie's comment when they reached home. Not so much as a word about the assembly. She had met and stood up with half a dozen eligible gentlemen. Any normal girl would have been gurgling or at least repining.

"Let us wait and see what the weather has in store for us."

Over the ensuing week Bea set a routine of riding in the morning, to induce her charge to participate in social matters for the remainder of the day. There was the girl's toilet to smarten up. Southam had not stinted in supplying funds, nor did Beatrice stint in spending it on silks and muslins, gloves and shawls and bonnets.

Lord Horatio was good to his word. He came twice to "give the youngster a whirl" in his curricle, as

28

he described it. Of more importance, he brought his nephew, the Duke of Cleremont, with him to call one afternoon. The duke had the family looks—tall, slender, with dark hair and dark blue eyes. Yet these promising parts did not assemble into anything that would earn him the description handsome. He was all arms and legs, clumsy in his movements and awkward in his manners. His jackets were well cut, but between wrinkles, dust, and the scent of the stable, they were not what a gentleman's jackets should be. It was no secret among those interested in such matters that Weston refused the duke his services, fearing the results would put off other clients.

Lord Horatio performed the introduction, then let nature take its course. He was more comfortable having a glass of sherry with Bea before the Rumford grate.

Gillie saw nothing amiss in the duke's looks or manner, nor did she see anything intimidating in his title and numerous estates. "Your uncle tells me you have a fine stable at Ardmore Hall, Duke," she said the moment he had performed his graceless bow and stumbled onto a chair.

"No," he said. "Only a small stable at Ardmore Hall. A dozen stalls."

"What's in them?" she demanded.

"Percherons, mostly. Ardmore's just a farm. Dandy cattle—cows, I mean. I don't go to Ireland very often, except to a breeding farm I know of there. Evendon, in Suffolk, is where I keep my cattle."

"Your horse cattle," she said, not at all confused by this lack of specifying.

He nodded. "Two dozen stalls. A fine Arabian stud. I bred Firefly from him. Took the Oaks at Epsom last year, and the One Thousand Guineas at Newmarket as well. Might have taken the Derby,

29

too, but I did not want to overwork her. Only two days apart. Mind you, she'll run against the colts at Ascot this year. She ain't afraid of going against the colts."

Racing was an unknown field to Gillie. She interrupted his spasmodic utterances to say, "What do you ride yourself, Duke?"

"Prefer mares to geldings for hacking. I hunt a gelding, though. More power. My hands are too weak for a stallion. Broke my thumb riding one once." He held up a crooked thumb for inspection. "Uncle tells me you ride a pony."

Gillie bristled at this slur on her mount. "Penny is not a pony! She is part thoroughbred, even if she is only thirteen hands high."

He gave a derisive snort. "Welsh or Shetland?" he asked, undeceived.

She ignored his jibe. "My brother, Lord Southam, rides an Arabian mare," she announced grandly.

The duke nodded. "Black Lady. Papa sold her to him."

"You bred Black Lady at Evendon?"

"Black Knight," he said cryptically. "The Arab stallion I was telling you about. Sire. Dame was Gray Lady."

"You didn't tell me anything about your stallion, except that you own him. What line is he from?"

"Godolphin Barb."

"Rawl thought he was from the Byerly Turk."

A glimmer of interest flashed in the duke's eyes. It wasn't often that he met a lady with whom he could have a conversation of more than two or three syllables. It was nice to finally meet one who spoke equine English. "You drive?" he asked.

"I'm learning. Your uncle is giving me lessons."

"A shocking bad fiddler. Cow-handed. Holds the reins too tight. Ruined more mouths than I care to think of, and don't treat the wounds properly, either. Bran."

Gillie nodded at this wisdom. "Mashed. Or at least cooked oats, till the mouth is healed. Where can you get good clean hay here in Bath? There were hawthorn twigs in Penny's hay today."

"Can't. Not in the city. I order mine from old Jed Hanks, just north of Guinea Lane. I'll send a load to your stable if you like."

This was condescension of a high order and appreciated as such. "Yes, I would, thank you."

"So, when would you like a driving lesson?"

"We ride in the morning—usually out the Old Roman Road. I should like to try some more challenging routes, but my aunt Bea is old, you know."

The duke looked across the room to the fetching widow and found nothing foolish in this statement. "A bit past it. We'll ride north."

"Drive, you mean."

"I meant ride, in the morning. Will your aunt let you out with me, or are you too young?"

"I'm not young!"

"I'm twenty-seven. Don't look it, they say, but I am. How old are you?"

"Nearly eighteen—in nine months. But I cannot like to abandon my aunt. She depends on me for company."

"Pity. Tomorrow afternoon, then?"

"All right," Gillie said with some pleasure, for she always appreciated an opportunity to try new cattle. "I'd best ask Aunt Bea first. She's nice but quite strange. She makes me go to the Assembly Rooms and to concerts and even the lending library." A snicker escaped her at these bizarre pastimes.

The duke shook his head in sympathy. "They get strange notions when they grow old. Can you ask her now? I want to leave."

"All right."

Mrs. Searle was not slow to give her permission
to this scheme. It also occurred to her that the duke
might replace her on some of those tedious morning
rides. She liked riding but was not such a fanatic
that she liked going out no matter how chilly the
weather or how menacing the sky. Any gentleman
staying with the redoubtable Lady Sappington must
be unexceptionable. That Tannie was also an extremely eligible duke was not overlooked, either.

The afternoon drives were soon established as
custom. The duke began replacing Beatrice in some
morning rides as well. To repay his hospitality, she
occasionally invited him to take dinner with them.
His demeanor was closely studied, and though the
chaperon detected no tender looks or whispered
asides between the two, she observed that they got
on uncommonly well. Almost like brother and sister. She learned from Lady Sappington that the
duke would be going to London for the Season. It
seemed an excellent idea for Gillie to go as well.
With balls and other social doings that excluded
horses, something romantic might develop between
these two horse lovers.

Bea kept chipping away at Gillie's rough edges
to prepare her for the Season. She had some more
fashionable gowns made up and taught her to hold
a fan like a weapon of flirtation instead of a riding
crop. One item that must be attended to was teaching her the waltz, and to this end, Bea joined her
charge in a series of waltzing parties arranged by
mothers of young ladies preparing to make their
bows at Saint James's. To her considerable astonishment, the duke agreed to take part in the lessons.

"Won't do me any harm, I expect. A bit of an
awkward fellow, I know."

"Not in the saddle or in the riding box, either,"

Gillie said supportively. "Tannie reminds me of the swans at home, Aunt Bea. So graceful in their own element, and so awkward on land." The youngsters had achieved a first-name basis during their outings.

"Pity they don't have a mounted waltz." Tannie smiled lazily. "By jingo, Gillie, I think we're onto something."

"The horses put their forelegs around each other, you mean?" she asked, with a disparaging look.

"Course not! The riders do."

"They could only hold hands. A country dance would be better."

Bea listened with falling hopes. This pair had no more notion of romance than a cat had of flying. But as the days passed, and she sat on the sidelines at the waltzing lessons, she noticed that the duke wore a piqued expression when Gillie danced with anyone but him. She could not blame Gillie for trying to escape him. His waltzing was execrable. He seemed to have four feet, one of which was invariably on his partner's toes.

Bea went to the refreshment table for a glass of wine during a lull in the lessons and overheard a conversation between the duke and Gillie.

"You haven't stood up with me once!" the duke exclaimed angrily. He never bothered to lower his voice, no matter what he was saying or who was listening.

"I can't afford to. You've already destroyed two pairs of my dancing slippers."

"I don't see why we must come to these stupid parties. It is a fine afternoon. We could be out driving."

Gillie's reply was less loud, but Bea overheard her name and suspected that she was being blamed. "All right, then, I'll waltz with you next, but you must try to keep off my slippers, Tannie."

33

"I suppose Mr. Egerton never accidentally touches your slippers?" he asked ironically. "How does it come they are all dusty? You haven't danced with *me* all afternoon."

"I danced with you last time. The scuff marks will not come off. Oh *do* be careful! You're spilling wine all over your jacket."

"Damme, and it's brand-new! You didn't even notice," he added in an injured tone.

"It looks just like all your others," Gillie replied unconcernedly. Really the girl had no notion of flirting, to let that excellent opening pass.

"Well it isn't. It's new."

"It's all right, but your cravat is a mess. Don't you know how to tie a proper cravat?"

"It's my broken thumb.'

"Have your valet do it, then."

"He doesn't know how, either."

"Then get a new valet."

"What, give Huckam the heave-ho, when he can bandage an ankle better than any of my grooms? Not likely!" He pulled out his watch. "Only half an hour more of this torture. I expect Mrs. Searle is dragging you off to the Assembly Rooms this evening?"

"No, a concert." Her voice sounded like a yawn.

Mrs. Searle decided that Tannie was beginning to entertain proprietary feelings about Gillie. It was time to write to Southam and mention her plan of Gillie going to London for a Season.

Chapter Four

Bea's letter was duly received at Elmland. When Deborah Swann made her daily call, Southam showed it to her. "Mrs. Searle suggests sending Gillie to London for a Season. It might not be a bad idea," he said.

"She will be better off at home, married to Stuyvesant."

"I have been hearing things about Stuyvesant that make me less eager for that match, Deborah. He's a bit wild for Gillie."

"Marriage would settle him down. You cannot send her to London. Who would chaperon her?"

"We would. We could be married by May."

Deborah considered this scheme. "But what if she fails to find a match? Then she would be back here with us. You know I cannot rub along with Gillian, Southam. She goes out of her way to annoy me. Her flouting of my authority would be a wretched example for dear Effie and Alice. Could Mrs. Searle not find someone for her in Bath? There must be some eligible gentlemen there."

"It seems there are. Gillie mentions a good many

balls and assemblies. She is seeing some horsey fellow called Tannie."

"Tannie?" Miss Swann's pale brow wrinkled in consternation. "I don't recognize the name. He never visited the princesses. He cannot be anyone."

"Some relative of Lady Sappington."

"Some of those Sappingtons are very dirty dishes, Southam. Horse-mad, all of them. You may be sure he is some racetrack tout. I would put a stop to that if I were you."

Southam listened in alarm. "It will be as well to get Gillie away from him. Perhaps Mrs. Searle would chaperon her in London. They could use my house in Berkeley Square. I would remain here, of course."

Miss Swann pokered up at this suggested incursion into her domain. "That would look very odd, Southam. You scarcely know the lady."

"You said she was unexceptionable! Damme, I have entrusted Gillie to her care. She is Leonard's widow."

"Her character is good, but socially—well, marrying your cousin Leonard is as high as her connections go. I only meant for her to smarten up Gillian's toilet and manners. We do not want her moving into our house. We may never dislodge her. You know what leeches family connections can become. I daresay this is exactly what Mrs. Searle had in mind when she suggested London. A free Season for herself!"

Southam raked a hand impatiently through his hair. "What shall I do, then?"

"Write Mrs. Searle that you do not approve of a Season for Gillian. At the end of six weeks we shall see how Gillian behaves when she comes home. Stuyvesant may have her after all. He would not dislike getting his hands on her dowry."

"That hardly seems a good basis for a marriage!"

36

"It is no uncommon one," Deborah said, and took up her embroidery. "And about this Tannie person, you had best inquire exactly who he is and what sort of estate he has—if he even has one."

Lord Southam was on the fidgets. He felt derelict in having sent his sister off to a virtual stranger. His impression from the family had been that Mrs. Searle was unexceptionable, but that was many years ago. If she had become a conniving widow, letting Gillie run free with some reckless gambler, and if she was trying to get a free Season out of him ... She might have changed since Leonard's death. Really he ought to take a dart over to Bath and see for himself how matters stood.

He could make the trip in a day. Spend a day or two with Gillie, check out her beaux, and give Mrs. Searle a close scrutiny while he was there. Yes, he really should.

"I'm going to Bath tomorrow, Deborah," he said.

"Going to Bath! Don't be foolish, Southam. That is not necessary."

"I feel I must."

"I cannot get away tomorrow. Mama's sister is feeling poorly. You know I quite depend on Aunt Alexandra to tend Mama when I am away."

"There is no need for you to go. I shall be putting up at an inn. We could hardly stay there together."

"I would stay with Mrs. Searle, of course. Beatrice and I are old friends."

"We are already battening Gillie and Miss Pittfield on her. There are limits. I'll go alone. I shan't be gone long."

"This is foolishness, not at all necessary," she scolded.

"I'm going," Southam said. When he spoke in that final way, argument was futile.

Deborah tucked in her chin and said, "Very well, if you insist. I trust you will be back by Saturday?"

"That would only leave me one day there."

"How long does it take to have a chat with Gillie and reassure yourself that all is well? We are promised to dinner at the Comstocks' on Saturday evening."

"I shall send in my excuse. I should be back late Monday." Deborah's embroidery frame twitched in angry silence. Southam liked her least in this mood of self-righteous indignation. She had a way of pinching her nose and lips that always reminded him of a mare pulling her ears back. "Or perhaps Tuesday," he said.

Deborah's needle punched into the canvas with vehemence. She had learned by experience that when Southam was in this mood, rational discussion soon degenerated into a squabble. She did not squabble.

As Southam meant to leave on the morrow, there was no point writing to inform Mrs. Searle of his coming. He felt it was as well to pop in without warning and see exactly how things were going on. As he drove through the countryside, with spring burgeoning on every side, he felt impatience with Deborah's foot-dragging about their marriage. Damme, he was five-and-thirty years old. If he meant to have any enjoyment from his family, he should be starting his nursery. Still, he could hardly blame Deborah for not wanting to take on Gillie. The girl was hot at hand and ill-mannered. She could make Deb's life a hell. Some animosity had sprung up between them from the very beginning.

Fortunately Mrs. Searle had no complaints about managing Gillie. As he considered it, he had to wonder why. Was the woman so lax that she let Gillie do as she wanted? Was she taking proper precautions for Gillie's welfare? All his own fault, of course. He should not have sent Gillie to her. He had thought any friend of Deborah's must be well-bred and cautious. Deb's hint that the woman was conniving for a free Season in London didn't make her sound like the sort of person he wanted Gillie to be with. If he didn't like the look of things, he'd bundle Gillie up and take her home. Wouldn't Deborah love that!

What was he to do with Gillie? The more he thought about it, the less he liked the idea of her marrying Stuyvesant. She might never find a husband, and Deborah would not marry him till she was out of the house. Women!

When he reached Bath, he was relieved to see that at least Mrs. Searle lived in style, in a fine brick house on Saint Andrew's Terrace. He arrived late in the afternoon, but the lights in the saloon told him Mrs. Searle was at home. As he approached the door, he heard music. Odd she should be having a rout in the afternoon! It was not concert music, but the strains of a waltz, on piano, cello, and violin. A quick peek in at the saloon window showed heads and bodies moving about. Demmed odd! The word *ramshackle* came to mind, and when he lifted the knocker, he banged it rather hard.

The worries of his life made a scowl a familiar expression on his saturnine face. It was firmly in place when the butler opened the door.

"Lord Southam to see Mrs. Searle," he said.

The name was known to the butler. "I shall call madam. She is busy with a party at the moment, but she will be happy to see you," he said, and ushered Lord Southam into a small parlor to wait.

Bea felt a surge of excitement when she was given the message. "Lord Southam! And he didn't even let me know he was coming!" she exclaimed. Her pleasure was tinged with vexation as she hurried off to meet him.

She found him pacing the small parlor with his scowl firmly fixed in place. He removed it to greet her, but she was aware of a coolness in him. Bea's sense of ill-usage by Southam, which had dwindled over the weeks, was reactivated. Instead of warm greetings and loud thanks, she received a brief bow and a curt "Good afternoon, Mrs. Searle. I hope I am not come at an awkward moment. I had not thought to find you hostess to a ball so early in the day."

He noticed she was wearing an evening gown at four o'clock in the afternoon. A handsome gown, to be sure, of some gold-and-bronze material that shimmered when she moved. It was cut low enough in front to give a tantalizing glimpse of incipient bosoms. Good God! What did she wear in the evening, if this was her idea of an afternoon gown? Her face, though, was just as he remembered. She had hardly changed at all.

"No ball, Lord Southam, but a dancing lesson." So that was the cause of his stiff expression! He mistook the waltzing lesson for a wild, abandoned party.

One crow-black brow lifted in question. "A waltzing lesson, to judge by the music? At home we do not allow Gillie to waltz. She should have told you so." His tone suggested, "You should have known better."

"She did tell me so. As she is considered ripe for marriage, however, I do not see that a waltz is too risqué for her. And when she goes up to London—" She stopped and waited for his reponse to this venture. "You *did* receive my letter about giving Gillie a Season?"

"That is why I am here."

Their initial conversation was held standing up. "As you have come fifty-odd miles to discuss it, per-

40

haps you would like to sit down," she said, taking a seat on the sofa.

Southam sat on the chair facing it. "I fear I cannot go along with your scheme. I have no relative who is in a position to sponsor her." As he spoke, he continued to examine Mrs. Searle's toilet in a manner that annoyed her. It was early for evening clothes, of course, but it was her house, and he was here uninvited. She owed him no explanations.

"I wondered if that was why you had not planned to present her. I shall be going to London myself. I would be willing—"

He heard the echoes of Deborah's warnings and spoke firmly. "I'm afraid not, Mrs. Searle. My house hasn't been open for three years. It would hardly—"

"I did not mean in your house," she interjected swiftly. "Leonard's aunt lives in a more than respectable way. As it is your aim to get Gillie married as quickly—and one presumes as advantageously—as possible, London is surely the place for it."

He was somewhat mollified to hear her plan. "You are very kind, but my hope was only that you smarten her up a little." Again his eyes moved over her low-cut gown and the necklace of topaz and diamonds at her throat. "A little," he repeated, frowning.

"But to what end, if not to finding a husband?"

Left with nothing sensible to say, he resorted to the old plan of catching Stuyvesant. "There is a chap at home. . . ."

"Lord Stuyvesant? Gillie detests the man."

"She is young."

"Old enough to know what she likes and does not like!" she retorted sharply. How different this meeting was from what she had originally imagined it would be. How had she ever thought Sou-

41

tham was anything like Leonard? He was a prig. He and Deborah would get along just fine.

"May I see her?" he asked, to forestall further discussion on this tender point.

"Yes, certainly, she will be eager to see you. I hear the music has stopped." He followed her to the saloon, where the furniture had been rearranged to make room for six couples.

Glancing around at the youngsters, he found them no worse than he was accustomed to at Alderton. He soon spotted Gillie, and stared in disbelief. It was hard to believe that this fashionable creature was his Gillie. Her wild hair had been trimmed into fashionable curls. She wore a smile such as he had not seen since his betrothal to Deborah. Soon his eyes fell lower, and he discerned her gown. It was cut lower than he liked for his little sister, though to be fair, no lower than the other young ladies were wearing.

The party were invited to dinner at Mrs. Carrington's after the waltzing lesson, from whence they were to go directly to the Assembly Rooms, properly chaperoned by two of the mothers and Mrs. Searle. This arrangement made it necessary for them to wear their evening clothes to the waltzing party.

Gillie rushed forward and threw her arms around Southam's neck in a girlish display of welcome. "Rawl, I didn't know you were coming! Why didn't you write me? How are Effie and Alice, and Abe and Elmer?"

"They are all fine, and missing you very much. Deborah sends her regards," he added. Deborah would have sent her regards if she had not left Elmland in a huff. Her manners, honed amid royalty, had not lost their edge.

Gillie ignored this statement and went on to inquire after the various bloods in her brother's stable.

Bea spoke to the musicians and arranged a ten-minute intermission, to allow Southam a few words with his sister. She introduced some of the chaperons to him. She wanted to bring the duke forward as well, but he demurred.

"I'd only step on him or trip. I'll meet him later," he said humbly, and moved back against the wall to study Southam in silence. Southam was even more fearsome than he had anticipated. The sort of chap who never dropped anything, who talked loud among men, and always knew what to say, even to ladies.

At the end of ten minutes, Bea joined Southam and Gillie. "Our dancers are becoming impatient," she said. "Let us find a seat, Lord Southam. I'll tell you what Gillie and I have been doing."

"I'll stay with you," Gillie said eagerly.

"Now, my dear, you know we have two extra gentlemen, so that you ladies will all be in high demand. It would be unfair of you to deplete the ranks of ladies by even one."

Southam waited for Gillie's objection. "I expect you're right," she said with a smile. "Besides, I promised Tannie the next waltz." She looked around for him.

He came loping forward at an awkward stride. When Southam spotted him, a frown drew his brows together. He said, "So this is the Tannie you have been writing me about, Gillie. I am afraid I cannot say much for your taste."

Beatrice sat, listening and watching. She had purposely withheld any mention of the duke when she wrote to Southam. She did not wish to raise hopes she could not fulfill. Her curiosity was high to discover whether Southam was aware of Tannie's social position. She judged from that disparaging tone that he was not.

"He has wonderful nags, Rawl," Gillie confided.

43

"We go riding every day, and he lets me drive his curricle, too, but only in the countryside."

Southam directed a sharp look at Mrs. Searle. "Every day!"

Before Bea could reply, the duke reached his quarry and made a clumsy bow in Southam's direction, while reaching out his hand to Gillie. "Our dance, I believe," he said.

"I don't have the pleasure of your new friend's acquaintance, Gillie," Southam said. His voice was tense with displeasure. The raking gaze he bestowed on Tannie reduced the recipient to charred cinders.

"This is Tannie. I told you about him," Gillie said, in her offhand way. "Tannie, this is my brother, Lord Southam."

"Very pleased to make your acquaintance, sir," Tannie mumbled, and blushed.

"And *still* I do not have your friend's last name," Southam pointed out.

Gillie frowned a moment in perplexity. "I don't actually know it." Southam's mouth fell open. She turned to the duke and asked, "Would it be Evendon, like your Uncle Horatio?"

"That's right. Tannie's short for Tanford—my mama's maiden name," the duke explained.

Southam's face was as transparent as glass. Bea saw him search his mind to identify the name. The present duchess sprang from an undistinguished family and was noble only by virtue of her marriage. The name Tanford, from Northumberland, was obviously unknown to him, for his expression stiffened to hauteur as he raked the duke in a cold glance from head to toe. "Gillie, I think you and I—"

Bea jumped in to forestall offending this prime *parti*. "Perhaps you were acquainted with Tannie's papa, Lord Southam," she said hastily. "The late

44

Duke of Cleremont, and this, of course, is the present duke."

She watched as Southam blinked in astonishment, and his frozen features congealed to a delighted smile. "Ah, the Duke of Cleremont! Yes, indeed. I knew your papa well. I have a mount from his stable. And the duchess—I did not recognize her maiden name."

"Black Lady," the duke said. "The horse, I mean. Tanford was Mama's family name."

"Just so, from Northumberland."

"May we go now? The squares are forming," Tannie pointed out.

"Certainly! You youngsters run along. Enjoy yourselves. We must have a chat later, Duke," he called after their fleeing forms. The duke and Gillie scuttled off like a pair of miscreants.

Bea gave Southam a mocking smile and said, "The duke is a dear boy. Why did you frighten him with those black scowls, when I have been at such pains to make him comfortable here? He is an excellent *parti*, Southam, despite his creased jacket. Much better than Lord Stuyvesant."

He shook his head in confusion. "One would never guess it to look at him. He has all the countenance of a junior clerk at Whitehall. So that is old Cleremont's heir. Yes, a prime *parti*. What do you suppose he sees in little Gillie?"

"A lonesome youngster, like himself," she replied.

"Gillie lonesome? My house is full of people. She has her sisters and me, and Deborah."

"Of course," Mrs. Searle said, but she did not rescind her first statement. "You must be feeling peckish after your trip, Lord Southam. Would you care for some mutton?"

"I shan't disturb you at this busy time. I'll run along to the inn. May I return later?"

"I would ask you to dinner, but we are dining out

45

this evening. A few of my friends and I have arranged to take these young ladies to the Upper Rooms after dinner. I wanted Gillie to have some girlfriends, as well as beaux."

"That was very kind of you. I did wonder, when you were dressed for evening so early in the afternoon."

"I noticed your remark about a ball," she reminded him with a cool look but one not devoid of laughter.

Lord Southam looked younger and much more handsome when he smiled. "I did put my foot in it, did I not? I had to wonder at your wearing such a charming gown so early in the day. It is the business of our not being very well acquainted that accounts for my confusion."

"I wondered at your choosing me for the honor of chaperoning Gillie," she said frankly. The speech, in its polite way, demanded an explanation.

"Deborah felt you were the very one. Deborah Swann, my fiancée, and an old friend of yours, Mrs. Searle."

"Old fr—yes, I have known her for eons, though not well. Gillie told me of the betrothal. I must congratulate you." And more particularly, Deborah, she added to herself. "The only mystery remaining," she lied affably, "is that Deborah could not smarten Gillie up herself."

"They don't rub along, for some reason. Pity."

"That is strange, for I find Gillie extremely biddable and friendly."

"And Deborah, of course, usually gets along with everyone. She failed with Gillie, but she is looking after the rest of us at Elmland in excellent fashion."

"You would be easy work after the royal princesses," she replied.

Mrs. Carrington joined them and invited Lord

Southam to join her party for dinner. Her pleasure at meeting Gillie's brother and her invitation seemed genuine, so after a polite hesitation, he accepted.

"I shall run along to the inn and change," he said.

"Breeches and silk stockings," Mrs. Carrington reminded him. "They are very strict at the Upper Rooms."

"So my valet told me. He has packed them, I believe." He made his bows and left.

"A new beau, Bea?" Mrs. Carrington asked archly.

"A connection only, through Leonard. Southam is betrothed to an old school acquaintance of mine, Miss Swann."

"Pity," Mrs. Carrington said.

"Yes," Bea agreed.

"That is always the way, is it not? The best ones are already taken."

Chapter Five

Although Mrs. Searle was placed at Southam's
right hand for dinner, no meaningful conversation
was possible. A dozen young belles and beaux, even
if they are well-bred, will always fill the air with
merriment when they are anticipating a ball. Bea
gave Southam brief histories of the youngsters during those periods when he was not talking to the
hostess on his other side. Before leaving the table,
she inquired, "Will you be joining the dance, Lord
Southam?, or will you go to the card parlor?"

"I'm not much of a hand at dancing," he replied,
yet he resented the suggestion that he was past it.
It had been a long time since he had gone dancing
with anyone but Deborah. She approved of assemblies for what she called the youngsters, but her
own participation in them, and Southam's, was
usually limited to opening the dance, then removing to the card parlor.

"Hand? Surely 'foot' is more to the point." She
laughed. He remembered that laugh—light, silvery.
What an attractive lady she was, for her age. "Why
do you not come with Mrs. Carrington and myself?

Give your little sister a chance to show you how popular she is here in Bath. Tannie does not usually attend these dos, but because of this dinner party, he is coming this evening. It will be an opportunity to know him better. He improves on longer acquaintance. One learns to duck and dodge his unintentional assaults."

"I should like to know him better." Glancing along the table, he was gratified to see that Gillie was as pretty and lively as any of the other young debs—and as popular. Mrs. Searle had done a remarkable job of trimming her into line. "Yes, I'll join you."

Quizzing glasses were raised around the room when Mrs. Searle and Lord Southam led the party of youngsters into the assembly. "You are causing quite a stir, sir," Beatrice informed him. "This being Bath, within sixty seconds the quizzes will have figured out that you are Gillie's brother."

Unaccustomed to so much attention, Southam was uncomfortable with it. He noticed, though, that Mrs. Searle was in her element. She sailed through the room like a frigate in full rig, nodding and smiling to her friends, and with her fingers laid proprietarily on his arm. He was aware of jealous glances from the men and felt a little spurt of pride in his companion's beauty.

Southam anticipated a dance with Mrs. Searle and perhaps one with his hostess for civility's sake. He realized, after the party was ensconsed at tables in the Upper Rooms, that the older folks in Bath did not take a backseat to the youngsters. Mrs. Searle was whisked away from the table as soon as they arrived.

Mrs. Carrington inclined her head toward him and said, "That is Mr. Reynolds, one of Mrs. Searle's court. He has retired from London—something to do with the law—and bought a handsome estate north of Bath. Extremely eligible."

49

He looked surprised to learn that Mrs. Searle had her circle of admirers. "At her age!" he exclaimed, not well pleased.

"Why, she is only thirty, and so very pretty. Naturally she will not molder into the grave without making another match. Though I have often thought Sir Harold Whitehead has the inner track. A baronet, but not so deep in the pockets as Reynolds. There is no saying with Bea. She never had any hankering for a handle to her name. She has turned down dozens of offers. She is quite a dasher, I promise you."

As he watched from the sidelines, Mrs. Searle negotiated the steps of the country dance with every evidence of youthful vigor. Neither her small, lithe waist nor her lively performance revealed the least sign of advancing senility. Had he not been familiar with her background, he would have taken her for Gillie's friend, not her chaperon. This had been an excellent notion of Deborah's, to send Gillie here. What the girl required was a good-natured lady who enjoyed youthful outings herself. Gillie's social life had been sorely restricted in Alderton.

He prepared himself to replace Mr. Reynolds at the end of the set, but before Mrs. Searle reached the table, she had been accosted by another gentleman. Fellow looked like a demmed caper merchant, with his oiled hair and greasy smile.

Mrs. Carrington leaned forward and said, "That is Sir Harold Whitehead that I told you about. He is put out that Bea stood up first with Mr. Reynolds this evening. And only see how Miss Tobin is scowling! She wouldn't say no if Sir Harold asked her to dance—or to marry him, either."

The place was a regular hotbed of romance. It struck Southam as unseemly for his cousin's widow to be so popular and gay. Why, she was flirting with Whitehead! Upon my word, he

50

thought, I am not at all sure this lady is any better than she should be.

His anger subsided when she returned to the table at the end of the set and said, "Why are you not dancing, Lord Southam? Can you not see all the ladies languishing for want of a partner? We do not often have the honor of an earl at our little assemblies. I hope you are not too high and mighty to stand up with me?"

"I have already warned you I am not much of a hand at jigging, but if you are willing to take the chance, I will be more than happy to oblige you."

She gave him her hand with a teasing smile and replied, "I never hesitate to take a chance, Lord Southam. You do not look that dangerous to me."

"Deborah tells me I have two left feet."

"Only two? Tannie has four, and I have waltzed with him when one of the girls for the waltzing class failed to attend."

"I can only offer you two, but I assure you they are both left feet."

"That attitude is enough to insure failure. I expect you are an excellent dancer." She smiled and led him to the dance floor, where he acquitted himself without disgrace. Strangely he seemed to dance better than usual. Perhaps it was because Mrs. Searle was such a good dancer herself.

"I was a little surprised to see the youngsters waltzing this afternoon," he mentioned when the steps of the cotillion permitted them to converse.

She gave him an arch look. "Your surprise was more than evident, Lord Southam. You looked as if you had stumbled into a house of ill repute, only because I was wearing an evening gown."

"My understanding was that Bath was very strict, even more so than the provinces. I had not thought learning the waltz would be a priority."

"Why, waltzing is allowed at Almack's, the strictest club in all of England! We must not be overly rigid."

"It was not the way in my day."

"Nor in mine, either, but things change, and we must change with them or become hopelessly outdated. The old-timers are forever telling me that morality has gone to hell in a hand basket, but for myself, I enjoy the greater freedom that prevails now. Especially to a widow. I will admit, however, that in Bath the waltz is only done in private homes. You will not see any waltzing here at the Assembly Rooms."

"Pity."

"I joined Gillie up for the dancing class in hopes that you would give her a Season, Lord Southam," she said, and looked for his reaction.

"As you know, that was not my intention. Now that she has nabbed Cleremont without aid of a Season . . ."

They parted, and when the dance permitted, she continued the conversation. "She has not nabbed him. She has caught his interest, but he will be going to London in May."

"That gives her a few weeks."

"Unfortunately, it does not. The duke is leaving soon for Newmarket. He has some nags entered in the races and will be going before then to work with his trainer. At this time of year he is darting hither and thither to small meets as well." Again the demands of the dance took them apart. Southam found this method of conversing difficult, but Mrs. Searle apparently had no trouble with it. When they met again, she continued her persuasions. "He is far from reaching the sticking point. As far as that goes, I am not at all sure Gillie would have him."

"She'll have him all right," he said firmly. Bea just looked at him uncertainly. She disliked that decisive tone. "She mentioned she rides and drives with him daily," he reminded her.

"Not every day. They are good friends, but Tannie doesn't realize yet that he is in love with her, you see. As to Gillie, she is in love with his team, which is not precisely the state of affairs that would lead to acceptance if he offered." She wafted away to the steps of the dance.

When they met again, Southam had his answer ready. "He's not likely to hand over the team without including himself in the parcel. He ain't that big a booby."

Beatrice drew a deep sigh. "Why is it that men, who can run vast estates, cannot understand the simple elements of making a match?"

Southam cocked his head and answered frivolously, "It's because animals and acres of crop and forest don't insist on falling in love, I expect. If you ladies were running things, you would insist on only breeding a prime stallion with one mare."

At the end of the dance the party went to the tearoom, where Bea made sure Southam and the duke were seated at the same table. Southam was at pains to draw the duke out. "I hear you are interested in racing," he said, smiling.

"My name is up for the Jockey Club." As this came perilously near to boasting, something the duke abhorred, he added, "Daresay I shan't be let in for a decade yet."

"One can only try," Southam said supportively. "This is an interesting time for you—the five classics."

"Four in spring. The Saint Leger is run in September." The duke wanted to make a favorable impression on Gillie's brother. This, unfortunately, required conversation of more than two or three syllables. Racing was the only area in which he felt

53

competent to discourse rationally, so he rattled on. "One and three-quarters miles."

"I thought it was one and a half," Southam said.

"Derby's one and a half. Oaks is one and a half. Ascot's two and a half. All ages and sexes. Gold Cup."

"Just so. Well, I daresay you are looking forward to the Season."

"I have a sweet filly running in the Oaks. My Firefly took it last year. Three-year-old. Well, has to be, what? Running her sister, Flame, this year."

"I meant the social Season, in London."

"Oh, that Season. Mmm." No comment occurred to the duke on that Season. "Are you going to Bournemouth?" he asked.

Southam frowned in perplexity. "Bournemouth?"

"Hurdle races start this week."

"No, I shan't be attending those."

The duke gave Gillie a commiserating look and turned to speak to her. Southam ran out of ideas, and the conversation lapsed, to the mixed relief and regret of both participants.

Nothing of great interest occurred over the remainder of the evening. At eleven sharp the music stopped, and the guests left. Southam accompanied the ladies to Saint Andrew's Terrace. He accepted Mrs. Searle's invitation to join her for a glass of wine, apologizing for the lateness of the hour.

"It is only eleven-thirty!" she said, laughing. "Your carriage does not turn into a pumpkin at midnight, I hope. Good gracious, in London the parties go on till three or four in the morning. Here in Bath we frequently go out for a late supper after an assembly. Of course, when we are chaperoning the young debs, we must curtail our activities."

"I hope having Gillie is not too great a restraint on your amusements."

"Not at all. I enjoy her company." She turned to Gillie. "You had best run up to bed now, dear," she said.

Gillie came to kiss her good-night. "It was a lovely party, Aunt Bea. Goodnight, Rawl." She stopped before leaving and said to her brother, "I don't suppose we could go to Bournemouth?"

"Did the duke suggest it?" he asked.

"He asked you if you were going."

"No, best not. Deborah expects me home Monday."

Gillie's face stiffened, and she left without further entreaties.

Southam noticed with chagrin that his sister showed more warmth for this new friend than for himself. "Why does she call you Aunt Bea?" he asked, to conceal his annoyance.

"Because we wanted some friendlier term than Mrs. Searle, after we had become bosom bows. I could not permit her to use my first name without some handle. Such familiar terms between a chaperon and her charge might lead to trouble."

"You are cousins. She might have called you Cousin."

Bea shrugged. "We are connections, Lord Southam. I am neither her cousin nor her aunt."

"Nor mine, either, but I hope, now that we are friendlier, that you will permit me to call you Beatrice."

"You are old enough to rob it of impropriety," she answered saucily.

"I notice that here in Bath age is no deterrent to merry-making."

"No, indeed. I greatly enjoy my maturity. In fact, I am happy to be rid of the burden of youth. Older ladies, especially if they are widows, are not so en-

55

cumbered with rules as are debs. So long as one heeds the usual proprieties, a widow may do pretty well as she pleases."

"Now that Gillie has left, let me ask you frankly, is she a nuisance for you? Does she tie you down more than you like?"

"Not at all. It is an interesting change, to hobnob with the younger set. Having missed out on motherhood, I am enjoying the privileges without the total responsibility."

"It is truly remarkable how well she has taken to you."

"I hope I am not that hard to get along with!" she exclaimed.

"That was not my meaning. It was meant as a compliment. She is a difficult girl to handle."

"Not really. It boils down to understanding her. She cares more for horses than most girls her age. If one hopes to engage her in social doings, one must wedge them in sideways, under the guise of horsey doings, or with an outing involving horses in the offing. When she catches some other lady throwing her hankie at the duke, she will realize he is a man and she is a woman. Then she will go after him hammer and tong, even if he does not wear a bridle."

"I fear the idea has not occurred to her yet. A pity he will be leaving so soon."

"A pity Gillie cannot have a Season," she replied, watching him from the corner of her eye. She hoped to win him over by repetition.

"I'll speak to Deborah about it," he said, thinking aloud.

Bea felt a stab of anger but bit back the hot retort that rose to her lips. "I expect you can let me know soon, as you will be returning to Elmland on Monday. That is when Deborah is expecting you back, is it not?" He nodded. "There are many details that must be attended to if Gillie is allowed to go. Her name must be entered at Saint James's. I would have to be in touch with Mrs. Louden to arrange her ball and be in touch with other chaperons."

"Have you spoken of all this to Gillie? She will feel sorely done by if she is not allowed to go."

"I am not a complete widgeon! Of course I haven't," she snapped. "But you *will* speak to Deborah as soon as you return, I hope. Even she might approve, when the prize is a duke."

Southam noticed her piqued tone. "Why do you say *even* she, as if Deborah were unreasonable? She is greatly interested in seeing Gillie settled."

"Then I expect she may give her permission, if you approach her nicely."

There was some mischief lurking in those green eyes. "Give her permission"—was that it? She was saying Deborah had the ring through his nose? "It is not a question of permission. The decision is mine. I am Deborah's brother and guardian. Naturally my fiancée is involved in such decisions, however. She knows more about such things than I, from having lived so long in London."

"Of course. Yet I cannot think she learned much about making matches at the palace. The royal princesses are all wilting on the vine, except Princess Elizabeth, and she was nearing fifty before she nabbed her beau."

"You forget Deborah had a Season herself, Cousin."

"She did not make a match, though." She smiled saucily.

"It was not for lack of offers!" he defended swiftly. "She has a poor opinion of the beaux met there. Fops and Corinthians. She prefers provincial gentlemen, for their steadiness of character."

57

"Like Stuyvesant?" Bea asked ironically. "Or do you mean like yourself, Southam? Certainly one cannot accuse you of foppishness. No, there is no need to lower your brow at me. That was not a slur on your toilet!"

His blackening mood lifted as he watched her green eyes twinkle with amusement. "One cannot accuse the duke of overdressing, either," he said, smiling. "Lord, did you ever see such a disheveled boy in your life? He looks as if he'd been rolling around a cow byre."

"No, a stable! Gillie wasn't much better when she arrived here. If we do bring off this match, we must find them a valet and dresser to turn them out in style."

"It would be an excellent thing for her," Southam said, warming to the idea. "Gillie a duchess, imagine! Most gents are put off by her stable ways, but the duke would feel right at home. It seems to me they are made for each other."

Bea gave him a conning look. "You know how to bring the match off, Southam. Send her to London. As you said, the decision is yours."

He did not reply to this taunt, but said, "I wish he were not going to Bournemouth so soon."

"If wishes were horses . . ."

"Then the duke would love them," he finished, laughing. "I have overstayed my welcome. You must forgive me."

She shrugged. "Not at all. My guests often stay much later than this, but you have had a fagging day. Will you call tomorrow to see Gillie?"

He nodded. "Is eleven too early?"

"Gillie will be riding with the duke, but I shall be here if you want to call. I'll take you on the strut on Milsom Street and make all my beaux jealous. Or we could stay here and have a private coze," she added. This would give her another opportunity to

58

try to tease him into accepting the London idea. A smile moved her lips as she saw Southam try to figure out her aim.

Southam decided there was some enchantment in her smile. It suggested all manner of delightful things, not all of them having to do with Gillie. Deborah would not approve of his spending a morning alone with this enchantress. "I'll see you at eleven, then," he said, and rose to take his leave.

As the carriage jogged through the streets to the White Hart, Southam reviewed the evening. His thoughts soon settled on Mrs. Searle. He knew in his bones that she had changed from her school days with Deborah, or his fiancée would not have suggested her as Gillie's chaperon. She was too dashing, too free in her manners, too flirtatious.

It would be Leonard who had worked the change, of course. Reckless, handsome Leonard. He must have seen the potential in Beatrice, or he never would have married her. No denying he was a highflyer. Just how high, he wondered, did the widow soar? She mentioned more than once how she enjoyed her freedom.

She was too young to be past temptations of the flesh. Did she indulge in discreet amours, taking care that the proprieties were maintained? In Bath the proprieties would be of great concern. At least she would not do anything outrageous with Gillie around. Was that why she had suggested they remain at home tomorrow morning when Gillie was out? Good lord! Surely she wasn't planning to have an affair with him!

He had sensed some incipient seduction in her green eyes. It was no more than flirtation really. Very likely that was all she had in mind. Well, he had nothing against flirtation. He used to be a bit of a dasher himself in his salad days, before he suddenly had the care of Elmdale and his three half sisters thrust on him. And before Deborah. Naturally an engaged man did not flirt with other ladies—not in front of his fiancée in any case.

Soon he would be married. This might be his last chance for a flirtation. He could think of no one more delightful than Mrs. Searle for a partner. He must take care it did not go beyond flirtation.

Chapter Six

Lord Southam's valet was surprised, the next morning, to receive a scolding for not having packed his lordship's new jacket.

"You only wear it to church on Sunday," Scrumm objected.

"Just what did you pack?" Southam demanded.

"The jacket you're wearing and your monkey suit."

"Only knee breeches and silk hose for evening?"

"Miss Swann said that was what was required for the assemblies in Bath."

"No one is wearing knee breeches to private parties. Damme, I'll look like an antique. When did Miss Swann speak to you?"

"She sent me up a note the last day she was at Elmdale." Scrumm's eyes glinted. "Miss Swann didn't think there'd be any private parties. I tossed in your black pantaloons and evening jacket, just in case," he said.

"Thank God for that! Help me with this cravat, Scrumm. I want something different from that hard ball of a knot I usually wear. I noticed a gent at breakfast with a sort of folded, softer look."

"The Oriental," Scrumm nodded. "I learned it off Stuyvesant's man. Tried to get you to try it a month ago," he mentioned.

"So you did."

"You said it looked like a nun's wimple."

"I've changed my mind," Southam said with a glassy stare.

Scrumm performed this sartorial miracle and stood back to admire his handiwork. "The Oriental requires a wider linen, but that's the general style of it. It'd look more stylish with shorter hair. The Brutus-do that Stuyvesant sports—that'd suit your lordship." Scrumm waited for some scalding putdown, and was surprised to see instead a contemplative expression. His efforts to smarten up his lordship seldom met with success. A pity to see such a fine-looking young lad turn out so rusty.

Southam was tempted. He glanced at his watch. "It is nearly eleven. I haven't time. You might see if you can find some of those wider cravats, however, while I'm gone."

"I'll do that." Made brave by this small success, Scrumm ventured further.

"There's a man comes to the inn here to do gents' hair. You could slip in before you dress for dinner this evening. You need an appointment."

Southam examined himself in the mirror. Yes, his hair was an inch longer than the men in Bath were wearing it. Even Mr. Reynolds, who looked every day of forty-five, was wearing the Brutus-do. "Set me up for six-thirty," he said.

Scrumm's head jerked in pleasure. There was life in the master yet. "When I'm buying the wide cravats, would you like me to pick up a spotted Belcher kerchief for you? You see them everywhere nowadays—except in Alderton."

Southam gave him a killing stare. "I think not, Scrumm. I am not a dancing master after all." He picked up his curled beaver and gloves. The gloves, he noticed, were discolored at the ends of the fingers. "You might see if you can find me a new pair of York tan gloves. You know my size."

A newly tied cravat was not sufficient change to make Southam uncomfortable when he was admitted to Mrs. Searle's saloon. He entered with an easy smile. Mrs. Searle sat alone in her morning parlor, glancing through the journals. She looked entirely enticing in a green sarcenet gown a shade darker than her eyes. An elegant paisley shawl lay beside her on the sofa. Above the gown her ivory skin seemed almost luminous. A lovely complexion she had.

"Good morning, Cousin. Did you get our girl off with the duke?" he asked, making a brief and rather graceless bow.

"Indeed I did." Her flashing eyes just skimmed over the cravat. "Very handsome," she said. "Come and sit down." She patted the sofa seat beside her, but there was no air of flirtation in her manner. Just so would she have spoken to Gillie. "Why do you call me Cousin? I thought we had agreed there was no impropriety in your calling me Beatrice."

Why had he? Was it to dilute the guilty feeling he had when he was with her? To create some informality without suggesting intimacy? "You are my cousin Leonard's widow. It seems appropriate," he parried, trying to give an impression it had slipped out by chance.

She nodded indifferently. "I fear I have some bad news for you. The duke is leaving for Bournemouth tomorrow! Is that not wretched luck?"

"How long is he staying?" he asked, taking up the proffered seat.

"A week. And soon he will be going to Newmar-

63

ket. I fear he may forget all about Gillie amid such stiff competition."

"There won't be many ladies there before the races."

"Ladies? Don't be absurd. I mean fillies. Really there is not a single whiff of April or May between the pair of them, Southam. The only odor is horse-flesh. Tannie was jawing at her for being two minutes late, and she hadn't the wits to let her lower lip tremble. She shot back, sharp as a barking dog, that she'd often had to wait longer for him. I fear this is a lost cause." She shook her head and felt the coffeepot. It was cold.

"We must do something to waken her up."

They sat, thinking. "Would you like some coffee?" she asked. "Perhaps it will sharpen our wits."

"Coffee is not good for you," he said automatically. Deborah was vehemently against the indiscriminate serving of coffee. She permitted one cup in the morning. "It keeps you awake."

Beatrice blinked in surprise. "I hope you were not planning to fall asleep on me at eleven o'clock in the morning! You make me wonder what you did when you left here, Southam. Did you have a very late night? Slipped the leash, did you? One last prowl before you are caught in parson's mouse-trap?"

"I went straight home to bed!" he exclaimed, shocked at her racy ideas.

She disliked that Puritan face and decided to tease him. "That is where one usually goes with a lightskirt, is it not?"

"Upon my word! You have a fine idea of my character."

She tilted her head and laughed at him. "I was *joking*, Southam. Now before you feel constrained to deliver me a lecture, let me assure you I do not talk so broad in front of your little sister. Between us enlightened adults, however, there is nothing amiss in a joke, I hope."

He lifted his brows and gazed at her. "Nothing amiss in such jokes to Leonard's cousin," he agreed. "I fear certain gentlemen might misread you."

"Very likely, but I do not associate with rakes or rattles of that sort. Now—no, before we begin, I shall have coffee. Would you like some tea?"

"I'll have coffee if that's what you're having."

Over coffee they racked their brains for some means of advancing Gillie's romance at top speed. "A little jealousy might help," Bea said. She sat with her chin in her hands, staring at her lap.

Even in that mundane pose, Southam found some charm in her. He looked at her long lashes, curling over her lids. Sunlight from the window painted her raven hair in hues of indigo and amber, with flashes of crimson. Odd that jet black hair should hold so many shades.

She looked up as the silence stretched and found him gazing at her. "You mean, another beau for competition?" he asked.

"No, stoopid! Tannie is already half in love with her. I mean, another girl to make Gillie look lively. All the mamas are after him like foxes after a hare. They recognize a prime *parti* when they see him, if their foolish daughters do not. The difficulty is that Tannie never looks at them unless they are riding. And then he only looks to see how they sit their mount."

"Then we should enlarge the riding parties."

"Except that he is leaving for Bournemouth tomorrow."

Southam rubbed his chin with his fist and took his decision. "We'll just have to follow him."

Her head lifted, and her eyes were like smiling emeralds. "Go to Bournemouth, you mean?" she asked.

"Why not?"

"It's fifty miles away! It would take a day to get there. And what is there to do, other than looking at the hurdle races?"

"We need not attend all the races. We'll take Miss Pittfield with us. She can play propriety. Why, it is a famous watering place. There must be many facilities for tourists. There is the New Forest for drives. . . ."

"We? Did you mean for *me* to go with you?" she asked, startled. "I thought you meant you and Gillie."

Southam gave a conscious look. In his mind it was a holiday with Beatrice he was envisaging. Gillie and Tannie had fallen to the bottom of his mind. "Yes. I would like to repay you in some manner for having Gillie. It will be a short holiday, at my expense."

Bea drew her brows together in consideration. "Holidaying with a gentleman at his expense sounds a trifle—irregular," she said. "I don't know what my friends would think."

"Why, they would think you are moving heaven and bending earth to land the duke for your charge and commend you for your efforts. If it is the proprieties that deter you, let me remind you Miss Pittfield would be along."

"Yes, it is the proprieties," she admitted. "I would love to go. Naturally I did not mean your intentions were evil, Southam. You are engaged to Deborah." Her frown deepened. "*She* might not like it," she warned, and looked for his reaction.

"I'll handle Deborah," he said airily. His tone said, "If she don't like it, then she can lump it." But in his mind he knew she would dislike it very much, and he had no intention of telling her.

"I suppose there is no harm in it," she said pensively. "Yes, why not? It might be the very thing to seal the romance. I doubt the place will be crowded in March, but perhaps we ought to send a request for rooms today. I have a book of travel here somewhere that will tell us what is for hire."

She called her servant to fetch the book. She and Southam pored over it while they had their coffee. When Beatrice lifted the pot to pour herself another cup, Southam held his cup out without thinking.

"The Royal Bath on the east cliff has fine views of the sea," she read. "The prices are a little stiff."

"We'll want a view of the sea. We'll take it. I shall make the arrangements."

A holiday mood already prevailed in the parlor. Beatrice had never been to Bournemouth, and a holiday at this fashionable resort town, without expense, put her in a good mood. She chattered idly, really thinking out loud. "It might be considered a trifle fast, but then, Miss Pittfield will be along. It was not as though we were going alone, Southam, just you and I with Gillie. Your having a title and a fiancée will lessen the odium of it as well."

"If you are truly worried . . ."

She shook away the wisps of concern. "No. Why should I be? After all, I went to Brighton with Sir Harold Whitehead."

A loud exclamation rent the air. "What!"

"Sir Harold and his mama and a large party. Quite unexceptionable, but Harold and I did stay at the same hotel, so he cannot cut up stiff over this."

"Is he in a position to question your actions?" he inquired testily.

"We are not engaged, if that is your meaning. It is only that gentlemen *do* seem to feel they have the right to question their lady friends' actions."

"If he has anything to say, let him say it to me," Southam declared with a kindling eye.

"That won't be necessary. I manage my own life. You won't forget to send a note off about the rooms?"

"I'll do it this instant."

Beatrice led him to her study, and while he was composing his note, Gillie and Tannie returned home from their ride. Southam, hearing the racket, came out and dispatched the note with his groom.

The young couple wore no traces of dalliance. "You demmed near drove that dung cart off the road. I told you to ease over farther to the right," Tannie was saying.

Gillie gave him a blighting stare and replied, "There was a ditch. Did you want me to drive us into the ditch?"

"We missed that cart wheel by inches. No, by an inch."

"We missed it. That's the important thing."

Southam and Beatrice exchanged a forlorn look. "Can you stay to lunch, Tannie?" she said, hoping for a better mood to prevail under her managing hand.

"I'm meeting Duncan McIvor for lunch. He's hiring a nag for his sister this afternoon. We're going over to the stable to look over the cattle."

No thanks for her offer. Nothing. The boy was hopeless, and Gillie looked as if she couldn't care less.

"Shall we see you this evening, then?" Bea persisted.

"The McIvors have invited me for dinner. Thank you anyway," he added, to impress Southam.

"And tomorrow you're going to Bournemouth," Gillie added. "Will you ride with me in the morning, Aunt Bea?"

"Mrs. Searle won't be here," Southam announced. Gillie looked aghast. Before she could object, he

68

added, "She will be going to Bournemouth with us, Gillie."

"To Bournemouth! Rawl, you're taking me! Oh, thank you." She pelted forward and threw her arms around his neck.

"Very glad to hear it," Tannie said, smiling vaguely. "Where will you be staying? We might get together. McIvor and I are putting up at the Lansdown. His pockets are pretty well to let," he added.

"We shall be at the Royal Bath," Beatrice told him.

Tannie drew out his watch and said, "I'd best be going. No saying what tired old dray horse McIvor will hire if I ain't there to advise him. Not that I would like to see his sister astride a decent bit o'blood. She lamed his Lancer, trying to follow him over a fence at Uncle Horatio's place. Gudgeon."

On this remark he rammed his hat on his head, made a bow even less graceful than Southam's, and took his leave. "I look forward to seeing you at Bournemouth, Mrs. Searle, Southam." He forgot to include Gillie in this wish.

She neither noticed nor cared. She was too excited at the pending adventure. "I have never seen hurdle races. I bet Penny could beat them all. I wonder if they have betting. Tannie told me his uncle Horatio made a monkey last year, then blew the lot on the last race. Gudgeon."

It seemed the only change in her demeanor due to her association with the duke was an increase in unladylike cant terms.

"You should not use such language about your elders, Gillie," Bea said.

"I have heard Tannie call him worse names."

Gillie went to toss her bonnet and pelisse at the butler, and during her short absence, Bea whispered, "Jealousy" to Southam. When Gillie returned, Bea gave him a wink and said to Gillie,

"This Duncan McIvor, he would be Miss Althea McIvor's brother, would he not?"

"I believe so. Duncan has three sisters."

"The elder is married, and the younger is not out. It would be Althea that Tannie is interested in, I daresay."

Gillie looked at her with a sapient eye. "Not likely. She sits her mare like a bag of oats, jiggling all over."

Southam took over. "That may be of interest if he meant to hire Miss Althea as a jockey. I take it your meaning is that he has a tendre for her, Cousin?"

"I expect so," Bea said offhandedly. "She is monstrously pretty, with her blond curls and blue eyes. And so ladylike, don't you think, Gillie?"

"She is pretty enough," Gillie said grudgingly.

"I notice Tannie alway stands up with her first at the waltzing parties."

"He asks me first," Gillie shot back. "He's an awful dancer."

"Such fripperies are important in a lady, but less so in a gentleman," Southam said. "Naturally a gentleman wants his bride to appear to have all the social graces. Especially when he is so eligible as the duke. I daresay all the ladies are tossing their bonnets at him, eh Cousin?"

"It is all the mothers talk of," she agreed. "What a prime catch for some fortunate lady. Three vast estates, a large fortune, and, of course, one of the finest stables in the country." She peered at Gillie as she named this last advantage.

"I never heard Tannie complain of the girls bothering him," Gillie objected.

"Complain!" Bea laughed.

Gillie saw nothing amiss in her choice of word. "I don't think he is interested in Althea at all," she said.

70

"It would be gauche of him to praise another lady to you, Gillie," Bea pointed out. "You tend to forget it, but you are a lady yourself. You won't hear a whisper of the romance till Miss Althea comes flashing the diamond under your nose, crowing of her catch."

Gillie frowned and took up Southam's cup without thinking. "I wonder if *she* is going to Bournemouth," she said, eyes narrowing in suspicion.

The two conspirators exchanged a triumphant glance. At least she recognized that competition was out there. Gillie sipped and put the cup down. "Are you drinking coffee in the middle of the morning, Rawl? You know Deborah doesn't let you."

A slight flush colored his cheeks. "I do as I please," he said.

"Yes, when Deborah is not here to keep a sharp eye on you." Gillie laughed. "Did you write her that you shan't be home by Monday?"

"Not yet. I'll drop her a line before we leave."

"I'm glad we will get away before she hears, or she'd write forbidding it."

"Go and wash your face," Southam said grimly. "You're covered in dust. No wonder the duke has no interest in you."

"He has an interest in me. He calls on me more than anyone else."

"Aye, as a fellow horseman, but not as a suitor."

"What would I want a suitor for?" she riposted, and stalked out of the room.

"That's put a bee in her bonnet," Southam said, and took up his cup to sip cold coffee. He was unhappy at the impression Gillie had left behind that he was completely under Deborah's paw. Such nonsense! He did as he liked; it was just that Deborah was such a sensible lady and took such a strong interest in him and his family. He had never cared much for coffee anyway. As to Bournemouth, she

71

wouldn't object when she learned the reason. Deborah was all for advancing the family in the traditional ways, such as advantageous matches. She would be delighted to be related to a duke, and even more so to get Gillie bounced off.

"What are we doing this afternoon?" he inquired.

"Gillie and I will be preparing for this holiday."

"It won't take long to throw a few gowns into a trunk."

"I see you have never traveled with a lady of fashion before, Southam," she replied with another of those flirtatious glances that always sent his blood racing. "Your education is sorely inadequate. Gowns must be selected, pressed, packed in silver paper. Accessories must be chosen, probably new silk stockings purchased, for those that match one's favorite gown are bound to have sprung a hole. Why, you will be fortunate if we are ready to leave by morning."

"Surely you are joking!"

"Indeed I am not. You gentlemen who have only to pull on your blue jacket and run a brush through your hair have no notion how difficult it is for a lady to turn out in style."

"Such intensive efforts will leave you hungry. You must be planning to eat dinner at least. Let us go out for dinner."

"There is no point," she said. "Tannie is dining with the McIvors. You are welcome to dine here if you are at loose ends."

"I don't want to put you to any trouble."

"I did not wish to cramp your style, or I would have suggested it sooner." Again those laughing green eyes studied him. "I thought you might have more interesting company."

"Now you are putting ideas in my head, Cousin."

"Ah, well, in that case you had best dine here,

where Gillie and I can keep an eye on you. I would not want to be responsible for your going astray so close to your wedding."

"Sevenish?" he asked.

"I usually dine at eight, but as you are still making the transfer from country hours, let us compromise and say seven-thirty."

"I look forward to it."

His bow, when he left, was less countrified than before. Or perhaps it was just his anticipatory smile that made it seem better.

When she sat alone after his departure, Bea felt that if she had six weeks with Southam, as she was having with his sister, she could whip him into shape, too. But then, why should she go to so much bother for Deborah Swann?

Chapter Seven

"Rawl, you've got a new hairstyle!" Gillie exclaimed, when her brother entered that evening. His hair was clipped short and brushed forward.

"My hair needed cutting. This is the way barbers do it in Bath," he said. His eyes flew warily to Bea, who was examining him with interest.

"The Brutus suits you," she said. Her feminine intuition sensed his lack of ease and his unconscious turning to her for approval.

"And you're wearing a more stylish cravat," Gillie added.

"Scrumm bought it for me this afternoon. Trying to smarten me up. I daresay he is ashamed of me in my provincial garb. Next he will be sticking wadding in my shoulders and buying me top boots with a white edge."

"It looks nice. Does he not look nice, Aunt Bea?"

"Very handsome," she conceded. "Deborah will not recognize you when you return. And speaking of Deborah, there is a letter for you in the evening post. She sent it in my care, as she was unsure what inn you were putting up at."

When a servant brought the letter, she was surprised to see Southam stick it in his pocket unread. "It might be important, Southam," she said.

He took it out and read it. His countenance did not assume any air of excitement but only a certain rigidity about the jaws. Deborah wrote that she was sorry to upset him, but it had been necessary to dismiss one of his footmen. She had caught Tolliver stealing a bottle of Southam's best sherry. He had tried to bam her that it was for Cook; Cook had supported him in this patent untruth. As Southam knew very well, Cook was not allowed to use the family drinking sherry for her cooking. Deborah had added two teaspoons of salt to the bottle, to insure that it was used for cooking and not for purposes of debauchery. She had told Cook that in future she must use only the cheap sherry for cooking, etc. Demmed interfering of Deborah! What the devil had she been doing at the house when he was away?

"Not bad news, I hope?" Bea inquired.

"Merely a domestic crisis. Deborah handled it."

"Which of the servants has she had a fight with now?" Gillie asked.

"Don't be impertinent," he said curtly, and rammed the letter into his pocket.

Gillie fastened a demanding pair of eyes on her brother. "I hope it wasn't Abe or Elmer."

"Of course it wasn't a groom. What would Deborah be doing in the stable?"

"I wonder what she was doing at the house," Gillie continued, then answered her own question. "Cook's birthday! I expect you gave her Armitage's birthday envelope to deliver."

In the confusion of his unplanned trip, Southam had forgotten this minor domestic celebration. He doubted Deborah had remembered it, either, but he knew now why the footman had been taking the bottle of sherry. The servants would have their own little celebration for Armitage. The sherry incident must have put a fine crimp in it. He'd have to apologize to Armitage. He'd send her a little something extra for her birthday and ask her to have the dismissed footman recalled. Deborah was only trying to be helpful, of course, but at times her help could be a demmed nuisance.

"Exactly," Southam said.

It was obvious to the meanest intelligence that he was lying, and that he was upset.

Before Gillie caused any further deterioration in her brother's mood, Bea changed the subject by calling for sherry. "You will observe, if you please, that I have taught your savage sister to sip her sherry without wincing," she said, handing Southam a glass. "She demanded ale the evening she arrived."

"I still prefer it," Gillie said, but she said it with a smile.

The conversation turned to their holiday and continued on that subject through dinner. To push Gillie into the proper frame of mind, Bea said casually, "Sir Harold Whitehead and his mama called on me this afternoon. She mentioned that Mrs. McIvor hired a pianist for her dinner party. That would be to allow the youngsters to dance this evening, to throw Tannie and Miss Althea together."

"And she didn't invite me!" Gillie said, not angry, but slightly miffed.

As Bea knew perfectly well that the entertainment was to be a concert and doubted very much that either Duncan or Tannie would attend, she tried to smooth it over. "I believe she had her guest list made up a week ago. No doubt the dancing was a last-minute thing, when she learned Tannie was to attend."

Southam was more interested to hear that Sir Harold had been allowed to call, when he himself had been turned out. "I trust Sir Harold and his mama did not remain long enough to delay your packing for Bournemouth," he said.

"Only long enough to invite me to a card party tomorrow evening, which I, of course, was obliged to decline. I gauged their reaction closely when I explained the reason. You will be happy to learn, Southam, you are considered completely harmless. No eyebrows rose—well, not more than an inch or so. Sir Harold harrumphed in displeasure, at which point I hastily inserted that Miss Pittfield would accompany us."

Southam was obliged, by Gillie's presence, to hear this slight in silence. "Where is Miss Pittfield?" he inquired. "I have not seen her since my arrival."

"She dines with us when we are at home alone," Bea explained. "She tells me she does not dine with company at Elmland. She seems to consider you company, Southam. She insisted on eating with the housekeeper this evening."

"Miss Pittfield came to us as a governess years ago. We consider her part of the family, but she stands high on her dignity. From time to time she takes these freakish notions."

"It began the day Deborah asked her whether she was paid," Gillie explained. "Deborah told her that as she still receives a salary, she should consider herself a servant. In case you hadn't noticed, Rawl, it is when Deborah dines with us that Miss Pittfield eats with the housekeeper."

Southam directed a quelling glare on his sister.

"You are obviously mistaken. Deborah is not with us this evening."

Beatrice would like to have heard more of this. A hostess's job was to maintain a pleasant atmosphere, however, and she dutifully changed the subject. "If you want to have a word with Miss Pittfield later, you will find her in the housekeeper's parlor, chirping merry over this unexpected holiday."

"I trust her eyebrows did not rise, either, when you told her of it?" Southam asked.

"She thought it an excellent idea. Do you a world of good, she said."

A few subtle hints let Southam know he was not to linger long after dinner. Phrases like "an early night before traveling" and "still a few things to pack" left him in no doubt. He took only one glass of port after dinner and planned to leave within a half hour of joining the ladies. He wanted a few moments alone with Bea before leaving, telling himself they had planning to do to hasten Gillie's romance. Yet some deeper well of truth in him admitted that he also wanted a little flirtation. No harm in it. Mrs. Searle was an engaging lady. Why, a married man would do no less.

When he went to the saloon, he was surprised and not at all pleased to see Sir Harold Whitehead ensconced in a chair, with Mr. Reynolds on the sofa beside Beatrice. Southam had made their acquaintance at the Upper Rooms, and said goodevening.

"I was just telling Beatrice," Mr. Reynolds said, "that I heard of her little trip—no thanks to Sir Harold. You should have told me, sly dog! I came to say farewell and urge her to return as soon as possible." He turned to Bea, "No need to tell you, madam, that the town will be a desert without you."

"How did you hear of it, if not from Sir Harold or his mama?" she asked.

"I daresay Sir Harold's mama told her crones. Word is buzzing along the grapevine: hang up the knocker in crape, don your mourning bands. Mrs. Searle is leaving us."

Southam noticed that Bea smiled at this absurdity. How could she tolerate these old fools? He saw a box of bonbons sitting on the sofa table and a bouquet of flowers—farewell tributes from her swains. All this had the aroma of romance.

"Next time I shall tell Mama to hold her tongue," Sir Harold said, with a jealous eye at Reynolds.

Reynolds, not to be outdone, began to pester Bea. "You have been to Brighton with Sir Harold; you are off to Bournemouth with Lord Southam; when am I to have the honor of making a trip with you, Beatrice?"

"Why, as soon as you acquire a mama, or maiden aunt, or sister to chaperon us, sir. You cannot expect me to traipse off alone with a gentleman!"

"Quite so, but that is not to say we could not take a dart to the coast, to Portishead or Avonmouth, some day and be home by evening."

"Portishead!" Sir Harold disparagingly. "Is that your idea of an outing? I am surprised you don't suggest touring the slums. What we ought to do is make up a party and go to visit the Lake District."

"An excellent notion!" Reynolds said. "You and your mama, Mrs. Searle and myself."

"And Mrs. Searle's chaperon!" Bea added, laughing. "You are shocking Lord Southam, gentlemen. He will expect me to reach down and tie my garter in public, the way you natter on."

79

She gave them a cup of tea. As soon as this was taken, she summarily dismissed them. Southam was the last to go. Between Deborah's letter and Bea's beaux, he was in a vile humor and did very little to conceal it.

"Where has Gillie taken herself off to?" he asked curtly.

"She is having Miss Pittfield do her hair up in papers, to present a ravishing picture tomorrow."

"Just as well she missed that visit from your beaux. Are they accustomed to cluttering up your saloon in the evening?"

Her eyes narrowed at his tone. "Why, no, they are not so inconsiderate. I more usually go out or have a larger party in for dinner. They came this evening to wish me a pleasant trip."

"Did you ever think of hiring a chaperon, Mrs. Searle?"

Her green eyes flashed dangerously. "For your information, Southam, I *am* a chaperon. You have not forgotten, surely, that you sent your young sister to me. If you feel me competent to guide and protect *her*, then common sense must tell you that I can chaperon myself."

"I didn't care overly much for the way those two old roués were speaking."

"Then you ought to have left!" she shot back angrily. "I am not about to take lessons in propriety from a provincial, even if he has a handle to his name. My friends are not roués; they are gentlemen. They would no more try to take advantage of me than they would dare to read me this lecture you are attempting to deliver. You were surly and rude throughout their entire visit. Whatever was in that letter you received, it is obvious it has upset you considerably. I pray you will get it straightened out before we leave for Bournemouth."

80

"This has nothing to do with the letter."

"Then what has it to do with? Are you criticizing my friends, my morals, what? If you feel I am not straitlaced enough to guard Gillie, then you may take her home, for I do not intend to change my ways to suit you. You are not even a relation, but only a slight connection through Leonard."

"It was only meant as a word of warning. I thought perhaps you did not realize . . ."

"Live all my life in Bath and not realize that tongues wag at the slightest hint of impropriety? Whatever I may choose to do in my private life, you may be very sure I give no cause for scandal. Now, if you will excuse me, Southam, I am tired. I have to speak to my housekeeper about managing the house while I am away."

"I'm sorry if I upset you, Cousin," he said gently, for he knew her anger was justified. "You are quite right, of course. And I have no qualms about your guardianship of Gillie."

"Do you want a word with Miss Pittfield before leaving?"

"I'll see her tomorrow. There is no need to detain you further."

She accompanied him to the door, where she handed him his hat and gloves. As she was to be confined in a carriage with him for the better part of the next day, Beatrice wanted to patch up the little quarrel. "Was there bad news in your letter?" she asked in a more friendly tone.

"Only a fracas over a bottle of sherry," he said, shaking his head at the troublesome triviality.

"I won't suggest you are such a nipcheese as to salt the cooking sherry, thus forcing your servants to pilfer a bottle, so I conclude you have a tippler on your staff. They can be the very devil, but I am sure Deborah has given him a stiff lecture."

"Yes," he replied as calmly as her words allowed.

They made their adieux and parted friends. Southam was unhappy with his behavior. It was outrageous of him to complain of Mrs. Searle's private life, when he had battened Gillie on her with no real excuse. No wonder she fired up at him. How her eyes had flamed! Still, it was a trifle fast, her running about here and there with gentlemen. Was she having an affair with one of them? That remark, let out in the heat of argument, about maintaining an air of propriety whatever she was doing, was ambiguous to say the least. Reynolds, he thought, had the inner track.

Not much of a catch for the dashing Beatrice Searle. With her looks and charm she could do better for herself. Any gentleman would be proud to escort her. Some ladies were made for wives, and some were made for mistresses, and to him, Beatrice seemed the ideal mistress. Beautiful, certainly. A widow, therefore not a prude. They would be together at the inn for a few days. Gillie was sharing a room with Miss Pittfield, and Beatrice had a private room—next door to his own. On the surface, there was nothing to cause scandal. Beatrice boasted of her discretion. It almost seemed an invitation. . . .

Then he thought of Deborah and was unhappy with her behavior. She hadn't used to be so demmed interfering. Surely Gillie was mistaken about her having spoken to Miss Pittfield about her paltry salary. Pittfield, though only a connection, was like a second mother to him. He felt badly about Armitage's ruined birthday as well. Have to write that note off tonight and include a few extra pounds. Would his future life be peppered with such upsets? Deborah, as mistress of Elmland, was supposed to smooth matters on the home front, but since their betrothal it seemed he was constantly involved in minor domestic frictions.

Mrs. Searle, Beatrice, ran a smooth and comfortable house. No salting of the sherry in her kitchen. Whoever decreed that comparisons were odious was right, but they were also inevitable, and for the first time since the advent of Deborah Swann into his life, Southam felt a doubt that he had chosen wisely.

Chapter Eight

The fifty-mile trip in Southam's well-sprung chaise was pleasant. They drove through the spring countryside, with gently rolling hills and rich meadows enlivened by many villages. Until they reached Frome, the roads were busy, but as they approached the broad Vale of Blackmore, the rich pasturelands ahead were less traveled and promised fewer congenial inns, so they took lunch at Wincanton. Afternoon was drawing to a close when the outcroppings of pinewoods alerted them they were nearing their destination. From the rising ground they looked down on a fashionable watering place situated at the mouth of a valley. Hills of pine lifted above, surrounding and protecting it from harsh winds. Beyond the coast, water shimmered gold and orange and crimson in the sunlight.

"Our hotel is on the east cliff," Bea said.

"Yes, John Groom has studied the maps. He will get us there with no trouble," Southam replied.

"I'm starved!" Gillie whined. She was restless from her long incarceration. Bea shot her a warning look. "Pardon me, Aunt Bea. I am feeling peckish. Or must I wait till you ask me?"

"Southam is your host on this trip, Gillie. I would have to admit I am feeling peckish myself if our host asked me."

"Your hints are noted, ladies." He turned to Gillie and added, "This is what happens to young girls who don't eat their vegetables."

They were soon let down in front of the stylish Royal Bath and went in to claim their rooms. After arranging for a private parlor for dinner, Southam took charge of the keys. He led the way upstairs, opened one door, and handed the key to Miss Pittfield.

When Bea made a move to enter as well, he said, "I have hired a separate room for you, Cousin."

She followed him along the hallway to another room. "You are extravagant, Southam!" she exclaimed when he opened the door for her. The room was large and elegantly appointed, with a view of the sea from the east windows. "I would have been perfectly happy sharing a room with Gillie and Miss Pittfield."

She took his flush for pleasure at her praise. "You will want a little privacy from time to time," he said. "Gillie is a renowned chatterbox."

"It is a charming room, but I don't know that I will be quite comfortable sleeping alone here. One hears of break-ins and things in a holiday hotel. The lock looks stout enough," she said, examining it. Her examination prevented her from noticing the gleam of interest in Southam's eyes.

"You will know where to find me if you hear anyone scratching at your door. I am in the next room," he said.

She glanced up then, not suspicious but just acknowledging the information. "I shall bear that in mind. Shall we dress formally for dinner? Let us do it. It will add a festive note to the commencement of our holiday."

"I trust you don't mean I should wear my knee breeches and silk stockings. I left them behind."

"Good gracious, no! We are away from the antique customs and prying eyes of Bath now. We shall enjoy ourselves like modern folks."

Another gleam shot forth from his eyes. She noticed it this time. "*Respectable* modern folks," she added playfully, and turned him around to lead him out the door.

"We'll meet downstairs in half an hour?"

She just looked, shaking her head. "I am not a magician, Southam. It will take at least an hour before I am fit to be seen in public. My housekeeper usually acts as my dresser. I am perfectly capable of making my own toilet, but it will take me more than thirty minutes. We shall meet in one hour in your parlor."

"You don't look that frazzled," he said, using it as an excuse to study her. His gaze lingered on her green eyes and arched eyebrows, so dainty and perfect, they might have been sketched on in charcoal.

"If that is a compliment, which I very much doubt, I thank you. If it is a hint that one hour is too long to wait, then I can only assume that Deborah has spoiled you wretchedly."

"She is punctual, I'll say that for her."

"That is grudging praise, sir! I begin to see that you are not the only one in this engagement who has to put up with—" She came to a guilty halt in midsentence. "You are not at all gallant," she said, trying to pass it off without undue embarrassment. Then she turned him around and shoved him out the door.

"And you, Cousin, are a tyrant! Take care, or I'll lock you in." He dangled her key from his fingers. Bea reached out and grabbed it.

86

When the door was closed behind him, she made a grimace at her blunder. She must be more fatigued than she realized. What a thing to say to an infatuated groom-to-be! Though, as she considered the matter, she realized she had heard very little raving about Deborah from Southam. She was beginning to wonder whether he was not undertaking a marriage of convenience. His scant compliments on his beloved were all to do with her help in managing his household. Her own knowledge of Deborah Swann told her that she was not the sort of lady to engender a wild passion, nor would her years among the spinster princesses have sharpened her up much in that respect.

Pity, for beneath Southam's demure facade, she sensed a more interesting man trying to get out. The new haircut and stylish cravats were but an outer manifestation of a deeper change occurring beneath. She rang for water and made a leisurely toilet.

Bea had long since given over any claim to being anything but a matron. Her gowns were not the pastel hues favored by debs, but the rich jewel tones of a mature lady of fashion. She wore a low-cut gown of claret silk that enhanced the creamy velvet of her throat. It was cinched tightly at the waist and hung in elegant folds to the ground. She never traveled with her diamonds, except to London for the Season. For such a trip as this she wore the pearls given to her by Southam as a wedding gift. They hardly showed at a distance, but at close range, their iridescent hues glimmered attractively. She attached a set of garnet ear pendants. Her only other jewelry was her wedding band of diamond baguettes.

With a last pat of her hair, she turned down the lamp, set the door on the lock, and went along to

Gillie's room. Two taps were enough to tell her Gillie and Miss Pittfield had already gone below stairs, so she went along, not hurrying but glancing around the lobby at the other guests. She was directed to Lord Southam's parlor and proceeded toward it.

"What kept you!" Gillie demanded. "We've been waiting for ages."

"You cannot claim you are starving at least," Miss Pittfield said, "for you have eaten a plate of macaroons."

Southam was standing at the window with a glass of wine in his fingers, looking out at the street. His head turned, his eyes made a slow examination of Bea, and a smile moved over his saturnine features. "Well worth the wait," he said, with a small bow.

She felt he was looking straight through her gown. The intimacy in that gaze warmed her cheeks. When Miss Pittfield cleared her throat, Bea felt that the whole room was aware of the awkward moment. "You are also looking elegant, Southam. I see you are wearing the new cravat your valet purchased. We must keep an eye on him, Gillie, or your brother will take to sprinkling himself with Steak's Lavender Water and carrying a bouquet."

Southam smiled blandly at these charges and went to the table. He poured a glass of wine and carried it to Bea. "I have taken the liberty of ordering dinner, to soothe the savage beast," he said, a glance just flickering off his ravenous sister.

"Roast beef!" Gillie said. "I told Rawl you like it, Aunt Bea."

"Indeed I do. I'm sorry if I kept you all waiting."

Southam drew her a chair and sat down across from her.

"What are we doing tonight?" Gillie asked. Southam looked to Beatrice for instructions.

"There's a dance, here at the Royal Bath," Miss Pittfield mentioned.

"Till we have time to canvass the town tomorrow and see what it offers, it might be best to stay here tonight," Southam commented idly.

Gillie stared into her wine glass. "There wouldn't be any races at night. And Tannie knows where we are staying."

"Perhaps he'll drop in," Bea said, to cheer her.

Dinner arrived and was attacked with vigor. Bea was aware of Southam's dark eyes moving too often in her direction as they ate and talked and lingering longer than they should. He made her uncomfortably aware of her low-cut gown. Over coffee he was staring again. When he lifted his eyes, he found Bea examining him.

"Have you been wondering whether these are the pearls you gave me as a wedding gift, Southam?" she asked. Her tone was ostensibly polite, but he sensed an undercurrent of censure in it. "I have noticed you examining them from time to time. They are indeed the same ones. I am very fond of them."

"I am happy they proved useful."

"Pearls always come in handy," Miss Pittfield said.

The waiter came to remove their plates and announce the dessert choices. Gillie, who had a large sweet tooth, could not choose between the Chantilly cream and more macaroons, so she ordered both, and so did Miss Pittfield.

"I, being a confirmed provincial, will have the apple tart and a wedge of cheddar," Southam said.

"And I, being an aging lady, will have just coffee, or I shall not be able to get my gown buttoned," Bea said.

"Why, you are thin as a rail, Cousin," Southam objected.

"High praise indeed! Next you will be saying I look like a skeleton."

He turned a laughing eye on her. "That was not the simile that occurred to me, I promise you."

"I shan't ask what simile did occur."

"A cat," he said promptly.

"You're making Aunt Bea blush, Rawl," Gillie said. "Don't you know you should never say anything to make a lady blush?"

"If a gentleman is so uncouth," Bea added, "then a lady does not hear it. Though if I had heard it, I would show him my claws. At least he did not say an *old* cat."

"I was referring to your eyes," he said.

Dessert and coffee were brought in. There was no longer any discussion over the taking of coffee. Southam held his cup out without even thinking. Hard on the heels of the waiter came the duke, bumping into the servant and knocking the cheese plate off his tray. It clattered across the floor, with cheese slices flying in all directions.

"Watch what you're about. You nearly knocked me over!" the duke scolded.

"Sorry, sir." The waiter turned to Southam. "I'll get fresh cheese, milord."

"And another cup for our guest. Or perhaps you would prefer a glass of wine, Duke? How about some dessert?"

The waiter's head slewed around to the ungainly guest. In his snuff-brown eyes there was more doubt than amazement that this buffoon was a duke.

"Whatever you are having," the duke said. "To drink, I mean. I've just had dinner."

"Another cup," Southam informed the waiter.

"How long have you been here? Why did you not send a note and let me know you had arrived?" Tannie said. In his shyness he directed his words to Gillie, the least intimidating of the group.

"We arrived late this afternoon. We just changed and came straight down to dinner."

While they were discussing the trip, the waiter returned with another cup and the cheese. Later Gillie asked the duke, "What are you and Duncan doing this evening?"

"A bunch of us are poking around town to see who is here for the races. We will be stopping at all the inns, I expect. We came across my uncle Horatio. He is putting up at the Carlton with some friend who stays there year around."

"Good! I look forward to seeing him. There is a rout being held at this inn," Gillie said.

"Do you have to go?"

The duke, as usual, spoke in his normal voice. Bea used her chaperon's prerogative to join the conversation. "You must know, Gillie cannot knock about town with a bunch of gentlemen. We shall visit the rout here for an hour. I do hope your friends can spare you to us for that long?"

"They would be honored, ma'am. That is to say, I would be honored."

Bea and Southam exchanged a satisfied look. The instant Southam put down his fork, Bea said, "Let's you and I take our coffee to the sofa, Southam. I never like lingering at the table after dinner, with all the confusion of used plates."

"I haven't had my cheese."

She picked up a slice and put it on his saucer.

He looked confused, but followed her lead. Bea caught Miss Pittfield's eyes and beckoned her from the table as well. Miss Pittfield was no stranger to the plan of nabbing the duke. She joined them, wearing a cagey smile.

"He didn't put up any resistance to staying for the rout," Miss Pittfield said, smiling.

"As he had already acceded to that, why are we here, juggling our cups on our knees, when there is a plate of cheddar on the table?" Southam demanded.

"Because we want to leave them alone, ninny-hammer," Bea explained. "Nothing will develop with three chaperons staring at the poor boy."

"He will hardly fall to his knees and crop out into a proposal at the dinner table."

"One would think he had never been young," Miss Pittfield said to Bea. She would not normally be so familiar in front of her employer. Her weeks with Mrs. Searle had lent her behavior a more casual air, though she was never less than a lady.

"Nor ever even had a cap flung at him in his life, since he does not recognize the most basic elements of catching a husband," Bea added, shaking her head at his naïveté. "The idea, Southam, is to throw the couple alone together as often as possible, and let nature take her course."

"If nature don't oblige you, then I expect you have a few more tricks to prod her along?"

"There! He is moving to sit next to her," Bea exclaimed, but in a lowered voice. "Even Tannie, that awkward colt, knows the moves."

"He just wants more sugar for his coffee," Southam said, when Tannie reached for the sugar bowl.

"That is the pretext, Southam, not the reason. Really, I begin to wonder how you ever managed to get a ring around Deborah's finger, you are so uninformed in flirtation."

"I daresay she engineered the whole affair." He laughed. "Though to be fair, I cannot remember her pulling off such stunts as this."

Miss Pittfield took a deep breath and uttered a speech that shocked her for its boldness. "Why do you think Miss Swann suddenly developed an interest in old sermons, Lord Southam, and you with two hundred of them in your library? Did you not notice the interest died as soon as she got her ring?"

He laughed, taking it for a prime joke. "I was maneuvered into love," he said.

Miss Pittfield looked at Bea and lifted her brow. "Well, he was maneuvered at any rate," the look said.

Bea observed the look and filed it away for future consideration. Soon she was preoccupied with something quite different. She touched Southam's elbow. "Do you notice anything unusual?" she asked.

He followed the direction of her gaze to the table. "I don't see him on his knees."

"You don't hear him, either, but his lips are moving. Tannie usually speaks at the top of his lungs. He must be saying something personal, something he doesn't want us to hear."

Southam blinked. "By God, you're right! You ladies are regular Napoleons for strategy."

"Wellingtons, if you please!" she replied. "We plan to *win* this battle—or should I say engagement?"

Miss Pittfield leaned toward the table, eyes gleaming. "Look at that!" she whispered. "Gillie is pouting! She never pouted in her life before. When she is in one of her moods, she wears a face like a sulky dog."

"That expression she is wearing is officially known as a moue, Miss Pittfield," Bea said. "I take that as an excellent harbinger of love. Where the deuce did she learn it?"

Southam cast a teasing eye on her. "Are you not her mentor, Cousin? I assumed she had learned these tricks from you. I promise you she didn't leave Elmland with them."

"That is why you sent her to me, is it not? To smarten her up. I cannot take credit for the moue, however. I do not pout to advantage. Something to do with the shape of my lips, I believe. Leonard was used to tell me I looked like a tired camel when I tried it, so I left it off. We Irish employ the more direct approach of temper tantrums instead."

"I prefer directness myself," Southam said.

"The last resort of the unsubtle," Bea sniffed playfully.

The duke suddenly rose and held Gillie's chair. "Is it all right if I go out to the lobby with Tannie, Aunt Bea? We want to see if any of his friends are staying here, and get them to join us," Gillie said.

"Excellent! Run along," Southam answered.

Bea shot him a killing look. "You'll look after her for us, Tannie?" she said. "We depend on your good judgment not to introduce Gillie to anyone undesirable."

"Certainly, ma'am. I shall keep a sharp eye on her."

"Very well, then. We shall join you shortly at the rout."

The duke bobbed his thanks and left, holding on to Gillie's arm as if he were a constable and she in his custody.

Bea turned to Southam. "Did you have to make it so obvious we were thrilled? A little hesitation would have made his prize seem dearer. That was rather clever of me to have given him the idea he

94

was responsible for her safety, was it not? He will be conscious of his duty. That sense of responsibility will make him take a proprietary interest in Gillie."

"Lord, Mrs. Searle, you are as sharp as a needle!" Miss Pittfield said, staring in wonder.

"The word schemer comes to mind," Southam said, also impressed.

"You did not think a Miss Watkins, of no particular fame or fortune, had won Leonard Searle without knowing what she was about, did you?" Bea laughed. "I hope you are making notes, Southam. You have two more sisters to have bounced off one of these days."

"I shall certainly send them to you, Cousin. If one of 'em don't come home a princess, I shall be mighty surprised."

"All in a night's work. And now, if you will excuse, me, I shall go to my room."

"Are we not going to the rout?" Southam demanded. He was aware of a sharp sense of disappointment. He had been looking forward to dancing with her.

"Of course we are going to the rout. Gillie is not the only lady in search of a match. Miss Pittfield and I are also on the qui vive for a husband, are we not, Miss Pittfield? I am going upstairs to rouge my cheeks and douse myself with perfume. I spotted a very handsome gentleman in the lobby as I came down to dinner. He nodded and smiled. I fully expect that he will approach me later in the evening and ask if he has not met me somewhere before, for I look very familiar. He will use that tired old ploy as a springboard to introduction. He will list half a dozen places we might have met, which will give me a very good idea of his background. If I like the places, I shall accept his offer to stand up for a dance."

"Napoleon be demmed," Southam said. "You are the reincarnation of the wily Odysseus."

"Could you not have said Cleopatra, or at least the Empress Josephine?" she pouted.

A reluctant grin tugged at his lips. "If that ain't a moue, Cousin, I'll eat my hat."

"I wish you would. Now that you have got a decent haircut, that old curled beaver should follow your shorn tresses and narrow cravats into the dustbin." She turned to speak to Miss Pittfield. "Are you coming upstairs, too, or will you go directly to the dance hall?"

"Do you want me to go and chaperon Gillie? Otherwise, I shall just retire."

"Retire? I am shocked at your lack of initiative, Miss Pittfield," Beatrice scolded. "Come and share my rouge pot. There is no saying who will be at the rout. You might nab a *parti*, too, for you are looking very elegant this evening. Retire indeed! It is only nine o'clock."

"Well, if you are sure I shan't be in the way . . ."

"In whose way?" Bea asked, astonished. "We are paying guests. We have as much right to a crack at the gentlemen as anyone else."

"I shall wait for you here," Southam said.

"No, no, run along to the dance, Southam. Miss Pittfield and I shall chaperon each other."

"No, I had best—"

"Go! No other gentleman will bother with us if he thinks we are with you." She turned back to Miss Pittfield. "Really, your cousin has no notion of how to get along in society. Someone ought to give him a Season, to rub off the rough edges."

"Oh, Lord Southam has already been caught. There is no point wasting time or money on him," Miss Pittfield said roguishly.

The ladies left, laughing like schoolgirls. Southam remained behind, sipping his coffee. A rueful smile played over his features. What a lively, enchanting creature she was. Such charm—even dour Miss Pittfield had come to life. Beatrice was not only charming and beautiful but also clever. Beneath the jokes and chatter there was obviously a deal of experience in the art of enticing gentlemen. But did she really plan to let some stranger attach himself to her? A bit rackety, that. He would wait and accompany her to the rout.

Chapter Nine

Southam was waiting, as threatened, when Bea and Miss Pittfield came downstairs. He went forth to meet them in the crowded lobby.

"You must have applied that rouge with a light touch, Cousin. I cannot see any trace of it," he said, by way of a compliment.

"Did you think I would draw two red circles on my cheeks, like a clown at Astley's Circus, Southam, to draw attention to it?"

"You do not take a compliment gracefully for a lady whom I imagine has heard a good many of them in her day."

"I suggest the fault is in the complimenter. 'In her day' suggests that her day is past. As to mentioning my resort to the rouge pot, some things are best noted in silence."

"You said you were going above stairs to rouge your cheeks! How was I to surmise from that that it was a secret?"

"A secret *entre nous*, not to be hollered in front of the world."

"What do you care what this lot think of you?" he said with a disparaging glance at the throng.

With a lady on either arm he proceeded in state to the dancing hall, where a rowdy country dance was in progress. The crew assembled for the rout at the Royal Bath were not those members of the haut ton encountered in the polite saloons of London. There was a smattering of society so crazed over horses that they would come to Bournemouth in March for some undistinguished hurdle races, but their numbers were few. Most of the people were impoverished gentility who wanted a holiday at the seaside and could not afford it in season, so they had come in March, before it was taken over by wealthier patrons.

They took up seats by the wall to await the dance's termination. "We'll have the next waltz," Southam said, inclining his head toward Beatrice.

"And leave Miss Pittfield sitting alone? Indeed we will not!"

"Tannie can dance with her."

"That is even worse! We cannot leave Gillie unattended."

"Why are we here, then, if we cannot dance?" he asked, becoming grumpy from frustration, for of course she was right. "I don't see why you asked Miss Pittfield to join us," he said in a low voice.

"No wonder your servants pinch the sherry, if you treat them so shabbily," she hissed back in a low voice. Under cover of the music, a private conversation was possible, as Miss Pittfield was on Southam's far side. "Miss Pittfield is a lady, Southam. Her lot is dreary enough without confining her to her room at nine o'clock in the evening."

He rose suddenly, excused himself, and disappeared. Beatrice thought he had taken a huff and feared she had pushed him too far. She moved over to the chair beside Miss Pittfield.

99

"Where did Southam go?" Miss Pittfield asked.

"Probably out to blow a cloud. It is rather warm and noisy in here."

"He never did care much for dances. I was surprised he suggested we come."

The ladies enjoyed themselves, quizzing the dancers and the chaperons to their hearts' content and not omitting the single gentlemen ranged along the wall, either. As the music drew to a close, Southam suddenly appeared before them. He had in tow an elderly gentleman who looked as if he might be a schoolmaster or a minor civil servant. Though he was obviously genteel, his jacket was lacking in nap, and his hair had not seen scissors in some weeks. Bea thought he must be some poor relation and waited with little interest to meet him.

"Cousin, Miss Pittfield, I would like you to meet Mr. FitzGeorge," Southam said. "He owns an apothecary shop in Poole. He has come to Bournemouth for the hurdle races. Putting up here at the Royal Bath, like ourselves. Is that not a coincidence?"

Bea searched her mind in vain for the great coincidence that made this introduction eligible. "How nice to meet you, Mr. FitzGeorge," she said, smiling gamely in her confusion.

Southam steered FitzGeorge to the chair beside Miss Pittfield. "Here is the very gentleman who can suggest a remedy for that—er, cough you have been complaining of, Miss Pittfield. Ah, they are tuning up their fiddles for a waltz. Miss Pittfield, I'm sure you will give Mr. FitzGeorge the pleasure of a dance. He is an old bachelor like myself and doesn't know any ladies here." He turned back to Bea. "Cousin, will you do me the honor?"

Bea bit back a laugh and accepted his arm. "You are a complete hand, Southam!" she said, laughing, when they had escaped. "Where on earth did you find him?"

"In the taproom. He was sitting alone, peacefully enjoying an ale when I shanghaied him. Mind you, I vetted him before entrusting Miss Pittfield to his care. He has a brother a vicar in Poole. That speaks well for his family's character. His business is thriving, too. He has twenty thousand pounds. Not bad!"

"How did you find out all that in five minutes?"

"Getting the offer is the lady's job. Checking out the victim is the man's. If you have trained Miss Pittfield well, she'll have her offer before we leave town."

"You not only vetted him; you found him and dragged him to the rout. You are encroaching on the ladies' territory. I must say, you learn quickly," she said, as he drew her into his arms for the waltz.

His dark eyes smiled indulgently into hers. "I am making rapid strides under your tutelage, Cousin."

"You must put these lessons to good use when you go home. With persistence you may even get that reluctant bride of yours to the altar before she is too old to provide you an heir."

Southam found that reference to Deborah bothersome. He chose to ignore it. "The handsome gent from the lobby hasn't come forward yet to discuss the various venues where you and he might have met but didn't?"

"He was about to make his move when you brought in Mr. FitzGeorge."

"Slow top! Did he think a prime flirt like yourself would sit a whole five minutes without finding a partner?"

"Indeed he did not. He had first to establish by questioning glances that he was 'recognizing' me. He looked quite brokenhearted when you came rushing back so soon and spoiled his chances."

"Are you serious?" he asked, frowning.

"You mean, about my handsome gent? No, I would hardly call it serious. I had not planned to marry him. It was only a seaside flirtation I had in mind. There is something to be said for variety, don't you think? Sir Harold and Mr. Reynolds are all very well in their way, but their stories are familiar to me by now. They lack spice."

"If it is only a seaside flirtation you have in mind, why look further than myself? You must not think I cannot provide you with flirtation, only because I am engaged to your friend." His tone was facetious, and Bea replied in the same spirit.

She considered his suggestion a moment, then shook her head firmly. "No, it is not the same thing at all. There must be at least the possibility of something beyond flirtation developing, or the whole game loses its zest."

A reckless smile flashed, and he said, "It can go as far as you like, only stopping short of an offer, of course, as I am already taken."

"You misunderstand the game, sir. If I am not to have the pleasure of breaking your heart, what is the point?"

He studied her a long moment, then said, "I wager you could do that too, Cousin."

She lifted her head and met his gaze, while the music reeled around them and they swirled in giddy circles. Southam was a surprisingly agile dancer. "You tempt me, Southam, for I begin to see Deborah has not won herself the prize I thought she had. You, sir, are a gazetted flirt. Take care, or I shall take you up on that offer of breaking your heart."

"I'm game. Did you realize you slipped into an unwitting compliment there, Beatrice? That is the first indication that you thought me a prize."

"Don't let it go to your head. A title and a large

102

estate are always considered a prize, even if the man who goes with them is a booby."

"A booby! Upon my word, you are hard on me! I have sunk from a provincial to a gazetted flirt to a booby in two minutes. Have I no redeeming features?"

"Can we not find something more interesting to talk about than you?" she scolded. She looked around the floor and spotted the apothecary. "FitzGeorge waltzes well," she said. "And only look how lightly Miss Pittfield moves. She has been practicing with Gillie. I told her it might come in handy."

"A booby!" he repeated, in accents of deep injury.

"And a bore. No, Southam, we are *not* going to discuss your interesting character, no matter how much you harp on it. I shall have the next waltz with Mr. FitzGeorge, and you must stand up with either Gillie or Miss Pittfield."

"Yes, *you* get to gallivant with Mr. FitzGeorge, while I am forced to stand up with my sister or her chaperon. Slim possibilities there for a gazetted flirt. I daresay this is some deep ploy to ditch me and take up with your handsome gent."

Her eyes sparkled, and her smile brought out a hitherto unseen dimple at the corner of her lips. "Just so, Southam. You are coming to know me uncomfortably well."

The music stopped, but he held her a moment longer in his arms. "Not so well as I would like to, Cousin."

Beatrice noticed he was no longer smiling. His tone, too, suggested something different—she could hardly put a word to it. Was it possible Southam was getting some ideas he shouldn't? His conversation had bordered on the unseemly. All in fun, of course, but then a man would oftentimes float a serious notion under the guise of a joke, to see how it

103

went off. Her eyes flashed dangerously. "If you try to get to know me more intimately, you might be surprised, Southam." She disengaged herself from his arms.

He replied, "I like surprises. As you said, the spice of the unfamiliar."

"I don't think you would care for Irish spice," she said, leveling a cool stare on him.

"One never knows till he tries. I am very fond of Irish whisky."

"But I was speaking of Irish *temper*, Southam."

She turned and walked hastily back to their chairs by the wall. She spoke to Miss Pittfield and Mr. FitzGeorge, making it clear by her friendly manner that she would not refuse a dance with the apothecary. Gillie stood up with her brother, and Tannie did his duty with Miss Pittfield, not by standing up with her, but by sitting at her side in nearly total silence for the duration of the cotillion.

The original party, minus Mr. FitzGeorge, regrouped at the end of the cotillion. Tannie said, "I'll be running along now, Gillie. We cannot stand up together again, I suppose. Foolishness. Why do people make us go to dances, if we are not allowed to dance? I'll call on you after lunch tomorrow and take you to the hurdle races if that is all right."

His speech was, of course, overheard by them all. "We'll all go. That is why we're here," Southam said. "You can show us the way, Duke. We haven't been there before."

The duke left, and with only one escort for three ladies, the evening promised little further entertainment. They were tired from the long trip, and when Miss Pittfield said she was for bed, they all decided to go up. Gillie and Miss Pittfield said goodnight at their door and arranged to meet the others in the private parlor at nine for breakfast. Southam accompanied Bea to her room.

"It is still quite early," he said, taking her key and unlocking the door. "Shall we have some wine before retiring?" He pushed open the door.

Beatrice took a step into the room. "I don't feel like tackling those stairs again," she replied. Her hand was on the door, preparing to close it. As Southam had himself wedged in the doorway, she waited for him to leave.

He took her hand and looked into her eyes. "We don't have to go downstairs, Beatrice. They will bring wine up."

"Up to my room, you mean?" she asked, startled.

"What is the harm in it? It is not as though you are sharing a room with Gillie. She will not know."

"Is that why you hired a separate room for me?" She studied him, wondering if he was actually suggesting what she thought he was. Surely that was not the opinion Southam had of her! Yet his eyes held a lambent glow, and the soft curving of his lips spoke of nothing less than lovemaking.

"I hoped we might have a little privacy from time to time. We are not children, after all. If adults want some adult entertainment as a respite from chaperoning the youngsters, what is the harm? No one knows us here." As he spoke, he placed a hand proprietarily on her shoulder. His fingers tightened in an intimate gesture of encouragement, and he guided her into the room.

Bea took a deep breath. It was time to give him a taste of her Irish temper. She closed the door, for she was not the least frightened of him, and she did not want to provide a spectacle for anyone passing in the hall. Unfortunately Southam took the closing of the door for agreement. In his eager joy he acted swiftly and spontaneously, all decorum forgotten. He swept her into his arms for an ardent kiss. Taken by surprise, Beatrice was locked in his arms before she could push him away. His lips were hot, and his arms crushed her against his strong chest.

She hadn't been kissed—not like this—since Leonard's death. She had forgotten the potency of passion, but it came swarming over her senses, inundating her in a wave of sweetly remembered desire. Every sense was quickened, acutely aware of this attractive man who wanted her. As his passion swelled, she admitted she wanted him, too. She felt a weakening surrender invade her body. Her arms, though she did not hold him, felt too weak to push him away. They just hung by hers sides, as he molded her against him with both strong arms. Her lips, she knew, were encouraging, moving irresistibly against the commanding pressure of his. She should move her head aside at least, to escape this torment.

She tried, and he lifted one possessive hand to hold her head firm, while the kiss deepened to devastating passion. It flamed along her veins, intoxicating, strong, and hot as brandy. It robbed her of common sense and filled her mind instead with an old longing. A low moan echoed from her throat. Suddenly his lips grazed with rough tenderness across her cheek and whispered in her ear. "God, I have been wanting to do that forever!"

Free of his restraining arms, she took a fumbling step backward. Her breaths came in panting gasps, and her heart throbbed tumultuously. Southam looked into her wildly dazed eyes and smiled softly. "You have been feeling it, too, Beatrice. I knew I could not be mistaken."

She pinched her lips to firm their trembling and

106

took a deep breath. "How dare you!" she said in a menacing whisper.

Southam made the horrible error of laughing. "What is this, a Cheltenham tragedy? I prefer—"

She lifted her hand and struck him full on the cheek with such force that he fell back a step. "How dare you barge your way into my room and force yourself on me!" she demanded, her voice firming.

He rubbed his cheek in confusion. "I thought you wanted it!" He reached out and grabbed her hand. "Darling, you know you do. I was clumsy—overly eager. You drove me to it. You are the most ravishing, adorable girl."

She pulled away and put her hands over her ears, to block the temptation. "Get out! Get out of this room, and never come here again. I won't listen to this."

He smiled tolerantly and captured both her hands. "Then you haven't done this before? I own I was fiercely jealous of your Sir Harold."

Green sparks flashed from her eyes. "You have no right to be jealous of anyone! You are nothing to me, less than nothing. I am a decent, respectable widow. I should think respect for Leonard's memory must protect me if your own chivalry to a lady is so lacking. I have never been so insulted in my life. By God, if I had a gun, I'd shoot you."

A frown drew his brows together. "You're *serious*!" he exclaimed in a light, incredulous tone. "*You* are the one who closed the door behind us."

"Yes, because I did not want the whole inn to see me rake your hair with a chair."

"But you as well as said, at the dance—"

"I said nothing of the sort! We were joking."

"About having a flirtation and breaking my heart?" he asked, to recall the details of the conversation to her.

107

"You don't have a heart. You have only an ego as big as London. Let me tell you, Lord Southam, you are quite as deficient as a flirt as I have not the least doubt you will be as a husband. To start mauling me the instant the door was closed, as if I were some lightskirt you had bought and paid for."

"You didn't seem to mind!"

"I minded very much! You didn't give me a chance to say anything. I want you out of my room this instant. Tomorrow I shall return to Bath—alone."

"How?" he asked.

"By foot, if necessary."

As it sunk in that she was serious, Southam felt thoroughly ashamed of himself. He lifted his hands, palms out, in capitulation. "I made an error of judgment, and I am very sorry, Cousin. Your somewhat free manners led me astray. I would suggest in future you tame your flirtation if you don't wish to be misunderstood."

"There is no danger of a true gentleman misunderstanding me, sir. No one else has ever tried anything like this."

"I have said I am sorry. If you will stay here a few days longer to give Gillian a chance to win her duke, I will be eternally in your debt."

"Stay in the same inn with you? Not likely!"

His lips thinned in frustration and anger. A line formed from his nose to his lips. "I can control myself, Mrs. Searle. I am not an animal led by his appetites."

"I take leave to doubt that. What was and remains a mystery to me is how Deborah puts up with this sort of carrying on."

"Naturally she is not aware of it."

Bea frowned in perplexity. "I meant your mauling her about as you attacked me. If she permits

108

this sort of thing without benefit of marriage, she is a more foolish lady than I ever thought."

"I don't maul her about it. You make me sound like a wild animal."

"I see," she said, her fury mounting. His fiancée he treated with respect, while he took his appetites out on lightskirts and such unfortunate ladies as herself. She strode to the door and flung it open.

"You haven't given me your answer," he said. "What can I tell Gillie and Miss Pittfield if you are gone in the morning? I wish you would reconsider, for their sake. I would not dare to ask that you do it for mine. I promise I will not subject you to any further—mauling," he said, unhappy at the word.

"Perhaps I should stay. It will only set tongues wagging in Bath. . . . Very well, I shall remain a few days, but it is agreed between us, Lord Southam, that there is to be no more of this behavior."

"On my word as a gentleman." He bowed and left, before he fell into any further fracas.

Southam went to his room, feeling as foolish as he had ever felt in his life. He put his head in his hands and moaned in misery. He had behaved like a scoundrel, and to a lady whose good opinion he cherished. A lady, besides, who was an old friend of Deborah's and his sister's chaperone. What had come over him? Was he mad? And to have to face her tomorrow over breakfast. He half wished he had let her go back to Bath. Have to make the best of it. Behave most properly and hope that in the fullness of time, this whole embarrassment would be forgotten.

Alone in her room, Bea was even more shaken. She felt cheapened and thoroughly confused. Was it *her* fault? Surely Southam did not think she would countenance an adulterous affair? It must be at least partly her fault, for she knew from Leonard that Southam was far from being a scandalous sort of gentleman. His engagement to Deborah was proof of that. Less than ever could she imagine how Deborah had landed this tiger. He was a wild beast in his passion, whatever he said to the contrary. And beneath all the worry and confusion, one small spring of pleasure coiled, that she had aroused the beast in Southam. She doubted if Deborah had done so.

Chapter Ten

Mrs. Searle and Lord Southam were so polite to each other over breakfast that Gillie knew immediately they had had a falling-out.

"I expect you ladies would like to have a tour of the shops this morning," he said with a forced smile. "I will be very happy to accompany you."

Gillie knew Rawl hated visiting the shops. She also knew Aunt Bea loved it and found her reply as strange as Rawl's offer.

"I had planned to take Gillie to view the gardens and some of the walks this morning, but if you wish to go on the strut, Southam, you must not curtail your activities on our account," Bea said.

"An excellent idea. We'll all go," he said at once.

They spent the morning touring the east cliff. When they tired of driving, they got out and walked through some of the ravines. The walking was hard, whether on rock or the springy turf that covered some of the chines. They viewed the gardens, admired the rhododendrons and the sea, and agreed that they could feel the fresh sea air invigorating them. The ladies could also feel it removing the curl

111

from their coiffures, and Miss Pittfield could feel the damp seeping into her very bones. When Mrs. Searle accidentally wrenched the heel off her slipper, she was careful to moderate her anger to a mild "Oh, dear!"

Everyone agreed that they had had enough of invigorating air for one morning and used Mrs. Searle's ruined slipper as an excuse to return to town. Southam, with a great show of concern, suggested she call a doctor. "A cobbler would be more to the point," she said curtly.

"Well, have a good lie-down with your foot elevated on a pillow at least," he said. "I plan to drive over and have a look at Saint Peter's Church—unless you would like to go there tomorrow morning, Cousin?"

Bea disclaimed any interest in the church. The ladies got rid of Southam, and as soon as Bea changed her slippers, they went out to visit the shops. Gillie bought useless and gaudy souvenirs for her sisters, and Bea bought silk stockings. Miss Pittfield bought three postcards and mailed them home to her friends.

When the group met Southam at lunch hour, they were all in somewhat better spirits. Bea was not very keen on the hurdle races, but she meant to go the first time, just to see what they were like. Tannie called while they were finishing lunch. The next matter of business was to sort out who should go in what carriage.

"Why don't you run along with Gillie and the duke, Miss Pittfield," Southam suggested. "Mrs. Searle and I will follow behind in my carriage."

"Delighted, except I am driving my curricle," the duke said. "I can dart back to the inn and change it if—"

"No, no. You and Gillie run along. Miss Pittfield will go with Southam and myself," Bea said.

Southam swallowed his annoyance and smiled. He had hoped for some privacy, to apologize more thoroughly to Beatrice. With Miss Pittfield to provide harmless conversation in the carriage, he was almost totally ignored.

The racetrack with hurdles was set up at the edge of the New Forest. A motley throng had gathered. Stalls selling tea and gingerbread and ale dotted the length of the track. The gentlemen and Gillie took great pleasure in watching the horses racket over hurdles. Bea soon tired of this and turned her attention to the onlookers. When she spotted Sir Horatio Evendon, she strolled over for a word with him. He was sitting with some friends at an ad hoc tavern set up in the open air. Horatio introduced Bea to his colleagues and procured a glass for her. They discussed the races.

"Lightening, that's the lad who'll make my fortune," Horatio said. "He'd never win a penny in a flat race, but his short legs are an advantage in the hurdles. Less of them to be pulled up." He tossed his head, and a blackleg came forward to take his bet. "A hundred pounds on Lightening," he said. "He's running at odds of five to one."

"Horatio! Don't bet so much!" Bea objected. She was aware of his customary lack of funds.

When he drew out his purse, she saw it was full to overflowing. "I am high in the stirrups." He laughed. "I have a knack for this sport. Put your blunt on Lightening, and you will go home with your purse bulging, too, Bea."

"Well, I'll risk one guinea," she said, and handed her money over.

This lent a sharper interest to the race. She stood at the rail with the others, hollering her encouragement as the nags streaked by, flying over hurdles of various heights. Lightening won, and soon she was five pounds richer. She would like to have

113

remained and made more money, but could not like to abandon her own party for much longer. From the corner of her eye, she had noticed Southam glancing in her direction more than once. Soon he began stalking toward her, wearing a scowl. She hastily shoved her money at Horatio. "Bet it on some more races for me," she said. "I'll pick up my winnings when we meet. I expect we'll bump into each other again before we leave Bournemouth."

Southam disliked to see Bea with this batch of aging urchins. It was incredible to him that a lady would sit at a table with three such specimens, drinking ale in public. She might not be as loose as he had imagined, but her common sense was sorely lacking. Her acquaintance appeared to be with the worst looking of the lot, a swarthy-complexioned man with dark hair, just graying around the temples. As Southam had been monitoring her closely, he knew that was the gent who had introduced her to the others. He was not unhandsome, but his toilet did not suggest he was from the better class of society, either. His hair was a stranger to the scissors, and his jacket was shiny from use. Where did she meet such creatures?

"Southam, I would like you to meet—"

"Could you come at once, Cousin," he said, barely nodding to her companions. "Miss Pittfield is asking for you. She has a touch of migraine. We hoped you had some headache powders with you."

"Oh, dear! Poor Miss Pittfield. Yes, I shall come at once." She turned back to Horatio. "You won't forget to do as I asked?"

He winked and held up her money. "That I will, with pleasure, my dear." She waved to the others and left.

"What was that all about?" Southam demanded, as he hurried her away from danger.

114

"I won five guineas, Southam! Isn't that wonderful?"

"You're leaving your money with that tout! You'll never see it again. He'll take to his heels."

"He is not a tout. He is an old and dear friend, and he is very knowledgeable about racing. He just won five hundred pounds, imagine! I wish I had bet more. Why don't you place a bet, Southam?"

"I didn't come here to gamble," he said brusquely.

They joined the others. Bea said to Miss Pittfield, "I don't have any headache powders with me. What are we to do? I have some back at the hotel."

"Oh, no, you will not want to leave," Miss Pittfield said.

"There is a stall where you can get a cup of tea," Bea suggested.

"I'm fine," Miss Pittfield assured her. "I wish Lord Southam had not bothered you. I just mentioned the shouting was enough to bring on a migraine, and he immediately insisted I must have some medication. So foolish, and so unlike Southam," she said, shaking her head.

"It is so noisy and rackety, I shouldn't mind going back to the hotel," Bea said, and meant it.

"We'd have to take the carriage—how would Lord Southam get back?"

"Perhaps he could squeeze in with Tannie. I'll mention it."

"Only if you're sure you don't mind."

"Truth to tell, I have had more than enough of this hurdle racing. I'll speak to Southam."

"I'll go with you," he said at once, when she outlined the situation.

"And leave Gillie unchaperoned? No, either you or I must take Miss Pittfield back. One of us must stay."

"In that case, I shall stay. Don't bother to send

115

the carriage back. I'll hitch a drive with someone. The duke appears to know everyone here."

"We'll meet back at the hotel for dinner, then."

This solution pleased everyone. Southam was happy to have detached Beatrice from her ramshackle friends, and she was happy to be able to return to civilization. She had never cared overly much for the track. The ladies enjoyed a refreshing tea before the fire in Southam's private parlor.

"Did Southam mention what we might do this evening?" Bea asked.

"There is a concert in town, an Italian singer."

"Hmm. I am not terribly keen on Italian singers. Male or female?"

"Female."

"That explains it." Mrs. Pittfield looked a question at her. "Southam's interest in going, I mean. I daresay the female is pretty."

Miss Pittfield was never one to gossip, but from having lived with Mrs. Searle now for a few weeks, and being even more in her company during this trip, she was coming to think of Bea as a friend.

"Oh, Mrs. Searle, you cannot know Lord Southam, to say such a thing," she said. "He is not at all a womanizer. Far from it. Since becoming engaged to Miss Swann, he has got over all that. I admit he used to take notice of a pretty girl, but now . . . I don't know, the life has just gone out of him." She shook her head sadly.

"That is news to me," Bea said, and immediately regretted it.

"You don't mean he—"

"No, no! Of course not."

"Then why do you say it is news to you?" Her eyes gleamed with knowledge.

Bea lifted her cup to hide the telltale trace of pink that rose up her neck. "Nothing. I am just cross with him, that's all."

116

"I knew something had happened last night!" Miss Pittfield exclaimed, undeceived. "I knew it by the way the pair of you were being so polite and stiff this morning. I can hardly believe it! Miss Swann would have a fit if she ever found out."

"You may be very sure she shan't hear of it from me."

"I almost wish she would, for if there is one thing that might make her turn Southam off, it is womanizing. Other than that, I fear we are stuck with her."

Bea listened sharply. "You don't think it is a good match, then?"

"The worst match since the government forced Prinney to marry that ugly German princess. Miss Swann is so sly! She came nosing around when Southam was all at sixes and sevens after his mama's death, you must know. He was an easy piece of work for her. She soon convinced him the girls needed a mother. Then, no sooner did she get his ring than she started her campaign to get rid of Gillie. Gillie won't truckle under to her, you see. Gillie is old enough to see through her tricks. She brings gewgaws for Alice and Effie, so they make a great fuss of her when she comes. She would like to see the back of me as well, but I shall stay till Gillie's fate is settled. She'll not drive me off till she wears the title of Lady Southam. Oh, it was a black day when she landed in on us."

"But surely he must love her?"

"He thinks she is suitable." Miss Pittfield leaned closer and lifted her hand. "I'll tell you this, Mrs. Searle, in their six-month engagement, I have never once caught them so much as holding hands. They always leave the door open when they are alone together, so obviously there is nothing of a romantic nature going on. It is a marriage of convenience. Southam is too young, yes, and too hot-blooded, too,

117

to be happy with that cold cucumber. She caught him at a weak moment. I wish he could jettison her, but she'll cling like a barnacle."

Bea thought a moment, then ventured, "You mentioned she might be dissuaded if she heard of Southam fooling around with another woman."

"She *won't* hear of it. He'd never do it at home, where she could hear. And anyway, she keeps all the pretty girls away."

Bea gave a *tsk* of disgust for his lack of enterprise. "I feel no pity for a gentleman who will let himself be trampled on in this fashion."

"Gentleman! There is the mischief. He is too much of a gentleman to go back on his word, but if we could get Deborah to break it off . . ." She darted a hopeful glance at her companion.

"I hope you are not expecting *me* to make a sacrifice of myself. I blacken my character, then he marries his Deborah after all. Thank you, no. Let Southam solve his own problems—if he has the grit and wits to do it. Now, let us speak of more interesting things. Will you be seeing Mr. FitzGeorge again?"

"I'm too old a hag to make a cake of myself. I shan't—unless he comes to call," she added, and laughed. "My, don't we sound like a couple of debs, Mrs. Searle—at our ages! Not that you are so ancient as I."

"We ought both to know better."

Miss Pittfield decided to go and have a rest before dinner. Bea stayed below in the parlor, looking over the journals to see what entertainment the city offered to tourists. She looked up with interest when she heard a sharp rap on the door. "Come in," she called.

Lord Horatio stepped in. He was not wearing the reckless smile he had been wearing when last she saw him. "I lost my five guineas," she said ruefully.

He nodded. "You did, and I lost a deal more than that."

"Not the whole roll, Horatio! Surely you did not blow that whole wad you had won."

"Worse. I punted a thousand on tick. The blacklegs are after me. I want a word with Tannie, to see if he can bail me out. I cannot remain on where I am staying. The blackleg got that address out of me early on. These lads play rough. I'll have to hide till I get the money from Tannie. Do you know where I could find him tonight?"

"I expect to see him here this evening."

"This is too public for my taste." He peered about nervously.

"I'll give him a message, then. Where can he be in touch with you?"

"I am on the run. I'll get word to you or Tannie where I run to ground. I shall be hiding under an alias, like a common criminal. I shall be Mr. Jones for the nonce. Pray do not utter my name aloud to anyone. One never knows who may be listening."

"What happened? You were doing so well!"

"The last race was fixed, I fear. If I cannot raise the wind, I'll slip out of town. The bother of it is that the same lot will be at Newmarket in May. I cannot like to make myself persona non grata there. What is the point of living if a man cannot go to Newmarket for the races?"

"Tannie will bail you out. He is rich as Croesus."

"I'll pay him back, of course. I have a few ugly ancestors still hanging in frames in my saloon. I shan't mind losing them. The Van Dyck should be worth something."

They were interrupted by the sound of the doorknob being turned. Southam entered, looking daggers to see the racetrack tout in his private parlor.

Bea looked up, unperturbed. "Southam, allow me to introduce Lo—"

Evendon gave her a warning look and bounced forward. "Mr. Jones. I am delighted to meet you, sir. I was just leaving. You won't forget what I said, lass?"

"No, I shan't forget. And good luck, Mr. Jones."

Horatio winked and slipped out. She could see no harm in letting Southam know his true identity, but was willing to go along with Horatio's wish.

"That was your old and dear friend?" Southam asked. His face wore the haughty expression it had worn the evening he arrived in Bath.

"Yes, it was."

"Giving you another hot tip on the races, was he?"

"Why no. As a matter of fact, I lost my five guineas. That will be a lesson to me. Where is Gillie?"

"She will be along shortly. I hitched a ride with another chap."

"The tea is cold. Would you like to order some fresh?"

"That would hit the spot." He pulled the bell cord.

Taking tea seemed a good way to insure Bea's company for half an hour. Southam was still feeling awkward about the contretemps of the evening before and wanted to talk it away.

"What would you like to do this evening?" he asked, pulling out a chair and sitting beside her. "There is a concert at the King's Arms."

"Gillie would not care for an Italian soprano. There is a musical comedy at the George."

"Some of those provincial musical comedies are pretty risqué."

"This one is not. Friends of mine saw *The Mop Girl* at Bath last year. It is harmless. A lady runs away to the Mop Fair to escape an unwanted marriage and ends up marrying a lord. There are some lively tunes, some jokes, and a deal of nonsense."

120

"I'll arrange tickets, then, as soon as I have had tea."

The tea arrived soon after, and as soon as she had poured Southam a cup, Bea rose to leave.

"Aren't you going to join me?" he asked, surprised.

"I have already had three cups of tea with Miss Pittfield. Gillie should be along soon. She'll join you. I shall have a rest before dinner. And by the way, as you were so concerned about Miss Pittfield's headache," she added in a snide tone, "you will be happy to hear she has recovered completely. It was not so severe as you imagined."

"Why did you rush her away from the races, then?" he charged.

"Because I had had more than enough of rackety crowds and mud and the stench of horses."

"The rackety crowd at least seemed to amuse you."

"If you are referring to Mr. Jones, then you are right. He is always amusing, but I do not have to go to the races to meet him. He is a friend and frequent caller from Bath."

"I don't recall seeing him at your place."

"You were only in town a few days. He was here. How should you expect to see him in Bath?"

Gillie and the duke arrived in the middle of this spat. Both were in high good humor at the afternoon's outing. Bea contrived to get Tannie to walk her to the door and had a private word with him.

"Your uncle Horatio is in the suds, Tannie," she said. "Can you let him have a thousand pounds?"

"Lord, I don't have that kind of money on me."

"Can't you write a check?"

"I don't have the cash in the bank at the moment. My businessman will be advancing me funds for Newmarket, but not till next week. Where is Horatio?"

"I don't know. He'll get word to you. The message will be from Mr. Jones."

"Who is Mr. Jones?"

"Your uncle Horatio. He will be using that name."

"Queer nabs. He knows where I am putting up, so I expect I shall hear from him. Daresay we shall come up with something. I wish Uncle would not dip so deep. He always loses."

"You'd best go now. We are planning to attend a musical comedy this evening. I hope you will join us?"

"That sounds dashed good. I like a musical comedy."

"Then I shall see you this evening."

Bea did not lie down but tended to her toilet instead. As she sorted through her gowns, she thought of Southam and Deborah. It angered her that Deborah had hoodwinked him into an offer, but it angered her more that he had allowed himself to be hoodwinked. She would not lift a finger to help him. Why should she? Who was to say he'd have her if she did manage to free him from Miss Swann? He thought her worthy of a three-day fling, but that was no indication of any more serious intention. Oh, no, she was not about to bestir herself on Southam's behalf.

Chapter Eleven

The Mop Girl was a roaring success. The plot was entirely inane, the acting inferior, and the music poorly played, but overall it pleased the crowd who had come to be entertained. Millie was a delectable little blonde with just a trace of a lisp. No one was farouche enough to suggest that Lord Gallivant would not immediately fall in love with her, or even that a lord who dropped every second *h* was an unlikely nobleman. Southam's party left the theater in high spirits, to retire to the Royal Bath for a late supper.

It was not till this time that Bea could manage a private word with Tannie. "Did you see your uncle?" she asked.

"I received a note from Mr. Jones, but I daren't go to him. A rascal's following me. We were seen together at the track, Horatio and I. They are trying to learn from me where he is holed up. The man followed me to dinner, here to meet you, to the theater. As we entered the hotel again, I noticed the demmed—pardon me, ma'am—the curst fellow is still dogging my heels. He is worse than a shadow."

"Could you not send Horatio a note at least?"

"All I could say is that I haven't got the blunt—not yet, that is. I would not want the old boy to lose heart completely. I sent a footman off to London with a note for my man of business to send me some blunt."

"Could you sign a promissory note in the meanwhile, to get the fellow off Horatio's back—and yours? You are a duke after all."

"Offered to do it! The scoundrel wouldn't believe I am Duke of Cleremont. Who the devil does he think I am, if I am not me?"

As she examined Tannie's careless toilet and unprepossessing face, Bea could not entirely blame the scoundrel, whoever he was, for doubting Tannie's word. "Is there anyone who could vouch for you?"

"Southam," he said, with a diffident look. "I did not like to drag him into this. I mean to say, one don't like to trot out the dirty dishes when he is trying to make a good impression. Already knows I am an idiot, I shouldn't be surprised."

Bea was delighted to hear such a strong indication of serious intentions and hastily assured him it was no such a thing. Still, as Southam had taken an aversion to Horatio, it did not seem a good idea to involve him in this particular scheme.

"I would lend him the money myself if I had it," Bea said. "I could raise five hundred. I have that much left of last quarter's allowance. I shall need it before my next allowance comes due, however."

"No, no. I could not let you do it. There is no saying Mr. Jones will repay in cash. He will probably repay me with some curst old picture of a wart-nosed uncle. Mama tells me I am collecting up any such relics I can find, but you would have no use for such an ugly thing. Pay to be rid of it, I don't doubt."

"So what are we to do?"

"Keep Mr. Jones under wraps till I hear from my man of business. Let it be a lesson to Horatio—er, Mr. Jones."

Gillie came forward to hear what they were whispering about, and their private discussion was at an end. "Shall I call for you for the races tomorrow?" Tannie asked.

"Yes, please," Gillie said. "What are you doing in the morning, Tannie?"

"We can have a driving lesson if you like. There are some excellent drives hereabouts."

As this was permitted in Bath, there seemed nothing against allowing it in Bournemouth. Bea was happy to have a morning free of chaperoning duties. She thought she might visit a bank and try her hand at borrowing the money for Horatio. The duke would repay her within a few days, and she didn't like to see her old friend having to hide himself like a criminal, and, more importantly, missing the races that he so loved.

Tannie took his leave, and the remainder of the party went upstairs together. Southam just bowed at Bea's door and wished her a good night's sleep. This particular incident inevitably brought to mind the previous night's misdemeanor.

As Bea was putting on her nightdress, she heard a light rattle at her window. She took it for the sound of a branch brushing the pane and ignored it. It came again, louder, and unmistakably was not the wind.

She put on her peignoir and went to the window, where she saw a dark shadow standing below, tossing pebbles. Some gallant trying to make contact with his lady and mistaking the room? She raised the window and leaned out. "You have got the wrong room, sir!" she called.

"Nay, it's yourself I'm looking for," an uncouth

125

voice called back. "You know where he is hiding, the old crook. Best tell me, if you know what's good for you."

His menacing words alarmed her. She said, "Go away, or I shall call the proprietor!" Then she closed the window and drew the curtain. Her heart was beating rapidly, but she soon calmed it. It must be the blackleg from the racetrack, looking for Horatio. He had seen them together. As Tannie had failed to lead him to his quarry, he had decided to pester her, but he couldn't do much when she was safe in her room with the door locked. She checked the bolt. It was secure.

She proceeded with her nightly ritual of removing her combs and brushing out her raven hair. The man obviously meant business. Something must be done to pacify him. As she was about to go to bed, she heard a light tap at the door. Southam was the first name that occurred to her. Surely he was not about to repeat last night's performance? No, it must be something completely innocent. Perhaps Gillie was not feeling well! She had consumed the better part of a plate of macaroons before retiring. As soon as this idea darted into her head, she hurried to the door and opened it, just enough to show her her caller's face.

Three inches was wide enough for her caller to wedge his foot into the opening. His grimy fingers curled around the door and forced it open. She opened her lips to shout for help, but was assailed by visions of rousing the hotel. People rushing out, staring, gossiping, Southam running and making a great to-do of it. No, she could handle this person. The man did not intend to harm her. She would reason with him, make some arrangement for paying the debt.

"Who are you?" she demanded boldly.

"The name's Garrity," he replied, in the same way.

Bea found herself looking levelly into the eyes of a man no taller than herself, though considerably thicker. He was a dark-haired, swarthy fellow in a fustian jacket and leather waistcoat. She decided to take a high hand with him and not let him see she was frightened.

"Please state your business and leave. As you can see, I am preparing for bed." She casually picked up her hairbrush, as though to brush her hair. Her thinking was that with its bristles and hard silver back, it would make a useful weapon.

"Evendon owes me a thousand pounds. He ain't shabbing off without paying—not unless he goes in a casket. Ye'd best whiddle, lass, for I ain't talking through my hat."

"I have no idea where he is, but the young gentleman you have been harassing *is* the Duke -of Cleremont. I can vouch for him."

"Ho, and you with your rum togs are the Duchess of Wales, eh?" He subjected her to a scathing examination. "Jane Shore, more like. Me, I'm just a poor hard-working prince." He lowered his brows and advanced toward her, balling his hands into fists. "Where is he? And no tricks."

She lifted her brush and struck out at his head. The blackleg, accustomed to attack, deftly dodged aside and grabbed her wrist. All Bea's good intentions fled as panic seized her. "Help! Southam, Help!" she called out. Though the blood pounded in her ears, she thought she heard footsteps through the wall. She definitely heard a door slam.

The man looked at her angrily. He let go of her wrist and prepared to flee just as her door flew open. "I'm owed a thousand pounds, and I mean to have it, miss," he growled.

Before he got to the door, Southam was in the

room. Bea stood, staring with bated breath. The man was temporarily shocked into immobility. His victims were not usually top-of-the-trees gents like the one now glowering down at him. The light-skirt's patron, most likely. Such swells were trouble. They'd be calling in constables and laying charges. This gent, however, did not resort to accusations but raised his fist and darted forward.

The blackleg effortlessly dodged the blow. Being short, he had no hope of landing the swell a facer. His heavy, balled fist shot out into Southam's abdomen with all the force of his wiry body. A surprised, choking gasp hung on the air. Southam doubled over in pain, while the man stood, waiting for him to recover. Without thinking, Bea flew at him with her hairbrush. She landed one good crack on the side of his head before he wrenched the brush from her fingers and tossed it aside. He headed for the door but risked a parting shot to Mrs. Searle, "A thousand pounds. By tomorrow, or he'll be sorry." Then he was gone.

Southam, pale as paper, was just trying to stand upright. His hands clenched his abdomen. He lurched toward the door, trying to give chase.

"Sit down, Southam, before you fall down," Bea said weakly. "You haven't a hope of catching him. Are you all right?"

Southam sank onto the side of her bed and looked at her with accusing eyes. She poured him a glass of wine and took one herself, to steady her nerves. This brief pause gave her time to consider what story to tell him. She soon concluded the truth cast no dark reflections on her, and Southam would not give a tinker's curse if Tannie's uncle was dipped.

As she handed him the glass, she said, "Shall I call a doctor?"

"A constable might be more to the point," he replied, through clenched teeth.

"I doubt he'll return."

Southam took a sip of wine. He was hardly aware of the agony the blow caused. Anger drove everything else out of his head. "Think again. The thousand pounds—it is a gambling debt?"

"Of course."

"You don't have the money to pay it?"

"No. It's not—"

His brows drew together in a scowl. "How can you be short of money, with the sum Leonard left you?"

"He didn't leave me that much!"

"A widow should be able to live in some style on two thousand a year. She would if she did not gamble. Of all the asinine, foolish, dangerous things!"

"I do not gamble!" she shot back. How dare he read her this lecture! As if it were any of his business!

"I saw you with my own eyes. You admitted it!"

"One pound!"

"Cut line, Beatrice. One thousand, I believe, is the sum the tout mentioned."

Bea's hot anger cooled to reason. Let Southam go his length and make a fool of himself. She would enjoy seeing his pride humbled when he learned his mistake and had to come begging for absolution. "That is the sum," she said.

"I realize I am deeply in your debt for your chaperoning of Gillian. I shall pay the thousand pounds." He rose stiffly. "Naturally I shall be taking Gillian home to Elmland with me when we leave here."

"Of course. You would not want to leave her in the care of a hardened gambler," she replied with an ironic smile.

"It is nothing to laugh at! I was used to envy Leonard. I see now he had a deal to put up with."

129

"So he had, but then, Leonard was never such a stiff and pompous ass as yourself, Lord Southam."

His nostrils flared, and he clenched his lips with the effort to restrain his temper. "I shall give you the check tomorrow morning."

"Cash would be preferable. The person who called prefers cash, for obvious reasons."

"What reasons are those? My check is good."

"He did not believe Tannie was a duke; he may take the notion that you are not Lord Southam."

A tide of red rose up from his collar. "You have involved the duke in this degrading matter?"

"The duke is very much involved and has been from the beginning."

"I'll send that whey-faced wretch packing first thing in the morning. I might have known any *parti* introduced to Gillie through your graces would be ramshackle."

She swallowed this infamy, consoling herself with the prospect of his shame when he learned the truth. "He is innocently involved, Southam."

His scowl deepened. "You've been cadging from that boy as well?"

"Cadging is a hard word. I consider the thousand pounds a short-term loan. You will have your money within a day or two."

"The thousand pounds is a gift."

"I do not accept gifts of that magnitude from gentlemen."

"A payment, then."

"I wouldn't dream of it. Having Gillie was a pleasure. She has somehow managed to avoid that taint of self-rightous self-consequence you have picked up from your fiancée. You were used to be more amusing."

"There is no need to cast slurs on my fiancée, Mrs. Searle," he said haughtily.

"You did not hesitate to cast slurs on *me!*"

130

"I have not accused you unjustly of anything. If my words are offensive, then you should examine the cause of them, ma'am."

"And you should find out what the devil you are talking about before you make a jackass of yourself. Good night, Southam. I am sorry to have disturbed your rest."

She took him by the arm and led him to the door. He gave an abbreviated bow and left, still hunched in pain. Bea shook her head and smiled ruefully. Southam would feel a perfect ninny when he learned the truth tomorrow. A dish of humble pie would do wonders for his arrogance. She would let him stew for the next twelve hours or so, to show him the error of his hotheaded ways. Her only regret was that she had introduced Deborah's name into the conversation.

Bea finished her toilet and went to bed in good spirits. Tomorrow she would have the money for Horatio. Tannie could deliver it and repay her when he heard from his man of business. She might keep the truth from Southam until she had the money to give back. Just before she slept, she remembered Southam's words that had slipped out in anger: "I was used to envy Leonard." So he *had* had a tendre for her. . . .

Southam had more difficulty settling down. He quarreled with his conscience, first thinking he had been too hard on Mrs. Searle. Gambling was a disease; perhaps she couldn't help herself. He vacillated from that tolerant position to one of rage. How could she, a widow, put herself at the mercy of such wretches as that blackleg? She was in her nightdress, alone with him. How had the man got into her room? What would she have done if he had not been there to give her the money?

Was that why she tolerated the attentions of Sir Harold and Reynolds? Were they her bankers? Not without receiving something in payment. He had an idea what a pretty widow would use for coin in that circumstance. She had looked ravishing, with her dark hair streaming over her shoulders, and that white lacy thing she had on. Her green eyes had shone like diamonds when she went after that tout with her hairbrush. A regular hellion.

She had cut up stiff when he tried to make love to her. If she had been in his debt at the time, no doubt she would have been more compliant. Her attitude throughout the entire fracas had been noticeably lacking in either shame or sorrow. The woman was a hardened schemer, accustomed to such degrading exhibits as he had seen this night. Yes, he definitely must remove Gillie from her care. He was by no means sure the duke was all he should be, either. Surely she was not preying on that simple boy! He would have a word with the duke, and if he was involved in any way with the immoral Mrs. Searle, the duke could go to the devil.

Chapter Twelve

Southam, after a largely sleepless night, came down to breakfast late the next morning, pale and limping.

"What's the matter, Rawl? You look awful!" Gillie exclaimed.

"I had an accident. Bumped into the edge of my dresser last night," he said curtly. He darted a dark glance at Beatrice, who sat prim as a nun, sipping her coffee.

"You have not forgotten Gillie is driving out with the duke this morning?" Bea said, looking a question at him. The previous night's hard words about the "whey-faced wretch" left her in some little doubt as to whether Southam would permit this drive, in which case she must inform him as to Tannie's and her own true part in the matter of the gambling debt.

"I shall have a word with him before they leave."

"If you are planning to ask him about his intentions, Rawl, I wish you will not," Gillie said.

"Why not?" he snapped back. "It is a logical

question, when he is in your company for the better part of every day."

"Because I don't know whether I even want to marry him," she replied.

"Then you shouldn't be seeing so much of him."

"I didn't say I would not have him if he asked. I just don't want him to ask *yet*, till I'm sure."

"You had best make up your mind, for we shall be leaving this afternoon," he announced, taking up his cup of coffee.

"Leaving!" Gillie exclaimed. "We were to stay four days. Why are we leaving?"

"Because the place is full of riffraff. I should not have brought you here. Not that Bath is any better," he added.

Beatrice ignored this ill-natured shot at herself. Gillie complained a little longer, but she was missing Penny. She decided she would not mind so very much leaving Bournemouth. Riding was more fun than watching races.

"Aren't you going to eat anything, Southam?" Miss Pittfield inquired. She wondered about his bad temper. Did it have something to do with that letter from Deborah? He must have picked it up at the desk before coming to the table.

"I am not hungry."

"A blow from a wayward dresser will sometimes have that effect," Bea explained to Miss Pittfield. Southam gave her a quelling glare.

"What had Miss Swann to say, Southam?" Miss Pittfield asked.

"What do you mean?"

"Have you not picked up your letter? There is one for you at the desk. It has been forwarded from Bath."

"I haven't been to the desk," he said. Nor did he hasten in that direction. Indeed, his already bad humor seemed to worsen at the news. Why the devil does the woman have to hound me? he wondered. What new catastrophe has arisen, due to her interference? He knew he was diverting his anger with Mrs. Searle to the innocent Deborah but was unable to prevent it. It was true in any case. She was an interfering woman. He had decided to marry her to smooth the chaotic tenor of his life, but ever since the engagement, life at home had become a series of domestic calamities. Servants fighting, servants leaving, Gillie acting like a sulky child. And why the devil would Deborah not set a wedding date?

Beatrice examined him, wondering at his sullen silence. "You have no objection to Gillie's driving out with Tannie, then?" she asked.

"Let her have one last drive. We shall be leaving immediately after lunch. I have a little business to attend to this morning, or we would leave immediately."

Beatrice assumed the "business" was to arrange for the money from the bank. "Then I shall pack this morning," she said. "I shall just wait to say good-morning to Tannie before going upstairs." She would arrange to give Tannie the money before leaving town and see when he could repay her.

As soon as Southam had drunk his coffee, he went to get his letter from Deborah. He read it in the lobby, leaning against the desk. It was even worse than he had anticipated. She was "shocked and alarmed" to hear that he was prolonging his visit to Bath and demanded the details of what made this necessary. She was hurt to learn from the Comstocks that he had not informed them he was unable to attend their dinner party. At least she didn't know he had gone to Bournemouth. He had not mentioned that but only wrote that he would be staying a little longer in Bath. What would she not have to say about Bournemouth if she ever learned the whole truth?

It was a long letter, written in Deborah's spidery script, which was an effort to read. His eyes skimmed over various passages. Letter from Princess Augusta, talk of royal gardening, hints of Papa single-handedly solving some parliamentary crisis, and surely a portfolio to be forthcoming shortly. He had heard that before! He skipped down to the end and stiffened in horror. *She was joining him at Bath!* He must not worry about the inconvenience. She knew he would not remain unless some crisis had arisen. Her place was by his side, to help him in his time of trouble. Oh, Lord! That was all he needed! She would be leaving the following day. The letter had been forwarded from Bath, wasting a day. She would be arriving in Bath on the morrow! He crumpled up his billet-doux and tossed it into the cuspidor.

He looked up, his face a mask of frustration, to see Mrs. Searle studying him. She walked forward, her eyes just skimming off the crushed letter in the cuspidor. "Bad news, I take it?" she asked.

"On the contrary. Delightful news," he said through grim lips. "Deborah is joining me at Bath."

"Am I to have the pleasure of her company, or has she other friends in the city?"

"She didn't say. I rather think she means to stay with you," he said, pink with embarrassment.

"Lovely! I look forward to it." Her tone was not ironic; neither did it hold any tinge of pleasure. Resignation was the closest he could come to putting a word to it.

"Very likely she has written you, asking if it will be convenient."

"In that case my servants would have forwarded the letter, I think. It is no matter. As you will be rushing Gillie, and one assumes your fiancée, off to Elmland so soon, a short visit shan't bother me."

He feared Deborah would not want to leave im-

136

mediately. After the expense and bother of the trip, she would want to spend a few days of relaxation. "She will want a good visit with you first—her old school chum," he said, trying for a hearty air.

"We were never close, Southam. Ah, there is Tannie! I'll just say good-morning while you tell Gillie he is here."

This ruse gave her a moment alone with the duke. "I shall have the money in an hour," she said. "Cut your drive short, and you can take it to Mr. Jones before noon. We shall be leaving immediately after lunch."

"Where did you get it?"

"A loan from Southam, but I pray you will not mention it to him. It is a—sort of secret," she said. "There isn't time to explain now."

"Why are you leaving so soon?"

"It is difficult to explain, but"—she remembered Deborah's visit—"his fiancée is going to Bath to meet him."

"That don't sound difficult to explain."

"No." The duke rubbed his ear in confusion. "Hush! They are coming," she cautioned before he could pursue the matter.

Southam and Gillie came forward. A battle with his conscience made Southam realize the duke was too good a *parti* to cast aside only because Mrs. Searle had got her claws into him. He would see that that sort of thing came to a quick halt. He was as amiable as his present mood made possible. As soon as the youngsters left, Southam headed to a bank. It was no easy matter for anyone, even a lord, to procure such a large sum in cash with a strange bank. He was left cooling his heels for thirty minutes, while his temper mounted steadily higher. When he finally had the money, he went in search of Mrs. Searle.

As it was her last morning in Bournemouth, and

as Tannie could not give his uncle the money before he returned, Beatrice decided to have a stroll around the town. Packing would not take a whole morning. She and Miss Pittfield went to look over the shops and gardens. Southam returned to the Royal Bath to learn that the ladies were out. That was how much consideration she had for him! When he was giving her a thousand pounds, you would think she would at least have the common decency to be there to receive it.

He couldn't even give her a good chewing-out, because he had to keep her in good temper for Deborah's visit. Why the devil did Deborah want to come scrambling to Bath? No one had invited her. Didn't she trust him? That, he felt instinctively, was the real reason for her visit. She never had trusted him. Every time he glanced at a pretty girl, she was there, making some snide remark. "A pity Miss Simmons has those gap teeth." "Miss Lawson would be tolerably handsome were it not for that common streak that pops out from time to time. Always prattling of her sister's great catch. A mere baronet, really!"

What would she say if she knew he had tried to make love to Beatrice? His heart shriveled to consider it. He had an overwhelming fear that she would learn of it. Deborah always learned everything. He couldn't have a drink of ale in the local taproom without her calling him to account. "A man in your position, Southam! You must set a better example. To be idling away an afternoon in a tavern, like some retired Cit."

His mood did not improve when Beatrice returned carrying a hatbox. Out wasting her blunt, when she was a thousand pounds in hock. The woman had no management.

"Shopping, I see, Cousin?" he said, glinting a reminder of her penurious state at her.

"I could not resist this bonnet, Southam. The clerk told me it made me look young, and you know how folks of our age are always looking for tricks to rejuvenate us. Did you manage to complete your business successfully?"

"Yes, I got it." Miss Pittfield looked at him, inviting explanation. He could think of no feasible lie, so ignored her look.

Miss Pittfield sensed some conspiracy afoot between the two. She hoped it was of a romantic nature and left them alone, saying she had to attend to her packing if they were to leave after lunch.

"I should do the same," Bea said when they were alone. "There is time for a cup of tea first, I think. Will you join me, Southam?" She added in a low voice, "It would look odd for you to hand over the blunt here in the lobby. Such transactions want privacy."

He collared a servant to order tea and followed her into the parlor. "It seems a strange time for you to go on a shopping binge, when your pockets are to let."

"One bonnet is not a binge. Even two do not constitute a binge. It requires three bonnets to make a binge."

"You know what I mean," he said sternly.

"I know you are taking an overweening interest in my money. I am borrowing the thousand pounds for a short time. That does not give you the right to monitor what I do with my own funds."

"It is a gift, or payment if you like, not a loan."

He handed her the envelope. She took it with a curt, "It is a loan, and I thank you." She stored it in her reticule and sat down. "Would you like to see my new bonnet?" she asked, apparently forgetting his huge gift that easily.

"Not particularly."

"Then you can shut your eyes, for I am eager to

see it again." She opened the box and lifted out a delightful confection of chipped straw, with a wide satin ribbon and a tiny cluster of silk orange blossoms tucked in at the side. She placed it on her head and turned this way and that before the mirror, examining herself. "It will be a definite hit with the fogies in Bath," she said, putting her old bonnet into the empty box, while he watched, scowling. Though he did, in fact, think it was a very pretty bonnet. "What are you in the mopes about, Southam?"

He decided to try to reason her into common sense. "I cannot like your cavalier attitude about money, Cousin. Gambling can lead to God only knows what. You put yourself at the mercy of men—such creatures as Sir Harold and that Reynolds person, I suppose."

"Not to forget that Southam person," she added, smiling ironically. "The worst of the lot."

"I think you ought to leave Bath, go somewhere that you are not known, and begin a new life."

"I am very happy with my old life, Southam," she said unconcernedly. A slow smile crept over her lips and up to light her green eyes as he stared in frustration. "You are too absurd, you know, to think I have no more scruples or common sense than to squander Leonard's money on horses. I lost one pound, it is the only pound I have ever gambled on horses in my life. Other than whist for a penny a point, I am blameless."

"I would like to believe that. How do you explain that person in your bedroom last night?"

She tossed up her hands. "My bedroom seems to attract the undesirable element." She took pity on him and decided to explain. "He was trying to learn where Tannie's uncle is hiding. Evendon—he is presently going under the alias of Mr. Jones—is into the blacklegs for a thousand pounds, you see. When

Tannie would not reveal where Evendon is hiding out, Garrity tried to scare the information out of me. He saw us together at the races, I suppose."

He listened, staring in disbelief. "Why didn't you tell him if you know?" he asked suspiciously.

"Tell him! I am not such a Johnnie Raw! Mr. Jones had no money to pay. They would probably have beaten him."

"Where is Evendon? I'll take the money to him now."

"He is hiding out somewhere with a friend, but I don't know exactly where. Tannie knows. He'll deliver the blunt, and he will repay me as soon as his man brings him the money. Then I shall repay you, and you can quit monitoring my expenditures. And casting aspersions on my character," she added in a cooler tone.

"You led me on! You let me believe the worst!" he defended. He knew he should be angry with her for this stunt, but he was so relieved to know she was not a fallen woman that his charge lacked conviction. He even smiled sheepishly.

"Only to show you a lesson, sir! You are swift to accuse."

"I shall redress the offense as much as possible by being equally swift to apologize, Beatrice. I am sorry."

"More to the point, will you let Gillie finish her visit? In Bath, I mean."

"You mean, you actually want her?"

"Of course I do! She is a delightful child. It is not her fault if her brother is a gudgeon. Besides, I like to finish what I have begun. I have got her a good way toward landing a duke; I should like to finish it. *He* is serious, whatever about Gillie. He was afraid you would take a pet because his uncle is such a wastrel."

"I shall caution him not to support Evendon's expensive vices in future. As to Gillie, I would be happy if you would keep her for the present. She and Deborah cannot seem to rub along. Two women under the same roof—it seldom works."

"My only concern is whether Gillie wants to marry the duke," Bea said, frowning.

"She's a fool if she lets him slip through her fingers. She'll not do as well again."

"She is young—I would not push her into it if she is at all uncertain," Bea said.

"She has a few weeks to make up her mind."

"You forget, Tannie will be going to Newmarket shortly. Have you given any more thought to London?"

"I'll discuss it with Deborah. I'm sorry to land her in on you unannounced. I cannot imagine why she did not write and check with you first, for in the usual way, she is punctilious about such things."

When the tea arrived, they settled in for a friendly chat. Southam complimented her on her new bonnet, and she inquired as to the state of his wounds after last night's "accident."

"I am recovering. I felt a dashed fool, being beaten by that little ankle-biter."

"Garrity is short but stocky," she consoled. "And very fast-moving. He got my brush away from me before I could land a good blow."

"How did he get into your room?"

"I, like a greenhead, opened the door without asking who it was. I thought it might be you."

"Me?" he asked, with a conning grin. "Now that surprises me, that you would open the door to me."

"You or Miss Pittfield, with a message that Gillie was ill, since she stuffed herself with macaroons after the play."

"I am very sorry for that misunderstanding the night we arrived. I must have been mad."

She gave him a coquettish smile. "At least I cannot fault your taste, Southam." She rose and took up her hatbox. "Now I really am going to pack. I asked Tannie to return early, so he should have Gillie here soon."

"A pity we must cut short our trip. But with Deborah landing in on us . . ." He drew a weary sigh.

If he felt any pleasure in anticipating Deborah's visit, he was doing a wonderful job of concealing it. Bea was curious to see them together. "You must be eager to see her," she said.

"Yes! Yes, indeed. Very eager." He looked about as eager as a man on the way to the tooth drawer.

Beatrice left, and Southam sat on alone, wondering how he had got into this muddle. He felt a nervous qualm that he would not get out unscathed.

Chapter Thirteen

When Bea finished her packing, she went to Gillie's room to see if she had returned from her drive yet.

Miss Pittfield was there alone. "I've packed up Gillie's things," she said. "When she returns, all she will have to do is change out of her driving bonnet and she will be ready to leave."

"As soon as we have lunch," Bea said, glancing at her watch. "I told her to return early. I had thought she'd be here by now."

"The girl is scatterbrained, and the duke not much better."

"As you have things well in hand here, Miss Pittfield, let us go downstairs and have a glass of wine while we await Gillie." Bea wanted to be on hand when Tannie arrived, to give him the money.

They went down to the private parlor, where Southam was pacing the floor. "I thought they would be here by now," he said impatiently.

"Youngsters take little account of the time," Miss Pittfield said soothingly. "They'll be along any minute."

"We mean to have a glass of wine while we are waiting, Southam. Why don't you join us?" Bea suggested.

The wine was ordered and brought. One glass was drunk, then another, while they took turns looking at the clock and assuring each other the youngsters would be along any minute. At their regular lunching time Southam said, "The duke is not exactly a youngster. You specifically asked him to return early, Cousin. This disregard for your wishes promises an uncertainty of character that I cannot like."

"They may have had some minor mishap—overturned in a ditch, or some such thing," Bea said. "They are not far from civilization. If that is the case, they will either return soon or send us word. Have another glass of wine, and do stop pacing, Southam. You are making us fidgety."

Southam sat down to gulp another glass of wine. He was soon back at the window, pacing to and fro. At half an hour past their lunch hour, the ladies began to become nervous as well. "I hope they have not had a serious accident," Miss Pittfield said.

"Tannie is an excellent driver," Bea pointed out. "He may be a bit slack in other areas, but he certainly knows his horses."

Southam turned on her in alarm. "What do you mean, slack in other areas?"

"You know what I mean—a little careless of his appearance, hardly a great conversationalist. He does not care much what people think of him."

"You are not suggesting he might be taking advantage of her?"

She just looked at him, astonished. "Of course not! That was not my meaning."

"He is a good deal older than Gillie and more infatuated than she. By God, if he's trying anything—"

"Don't be such a ninny, Southam," she said

145

roundly. "The duke is a gentleman from the tip of his dusty hat to the toes of his boots. If he has inadvertently compromised Gillie, he will certainly marry her immediately."

Southam looked up, interested. Bea caught that hopeful gleam and leapt down his throat. "What a despicable creature you are! You would force Gillie to have him if you could. What you ought to do, if you are truly worried, is to go after them, as I plan to do." She jumped up and headed for the door, forgetting in the upset of the moment that her carriage was sitting in its stable at Bath.

"Do you know which way they went?" he asked.

Miss Pittfield spoke up. "She mentioned Branksome Wood Road, to the northwest of town. 'We haven't been out toward Branksome Woods,' she said. 'We shall take that road today.' Unless the duke was flinging dust in our eyes by having her tell us so," she added ominously.

"Not you, too, Miss Pittfield!" Bea exclaimed, chagrined.

Yet as she darted upstairs for her bonnet and pelisse, she did experience just one stab of alarm. She had thought that today, of all days, Tannie would make a special effort to be home early. His uncle was waiting for his money. It was true, Tannie was a rather uncertain fellow. If Gillie had laughed at his offer of marriage, for instance, and if the duke had a temper buried under his outer shell of indifference ... No, she would not let herself fall prey to such imaginings.

She had introduced the duke to Gillie; she had promoted and sponsored the whole idea. If anything happened to Gillie, it was her fault—and Southam would not hesitate to fling it in her face. At that moment she regretted she had ever met Lady Gillian.

Southam had his carriage at the door when she

146

came pelting downstairs. "Miss Pittfield will stay here in case they return. She knows which route we are taking and will have my valet hire a mount and come after us. How the devil does one get to the northwest edge of town from the east cliff?"

"You had best ask someone before we go."

Southam just hollered "Spring 'em," to his groom, and they wasted a quarter of an hour lurching through city streets before they stopped for directions. They were told to go up Westover Road to Bourne Avenue, and hence out the Branksome Wood Road. As they proceeded on their course, Southam watched out his side of the carriage and Bea out hers, checking for a sight of the duke's carriage in the ditch or at an inn.

"It is so late, they might have stopped for luncheon. If Tannie has stabled the rig, we won't see it," Bea mentioned.

"If that jackanapes is enjoying his luncheon while we are out scouring the countryside for him on an empty stomach, he will live to regret it."

"I am relieved to hear it. I thought you were going to say you would run him through."

"How well do you actually know the duke?"

"I have known his family for eons. His uncle speaks of him in the highest terms."

"This is the same uncle who is in hawk to the blacklegs for a thousand pounds? The man who is in hiding, causing his loutish friends to barge into your bedchamber at midnight? A fine recommendation!"

"Never mind ripping up at *me*, Southam! You were in alt to see I had got a duke interested in Gillie, and you need not bother denying it. You did not ask a single question about his character. You heard the magic words, 'the Duke of Cleremont,' and turned from a bear into a sycophant before my very eyes. It was disgusting."

147

"I am not a sycophant!" His objection was loud, for he knew there was a grain of truth in her charge.

"And the duke is not a rake. He is staying with his aunt, Lady Sappington, in Bath. She is a regular pillar of propriety. If there were any unsavory scandals in his past, I would have heard. Everyone knows he is seeing Gillie. They know she is under my protection." He gave her a leery look. "They have obviously had an accident, that's all. Stop! What is that?"

Southam pulled the check string, and the carriage slowed down to show them a pony cart pulled off to the side of the road. A young couple were eating sandwiches from a lunch box. Their carriage continued on its way.

"We should have begged some food from that couple. I am starved," Southam said wearily.

"I see where Gillie got her bad habits. I had to scold her for saying she was starved when she first came to me." She felt a fond nostalgia for those early, quiet days.

"She always had a large appetite. She was a great favorite in the kitchen at home," Southam replied, in the same nostalgic way. "I remember her sitting at the kitchen table, gnawing on chicken legs or ham bones at nine o'clock in the evening. She often stayed in the stable over the dinner hour."

"That would be where she acquired her taste for ale."

"Yes, she preferred it to wine. I remember the first time I caught her taking ale with my head groom. She was sitting on a tree stump discussing what to do in case of a breech birth—of a foal, I mean."

"I wish you would stop these reminiscences, Southam. You're making my flesh creep. You speak of her as if she were dead!"

"That is not what I am thinking. You are right. I have been promoting this marriage too eagerly. Gillie is too young. She's not ready for marriage. I shan't send her to London this year, either. I shall let her have another year at Elmland, and next year I shall take her to London to make her bows."

"What will Deborah have to say about that?" she asked.

He looked into the distance. "She can accept it or not. It is up to her. She cannot expect me to put my own little sister out of the house because she cannot get along with her. A man in my position has family duties that must take precedence over his own pleasure."

Bea regarded him with extreme skepticism. She thought that sounded remarkably like a rehearsed speech. That was what he would say to Deborah in an effort to shake her off. Knowing Deborah, however, she doubted that lady would give up her prize so easily.

The carriage rounded a bend at a fast speed, throwing Bea across the seat. Southam reached a hand out from the opposite bench to steady her, and missed seeing his sister. Bea recognized Gillie's bonnet and shouted, "Stop!"

Southam looked offended. "I am not attacking you, Cousin. I promised there would be no more of that sort of thing. I was merely steadying you. John Groom is driving too fast. Are you all right?"

"Of course I am all right, idiot! It's Gillie!" She pointed out the window. There, twenty or thirty yards into a meadow, stood Lady Gillian. She appeared to be gathering wood for a fire. The carriage stood by the side of the road, leaning at a perilous angle that spoke of a broken wheel.

"What the devil is she doing there?" Southam exclaimed.

He stopped the carriage, and they both clambered down. Bea smiled to herself, not only at finding Gillie but at Southam's hasty defense of his virtue. It indicated what was in his mind. He had certainly been behaving like a gentleman since that night in her room. She thought he had put any thoughts of that sort from his mind, but apparently his feelings for her were not quite dead, or he would not have leapt to his defense so swiftly. Bearing in mind his sudden decision to take Gillie home for a year against Deborah's express command, she foresaw an interesting time in Bath.

Gillie came running forward when she recognized them. Her face was coated in dust, her bonnet was askew, and her pelisse was destroyed. She went running into her brother's arms. "Rawl, thank God you have come. I knew I could depend on you."

Bea watched in satisfaction as he cradled her in his arms, with all the proper love and concern of a brother. Then he put her at arm's length and examined her. "Are you all right? What has happened? We were afraid you might be seriously hurt." Not a word about fearing she had run off or been carried off by the duke.

"I'm fine, but I fear I may have broken Tannie's arm. It hurts like the devil, and he is as white as a bone, so he cannot be shamming it. We got to arguing, you see. He said I was driving too fast for such a cow-handed driver and pulled the reins right out of my hands. Naturally the team got excited and bolted when he made such a to-do. We both dropped the reins, so that we ended up in the ditch. I fear we have broken the shaft of his carriage."

"Why did you not send for help? There is plenty of traffic on this road."

"I had to look after Tannie first. He was quite unconscious, you must know, so I could not leave him. I stopped a rig half an hour ago. The man said he would send a wheeler up from Poole, but he hasn't come yet, so I have been looking for a branch of a proper size to use as a splint for the shaft. I meant to secure it with strips from my petticoat. It need only last till we can get to a stable or wheeler. I think this one might do it," she said, hefting a branch.

"Where is Tannie?" Bea asked.

"There is a little stream over there," she said, pointing to a stand of willows in the near distance. "The horses needed water. I unharnessed them and took them up there for a drink, and to be out of harm's way in case a carriage came around the bend too fast. I wanted to bathe Tannie's face with water, too. He managed to walk that far, with my help. I got the blanket from the carriage and wrapped him up well in it. We are quite ravenous. I'm sorry, Aunt Bea, but we are really feeling a good deal more than peckish, even if you didn't ask. I gave Tannie the three macaroons I had in my reticule from last night, for he was looking so pale and faint." She looked quite noble at this sacrifice.

"We'd best have a look at Tannie," Southam said, and Gillie led them forth.

She did not forget to holler at John Groom to pull farther off the road. The drivers here drove like lunatics. They found the duke rolled up in a horse blanket by the side of the stream. He was as pale and faint as Gillie had warned. He tried to rise, and Gillie ordered him back down.

"My fault entirely, Lord Southam," he said in a weak voice. "I am very sorry. Daresay you was worried sick about Gillie. And when you especially asked us to return early, too," he added to Bea.

"You are forgiven, as it was obviously unavoidable," Bea replied. "Can you make it to Southam's carriage, Duke? We must get that arm looked at."

"If Southam will lend me an arm to lean on, I'll make it, but I cannot leave my team here."

"I'll stay with the team," Gillie said.

"Can't stay alone," the duke replied sternly. "We could hitch the team to Southam's rig and lead them back to town."

"What about the carriage?" Gillie asked.

"Surely the duke is more important than the carriage, or the team for that matter," Bea said. The two youngsters looked at her as if she were mad.

Southam helped the duke up and assisted him to the intact carriage. It was arranged that Southam would drive his own carriage, and his groom would stay behind with the duke's team and rig till help could be sent from Bournemouth, in case the wheeler from Poole failed to come.

During the return trip Gillie was a perfect ministering angel, asking Tannie every two minutes whether he was comfortable and assuring him that his arm would soon be healed, and he'd be driving as well as ever. Bea had a sneaking suspicion that under cover of the horse blanket they were holding hands. Tannie's vulnerability seemed to have aroused something akin to love in Gillie. Rather ironic, as Southam had decided against the match at this time. She doubted that his opposition would stand long against Gillie's persuasions.

They took Tannie to his own hotel, laid him on his bed, and called the doctor. When he came, the others went downstairs. Gillie would not leave the premises until she heard the doctor's opinion.

"If he is to lose that arm," she said, eyes wide with horror, "I must be here to comfort him, Rawl. He would never be able to drive again. Not so well as he drives now, though I am sure he would manage it somehow with only one arm. And it is all my fault! He told me to give him the reins, and I refused." Her lower lip wobbled, and her eyes filled with moisture.

"Let us have lunch while we wait for the doctor's verdict," Southam said.

"Oh, yes. I am weak with hunger," Gillie agreed. Her concern for Tannie had not deprived her of a hearty appetite.

"We ought to send word to Miss Pittfield," Bea said, and took care of that detail while Southam ordered lunch.

There were a few other matters that needed attention as well. Tannie was obviously not in any condition to take Horatio's money to him. That unfortunate gent was sitting alone in some room, afraid to stick his nose out the door. Bea decided she would have to learn the location and take the money to him herself. Another matter of considerable importance was the remove to Bath.

She mentioned that over lunch. "When shall we leave for Bath?" she asked Southam.

"It is pointless to set out so late in the day," he said.

"You will not want to leave Deborah there alone, though."

He clenched his lips. "I'll send a message telling her what happened. She came uninvited. It is not our fault if an unforeseen accident detains us. What can we do? We cannot leave that poor boy alone, at least till we discover how serious this accident is. It is Gillie's fault. We must stay."

Gillie burst into sniffles but gave him a thankful gaze and squeezed his hand.

When the doctor came down, Southam invited him to take coffee with them, while he outlined the duke's condition.

"It is a very serious sprain, but thank God, no bones are broken. He will recover eventually."

"How long?" Gillie asked eagerly.

"A month should see him back in fighting trim. I don't want that arm jostled with rough driving

153

for a couple of weeks, but he can be up and about in a day or two. I have bandaged up his arm and shoulder, and given him a draft of laudanum to deaden the pain. He will soon be sleeping like a baby. If you wish to have a word with him, best do it now, while he is still awake."

It was arranged that the doctor would return that evening, and meanwhile there was nothing more to be done. The duke's valet would be with him to see to his needs. The doctor had already had a word with him.

The party went upstairs to say good-bye while Tannie was still awake. He was already groggy. Bea did not think he would have called Gillie an angel and kissed her hand in front of them all if he had been perfectly alert. She managed to get Horatio's address from him, a disreputable establishment called the Old Fox, on Littledown Road. She assured him she would see that Horatio got the money.

"We'll come back this evening," Gillie said before leaving. "Is there anything you want, Tannie? Sugarplums or oranges or cigars?"

"Just make sure my team are unharmed," he said, his eyelids beginning to slide closed.

"Naturally! As if I would not check up on that!"

Chapter Fourteen

As they drove back to the Royal Bath, Southam expressed his concern at leaving Tannie in the hands of his valet, with no friend or family to assist him.

Gillie encouraged this line of thought. "There is no counting on Duncan McIvor and that set. They won't want to miss the races," she said, but in no condemning way.

It occurred to Beatrice that Horatio could stay with his nephew, leaving them free to return to Bath without feeling they were abandoning an invalid. Not knowing Horatio's plans, she did not mention it until she had a chance to talk to him. Her eagerness to take him the money was rising. Horatio would think they had all forgotten him. The blacklegs might have discovered his hiding place by now and beaten him to a pulp. By the time they reached the hotel, she was on nettles to get on with her errand. She did not relish going alone, but Southam was already distracted enough. She would be perfectly safe in his carriage.

"I must jot a line to Deborah to explain our delay," he said as he stood at the carriage door to hand the ladies down.

Beatrice did not dismount. "Could I borrow your carriage for half an hour, Southam?" she asked. "There is something I must attend to before we leave."

"Certainly," he replied, hardly noticing what she said.

With so many matters preying on their minds, neither of them observed the stocky, swarthy man in the leather waistcoat and fustian jacket loitering around the front of the hotel. Garrity had more than one defaulting bettor to look after. He had temporarily lost track of his leads to Evendon, but he knew where to find one of them. When he saw Beatrice leave in the carriage, he jumped into a hansom cab and followed her.

Once Southam had written his note, he began to wonder why Beatrice had wanted the carriage. She didn't know anyone in Bournemouth, so it could not be a social visit. Surely she had not chosen this inopportune moment to go shopping, and alone. Where could she be? He had marked the direction the carriage was heading—not south to the Cliff Promenade, but north, away from the center of town. With rising concern, he went out to the street and began to walk rapidly off in the same direction, his eyes peeling the streets for a sign of his carriage. When he had walked two blocks, he realized he would never catch her up and hailed a cab. He explained that he was looking for a black crested carriage and told the driver to whip the team up, to cover the maximum length of road in the shortest time.

Meanwhile Beatrice was driven through the better part of the city into a less populated area, clutching her reticule with the thousand pounds in it to her chest. Garrity's cab followed close behind, unobserved.

She dismounted at a second-rate hotel and asked John Groom to wait for her. Garrity got out and sauntered nonchalantly along, keeping an eye on her groom. It did not look suspicious for the tout to enter the dingy Old Fox Inn. Indeed, he looked more at home there than Mrs. Searle and her fine rig. Southam's groom didn't give him a second glance. Garrity picked up speed once he was inside. Mrs. Searle had already spoken to the clerk and was heading down a corridor to the right. The blackleg hurried after her.

She tapped quietly at the door; immediately Horatio opened it and Beatrice entered. The blackleg recognized him and slid forward, putting his ear to the door. He had to establish how many people were in the room before he went charging in.

"Did you think we had abandoned you, Horatio?" Beatrice said.

"Not for a minute, though I own I was becoming impatient. Did Tannie get the money?"

"No, I got it. I have it right here."

"That's my darling girl. Come here and I'll kiss you for that. You've saved my old neck." He gave her a loud smack on the cheek.

"I have a favor to ask of you in return, Horatio," she said.

"Ask away. You have just done me a large favor. I knew I might depend on you, lass."

"Tannie is hurt," she said, and explained the situation. Horatio agreed to go to him that night and see him safely back to Bath when he was well enough to travel.

Garrity, lurking at the door, heard only two voices, one of them a lady's. He quietly opened the door and entered. "So there you are, Evendon," he said. "And with enough money in your hands to choke a horse."

"I hope it chokes a swine instead," Horatio said, and flung it at him.

The man scrambled about the floor, picking up the bills and counting them carefully. When he had ascertained that it was all there, he said, "I can give you a hot tip on the four o'clock race. Fair Lady is paying seven-to-one. A newcomer, but I hear from her owner that she is a sweet goer."

"Be off, man," Horatio said, and cuffed his ear.

"No hard feelings, mate. Business is business."

The blackleg scuttled out, stuffing his ill-got gains into his jacket. As his cab had left, he had to walk back to town. Southam noticed the hurrying form as his cab passed. He had seen that dark phiz before. He stopped the cab, jumped out and grabbed the man by the throat.

"Where is she?" he demanded. "If you have touched a hair of her head, I'll kill you."

"Here, watch who you're mauling, mate. You mean the saucy piece in the fancy rig?" He pointed his thumb down the street. Southam saw his carriage standing outside a disreputable-looking inn.

"Yes—No! The lady who was in that carriage."

"She's with the old bleater in his room. Never fear he'd harm her. His darling girl, he called her. Kissing and sweet talk is the worst she's suffering. Take a right turn at the desk, and down two doors. That's where you will find her."

Southam released his hold on the blackleg and pelted forward. His groom recognized him and called out. Southam didn't stop but called as he ran, "Is Mrs. Searle in there?"

"Aye. This is where she asked me to bring her. I didn't think much of the—" He stopped, for Lord Southam was already beyond hearing. Looked as if the hounds of hell were after him. Something queer afoot, from the looks of him.

Southam darted down the hall and flung open the second door on the left. He saw Beatrice sitting at her ease with the racetrack tout ancient enough to be her father, though not an unattractive man in a raffish way. They were having a glass of wine and chatting as if they were bosom bows.

"So this is where you are!" he charged.

Beatrice, not realizing she was being rescued, replied nonchalantly. "Yes, this is where I am. As you are here Southam, let me introduce—"

"I have no wish to meet your paramour," he said stiffly. "What you do when you are in Bath is your business. Here, you are under my protection."

"Paramour!" she gasped, choking on her wine.

Horatio shook his head in wonder. "I've been called a blackamoor in my time, but what the deuce is a paramour? Sounds like a dashed insult."

"You must apologize for that, Lord Southam," Bea said, rising haughtily from her chair.

"I'll be demmed if I'll apologize to either of you."

"You will apologize to the lady if you are a gentleman," Horatio said, bristling up at this highhanded young buck.

Southam just reached out his hand and grasped Bea's fingers. "I am taking you back to the hotel."

She wrenched her hand away. "You are taking me nowhere, sir!" she stated firmly. Her Irish temper soared at his high-handed tactics. "I shall leave when I am ready. I'm not your sister, or your fiancée, that you can tell me what I may and may not do."

He took a deep breath to calm his nerves and said through clenched teeth, "Beatrice, come with me—now!"

"The lady said no," Horatio pointed out.

"Shut your face, you old fool."

159

"Now see here, laddie, you want to show a little respect for your elders."

"Southam!" Beatrice said, glaring at him. "You will apologize at once, and stop making a fool of yourself."

"Apologize be demmed. I'd blacken his daylights if I weren't too much of a gentleman to strike an old man."

"Don't let that stop you!" Horatio said, bristling.

"Just as you wish," Southam replied, and struck the man a blow across the cheek. It was not hard enough to hurt, yet too hard to be ignored.

Lord Horatio was a gentleman, whatever his looks or financial condition; he took the only course open to a gentleman who has received such an insult. "Name your second, sir. My man will call on you at the earliest opportunity."

"Horatio! Not a duel, for God's sake!" Bea howled.

"He struck me in the face. You saw it." He turned back to Southam. "Name your second, sir."

"The Duke of Cleremont," Southam said.

Horatio stared to hear his nephew's name. "Mr. Runciman will call on him," he said.

"I never heard such foolishness in my life," Beatrice said, and marched out the door, confident that no duel would take place when the duke was flat on his back and likely to be hors de combat for some time.

In the carriage she sat like a stone during the first few blocks. Southam, too, kept a sullen silence. He was by now thoroughly ashamed of himself and also highly curious to learn what Beatrice had been doing with that old man who called her his darling girl and kissed her.

Curiosity finally got the better of him and he said, "I think you owe me an explanation, Cousin."

"I owe you a good thrashing. What were you

160

thinking of, to involve Tannie, who is sick as a dog, in a duel with his uncle."

"His uncle!"

"Of course. Lord Horatio is his uncle. I was taking him the thousand pounds I borrowed from you, since Tannie was unable to do it."

"Good God, you might have told me so!"

"You might have waited for an explanation before you started beating up an old man."

"I did not beat him up. I tapped him on the cheek. He is the one who started this business of a duel."

"What did you expect, when you slapped him?"

"I expected him to apologize."

"For what? For sitting innocently in his own room? It is all your own fault, and you know it perfectly well. You must apologize and withdraw the challenge."

"I did not make the challenge; therefore I cannot withdraw it. It is for Lord Horatio to pull in his horns and admit he is in the wrong."

"He is *not* in the wrong. You apologize, and I shall see to it that he withdraws the challenge."

"You have that sort of influence with the old bleater, do you?"

"He owes me a thousand pounds. He'll do as I say."

"He owes *me* a thousand pounds."

"No, *I* owe you a thousand pounds, and that does not mean I shall do as you say."

"What's sauce for the goose . . ."

"I don't want you to mention this to Tannie. He is not well enough to be bothered with this foolishness. In fact, you had best turn this carriage around, or Horatio will have sent Mr. Runciman off to see the duke. Why on earth did you say Tannie, of all people?"

"I don't know anyone else in Bournemouth!" he shouted.

"This is a fine pickle. What will Lady Sappington say when she hears of this? What will Deborah say?" She pinned him with a wicked eye. "I shouldn't blame her in the least if she turns you off."

Southam heard the magic words and felt strongly inclined to go on with the duel. "I'll have Tannie suggest someone else to take his place as my second," he said.

Beatrice sniffed and turned her head aside to look out the window. It was all a tempest in a teapot. Horatio and Southam would meet at Tannie's hotel this evening and straighten the misunderstanding out between them. Neither one, she felt sure, really wanted to fight. As they went into the hotel, she said, "It would be scandalous for you to have a duel with a man so much older than yourself. It would alienate the duke's family, and prevent Gillie from making the match."

He held the door as she sailed into the hotel. "She is too young to marry," he said. "I have not agreed to the match. In fact, I told you earlier that I plan to take Gillie home for a year."

"You know perfectly well you'd leap at it if she expressed any real interest. And furthermore, it will not do my reputation any good to be involved in this imbroglio."

"There is no need for your name to arise. The altercation was over a gambling debt."

"I can see Tannie keeping that under his hat. He'll let it out the first time he opens his mouth."

"You should choose your male friends with more care, Cousin."

"I did not choose the friend who has caused this fracas. He just happens to be my late husband's cousin," she snapped, and swept past him to run upstairs.

Southam went into the taproom to drown his sor-

162

rows in ale. He had made a fine botch of things. Deborah was waiting for him at Bath, while he was mired in a duel in Bournemouth with the uncle of the best catch his sister was ever likely to make. A duke of vast wealth and prestige. Deborah would kill him if he botched that match. She very likely *would* turn him off, he thought hopefully. But then, Beatrice would not have him, either. He was demmed if he did, and demmed if he didn't. He ordered another ale, and found it gave him a thumping headache. He wished he had never come to Bournemouth.

Chapter Fifteen

Beatrice feared that if she had to face Southam over the dinner table that evening, she would strike him. For that reason, she claimed fatigue and ate in her room. When Miss Pittfield visited her after dinner, she knew from Bea's air of distraction that something was amiss. After a few prevarications, Bea told her the story of Southam's duel.

Miss Pittfield sat stunned by the news. "Southam involved in a duel! Surely you jest, Mrs. Searle."

"I assure you that is not my idea of a joke, ma'am."

"So that is why he didn't eat his dinner," Miss Pittfield said. "He sat like a man in a daze, pushing his food around his plate like a child. He's gone mad, that's what it is. We must talk him out of it."

"Of course, but that is only half the problem. We shall also have to talk Lord Horatio out of it, for it was he who issued the challenge, and you know how foolishly gentlemen behave when their honor is involved."

"Yes, when they start prating of honor, you know they are about to do something ridiculous and indefensible so far as common sense goes. Honor has caused more mischief among men than any other thing—except perhaps women."

"I fear the duel will give Miss Swann a disgust of him," Bea said, looking from the corner of her eye. She knew she was not imagining that light of hope that gleamed on her caller's face. "I daresay the best thing would be to get it all sewed up here tomorrow before we return to Bath."

Miss Pittfield listened, fell silent a moment, then spoke. "Much better to do it in Bath." To give this suggestion an air of innocence, she added, "There is no saying. It might all blow over, and it would be a shame to rush them into a duel if a breathing spell might prevent it."

"Perhaps you are right. We'll encourage Southam to return to Bath tomorrow morning as planned and delay the duel until Lord Horatio brings the duke back to his aunt."

"How long do you figure that will take?"

"A week, perhaps. That should be enough to cool tempers."

"Meanwhile there will be gossip of a duel," Miss Pittfield said, not quite smiling.

"It will mean that Miss Swann stays with us for that week," Bea said, and drew a discontented sigh.

"It will be worth it, if it means we do not have to live with her for the rest of our lives," Miss Pittfield said, and laughed at her daring.

The truth was out now, and the two ladies could get down to some decent gossip and planning, with no *honor* to disturb their enjoyment.

After dinner Southam took Gillie to visit Tannie. He trusted the duke would not discuss the duel in front of Gillie, nor did he. He had written the duke a note before dinner. His servant had brought back a reply announcing Tannie's willingness to help.

165

He had suggested Duncan McIvor as a replacement for himself.

It was a relief to see that Tannie was in good spirits and not suffering unduly. He spoke of returning to Bath in two or three days.

Lord Horatio bowed stiffly when they entered, and immediately excused himself. When the guests were leaving, Tannie said in a meaningful voice, "Mr. McIvor will drop around at your hotel this evening if it is convenient, Lord Southam. There is something he would like to discuss with you. I suggested nine-thirty in the taproom of the Royal Bath."

"I'll be there," Southam replied.

Gillie proceeded to the door, and Tannie said quietly, "I say, Lord Southam, you won't kill Uncle, I hope? Mama would dislike it very much. So would I, for that matter."

"I have no intention of shooting to kill. Indeed, I do not wish for this duel. It was your uncle who issued the challenge."

"That is odd! Uncle will usually walk a mile to avoid a duel. Since he killed Lord Peter Almquist ten years ago, he has never fought a duel. Mind you, he keeps his shooting up, just in case. A dead shot. He can take the eye out of a pigeon from a hundred yards."

Southam swallowed in astonishment and left, his eagerness for the duel greatly diminished. He was a fair shot himself, but he doubted whether he would have the sangfroid to aim his gun at a fellow human being. He would have to apologize. There was nothing else for it. He could not risk getting himself killed for no reason. He had his three sisters to look after. He'd ask Mr. McIvor this evening to deliver his apologies, and hope that Lord Horatio's blood lust would not insist on the match.

At nine-thirty Southam was waiting in the taproom. He had seen McIvor with the duke and recognized him when he came in. He was a tall, slender gentleman who fancied himself a Corinthian. His blond curls and blue eyes had earned him the reputation of being handsome, though Southam thought him a green boy.

McIvor was thrilled with the dashing role thrust upon him. In his set, however, no air of passion was ever allowed to betray itself. Even Miss Whitcombe, the lady with whom he was utterly infatuated, was only allowed to be "tolerable." He wore a face of ennui when he accosted Lord Southam. "Dashed nuisance, this duel," he said, drawing out a chair. "Still, when old Evendon feels the killing fit come on him, we must all hop to his command."

Southam's blood ran cold at the thoughtless remark. It was easy to believe the worst of that ramshackle old gent who had been kissing Beatrice—and she allowing it! Still, he must at least make an effort to patch up the difference. "I fear I thrust this duel on him," he said. "As the duke and my sister are friends, I wish to tender an apology for striking him."

McIvor was not at all happy to see all his glory wither away to dust. "What, apologize to old Evendon? Dear boy, not to be thought of. Wouldn't accept it, not for a minute. Only make a cake of yourself."

"He is an old man. It doesn't seem right."

Duncan stuck the knob of his cane under his chin and stared at Southam. "Bad shot, are you?"

"Certainly not!"

"Gun-shy?"

"No!"

"Then why apologize?"

"Because I say so, Mr. McIvor."

"Right. I'll speak to Runciman then, Even-

167

don's second, and see if we can patch it up. I'll do it now, and be back within an hour. Runciman is always to be found in the card room at the Carlton."

The hour of uncertainty seemed very long to Southam. Long enough for the trip to the dueling ground, the twelve paces, the fatal shot, even the funeral, where the chief mourner was not his fiancée but Beatrice, with a lace-edged hankie held to her moist eyes. "All my fault!" she moaned, inconsolable in her grief. She had not shed such a shower of tears for Leonard.

He judged from McIvor's jaunty air when he returned that the interview had gone well, that the duel was off. "What did he say?" Southam demanded eagerly.

"All a waste of time. He says you struck Evendon. No gentleman in his right mind will accept an apology for that. You cannot grovel! I mean to say, you don't want to look like a lily-livered coward! I did manage to get you a few days grace to practice up your shooting. Duel will take place Saturday in Bath. West bank of the Avon, just above Walcot Cemetery, six-thirty a.m. Will you be wanting your own doctor?"

"I should think so," Southam replied in a hollow voice. "A very good one. I leave the choice to you, as I am not familiar with the local sawbones in Bath."

"Leave everything to me, Lord Southam. I have a copy of the *Code Duello*. I'll swat up on it. Pity you could not dash up to London for a few lessons at Manton's Shooting Gallery, but there is a chap at the north end of Marlboro Lane in Bath who will teach you to culp a wafer right enough."

"I know how to shoot, Mr. McIvor." His tone implied that if he had his pistols with him, one of them would die on the spot.

168

"Carry your dueling pistols with you?"

"No."

"I'll borrow Tannie's. Get 'em oiled up. I'll call on you in Bath the day after tomorrow to put the final polish on the affair. Pleasure serving you, Lord Southam." He rose, eager to dart off and boast of the affair to his chums. "I must run now."

After a largely sleepless night, Southam was in no mood for chatter when the party met for breakfast in the morning. He arrived late and left early, after doing no more than sipping half a cup of coffee. "I must to go up to my room and have a look to see I haven't forgotten anything," he said.

Beatrice wanted to speak to him in private and left before the others. She went directly to Southam's room and knocked on the door.

"Have you spoken to Mr. McIvor yet?" she asked, when he admitted her.

"I had him deliver an apology. It was not accepted. The duel is still on."

"Horatio did not accept an apology? I can't believe it!"

His glare soon convinced her. "You neglected to mention he is a crack shot. Killed the last man he went up against."

"That was eons ago."

"He's kept in practice, McIvor tells me."

"Shooting birds, not men! Are you a good shot, Southam?"

"Fairly good. I hunt. The duel is to be held Saturday morning in Bath."

"Excellent!" His eyes widened in surprised dismay. "That it is to be delayed, I mean. It will give me time. . . ."

"To arrange my funeral?" he sneered.

"Don't worry. I shan't let him kill you."

"I am not hiding behind a lady's skirts!" he said

angrily. "If he means to shoot to kill, I shall brush up on my shooting, and we'll see which of us topples over."

She left, not frowning, but not smiling, either. She was surprised that Horatio had not accepted an apology. It must have been a very haughty sort of apology. Horatio had his pride, too, but she felt secure that she could get around him. No hurry.

Chapter Sixteen

A drizzling rain made the trip to Bath thoroughly miserable. Southam sat with his chin hunched into his collar in one corner of the carriage, Gillie stared out at the rain in another. The only conversation that occurred was between Bea and Miss Pittfield. With two witnesses they could not have the sort of talk they wished, so they were mostly silent as well. Yet, with all this monotony and discomfort, no one really looked forward to the termination of the journey, knowing what awaited them in Bath.

The Honorable Miss Swann sat in state by the fire in Mrs. Searle's saloon when they arrived. The reflection from dancing flames lent some liveliness to her pale charms. Sensing trouble in her romance, Miss Swann had made a careful toilet and wore a smile of welcome. She had seen, in Beatrice's bedroom, a recent portrait of her old school chum and realized that time had been kind to her. Her callers, many of them gentlemen, revealed that Beatrice was popular. Idle comments also revealed that Southam had been dancing with Mrs. Searle.

This was not the moment to be on her high horse. That could wait till she got Southam back home.

She rushed forward and threw herself into Southam's arms the moment he was in the door. "Southam! How delightful to see you again. I missed you so much that I decided to join you. I hope you are not displeased with my impetuosity!" she added with an air of stately archness.

"I am delighted that you came, Deborah," he said, amazed at this new warmth in her. "I only wish you had let me know, and I would have been here to meet you."

"That was horrid of me." She turned to Bea, smiling fondly. "And such an imposition. But then, Beatrice and I have been friends forever. We shall have a long chat later and get caught up on all our school friends."

"Hello, Miss Swann," Gillie said, drawing off her pelisse.

"Gillian! How I have missed this dear child. I have a dozen messages for you from your sisters. Let us all go in by the fire, for I see you are sodden." She was not sorry to see Beatrice with her moist hair drooping most unattractively around her ears. She helped Southam off with his coat, a thing she had never done before in her life, to remind Beatrice that she was Southam's fiancée.

"Come in by the fire and tell me all about Gillie's duke, and his driving accident," she continued. "Your letter barely skimmed the surface, Southam. I was happy to see you stayed over with him. The proper thing to do—you knew I would insist upon it. I did not at all mind being alone here, in Beatrice's charming little house. Quite like a doll's house, so cozy."

As they took their places by the fire, Deborah noticed that Southam had changed his hairstyle and was wearing more modish cravats. What had brought about this change? She had soon fingered Beatrice as the culprit.

Beatrice excused herself to freshen up. In her mind she had turned Deborah into a conniving hussy, but seeing her in the flesh made her think again. Deborah seemed genuinely fond of Southam. In fact, she seemed to be in love with him. She was prettier than Bea remembered—not a beauty precisely, but she had countenance and an air of elegance. Time had improved her. Her major fault as a girl had been her matronly manner, but now that she was older, the manner was less galling.

It had all been a daydream. She was not going to see Deborah turn Southam off. Indeed, it would be horrid even to try anything in that line. Some attraction had sprung up between Southam and herself, but it was just the charm of novelty. He had been engaged to Deborah for six months, whereas he had not seen her in years. Being together a good deal, some intimacy had developed. Now that Deborah was here, it was over.

Bea tidied herself but did not try to set up as competition. She drew her moist hair back severely from her face and took no particular care for her gown. Her old green crepe was good enough. She usually wore her pearls with it, but she set them aside and chose a simple golden locket on a chain instead. Examining herself in the mirror, she thought she looked a little like a nun.

When she returned below stairs, she found Southam and Deborah alone, chatting by the fire. It was a cozy scene, suggesting marital intimacy. He had not bothered to change. Could he not bear to leave her side? Bea entered, smiling politely.

"Are you telling Deborah of our adventures in Bournemouth, Southam?" she asked. She poured herself a glass of wine, as they were having some.

173

Southam looked up in alarm. "What do you mean?" he demanded.

"Why, the hurdle races, and Tannie's accident, and the lovely drives around the cliffs. They are very interesting, Deborah. One may drive along the top, or drive down through ravines, catching glimpses of the sea from time to time. Beautiful gardens. Very unusual."

Southam relaxed visibly. "We took Gillie to a play," he told Deborah. "Something about a mop girl. A foolish thing."

"Of more interest to me is that you have found Gillian a ducal *parti*," Deborah said. "I have been to call on Lady Sappington."

"I didn't know you were acquainted with her," Southam said, surprised.

"Papa knows Lord Sappington. When I discovered that the boy you casually called Tannie is the Duke of Cleremont, I went to introduce myself. I wanted her to know that although Gillian was staying with Bea—no offense, Beatrice—she has influential friends. Lady Sappington is charming."

Beatrice blinked to hear that Lady Gillian required the sponsorship of Miss Swann, to say nothing of the implied indignity of Deborah's staying in her home. This was the Deborah she remembered. Officious, interfering, lording it over the world.

"You have had several callers, Beatrice," she continued. "But then, you always were one to have a large circle of admirers," she added condescendingly. Something in her voice suggested the circle was not so discriminating as one could wish. She continued to make it quite clear. "A Mr. Baker came by. Some sort of retired merchant, I believe?"

"He is not retired," Beatrice said coolly. "He

is the proprietor of the Baker Art Gallery in Bath."

"No need to apologize. One meets counter-jumpers in the best homes nowadays," she replied, immune to a snub.

"I was not apologizing. Mr. Baker is also our member of Parliament."

"Odd he did not say so. One would think he would have recognized my name, as Papa is so prominent in politics. Perhaps he only knows my father by his title. I should have thought even he would know the family name of the house of Norland is Swann. Princess Sophia and I looked into the origins of the Norlands. We suspected we were related, and of course we were. One of my aunts, several generations ago, was married to one of her uncles. I must answer dear Sophia's letter."

Deborah then turned her attention to her fiancé. "Run along to the inn and change for dinner, Southam. You will take a chill, sitting in that damp jacket. Do you not have a decent cravat? That one you are wearing looks so very odd, as if it were made up from a serviette. And your hair!"

"This Brutus-do is all the crack," Southam defended.

"Only in Bath," Deborah said with a tolerant shake of her head. She turned to Beatrice. "He would turn out like a scarecrow if I didn't hound him into elegance."

"I see a fiancée has her hands full," Beatrice said blandly.

"I'll leave you ladies now and return after dinner," Southam said, rising to take his leave.

"Why, you'll be joining us for dinner, I hope!" Deborah said.

Beatrice felt her gorge rise at the impertinence.

175

She leveled a cool look at Southam and said, "If it is an invitation from the *hostess* you are waiting for, Southam, then let me add, I shall be very happy if you would join us."

"Thank you, ma'am," he said, suppressing his anger with Deborah. "In that case I shan't bother going to the hotel to change if you don't mind."

"Oh, really, Southam!" Deborah said. "You cannot come to the table looking like that."

"Why don't you use your usual room to freshen up, Southam," Beatrice suggested. She knew Deborah would dislike that air of intimacy and could not have cared less. The woman was insufferable, inviting a guest to *her* table!

Deborah's eyes snapped. "That sounds so cozy," she said, smiling determinedly. "As though you run quite tame here, Southam."

Beatrice replied in the same smiling way. "As you and I are such old chums, Deborah, I did not stand on my dignity with your fiancé."

"I should hope not. Very well, then, Southam. You run along to your *usual* room, while Beatrice and I have a good coze, and I find out what you have been doing here in Bath."

He made good his escape, fearful of what might be going forth before the grate. The conversation was not as frightening as he feared.

"Tell me all about the Duke of Cleremont, Beatrice," Deborah said.

"He is not so very handsome. His passion is horses, which suits Gillie very well, of course."

"What of his fortune, his estates?"

Beatrice gave a brief outline. "This is based only on gossip," she said, "for I have not personally quizzed Tannie on the matter."

"Of course not. We must be more subtle than that. I shall have Papa look into it. You have done very well," Deborah congratulated. "I despaired of ever getting Gillie bounced off. She failed to attach an excellent *parti* at home, you must know."

"She is only seventeen! There is no rush."

"The sooner we can wrap it up, the better. We do not want to let a duke slip through our fingers. Quite an ornament to hang on the family tree."

As Beatrice approved of the match, she did not bother to say all the disagreeable things she wanted to. They chatted without coming to cuffs until the others came downstairs and dinner was announced. The conversation was lively, with tales of their visit to Bournemouth and Deborah's news from home.

In the evening Sir Harold Whitehead, who had seen Southam's carriage enter town, came to call. After some general conversation, he said. "Do you know, I heard the most extraordinary thing. Upon my soul, I could scarcely believe it. There is a rumor afoot that old Evendon has got himself involved in a duel over a lady. Who would be fool enough to challenge him? He has got a notch or two on his pistol. Killed his man last time."

Southam and Bea exchanged a guilty look. "Really!" Bea said in a weak voice. "Where did you hear this, Harold?"

"Why the story came from Bournemouth. My cousin was at the hurdle races. I was hoping you might be able to give me the details. I am eager to hear what lady Horatio has in his eye."

"Lady!" Beatrice exclaimed in horror.

"Shocking, eh?" Sir Harold said. "One would have thought it would have to do with horses. Did you not hear it discussed there?"

"We heard nothing about it," Southam said firmly.

Deborah pokered up. "Disgusting! Dueling ought to be outlawed. Papa is working on a bill to present

177

to Parliament. I know it will have the Prince Regent's support, for he has often expressed himself against that barbarous custom. I trust the duke was not hurt in a duel? You could not allow Gillie to marry him if he is that rackety sort of creature, Southam."

"I wrote the details to you. He had an accident in his curricle," Southam said.

"Dueling is bad enough," Deborah continued, "but for grown men to be killing each other over a woman! I shall not say lady, for no lady would let herself fall into such a compromising position."

"You are hard on ladies, Deborah," Bea said. "She may have had no say in the matter."

"I repeat, no *lady* would let herself fall into a compromising position."

This categorical statement terminated the discussion. Tea was served, and when Sir Harold took his leave, Miss Pittfield took Gillian up to bed.

Beatrice soon excused herself. "You won't mind if I leave you alone with Southam, Deborah? You are engaged after all."

"I shan't be long," Deborah replied.

As soon as she was alone with Southam, she turned a steely eye on him. "How soon can we wrap up Gillie's match and go home, Southam?"

"We can hardly do so before the duke returns from Bournemouth."

"Pity."

"There is no reason you must stay, if—"

She laughed gaily, to conceal her annoyance. "Nonsense! I will not desert you. When do you expect him?"

"He mentioned a day or two."

"That will give me time to pay a few more calls on Lady Sappington. Perhaps we can take in a dance at the Upper Rooms, as you are so fond of going there," she said. Her tone was a rebuke.

He recognized that tone as one that required explanation. "Beatrice and I took Gillie," he said.

"That is well enough, I daresay, but why did you go to Bournemouth?"

"The duke wished it," he said, knowing this was the best excuse in the world.

"And Beatrice invited herself along. Really that woman is not quite the thing. I had no idea she had become so rackety. You would not believe the sort of Cits who have been calling on her. And that Whitehead creature, with his talk of duels. I daresay Evendon is some chum of hers."

"He is the duke's uncle."

"I know that! I have been reading the peerage to check up on the duke. There are some relatives that one does not associate with too closely, however. Still, Beatrice has served her purpose well. As soon as we get Gillie settled, you and I shall have our banns posted. And now you must run along, Southam. I want a word with Beatrice before she retires. Now that I am here, she can resume running around with her own set. I daresay she will be happy for that. You and I shall chaperon Gillie. We'll take her to call on Lady Sappington tomorrow. The duke's accident will make an unexceptionable excuse. If we go just before teatime, she might invite us to stay to tea."

Southam listened, hearing much that displeased him. Such scheming was new to him. Yet he read it in echoes of how Deborah had won him. Before teatime was usually when she came to call in the days when she was courting him, usually with some excuse that appeared feasible to an unsuspecting soul.

"Gillie has her routine established," he said. "She rides and drives, and joins with a young bunch of girls here who have waltzing parties."

"Waltzing! She is not even out. Really, I knew Beatrice was not fastidious, but I never imagined she was that foolhardy."

"All the debs-to-be participate. They are learning the steps before they go to make their bows. It is where Gillie met the duke." Not really a lie. She had met him there many times.

The magic word absolved the dance lessons of shame. "In that case I daresay it is all right. But she must mind her manners. It is of paramount importance for her to impress Lady Sappington favorably. She is the duke's mother's favorite sister. Her opinion will count for a good deal."

Southam's lips thinned. "Gillie is plenty good enough for him. If Lady Sappington don't like her, I cannot think it would make a tuppence of difference to the duke."

Deborah just tossed up her hands and laughed. "I did not arrive a moment too soon. Run along, Southam. Call for me tomorrow at ten. And, dear, you *will* do something about that cravat? And perhaps if you brushed your hair back, it would not look so odd."

She put her two hands to his forehead and brushed the offending hair back with her fingers. While she had him in this pose, she bestowed a chaste kiss on his lips. "Did you miss me, Southam?" she asked.

His answer stuck in his throat. "Do you have to ask?" he parried.

"Indeed I do, for you did not say so!" she said, pouting.

He raised her hand and kissed her fingers, for he could not face kissing her lips. Deborah was satisfied with this meager token of affection and sent him off. She darted upstairs, where she thoroughly annoyed her hostess by telling her, in effect, that her services were no longer required.

Before she closed her eyes, Beatrice had reversed her decision to leave Southam to his fate. Annoying as he could be at times, he did not deserve a lifetime of Deborah Swann. She almost felt that death at the hands of Horatio might be better. At least it would be over quickly.

Chapter Seventeen

For the following two days the calm of Saint Andrew's Terrace was shattered by the machinations
of the Honorable Deborah Swann. She bullied Gillie into accompanying her to call on Lady Sappington (where she failed to obtain an invitation to tea);
she condescended to Beatrice's callers and invited
her own cousins to dinner without asking Mrs.
Searle's permission. Gillie resumed her old sullen
ways. Throughout the ordeal Southam was in a
state of prolonged shock. Between guilt for his
thoughts and forebodings of the duel to come, he
was not up to coping with his fiancée. He did more
or less as she demanded, but he did it from a sense
of guilt, and he did it with a poor grace. He continued wearing his new cravats and hairdo.

The household, with the exception of Deborah,
felt as if they were sitting on a keg of gunpowder,
waiting for Lord Horatio and the duke to return to
town. Rumors of Evendon's duel were running like
wildfire through town, taking on melodramatic
hues as imagination dictated, since there was no
hard news. The lady's husband had caught her and

Evendon in flagrante delicto and demanded satisfaction. No, no, it was not a married lady at all. It was a young girl, and her papa was the challenger. It was an actress, it was a lightskirt, but fortunately it was never a widow, and the partner in crime was never Lord Southam.

Late on Thursday afternoon the duke finally arrived home and came to call on Gillie, with his arm hung up in a strip of black cotton. He was discomfited to find Mrs. Searle's saloon full of people. Southam was there and the Honorable Miss Swann, along with Miss Pittfield and Mrs. Searle and Gillie. He felt like turning tail and leaving when he beheld such a flock of ladies.

He was presented and made an awkward bow. Southam asked how the arm was coming along; he said it hardly hurt at all, except when he moved his fingers. He moved his fingers to demonstrate and grimaced with the pain. As soon as possible he took refuge beside Gillie on the sofa, but he was not allowed any peace. Miss Swann immediately moved over to join him.

"I hope you have had an expert look at that arm, Duke. Such a wound as that might cripple you for life."

He looked at her in alarm. "It is only a sprain!"

"A friend of Princess Augusta fell from his mount and sprained his wrist. He never rode again," she announced dolefully. "And that was with the assistance of Dr. Croft, the royal physician."

"Then I shall steer clear of him!" Tannie exclaimed.

She laughed merrily at this unintentional crumb of ducal wit. "You are too amusing, Duke. How Dr. Croft will laugh to hear that! And how is your dear aunt, Lady Sappington?"

"She is jogging along well enough. Except she complains that every time she is about to sit down and have a read, some curst female she don't even know comes landing in on her, and stays forever. Yesterday the woman came just at teatime, and had to be shown to the door."

"Some people have no discernment," Miss Swann said, shaking her head at such a lack of breeding. "I know just how she feels."

"I wonder we did not meet this lady, for we were there about that time, Miss Swann," Gillie said innocently.

"No doubt she came after we left, well before teatime, my dear."

The tea tray was brought in, and to escape Miss Swann, the duke went to the hostess to take a cup. "My uncle is back," he said to Bea in a low voice as she poured his tea. "I wish you will take a drive out and speak to him, Mrs. Searle. He would listen to you if he would listen to anyone."

"I shall go tomorrow morning, Tannie," she said, smiling as she poured milk in his tea. "What sort of mood is he in?"

"A foul one, I fear. One can hardly blame him. I mean to say, Southam struck him in the face. I think Southam ought to apologize."

"He did apologize. Sugar?"

"Four spoons, please. And if you'd just give it a stir for me. Cursed arm. Indeed he did not apologize! He never went near Horatio."

"He sent his apology through Mr. McIvor."

"The devil you say! Well, if that don't beat the Dutch. Between Duncan and Runciman, they will put either Uncle or Southam in his grave. Let us meet at Uncle's place tomorrow at ten and see if we can straighten it out."

"An excellent idea."

"Who is that appalling woman with Gillie?"

"Miss Swann, Southam's intended."

"Good God! No wonder he wants Uncle to kill him."

"Not a word in her direction about this duel, Tannie. She would dislike it very much."

"You need not fear. I shan't be talking to her if I can avoid it. Does Gillie know about the duel?"

"No one knows except us and Miss Pittfield."

"Mum's the word." He looked over his shoulder at Miss Swann. "If Southam marries that woman—you mean to say Gillie will have to live with her?"

"Of course. Where else would she live?"

"Poor child. Bad as I am, I daresay she'd be no worse off with me." He shook his head ruefully and took his tea to a far corner of the room, thus delaying his coze with Gillie until she could escape and join him.

His visit was brief, and when he left, Miss Swann announced to the room that the duke was "A dear, charming boy, quite unexceptionable. So friendly, and such a ready wit. I must write his little joke about Dr. Croft to the princesses. They like a joke as well as anyone. People who only know them from afar are out in their reckoning if they think the princesses lack humor."

A glazed look came over her listeners' eyes as she wandered off into various examples of royal wit, then brightened remarkably when she decided to just jot down the duke's little joke while it was fresh in her mind. She went no farther than the drop leaf desk in the corner of the saloon for her jotting, but at least it removed her from the conversation area.

Beatrice soon made an excuse from the room. She directed a commanding gaze at Southam to follow her. Within two minutes she had him alone in her study. It was the first time they had been alone since Deborah's arrival.

She wasted not a moment but said immediately, "You said you apologized to Horatio."

185

"I asked McIvor to deliver my apologies."

"Tannie says the apology was not delivered. He thinks Evendon would agree to call off the duel if you would apologize properly."

"I will not grovel!"

"No one is asking you to. Tannie and I are to meet at Horatio's at ten tomorrow morning to try to arrange things. Write an apology, and I shall deliver it for you."

Southam scowled and paced the room, as though trying to come to a decision.

"You cannot be unaware that Bath is rife with scandal about this matter, Southam," she reminded him. "How long do you think your identity will remain a secret if the duel actually takes place?"

"I am not unduly concerned for my reputation."

"Then you might give a thought to *mine*!" she retorted sharply. "Once your name arises, mine will be right behind it. I was the lady who went to Bournemouth with you. I have to go on living here after you leave. You must swallow that unappetizing mouthful of pride and apologize. You owe me that much."

Southam listened and acknowledged that she was right. "Very well. I shall apologize, as I *am* sorry I lost my temper."

Beatrice breathed a sigh of relief. "Do it now, and give me the letter. I shall probably be gone by the time you arrive tomorrow morning."

"I'll call later in the day to learn what Evendon has to say."

"I don't like to be uncivil, Southam, but once this matter is hushed up, I trust you will be taking your fiancée home to Alderton, or she will undo all the good we have done in attaching Tannie."

"You are referring to those ill-timed visits to Lady Sappington. I refused to accompany her, but

186

she somehow bulldozed Gillie into it. I'm sorry she is so—I realize her staying here is a great imposition. As she has cousins in town, I wonder she does not stay with them."

"She wants to be with Gillie," Bea said, though she knew by this time that what Deborah really wanted was to keep an eye on her. "I can endure it for another day or two." This sounded ruder than she meant it to. "I don't mean to disparage your fiancée, Southam. Certainly her intentions are of the best. I daresay she suits you very well, but my temperament is not so stolid as yours. I am not accustomed to being told what to do in my own house."

There was a sound in the hall, and they both looked guiltily toward the door, then back at each other. "That might be her," Bea whispered. "Quick, sit at the desk—I shall say I was just showing you where you could write your note."

"She'll want to know what I'm writing."

"Tell her you're writing to your steward at Elmland."

The door opened just as Southam lunged toward the desk and picked up a pen. Deborah's head peeped in. "Am I interrupting something?" she asked. Her tone was playful, but she looked sharply to see what was afoot.

"Finished your jotting so soon, Deborah?" Bea asked. "Southam had to write a note home. I suggested he use my study."

Deborah gave her hostess a knowing look and went straight to the desk, to hang over Southam's shoulder. "Writing with a dry pen, Southam?" she teased. "If I were of a suspicious nature, I would wonder if you are telling me the truth."

Southam's nerves were already stretched to the breaking point. To have his knuckles rapped in front of Beatrice was enough to snap his control.

His head turned slowly, and when he lifted it, his eyes were like ice. "What are you suggesting, Deborah? That Mrs. Searle and I were attempting to hide something from you? What is it that you suspect? That we were making love?"

Deborah emitted a gasp of surprise. "Really, Southam! What will Beatrice think of you?"

"What will she think of *you*, is more to the point." He turned his back on her, opened the inkwell and stuck the pen into it.

Beatrice slipped quietly into the hall. She heard Deborah's voice raised in complaint as she left. It was a quarter of an hour before the couple returned. Southam looked as if he had swallowed hot coals, and Deborah appeared slightly subdued.

Southam went to Beatrice and said, "I have placed my letter to Elmland on your letter salver in the hall. Perhaps you would be kind enough to post it with your letters tomorrow?"

"Certainly, Southam. I'm afraid the tea has grown cold. Shall I call for some fresh, or would you like wine instead?"

"I expect you are having coffee, Bea?" Southam said. "I'll join you in that."

Deborah's nostrils pinched, but she was still sufficiently cowed from her lecture that she did not object. "Nothing for me, thank you," she said, and went to join Miss Pittfield and Gillie.

The butler brought in coffee, and Bea poured. She said, "Should my ears be burning, or did Deborah reserve her wrath for *you*? No, don't answer that. I am not permitted to complain of a guest in my house, and a fiancé must never find his lady anything but perfect. I shall ask instead how you managed to get your letter written when you had company with you."

"It was accomplished by poor manners. I told her

188

to hush, for I could not think what I was writing when she was nattering at me."

Bea shook her head ruefully. "The same result might have been achieved by a compliment. You should have told her you were too distracted by her charming presence to concentrate. You will make a very unsatisfactory husband, Southam. There is no romance in you."

"Then it is only fair of me to show my true colors before marriage."

"No, it would be better to change them. I want you to take your cup and join Deborah. Be nice to her, Southam, for I suspect you were rather nasty in the study. Run along now," she said, shooing him away with a flutter of her fingers. Her smile was warm and charming. He had not the least desire to leave, but he knew he ought to, and he did.

"Coffee after dinner, Southam?" Deborah chided, when he sat at her side. "No wonder your temper is so uneven. I have noticed you are edgy lately. You have not been sleeping properly."

Deborah's stiff demeanor was like a dash of cold water after Bea's charm and humor. "I have been sleeping marvelously," he lied, and took a long drink. "My nightcap from now on will be coffee."

"We shall see about *that*," she replied blandly. "Not in my house," her expression said.

Southam found it impossible to say anything nice. It took all his control not to say something nasty, so he left very soon and returned to his hotel. He felt like a trout, caught on the hook, wiggling futilely to free himself. She'd *never* call the engagement off. She knew, she must have sense by now, that he didn't care for her. Her response was to rush the wedding forward. That was why she was courting Lady Sappington and pretending to find Tannie witty. She had decreed that Gillie must be

out of the house before they married. But even forbidding Gillie's match wouldn't be enough to do
it. She was beginning to soften her position on that
matter.

In his mind he was back in Bea's study with a
suitably penitent Deborah. "You're angry with me,
Southam. I own I am just a little jealous of Beatrice. Those flashy women have a superficial charm
that men find attractive at first." Her white hands,
cold as ice, clung around his neck, drawing his head
down.

"I find her attractive," he had admitted.

"It is our long engagement that makes you impatient. If we were married, you would be happier,
more settled. How long do you think it will take
the duke—"

"I am not rushing Gillie. I would like her to remain at home another year, then make her bows in
London."

"Beatrice's idea?" Icicles hung from her voice.

"My idea."

"In that case we shall have our banns read as
soon as we go home." She must have seen the
look of horror on his face. She was as sharp as a
needle. "I know it is what you want, Southam,
and I submit to your wishes. I shall just have to
learn to rub along with Gillie. She is more man-
ageable since coming to Bath and more polished.
I notice an improvement. Quite possibly Stuyvesant will offer when he gets a look at her new
style."

"I must write this letter," he said, and strode to
the desk. She was behind him, peering over his
shoulder. "I cannot concentrate with you hanging
over my shoulder," he had said brusquely.

"Then I shall just take a magazine and wait in
the corner, quiet as a little mouse. You won't even
know I'm there."

Oh, but he knew. He could feel her steely eyes staring at his back. He could imagine she was slipping up behind him, putting a noose around his neck. How could he get out of this marriage that had become a nightmare to him? His fingers were writing the words that would cancel the duel—his last hope of salvation. He crumpled the page and threw it in the wastebasket. He drew out a fresh sheet of paper and wrote a different note.

Chapter Eighteen

"Going for a drive so early, Beatrice?" Miss Swann said the next morning at breakfast. "Southam will not be here for hours yet. Perhaps I shall go with you."

"It is not a social visit," Bea said, to be rid of her.

"Charity work? What is it, visiting an orphanage?"

Bea feared it must be a more unpleasant visit than that and said, "I am taking a few orphans to the tooth drawer. If you would care to come along, another woman would not go amiss. They do scream and bawl so, and of course one of them is bound to run away."

"Why do you not go with Beatrice, Miss Pittfield?" Deborah said. "I would go myself, but I really should answer the princess's letter. I shall tell what the duke said of Sir Richard Croft."

Miss Pittfield explained that she was accompanying Gillie and a friend, Miss Cardiff, on a visit to Sydney Gardens. After inquiring into the antecedents of Miss Cardiff, Deborah decided to stay home. "I shall set your servants to polishing the silver, Bea, for I noticed it is getting black. You are too good-natured. You do not scold your servants as you ought."

"I am fortunate to have you here to do it for me," Bea said, with a semblance of good humor.

As Bea was adjusting her bonnet at the mirror by the front door, Deborah joined her. "I noticed Southam's letter is missing from the salver, Beatrice. You wouldn't know what happened to it?"

The letter rested securely in Bea's reticule. Three or four other letters were on the tray, so she could not claim that Southam's had been put in the post. "He must have decided to post it himself," she said.

"I'll ask him," Deborah said, frowning.

As Bea was driven down the Old Roman Road toward Lord Horatio's place, she took no notice of the newly-leafed trees and the beauty of springtime swelling all around her. She was deep in her own thoughts, wondering how Deborah had come to notice the letter was missing. Was she checking the address to see it was, in fact, to Elmdale that Southam was writing? Surely she had not planned to read it! Really, the woman was impossible! How did Southam stand her? She knew her own life would be incomplete when he left. Her old flirts had ceased to amuse. She wanted more than that from life. She wanted another husband, and no one she had met since Leonard's death suited her so well as Southam.

At least she would not be saddled with Deborah Swann. She was in no doubt that Southam had fallen out of love with his fiancée, if he had ever been in love. His behavior was so far removed from loverlike that it seemed impossible he had ever cared for her. Was there anything that could unglue Deborah from Southam? Only the duel, and if it went forward, there was no saying what the results would be, but one result would certainly be the ruin of her own reputation. Quite possibly Southam would be dead, and even if he lived, the Cleremonts would not let the duke offer for Gillie. Horatio was an excellent shot; he could kill Southam, but he was not vengeful. He would be careful to miss the heart.

The carriage drew in at the gates of Horatio's estate. The house was slowly perishing into ruins. Its crumbling stone, heavily overgrown with vines, suggested a Gothic heap. The duke's stately carriage standing on the broken cobblestoned drive only increased awareness of the squalor surrounding it. The groom hopped down and assisted Bea from the carriage. When she was shown in, she found Horatio and Tannie in the saloon.

They rose to greet her. "G'day, lass," Horatio said. "Tannie tells me Southam means to apologize. I own I am relieved. I dislike to be brawling at my age. It lacks dignity."

"Indeed it does. I have brought Southam's letter of apology. He sent his apologies through his second earlier, but it seems they never reached you."

"Not so much as an echo. Some misunderstanding between our seconds, no doubt."

"You must not fight him, Horatio. It is too ridiculous and too much trouble."

She handed him Southam's letter. Horatio set it aside. "I'll glance at it later. The thing is over, so far as I am concerned. The proper way to handle it is for me to notify Runciman that I withdraw my challenge. He must speak to young McIvor, who will carry the word to Lord Southam. But *entre nous*, it is over. Shall we have a glass of wine to celebrate?"

After his stable Sir Horatio's wine cellar was his second pride. He produced an excellent claret and they drank a toast to a successful conclusion to the affair of the duel.

"I am glad you are reasonable, Uncle, for if you had killed Southam, I daresay it would have busted up two romances," the duke said. "Mine with Gillie, and Lord Southam's with the lady he is marrying. Gillie tells me she is a high stickler. Wouldn't stand still for anything rackety. A friend of the royal princesses, which just goes to show you. A dashed queer nabs, Southam. Striking *you*, marrying a woman I couldn't stand for a minute."

Evendon listened, frowning. "I took the notion he was sweet on you, Bea. Why else did he try to knock me down?"

She blushed and tried to pass it off. "He has a quick temper. He was out of reason cross with me, but he could hardly strike a lady, you must know. He is not quite that farouche. So he struck you instead and has regretted it a thousand times since. He is one of those gentlemen who flares up, but soon settles down again and is ashamed of himself."

Evendon refilled their glasses and kept her talking. "He sounds a thoroughly uncomfortable sort of gent. I am not at all sure Miss Swann is getting the better of the match."

"Wouldn't say so if you knew her," Tannie said, wiggling his fingers and grimacing.

"Miss Swann doesn't know how to handle him," Bea said. "He can be very good company. Really he has the patience of a saint to put up with her. I ought not to gossip, but we are old friends, Horatio. I do not hesitate to tell you I pity him."

Horatio examined her wistful face and felt he had figured out the score. Young Bea was head over ears in love with this young Southam hothead. Southam, he already knew, was in love with her. No one was fool enough to strike a man over a lady he wasn't in love with.

As he already knew what he wished to know, he

spoke of other things. "Is it to be a match between you and Bea's cousin, then, Tannie?"

"I meant to ask Southam's permission before the duel, in case you killed him. I shall do it very soon. I don't want Gillie to have to go and live with Miss Swann—that is, after she becomes Lady Southam. No one deserves a fate like that."

They talked a little longer, finishing the bottle of wine. "There is no hurry for me to return," Bea explained. "I am taking some orphans to the tooth drawer this morning."

"Poor devils," Horatio said.

"No, no, you misunderstand. That is the excuse I gave Miss Swann. She had some idea of accompanying me."

When the wine was finished, she left. Bea was in a languorous mood as she was driven home. Her conscience was easy. She had done the right, the only proper thing to prevent the duel, yet a corner of her heart regretted that she had smoothed the path for Deborah's marriage. She took what satisfaction she could from knowing that Gillie would have her duke if she wanted him. Since the duke had acquired his sprained arm, Gillie seemed in a more romantic frame of mind.

Of course she would accept. Deborah would see that the wedding was rushed forward. All the visitors, the wanted and the unwanted, would leave Bath, and she would turn her mind to the London Season. Perhaps this year she would make a match. Although she had had offers in the past, she had held out for love. She had never imagined she would find anyone to replace Leonard, but she had found him now and lost him, so she would settle for companionship and security.

"What had Southam to say?" Tannie asked idly, after Beatrice left.

Sir Horatio tore open the letter and glanced at it. His wiry brows drew together in consternation. "If this is an apology, I fear it is couched in terms I cannot accept! Have a listen to this. 'In the opinion of a lady whose respect I cherish, I did wrong to strike you. The lady feels I ought to apologize, and indeed I never had any intention of shooting to kill. If you wish to withdraw your challenge, I shall understand and not consider it pusillanimous behavior in a gentleman of advanced years.' It is signed Southam. Upon my word, he has added to the offenses with this studied piece of impertinence. Gentleman of advanced years indeed! I am only fifty-five. I could take his nose off at a hundred paces. I have a good mind to do it."

"I smell the hand of Miss Swann in this letter," Tannie said, snatching it and glancing it over. "That is odd, for Mrs. Searle told me Miss Swann knew nothing about the duel. She was particular that I not mention it to her. I wonder if Gillie—but she don't know about it, either."

"I wish I had read this before I gave Bea my assurance the duel is off. I wonder . . ."

"Mrs. Searle would never have allowed him to write such a thing, Uncle. She is down as a nail. A regular right one."

"Of course she is. She believed she was delivering a proper apology. Well, by God, this puts me in a fine pickle. I hardly know what to do."

"Have Runciman speak to Duncan. See what Southam means by this queer note."

"Runciman and Duncan are as much use as a bucket with a hole in the bottom. Bea tells me Southam apologized verbally long ago, but I was told nothing of it. I should like to speak to Southam myself, but I am afraid I'd knock him down if I saw him again. Tannie, perhaps you would speak to him? Feel him out and see if he is only stupid, or if he meant to insult me again."

"He ain't stupid, Uncle."

"Then I shall not withdraw the challenge."

"Well, I'll speak to him. There must be some mistake."

"Meanwhile, there is no point disturbing Bea with the details of this letter. Let us hope we get the matter settled without bloodshed. I am going out to the meadow now to practice my shooting. Not that I need the practice!"

Tannie looked at the letter again and left. He drove to Southam's hotel and found him just about to leave. "I have come from Lord Horatio," Tannie said apologetically. "About that note you wrote him, Lord Southam."

"Let us go to my room," Southam suggested. "This is not a matter to be discussed in public."

Tannie followed Southam to his room. "The thing is," the duke said, "it don't sound much like an apology, Lord Southam, if you don't mind my saying so. I mean to say, it's like saying if you did anything to cause offense, you're willing to be forgiven, which ain't— And you did—cause offense, I mean. Twice."

"I said that I never intended to shoot to kill."

"That is all well and good, but Uncle is this minute in his meadow shooting the wicks off of candles. You ought to make it a little clearer that you are apologizing, if you know what I mean, Lord Southam."

"Oh, dear," Southam said mildly. "The not-shooting-to-kill bit didn't do the trick. I was suggesting, not very clearly apparently, that we should both delope."

"Then why bother having the duel at all? Why not just say you're sorry and have done with it?"

Southam tossed up his hands helplessly. "It is

Miss Swann, ain't it?" the duke said. "That note sounds like her notion of an apology. Mrs. Searle would not have let you write such fustian. How did Miss Swann find out about the duel?"

"This has nothing to do with Miss Swann. It is between your uncle and myself. I have apologized twice. He has not seen fit to accept my apologies."

The duke frowned. "So you will go through with it. You don't want to send a little clearer apology?" he asked hopefully.

"I do not grovel. You might tell your uncle, however, that I shall not shoot to kill."

"Yes, well, when Uncle's dander is up, there is no saying he will be so obliging. You ought not to have called him an old man."

"He *is* an old man."

Tannie shook his head. "The thing to do is for me to replace Duncan as your second. I am recovered sufficiently now." His hope was to heal the breach before the duel, or failing that—and really Southam was being a perfect mule—he thought he might disable the dueling pistols in some manner. Pity old Runciman was mixed up in it, but Uncle must have a second. "Six-thirty tomorrow, then, on the banks of the Avon."

"Just north of Walcot Cemetery. You'll let me know what your uncle has to say?"

"Oh, certainly you will be hearing from me. I am your second now, Lord Southam."

"You can find me at Mrs. Searle's house this evening. And about my message to your uncle, Duke, I would prefer a written reply, just to insure that the message is perfectly clear."

"Sure I can't deliver an apology for you?" Tannie asked once more, ever hopeful.

"Tell him that I shall not shoot to kill."

"Hardly seems worth the trip, but I'll nip back out to Horatio's place and have a word with him."

* * *

Miss Swann remarked twice that evening that Southam seemed fidgety. After her second complaint, he said, "I am expecting a call from the duke this evening."

Deborah's thin lips parted in a smile. "Excellent! You will give our permission, of course."

"I did not say he was coming to ask for Gillie's hand!"

"Why else would he be calling to see you? You said you were expecting a call. We must ask Lady Sappington to dinner tomorrow."

"You forget, Deborah, you are only a guest in Beatrice's house."

"She will be thrilled to have such a tonish caller."

They both looked across the room to where Beatrice sat playing jackstraws with Gillie. Deborah had noticed that her hostess was also on the fidgets this evening. Bea had ruled against a game of whist, when they had a perfect table, with Miss Pittfield to make up the fourth. Deborah had thought Beatrice was waiting for one of her rackety beaux to call, but if that was the case, she was disappointed. No one came.

Deborah had also noticed some unsettling glances exchanged between her hostess and her fiancé. It was hard to pin down the mood in the room. Expectant, waiting, was the closest she could come to it. When the duke was announced, the Argus-eyed Miss Swann observed that Southam leapt an inch from his chair. He hardly allowed the duke to bow to Gillie, before he hustled him off to Bea's study for their private coze.

As Gillie was now practically a duchess, Deborah went to her and began complimenting her on her skill with the jackstraws. "I can only marvel at your steady hand, when the duke is this very minute speaking to your brother," she said. Deborah

200

noticed that Beatrice's hand was far from steady. One would think she were the one awaiting a proposal.

"I shouldn't think the meeting has anything to do with me," Gillie said offhandedly. Yet, despite her denials, she wore a triumphant smile.

"We shall soon know," Deborah said. "Any minute now, Southam will join us and ask you to go to the duke. Let us go upstairs and tidy your hair for the great moment, Gillie." Gillie spurned this idea.

The absence of Southam and the duke lasted for five minutes, which seemed the right interval for Southam to have made a few perfunctory inquiries about the duke's financial state and to outline Gillie's dowry. After that time the two gentlemen joined the ladies.

Gillie braced herself for the request to join the duke. Tannie sauntered casually to the games table and sat down to join the ladies. "By jingo, you made a botch of that straw, Gillie," he said. "I could have done better myself, and I have my arm in a sling."

Gillie looked surprised at this unromantic speech. "Hullo, Tannie," she said.

"Will you not take my place, Tannie?" Beatrice offered at once.

She withdrew in Southam's direction, with Deborah hard on her heels. It was Deborah who demanded the reason for the duke's call. "Was it not an offer after all?" she demanded.

"No, he was merely delivering me a letter," Southam replied.

"What letter?" she asked.

His eyes went to Beatrice. "A note from his uncle," he said vaguely. Beatrice had to bite her lips to refrain from demanding an explanation.

Deborah noticed that look they exchanged. She felt in her bones that some impropriety was adrift in the room and meant to get to the bottom of it.

"Excuse us, Beatrice," she said, putting a hand on Southam's elbow. "I must have a private word with my fiancé."

They went to the study. "You must explain this mystery to me, Southam," she said.

His eyes flew guiltily to the desk, where his open note lay, face up. Deborah followed his glance, and pounced on the note. She read it silently, and as she read, the blood drained from her face.

> Lord Southam: I do not consider your note an apology but an aggravation of the original offense. If you are a gentleman, you will be at the dueling grounds at six-thirty tomorrow morning. Horatio Evendon.

"A duel?" she asked on a high, incredulous note. "You cannot mean you are engaged in a duel with the duke's uncle! The duke will never offer for Gillie if you wound his uncle. Southam, I forbid it!"

"That is your main concern, Deborah? Lord Horatio is a dead shot."

"All the more reason to call it off."

"I am flattered at your concern for my safety. I have already apologized. As you see, Evendon has not accepted. I must meet him."

"What is this duel all about? Good God!" She stood silent a moment, staring. "This is the duel the whole town is prating about! Lord Horatio—Bournemouth." She clenched her lips, and her breathing became rapid. "I need not inquire for the identity of the alleged lady in the case. It is Mrs. Searle, of course."

"Beatrice is innocently involved—a misunderstanding."

"Innocent ladies do not cause duels, Southam. I cannot allow this foolish duel to occur. You forget my position. What will the princesses say? And

202

Papa! You know he is working on a bill to forbid dueling."

"It is not illegal yet."

"But it is immoral. You will destroy Gillie's chances for winning the duke, after all my hard work."

"Your work?" he asked ironically. "It seems to me, your major involvement in it was to send Gillie off to Mrs. Searle."

"I have visited Lady Sappington a dozen times! You must listen to reason, Southam."

"I did not issue the challenge. I apologized. My apology was not accepted. I must meet Lord Horatio."

Deborah quickly scanned her options. She could see only one avenue open to her, and she knew it was a treacherous one. "If you persist in this folly, Southam, our engagement is terminated," she announced with awful solemnity.

He was happy to see her eyes were dry. He inclined his head in a bow. "I am sorry to hear it, ma'am."

She turned and swept from the room. The last he saw of her was her skirt whisking angrily upstairs.

Southam went to the doorway of the saloon and beckoned Beatrice into the study. "What happened?" she demanded.

"Deborah found out about the duel."

"You surely did not tell her!"

"No, she read Horatio's note, which I, er, accidentally left open on the table."

"But you are not fighting! Horatio accepted your apology. What have you done to change his mind?"

He handed her Evendon's note. "The man's a rock. Nothing pleases him."

She quickly scanned the note. "What does he mean by this? Your note is an aggravation of the original offenses. What on earth did you write?"

203

"I cannot recall the exact wording. It sounded unexceptionable to me."

"I should have known better than to leave you to your own devices. I'll go to Horatio this very minute."

She turned to flee from the room. Southam grasped her wrist and turned her around. "You will do nothing of the sort, madam. I have been at considerable pains to arrange matters just as I wish."

Angry sparks flashed from her emerald eyes. "And what is it you wish, Southam, to get yourself killed, or to kill Horatio?"

"Duels do not always end in a death. Sometimes they denote a beginning."

"Horatio is a dead shot."

"Tannie mentioned his shooting the wicks off candles in his meadow this afternoon," he said musingly.

A gasp of fear issued from her throat, and her white hands went out to him. "Southam, if you have any regard for me at all, please, *please* don't do this foolish thing."

His hands covered over hers and squeezed as he gazed into her eyes, darkened now with fear. "If?" he asked, his voice rough. "*If?* You say *if* to me? You shatter-brained, idiotic, adorable hoyden! I would not be risking my life if I were not insanely in love with you."

A smile trembled on her lips, and a soft sigh escaped her. "Thank you for that, Southam. I am glad you said it, before—while you are still able to."

"Then I am not imagining that you feel the same way?"

"I thought I was concealing it rather well," she admitted ruefully.

"Ah, but love and a cough, you know, cannot be hidden for long. Now that we have both confessed our sins . . ." He drew her into his arms and crushed

204

her lips with a searing kiss. Beatrice opened herself to the luxury of that one stolen embrace, made more poignant by the sense of wrongdoing. It was a bittersweet experience. She had finally found the perfect husband, only to know she might lose him on the morrow.

When Southam finally lifted his head, his eyes looked wild and dazed. He moved his hand behind him and closed the study door, which had been left slightly ajar. "That was an excellent appetizer," he said, smiling in anticipation.

She moved from his arms and opened the door wide. "I know what you are thinking, Rawl, and I would like it, too, but with Gillie and Miss Pittfield in the house—to say nothing of your fiancée—it would really be too farouche."

"Oh, did I not mention it? Deborah has given me my congé."

She read that flash of mischief in his eyes and knew she did not have the whole of the story. Southam had some scheme to avoid death. She gave a *tsk* of annoyance. "She only did it to lumber me with the job of burying your corpse."

Southam followed her to the door. "Very likely, but I do not wish you to go to any undue trouble. A simple winding cloth will do well enough."

She put her hand over his. "You will be careful, Rawl?"

"How can I let him kill me, when I suddenly have so much to live for?"

"Horatio won't care a fig for your happiness. He would delope if he knew it would make me happy."

He lifted her hand and kissed her fingers. "I hope you know what you are talking about, my darling. A third apology from me would surely break some rule of a gentleman's code of honor. I cannot permit you to beg for my life. And now I must retire. I have an early date in the morning and require a long

205

night of tossing and turning to prepare myself for it. Say good-night to the others for me."

She took a long look at him, fearful that it would be her last. "If you let him kill you, I'll never speak to you again, Southam," she said, and smiled sadly.

"Of course you will. I'll come back and haunt you. That's a promise."

He gave her a last quick kiss and left.

Chapter Nineteen

He didn't say good-bye to Gillie, Beatrice thought, as she lay in bed, worrying over the duel. Surely Southam would have said good-bye to his sister if he thought he would never see her again. She felt in her bones he had some scheme to save himself, yet he had spoken of risking death. Horatio was shooting the wicks off candles in the meadow. Why practice his shooting if he meant to delope? Sleep was, of course, totally impossible. She listened to the long-case clock in the hallway downstairs chime the slow hours. One, two, three.

Southam had said an early meeting. How early would it be? Probably long before most folks were up, to avoid interruption. She wondered if the seconds had remembered to have a doctor standing by. There was plenty of time—a whole sleepless night— to visualize the scene. The gentlemen with their dark jacket collars turned up to hide their white shirtfronts, which made excellent targets. They would probably meet above Walcot Cemetery, where the last duel, three years before, had occurred. Duels were not a common event in staid, respectable Bath.

At four o'clock, a fine rain began to patter against her window. Was that better or worse for Southam's chances? At four-thirty it stopped. The dueling site would be encased in fog, with water dripping from the trees, to lend the proper lugubrious atmosphere. Beatrice thought she might drive out to the cemetery—but then, there was no saying that was the site chosen. And besides, the dueling ground was not actually at the cemetery, but in some secret enclave nearby. No, there was no point in going. She would suffer the woman's silent torment of waiting and worrying.

Her nerves were in tatters when she rose and got dressed at seven o'clock. She went downstairs, wanting only peace and quiet, and was immediately faced with a hostile Miss Swann. Deborah ignored her hostess, as if she were not in the room, and spoke to the servant.

"I have been ringing for half an hour," she said. "Why was my bell not answered?"

"We don't come on duty till seven, ma'am."

"Really!" It was a burst of annoyance. "I want my carriage at the door at eight-thirty. Breakfast in my room, at once." The servant curtsied and left.

Beatrice looked askance at her guest. She was glad to see she wore a traveling suit. Bea was in no mood for condescension, but felt some words of farewell ought to be exchanged.

"So, you are leaving, Deborah?" she said.

Deborah turned a wrathful face on her. "I would never have come if I had had the slightest idea what sort of woman you have become, Mrs. Searle. I rue the day I sent Lady Gillian to you. I shall not thank you for having me, nor apologize for not doing so. You only allowed Gillian to come here to get your

208

talons into Southam. The more fool he, for being so easily duped."

"Are you not concerned that he might, even now, be lying dead?"

"Not in the least. As it will prevent him from making a misalliance with yourself, it is the best thing that could happen to him."

"That sounds remarkably like a bitch in the manger. As we are being entirely frank, I have a few things to say as well. You only sent Gillie here because you did not want to be bothered with her. You knew she saw through your stunt of pretending an entirely spurious interest in Southam's family. You wanted a wealthy, titled husband, but you did not want the duties his family entailed. The best thing I ever did was to show Southam the error of his ways."

"Don't think he'll marry you! A woman who sullies her name by a duel and travels abroad with a gentleman without benefit of marriage will never be anything but a temporary diversion for a man like Southam. Foolish as he is, he won't marry you."

"There is such a thing as too much propriety, Miss Swann."

"How would you know?" Miss Swann retaliated, and sailed out of the door before Beatrice could think of a set-down.

Deborah was on thorns to get back to Alderton to call on Stuyvesant. Very likely it was love of herself that had caused him to shy off from having Gillian. He, a *real* gentleman, would sympathize with her in her hour of distress. The naughtiness of her having turned Southam off would lend her a dashing air that might appeal to Stuyvesant. Only a baron, unfortunately, but then, look how high her papa had soared on a baron's wings.

Beatrice didn't take breakfast. While she sipped

her coffee, Gillian came down. She was looking out of sorts, although she knew nothing of the duel.

"Did you know Deborah is leaving this morning?" she asked.

"Yes, she was just down, saying good-bye."

"Why is she leaving?"

"I expect she is eager to get home to her mother," Bea replied. She was too overwrought to go into the whole story.

Gillie heaped her plate from the sideboard, but she ate little. "What is the matter?" Bea asked.

"What did Tannie want last night when he talked to Rawl?"

"I don't know," Bea said, crossing her fingers.

"Rawl didn't say anything to you last night before he left?"

"Not about the duke."

"Tannie didn't say anything about wanting to marry me, then?"

So that was it! Bea could not in good conscience encourage the girl. Tannie's family might very well forbid the match when they learned of the duel. "Did Tannie say anything to you?" she parried. "You spent more time with him than anyone else."

"All he talked about was Newmarket. Am I going to be allowed to go to London?"

"I don't know."

"I expect Deborah won't allow it."

After picking at her gammon and eggs for ten minutes, Gillie left the table. She looked precariously close to tears. And she hadn't mentioned her morning ride, which was unusual. Was it possible the hoyden had finally tumbled into love with her duke?

At eight-thirty Deborah's carriage arrived. Beatrice did not go to the door to see her guest off.

She had had a fire lit in her study and sat gazing into the restive flames. If Southam was dead, she would put on her caps and become one of the righteous widows of Bath. She would not continue with her annual trips to London. She would give up any thought of marrying again. A marriage of convenience was not an agreeable thought, and loving someone was too painful. There was too much agony along with the joy of love. Better a peaceful, retired life, not caring too much for anyone.

At nine o'clock, there was a rattle of the door knocker, and Beatrice jumped up. Her heart hammered mercilessly in her breast. Oh, God! If he's dead—she waited to hear whose voice sounded in the hallway and heard Lord Horatio asking for her. He had wounded Southam then, or killed him, and had come to explain.

She was galvanized into action, flying out the door like a harpy. "How dare you come here! Get out of my house. I don't know you, from this day onward, Lord Horatio!"

He blinked in astonishment, and behind him she saw Southam advancing toward the door. Tannie accompanied him, propping him up. The jacket hanging over Southam's shoulders had a bullet hole in it, to the left of and above the heart. His left arm was in a white sling, but other than that, he looked normal. His color was high, and he walked without trouble.

She looked from one to the other. "What happened?" she demanded. "Did you delope, Southam? Horatio, why did you shoot him? Southam, come in here and sit down. Let me look at that arm." She spoke rapidly, without waiting for answers.

Southam looked along the hallway toward the door of the saloon. "Is Deborah about?"

"She's gone home."

"Ah!" He reached out and pulled off the sling. His shirt had a bullet hole matching that in his jacket. A smear of something resembling blood oozed around the bullet hole. "In that case, I am fine." He shucked into his jacket, moving his left arm in a way that would have been impossible for a wounded man.

"I don't understand," Beatrice said, staring at this miraculous performance.

They all proceeded to the saloon, the gentlemen exchanging laughing looks as they went. "It is all a hum, you see," Tannie exclaimed. Being the youngest, he could not control his glee. "We thought Miss Swann would still be here, and we had to convince her there was a duel."

"Was there not a duel?" Beatrice asked, frowning at that bullet hole in Southam's jacket—and there had been a blood smear on his shirt. It made her flesh crawl to think of it.

"Shots were fired," Horatio said, chuckling. "I knocked a leaf off a branch, and Southam accidentally brought down a squirrel."

"I didn't even see it. It was hiding," Southam explained.

"That's where we got the blood," Tannie said.

"Gruesome! So you deloped," Beatrice said, trying to make sense of this farce.

"You didn't think I'd kill your beau, now did you, lass?" Horatio teased. "It has taken you long enough to find one. I knew by the gleam in your eyes when you came to see me that you had settled on your man."

"But you refused to withdraw your challenge."

"How else were we to free this lad from his engagement? I did have a few bad moments when I read Southam's letter. Man of my age indeed! That 'pusillanimous' did not sit well, either. But when

212

Tannie explained the situation to me, I understood what Southam was up to."

Beatrice looked at her beloved knowingly. "So that is why you sent Horatio that strange letter of apology."

"I have apologized more properly to Sir Horatio since then. We agreed we could not have our families become the Montagues and Capulets, when the duke and Gillie are to marry."

"If she'll have me, that is to say," the duke added humbly.

"I think she will have you," Bea said. "She was out of reason cross this morning that you did not speak to her last night, Tannie. Shall I call her down?"

"If it ain't too much trouble."

"It begins to look as if I am de trop here, unless there is another lady in the house who is looking for a match," Horatio said.

Southam looked at him with interest. "There is Miss Pittfield. . . ."

"Is she a looker?" Horatio asked. He did not remain to find out, but took his leave. "I want the pair of you to marry very soon, you hear?" he said to Southam. "I am too old to be embroiled in duels and scandal broth. It keeps me busy just paying my debts. I have given Southam back his thousand pounds, Bea. Tannie has taken an ugly picture of his great-uncle to cover my Bournemouth losses. I am glad to be rid of it, I can tell you." He waved and strode off to his waiting carriage.

Gillie was called and came flying downstairs, too young to conceal her eagerness. "Would you like to go for a drive?" Tannie asked, jiggling uneasily from foot to foot. "You'll have to handle the ribbons yourself. And mind you don't put us in the ditch again."

"All right," Gillie said, frowning. This was not what she had expected to hear.

"You'd best get used to it," Tannie said. "I mean to say, we'll want to take our curricle to Newmarket, and I shan't be able to drive for a few weeks yet. You will like Newmarket, I think."

"Don't be silly. I cannot go to Newmarket with you."

As usual, the duke spoke in his normal voice. "Could if we was married," he said. Southam and Beatrice exchanged a disbelieving look at this offhand proposal.

"It sounds like fun. I'll think about it," Gillie said, and went for her bonnet.

Tannie smiled at Southam. "Said she'll think about it. Didn't turn me off, at least. I'll offer her her own phaeton, and perhaps a new hunter. Well, she'll have to have one, won't she? Can't be riding yours when she ain't at Elmland."

"That might very well turn the trick," Southam said, smiling at this blatant bribery.

After Southam and Bea had waved the youngsters off, she suggested they go to her study. "I had a fire built in there. I needed some warmth while I was awaiting word of your execution. If you ever pull a stunt like this on me again, Rawl, I shall not be responsible for the outcome. I didn't sleep a wink all night. I must look like the wrath of God."

They stood before the leaping flames. He studied her upturned face. His own expression was dreamy, like a man besotted. "You look charming, as usual," he assured her. "Perhaps just a trifle puffy under the eyes. And your hair has not seen a brush this morning, if I am not mistaken." His hands brushed her hair back from her face, then cupped her head.

"Don't forget to remind me of my charming

214

crow's-feet, and the chin not quite so firm as it once was."

He cocked his head to one side and continued studying her minutely. It was only the love glowing in his eyes that saved him from abuse, for his words were far from flattering. "Yes, we are getting well past it, you and I, Cousin. We won't want to waste a single day. I think—a special license and a quiet wedding here before we go on to Elmland. Or shall we indulge in a dart to the border and a wedding over the anvil, to put the cap on our degrading affair?"

"A special license, please. It is well you are spiriting me away from Bath, for my reputation here will not be worth a brass farthing, I promise you."

"Nor in Alderton, either, when my ex-fiancée is through with us."

"I trust your having a sister a duchess will return us to her good graces. No match for a royal princess, of course."

"I am afraid we must not count on Deborah's continued intimacy. At least I sincerely hope we may not."

They moved to the sofa and sat, chatting, while he drew her head to his shoulder and stroked her hair. "How did you come to offer for her, Rawl?"

"I hadn't met you yet. Again, I mean, for of course I saw you some years ago. I think I always loved you from afar."

His fingers cupped her chin and turned her face up to meet his. "I rather thought you did," she said frankly. "I was cross as a bear when you didn't bring Gillie yourself but sent her with Miss Pittfield. I had a whole feast prepared, to seduce you."

"If I had known that, I would have brought her."

"And you an engaged man. You are depraved."

215

"Yes, and I didn't even know it till you showed me. As we are a pair of depraved beings ..." He pulled her onto his knee, where he began to execute new depravities.

"Rawl! What are you doing? You can't do that!"

"We could if we was married," he countered, and did it anyway.

FREE Test Taking Tips DVD Offer

To help us better serve you, we have developed a Test Taking Tips DVD that we would like to give you for FREE. **This DVD covers world-class test taking tips that you can use to be even more successful when you are taking your test.**

All that we ask is that you email us your feedback about your study guide. Please let us know what you thought about it – whether that is good, bad or indifferent.

To get your **FREE Test Taking Tips DVD**, email freedvd@studyguideteam.com with "FREE DVD" in the subject line and the following information in the body of the email:

    a. The title of your study guide.

    b. Your product rating on a scale of 1-5, with 5 being the highest rating.

    c. Your feedback about the study guide. What did you think of it?

    d. Your full name and shipping address to send your free DVD.

If you have any questions or concerns, please don't hesitate to contact us at freedvd@studyguideteam.com.

Thanks again!

ASWB Masters Study Guide 2020 & 2021
2020 & 2021
Social Work ASWB Masters Exam Guide 2020 and 2021 with Practice Test Questions for the MSW Exam
[2nd Edition Prep Book]

Test Prep Books

Written and edited by Test Prep Books.

Test Prep Books is not associated with or endorsed by any official testing organization. Test Prep Books is a publisher of unofficial educational products. All test and organization names are trademarks of their respective owners. Content in this book is included for utilitarian purposes only and does not constitute an endorsement by Test Prep Books of any particular point of view.

Interested in buying more than 10 copies of our product? Contact us about bulk discounts:
bulkorders@studyguideteam.com

ISBN 13: 9781628459203
ISB 10: 1628459204

Table of Contents

Professional Relationships, Values, and Ethics -------------- *164*

Quick Overview

As you draw closer to taking your exam, effective preparation becomes more and more important. Thankfully, you have this study guide to help you get ready. Use this guide to help keep your studying on track and refer to it often.

This study guide contains several key sections that will help you be successful on your exam. The guide contains tips for what you should do the night before and the day of the test. Also included are test-taking tips. Knowing the right information is not always enough. Many well-prepared test takers struggle with exams. These tips will help equip you to accurately read, assess, and answer test questions.

A large part of the guide is devoted to showing you what content to expect on the exam and to helping you better understand that content. In this guide are practice test questions so that you can see how well you have grasped the content. Then, answer explanations are provided so that you can understand why you missed certain questions.

Don't try to cram the night before you take your exam. This is not a wise strategy for a few reasons. First, your retention of the information will be low. Your time would be better used by reviewing information you already know rather than trying to learn a lot of new information. Second, you will likely become stressed as you try to gain a large amount of knowledge in a short amount of time. Third, you will be depriving yourself of sleep. So be sure to go to bed at a reasonable time the night before. Being well-rested helps you focus and remain calm.

Be sure to eat a substantial breakfast the morning of the exam. If you are taking the exam in the afternoon, be sure to have a good lunch as well. Being hungry is distracting and can make it difficult to focus. You have hopefully spent lots of time preparing for the exam. Don't let an empty stomach get in the way of success!

When travelling to the testing center, leave earlier than needed. That way, you have a buffer in case you experience any delays. This will help you remain calm and will keep you from missing your appointment time at the testing center.

Be sure to pace yourself during the exam. Don't try to rush through the exam. There is no need to risk performing poorly on the exam just so you can leave the testing center early. Allow yourself to use all of the allotted time if needed.

Remain positive while taking the exam even if you feel like you are performing poorly. Thinking about the content you should have mastered will not help you perform better on the exam.

Once the exam is complete, take some time to relax. Even if you feel that you need to take the exam again, you will be well served by some down time before you begin studying again. It's often easier to convince yourself to study if you know that it will come with a reward!

Test-Taking Strategies

1. Predicting the Answer

When you feel confident in your preparation for a multiple-choice test, try predicting the answer before reading the answer choices. This is especially useful on questions that test objective factual knowledge. By predicting the answer before reading the available choices, you eliminate the possibility that you will be distracted or led astray by an incorrect answer choice. You will feel more confident in your selection if you read the question, predict the answer, and then find your prediction among the answer choices. After using this strategy, be sure to still read all of the answer choices carefully and completely. If you feel unprepared, you should not attempt to predict the answers. This would be a waste of time and an opportunity for your mind to wander in the wrong direction.

2. Reading the Whole Question

Too often, test takers scan a multiple-choice question, recognize a few familiar words, and immediately jump to the answer choices. Test authors are aware of this common impatience, and they will sometimes prey upon it. For instance, a test author might subtly turn the question into a negative, or he or she might redirect the focus of the question right at the end. The only way to avoid falling into these traps is to read the entirety of the question carefully before reading the answer choices.

3. Looking for Wrong Answers

Long and complicated multiple-choice questions can be intimidating. One way to simplify a difficult multiple-choice question is to eliminate all of the answer choices that are clearly wrong. In most sets of answers, there will be at least one selection that can be dismissed right away. If the test is administered on paper, the test taker could draw a line through it to indicate that it may be ignored; otherwise, the test taker will have to perform this operation mentally or on scratch paper. In either case, once the obviously incorrect answers have been eliminated, the remaining choices may be considered. Sometimes identifying the clearly wrong answers will give the test taker some information about the correct answer. For instance, if one of the remaining answer choices is a direct opposite of one of the eliminated answer choices, it may well be the correct answer. The opposite of obviously wrong is obviously right! Of course, this is not always the case. Some answers are obviously incorrect simply because they are irrelevant to the question being asked. Still, identifying and eliminating some incorrect answer choices is a good way to simplify a multiple-choice question.

4. Don't Overanalyze

Anxious test takers often overanalyze questions. When you are nervous, your brain will often run wild, causing you to make associations and discover clues that don't actually exist. If you feel that this may be a problem for you, do whatever you can to slow down during the test. Try taking a deep breath or counting to ten. As you read and consider the question, restrict yourself to the particular words used by the author. Avoid thought tangents about what the author *really* meant, or what he or she was *trying* to say. The only things that matter on a multiple-choice test are the words that are actually in the question. You must avoid reading too much into a multiple-choice question, or supposing that the writer meant something other than what he or she wrote.

5. No Need for Panic

It is wise to learn as many strategies as possible before taking a multiple-choice test, but it is likely that you will come across a few questions for which you simply don't know the answer. In this situation, avoid panicking. Because most multiple-choice tests include dozens of questions, the relative value of a single wrong answer is small. As much as possible, you should compartmentalize each question on a multiple-choice test. In other words, you should not allow your feelings about one question to affect your success on the others. When you find a question that you either don't understand or don't know how to answer, just take a deep breath and do your best. Read the entire question slowly and carefully. Try rephrasing the question a couple of different ways. Then, read all of the answer choices carefully. After eliminating obviously wrong answers, make a selection and move on to the next question.

6. Confusing Answer Choices

When working on a difficult multiple-choice question, there may be a tendency to focus on the answer choices that are the easiest to understand. Many people, whether consciously or not, gravitate to the answer choices that require the least concentration, knowledge, and memory. This is a mistake. When you come across an answer choice that is confusing, you should give it extra attention. A question might be confusing because you do not know the subject matter to which it refers. If this is the case, don't eliminate the answer before you have affirmatively settled on another. When you come across an answer choice of this type, set it aside as you look at the remaining choices. If you can confidently assert that one of the other choices is correct, you can leave the confusing answer aside. Otherwise, you will need to take a moment to try to better understand the confusing answer choice. Rephrasing is one way to tease out the sense of a confusing answer choice.

7. Your First Instinct

Many people struggle with multiple-choice tests because they overthink the questions. If you have studied sufficiently for the test, you should be prepared to trust your first instinct once you have carefully and completely read the question and all of the answer choices. There is a great deal of research suggesting that the mind can come to the correct conclusion very quickly once it has obtained all of the relevant information. At times, it may seem to you as if your intuition is working faster even than your reasoning mind. This may in fact be true. The knowledge you obtain while studying may be retrieved from your subconscious before you have a chance to work out the associations that support it. Verify your instinct by working out the reasons that it should be trusted.

8. Key Words

Many test takers struggle with multiple-choice questions because they have poor reading comprehension skills. Quickly reading and understanding a multiple-choice question requires a mixture of skill and experience. To help with this, try jotting down a few key words and phrases on a piece of scrap paper. Doing this concentrates the process of reading and forces the mind to weigh the relative importance of the question's parts. In selecting words and phrases to write down, the test taker thinks about the question more deeply and carefully. This is especially true for multiple-choice questions that are preceded by a long prompt.

9. Subtle Negatives

One of the oldest tricks in the multiple-choice test writer's book is to subtly reverse the meaning of a question with a word like *not* or *except*. If you are not paying attention to each word in the question, you can easily be led astray by this trick. For instance, a common question format is, "Which of the following is...?" Obviously, if the question instead is, "Which of the following is not...?," then the answer will be quite different. Even worse, the test makers are aware of the potential for this mistake and will include one answer choice that would be correct if the question were not negated or reversed. A test taker who misses the reversal will find what he or she believes to be a correct answer and will be so confident that he or she will fail to reread the question and discover the original error. The only way to avoid this is to practice a wide variety of multiple-choice questions and to pay close attention to each and every word.

10. Reading Every Answer Choice

It may seem obvious, but you should always read every one of the answer choices! Too many test takers fall into the habit of scanning the question and assuming that they understand the question because they recognize a few key words. From there, they pick the first answer choice that answers the question they believe they have read. Test takers who read all of the answer choices might discover that one of the latter answer choices is actually *more* correct. Moreover, reading all of the answer choices can remind you of facts related to the question that can help you arrive at the correct answer. Sometimes, a misstatement or incorrect detail in one of the latter answer choices will trigger your memory of the subject and will enable you to find the right answer. Failing to read all of the answer choices is like not reading all of the items on a restaurant menu: you might miss out on the perfect choice.

11. Spot the Hedges

One of the keys to success on multiple-choice tests is paying close attention to every word. This is never truer than with words like almost, most, some, and sometimes. These words are called "hedges" because they indicate that a statement is not totally true or not true in every place and time. An absolute statement will contain no hedges, but in many subjects, the answers are not always straightforward or absolute. There are always exceptions to the rules in these subjects. For this reason, you should favor those multiple-choice questions that contain hedging language. The presence of qualifying words indicates that the author is taking special care with his or her words, which is certainly important when composing the right answer. After all, there are many ways to be wrong, but there is only one way to be right! For this reason, it is wise to avoid answers that are absolute when taking a multiple-choice test. An absolute answer is one that says things are either all one way or all another. They often include words like *every*, *always*, *best*, and *never*. If you are taking a multiple-choice test in a subject that doesn't lend itself to absolute answers, be on your guard if you see any of these words.

12. Long Answers

In many subject areas, the answers are not simple. As already mentioned, the right answer often requires hedges. Another common feature of the answers to a complex or subjective question are qualifying clauses, which are groups of words that subtly modify the meaning of the sentence. If the question or answer choice describes a rule to which there are exceptions or the subject matter is complicated, ambiguous, or confusing, the correct answer will require many words in order to be expressed clearly and accurately. In essence, you should not be deterred by answer choices that seem excessively long. Oftentimes, the author of the text will not be able to write the correct answer without

offering some qualifications and modifications. Your job is to read the answer choices thoroughly and completely and to select the one that most accurately and precisely answers the question.

13. Restating to Understand

Sometimes, a question on a multiple-choice test is difficult not because of what it asks but because of how it is written. If this is the case, restate the question or answer choice in different words. This process serves a couple of important purposes. First, it forces you to concentrate on the core of the question. In order to rephrase the question accurately, you have to understand it well. Rephrasing the question will concentrate your mind on the key words and ideas. Second, it will present the information to your mind in a fresh way. This process may trigger your memory and render some useful scrap of information picked up while studying.

14. True Statements

Sometimes an answer choice will be true in itself, but it does not answer the question. This is one of the main reasons why it is essential to read the question carefully and completely before proceeding to the answer choices. Too often, test takers skip ahead to the answer choices and look for true statements. Having found one of these, they are content to select it without reference to the question above. Obviously, this provides an easy way for test makers to play tricks. The savvy test taker will always read the entire question before turning to the answer choices. Then, having settled on a correct answer choice, he or she will refer to the original question and ensure that the selected answer is relevant. The mistake of choosing a correct-but-irrelevant answer choice is especially common on questions related to specific pieces of objective knowledge. A prepared test taker will have a wealth of factual knowledge at his or her disposal, and should not be careless in its application.

15. No Patterns

One of the more dangerous ideas that circulates about multiple-choice tests is that the correct answers tend to fall into patterns. These erroneous ideas range from a belief that B and C are the most common right answers, to the idea that an unprepared test-taker should answer "A-B-A-C-A-D-A-B-A." It cannot be emphasized enough that pattern-seeking of this type is exactly the WRONG way to approach a multiple-choice test. To begin with, it is highly unlikely that the test maker will plot the correct answers according to some predetermined pattern. The questions are scrambled and delivered in a random order. Furthermore, even if the test maker was following a pattern in the assignation of correct answers, there is no reason why the test taker would know which pattern he or she was using. Any attempt to discern a pattern in the answer choices is a waste of time and a distraction from the real work of taking the test. A test taker would be much better served by extra preparation before the test than by reliance on a pattern in the answers.

FREE DVD OFFER

Don't forget that doing well on your exam includes both understanding the test content and understanding how to use what you know to do well on the test. We offer a completely FREE Test Taking Tips DVD that covers world class test taking tips that you can use to be even more successful when you are taking your test.

All that we ask is that you email us your feedback about your study guide. To get your **FREE Test Taking Tips DVD**, email freedvd@studyguideteam.com with "FREE DVD" in the subject line and the following information in the body of the email:

- The title of your study guide.
- Your product rating on a scale of 1-5, with 5 being the highest rating.
- Your feedback about the study guide. What did you think of it?
- Your full name and shipping address to send your free DVD.

Introduction to the ASWB Masters Exam

Function of the Test

An Association of Social Work Boards (ASWB) Master's exam is used for licensure as a master social worker, or the equivalent, in all fifty U.S. states as well as the District of Columbia, the U.S. Virgin Islands, Alberta, and British Columbia. The Master's exam is typically taken by a new graduate of a master's degree program in social work as part of the licensing process, but can also be taken by someone already in the field with an eye toward a new or upgraded license.

In 2016, 15,442 people took the ASWB Master's exam, and 81.2 percent of those test takers passed. The passing score is determined nationally, and not on a state-by-state or board-by-board basis.

Test Administration

ASWB exams are given by computer. They are not administered on any particular fixed dates. Instead, tests are given by appointment at Pearson Professional Centers worldwide. Students must first register for the test, then visit Pearson VUE's website to schedule an exam sitting.

Candidates with disabilities can receive appropriate accommodations while taking the ASWB Master's exam by applying for accommodations through the ASWB website. Candidates whose first language is not English can also seek arrangements for alternate language exams in most jurisdictions.

Candidates must wait 90 days before retaking the exam, although exceptions can be made when there is a serious, documented malfunction with the initial attempt, or if employment is at stake and the initial score was within five correct answers of passing.

Test Format

Each examination lasts four hours and contains 170 four-option, multiple-choice questions in four categories of practice. 150 of the 170 items are scored, while the remainder is used for test validation purposes. Candidates have four hours to complete the electronically administered test.

The four categories of practice for the Master's exam are as follows: Human Development, Diversity, and Behavior in the Environment; Assessment and Intervention Planning; Interventions with Clients/Client Systems; and Professional Relationships, Values, and Ethics. Each section comprises roughly one quarter of the exam. Details are contained in the Knowledge, Skills, and Abilities statement (KSA) published by ASWB.

Here's a table of the sections:

Category	Subcategories	% of Exam
Human Development, Diversity, and Behavior in the Environment	Human Growth and Development	27%
	Concepts of Abuse and Neglect	
	Diversity, Social/Economic Justice, and Oppression	
Assessment and Intervention Planning	Biopsychosocial History and Collateral Data	24%
	Assessment Methods and Techniques	
	Intervention Planning	
Interventions with Clients/Client Systems	Intervention Processes and Techniques for Use Across Systems	24%
	Intervention Processes and Techniques for Use with Larger Systems	
Professional Relationships, Values, and Ethics	Professional Values and Ethical Issues	25%
	Confidentiality	
	Professional Development and Use of Self	

Scoring

Like all ASWB exams, the Master's exam is scored pass/fail, with a certain number of correct answers required in order to pass. The pass point varies from exam to exam based on the difficulty of a given test, but it generally ranges somewhere between 93 and 107 correct answers out of 150 scored questions. There is no penalty for guessing, as the total number of correct answers is the only factor in a test taker's raw score.

Although different states and jurisdictions have different numbers in their rules as a required passing score, the performance required to pass the exam is actually no higher or lower in any one state than in any other. Instead, the score reported by ASWB to each state is scaled to that state's required score. In other words, a test taker who gets exactly the score needed to pass nationally would have that score reported as a 70 in a state that requires a 70 to pass, and reported as a 75 in a state that requires a 75 to pass.

Recent/Future Developments

The content of the ASWB exams is constantly being updated to incorporate new information from the field of social work, such as changes in the new DSM-5. However, no other structural or testing procedure changes have been announced for the immediate future.

Study Prep Plan for the ASWB Masters Exam

1   **Schedule -** Use one of our study schedules below or come up with one of your own.

2   **Relax -** Test anxiety can hurt even the best students. There are many ways to reduce stress. Find the one that works best for you.

3   **Execute -** Once you have a good plan in place, be sure to stick to it.

One Week Study Schedule

Day 1	Human Development, Diversity, and Behavior
Day 2	Assessment and Intervention Planning
Day 3	Interventions with Clients/Client Systems
Day 4	Professional Relationships, Values, and Ethics
Day 5	Practice Questions
Day 6	Review Answer Explanations
Day 7	Take Your Exam!

Two Week Study Schedule

Day 1	Human Growth and Development	Day 8	Intervention Processes and Techniques
Day 2	Concepts of Abuse and Neglect	Day 9	Professional Values and Ethical Issues
Day 3	Diversity, Social/Economic Justice, and Oppression	Day 10	Confidentiality
Day 4	Biopsychosocial History and Collateral Data	Day 11	Professional Development
Day 5	Assessment Methods and Techniques	Day 12	Practice Questions
Day 6	Intervention Planning	Day 13	Review Answer Explanations
Day 7	Intervention Processes and Techniques	Day 14	Take Your Exam!

One Month Study Schedule

Day 1	Human Development Throughout the Lifespan	Day 11	Basic Medical Terminology	Day 21	Social Policy Development and Analysis
Day 2	Sexual Development Throughout the Lifespan	Day 12	Obtaining Sensitive Information	Day 22	Government Structures
Day 3	Spiritual Development Throughout the Lifespan	Day 13	Objective and Subjective Data	Day 23	Quality Assurance
Day 4	Factors Influencing Self-Image	Day 14	Intervention/Treatment Modalities	Day 24	Practice Questions
Day 5	Family Life Cycle	Day 15	Psychotherapies	Day 25	Professional Values and Principles
Day 6	Abuse and Neglect Throughout the Lifespan	Day 16	Practice Questions	Day 26	Client's Right to Refuse Services
Day 7	Impact of Social Institutions on Society	Day 17	Cognitive and Behavorial Interventions	Day 27	Professional Boundaries
Day 8	Practice Questions	Day 18	Partializing Techniques	Day 28	Client's Role in the Problem-Solving Process
Day 9	Biopsychosocial Assessment	Day 19	Family Therapy Models, Interventions, and Approaches	Day 29	Practice Questions
Day 10	Mental Status Examination	Day 20	Evidence-Based Practice	Day 30	Take Your Exam!

Human Development, Diversity and Behavior in the Environment

Human Growth and Development

Human Development Throughout the Lifespan

There are a number of theories on human growth and development. The most important theories are addressed in this section.

Freud's Model of Development

Freud is known for his research on stages of human development and his assertion that there were five stages of psychosexual development:

Oral Stage (birth to 18 months)
- An infant's focus of gratification involves the mouth.
- The primary need is security.
- Security needs are met when caretakers provide the baby with essentials, such as food, shelter, warmth and cleanliness.

Anal Stage (18 months to age 3)
- A child's focus of gratification involves the anus and the bladder.
- These organs represent sensual satisfaction.
- Internal conflict arises when the child begins the process of toilet training.

Phallic Stage (age 3 to age 6)
- The child engages in exploration of his/her body with greater interest in genitals.
- Oedipus and Electra complexes may occur.
- There is a pseudo-sexual attraction to the parent of the opposite gender.
- Conflict arises when the child realizes he/she has failed to win control over the parents' bond with one another.

Latent Stage (age 6 to puberty)
- The child's sexual interests become subdued or dormant.
- Energy is focused on school, hobbies, athletics, and mastering social skills.

Genital stage (puberty until death)
- The teen becomes aware of physical changes and onset of sexual feelings.
- The individual is less egocentric and more compassionate.
- There's a motivation to seek relationships that are emotionally and sexually satisfying.
- Success in this stage lays groundwork for future relationships that are healthy and long lasting.

13

Erikson's Model of Development

Erikson devised eight stages of psychosocial development. He emphasized the importance of social context, asserting that family and environment are major contributors to child development.

Trust vs. Mistrust (birth to 18 months)
- The primary goal is to learn to trust others.
- Trust occurs when a caretaker appropriately responds to a need in a timely, caring manner.
- Mistrust occurs when caretakers fail to meet the infant's basic needs.

Autonomy vs. Shame and Doubt (18 months to age 3)
- The primary goal is the development of self-control without loss of self-esteem.
- The toddler develops cooperation and self-expression skills.
- Failure to reach this goal leads to defiance, anger, and social problems.

Initiative vs. Guilt (age 3 to age 6)
- Initiative means confidently devising a plan and following it through to completion.
- Guilt is generated by fear that actions taken will result in disapproval.
- Failure to achieve initiative can lead to anxiety and fearfulness in new situations.

Industry vs. Inferiority (age 6 to age 11)
- Industry refers to purposeful, meaningful behavior.
- Inferiority refers to having a sense of unworthiness or uselessness.
- The child focuses on learning skills, such as making friends and self-care activities—e.g., dressing or bathing.
- Failure in this stage could lead to negative social or academic performance and the lack of self-confidence.

Identity vs. Role Confusion (age 12 to age 18)
- This stage involves the desire to fit in and to figure out one's own unique identity.
- Self-assessment of sexual identity, talents, and vocational direction occurs.
- Role confusion is the result of juggling multiple physical changes, increased responsibility, academic demands, and a need to understand how one fits into the greater picture.

Intimacy vs. Isolation (age 18 to age 40)
- This stage pertains to an ability to take risks by entering the work force, finding a long term relationship, and possibly becoming a parent.
- Failure to navigate this stage leads to isolation, loneliness, and depression.

Generativity vs. Stagnation (age 40 to age 60)
- This stage involves developing stability in areas of finance, career, and relationships, as well as a sense that one is contributing something valuable to society.
- Failure to achieve these objectives leads to unhappiness with one's status and feeling unimportant.

Ego Identity vs. Despair (mid sixties to death)
- Important life tasks, such as child rearing and career, are being completed.
- Reviewing and evaluating how one's life was spent occurs.

- Success in this stage provides a sense of fulfillment.
- Failure emerges if one is dissatisfied with accomplishments, which leads to depression or despair.

Erikson's Psychosocial Stages of Devleopment

Stage	Age	Psychosocial Crisis	Basic Virtue
1	Infancy (0 to 1½)	Trust vs. mistrust	Hope
2	Early Childhood (1½ to 3)	Autonomy vs. shame	Will
3	Play Age (3 to 5)	Initiative vs. guilt	Purpose
4	School Age (5 to 12)	Industry vs. inferiority	Competency
5	Adolescence (12 to 18)	Ego identity vs.role confusion	Fidelity
6	Young Adult (18 to 40)	Intimacy vs. isolation	Love
7	Adult hood (40 to 65)	Generativity vs. stagnation	Care
8	Maturity (65+)	Ego integrity vs. despair	Wisdom

Piaget's Model of Development

Piaget is best known for his concept that children's minds are not just smaller versions of adult minds, but instead grow and develop in different ways. His work has been influential within academic settings and has helped educators better determine what and how children can learn at various stages of their educational process. The following are the key ideas related to his research into the way cognition develops in children:

- Assimilation: A process by which a person accepts and organizes information, then incorporates new material into existing knowledge
- Accommodation: A process by which old ideas must be changed or replaced due to obtaining new information from the environment
- Schemas: A set of thoughts, ideas, or perceptions that fit together and are constantly challenged by gaining new information and creating change through knowledge

Piaget also recognized and defined the following *four stages of cognitive development*:

Stage 1: Sensorimotor Stage (birth to age 2)
- The infant becomes aware of being an entity separate from the environment.
- Object permanence occurs as the baby realizes that people or objects still exist, even if they are out of sight.
- Object permanence builds a sense of security as the baby learns that though mommy has left the room, she will still return.
- This reduces fear of abandonment and increases his/her confidence about the environment.

Stage 2: Pre-operational Stage (age 2 to age 7)
- The child moves from being barely verbal to using language to describe people, places, and things.
- The child remains egocentric and unable to clearly understand the viewpoint of others.
- The process of quantifying and qualifying emerges, and the child can sort, categorize, and analyze in a rough, unpolished form.

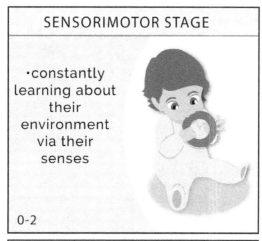

SENSORIMOTOR STAGE

·constantly learning about their environment via their senses

0-2

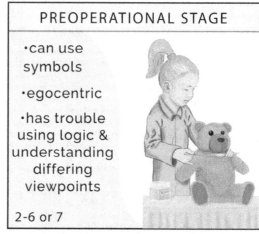

PREOPERATIONAL STAGE

·can use symbols

·egocentric

·has trouble using logic & understanding differing viewpoints

2-6 or 7

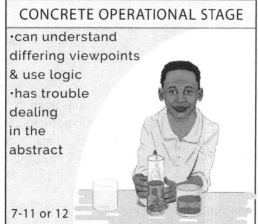

CONCRETE OPERATIONAL STAGE

·can understand differing viewpoints & use logic
·has trouble dealing in the abstract

7-11 or 12

FORMAL OPERATIONAL STAGE

·can think in   ·can solve problems
the abstract   systematically

12 - Adulthood

Stage 3: Concrete Operational Stage (age 7 to age 11)
- The ability to problem solve and reach logical conclusions evolves.
- By age 10 or 11, children begin to doubt magical stories, such as the Tooth Fairy or the Easter Bunny.
- Previously-held beliefs are questioned.

Stage 4: Formal Operational Stage (age 12 through remaining lifetime)
- More complex processes can now be assimilated.
- Egocentrism diminishes.
- One assimilates and accommodates beliefs that others have needs and feelings too.
- New schemas are created.
- The individual seeks his or her niche in life in terms of talents, goals, and preferences.

Ivan Pavlov (Classical Conditioning)

Another important concept of development has to do with learning and the way in which humans learn new behaviors. A famous psychologist, Ivan Pavlov, conducted research with dogs that proved to be ground-breaking in the field of classical conditioning. In his experiment, a ringing bell was paired with the presentation of food, which produced salivation in the dog. The ringing sound eventually produced salivation from the dog even in the absence of food. Salivation then became the conditioned response to hearing a bell, and thus, the theory of classical conditioning was developed. The important finding of this research is that we learn by association.

B.F. Skinner (Operant Conditioning)

Skinner also did important research in the field of learning, specifically operant conditioning. Operant conditioning theory focuses on behavioral changes that can be seen or measured. The basic concept is that behavior that is reinforced will increase, and behavior that is punished will decrease. There are several key concepts integral to an understanding of this form of learning:

- Positive Reinforcement: Anything that serves as a form of reward, including food, money, praise, or attention
- Negative reinforcement: An unpleasant stimulus that is removed when behavior is elicited, such as a man finally cutting the grass to stop his wife from nagging him about it
- Punishment: An unpleasant response from the environment—e.g., a slap, an unkind word, or a speeding ticket—that when encountered, increases the likelihood that a behavior will cease. Two problems arise with using punishment. Once the negative stimulus is removed, the behavior is likely to continue. Punishment can also cause humiliation, anger, resentment, and aggression.
- Superstition: An incorrect perception that one stimulus is connected to another. Skinner found that when teaching a rat to press a lever for food, if the rat chases its tail before pressing the lever, it will mistakenly believe that the tail chase is required and will do both behaviors each time it wants food.
- Shaping: The process of changing behavior gradually by rewarding approximations of the desired behavior, i.e., first rewarding a rat for moving closer to the lever

Skinner found that there are different schedules of reinforcement and that some work better than others. These include the following:

- Continuous rate: Person or animal is rewarded every time a behavior is demonstrated
- Fixed ratio: Reward is given after a fixed number of attempts
- Variable ratio: Reward is forthcoming at unpredictable rates, like a slot machine
- Fixed interval: Reward is given only after a specific amount of time has passed
- Variable interval: Reward is given after an unpredictable amount of time has passed
- Extinction: Occurs when a behavior disappears or is extinguished because it is no longer being reinforced. To stop tantrum behavior in toddlers, ignoring the behavior will decrease or stop the tantrum, if the desired reward is parental attention or parental aggravation.

Seasons of Life Theory (Levinson)

This theory of adult development is classified by development stages, with each stage defined by different, yet meaningful and developmentally necessary, tasks. There are transition periods where stages overlap.

The *pre-adulthood stage* ends at age twenty-two. Beginning at birth, this is the stage when a person develops and prepares for adulthood. It is a time of major growth and transition where the individual develops a state of independence.

The *early adulthood transition* is roughly age seventeen to twenty-two. Pre-adulthood is ending, and early adulthood is beginning, but the time of transition is actually part of both periods. Physical development is completed, but this time of transition can be compared to the infancy of a new period of development. During this stage, adolescence ends, and the individual begins to make decisions about adult life. He or she further develops independence and separates from the family of origin.

Early adulthood stage is roughly age seventeen to forty-five. This stage begins with the early adult transition. From a biological perspective, an individual's twenties and thirties are at the peak of the life cycle. This stage can be the time at which individuals have their greatest energy, but are also experiencing the greatest amount of stress as they try to establish families and careers simultaneously.

Midlife transition is roughly age forty to forty-five. This is a time of transition that bridges the end of early adulthood and the beginning of middle adulthood. At this time of life, people tend to become more reflective and compassionate and less concerned with external demands. Values may change, and it is possibly a time where crisis is experienced due to limited time to reach goals. Individuals become aware of death and leaving a legacy.

Middle adulthood stage is roughly age forty to sixty-five. There is a diminishment of biological capacities, but only minimally. Most individuals are able to continue to lead fulfilling and relatively energetic lives. Many take on a mentoring role and responsibility for the further development of young adults. Choices must be made about livelihood and retirement.

Late adulthood is at roughly age sixty. A transition period occurs from around sixty to sixty-five. Late adulthood is a time of reflection on other stages and on accomplishments. During this stage, retirement takes place, and the individual gives up his or her role in the workplace. Crisis occurs at this stage due to declining power and less accolades of work performed.

Social Clock Theory (Bernice Neugarten)

Neugarten proposed that every society has a *social clock*: an understood expectation for when certain life events should happen (e.g., getting married, buying a home, having children). When individuals do not adhere to this timeframe, they often experience stress, the sense of disappointing others, or the experience of an internal "clock ticking" and reminding them that time is running out.

Normal and Abnormal Physical, Cognitive Emotional, and Sexual Development Throughout the Lifespan

Typical and Atypical Physical Growth and Development

It is important to understand normal developmental milestones. While not all children progress at the same rate, one must have some guidelines in order to determine if the child has any developmental delays that prevent them from reaching goals by a certain age.

Infancy Through Age Five

During the first year of life, abundant changes occur. The child learns basic, but important, skills. The child is learning to manipulate objects, hold their head without support, crawl, and pull up into a standing position. The toddler should be able walk without assistance by eighteen months. By age two,

the child should be running and able to climb steps one stair at a time. By age three, the child should be curious and full of questions about how the world works or why people behave in certain ways. The child should have the balance and coordination to climb stairs using only one foot per stair. By age four, the child is increasingly independent, demonstrating skills like attending to toilet needs and dressing with some adult assistance.

School Age to Adolescence

By age five, speech is becoming more fluent, and the ability to draw simple figures improves. Dressing without help is achieved. By age six, speech should be fluent, and motor skills are strengthened. The youth is now able to navigate playground equipment and kick or throw a ball. Social skills, such as teamwork or friendship development, are evolving. The child must learn to deal with failure or frustration and find ways to be accepted by peers. They become more proficient in reading, math, and writing skills. Towards the end of this phase, around age twelve, secondary sexual characteristics, such as darker body hair or breast development may occur.

Adolescence

This is a period of extraordinary change. The process of *individuation* is occurring. The teen views themself as someone who will someday live independently of parents. More time is spent with peers and less with family. Identity formation arises, and the teen experiments with different kinds of clothing, music, and hairstyles to see what feels comfortable and what supports their view of the world. Sexuality is explored, and determinations are being made about sexual preferences and orientation. Sexual experimentation is common, and some teens actually form long-term intimate relationships, although others are satisfied to make shorter-term intimate connections. There is often a period of experimentation with drugs or alcohol. As the thinking process matures, there may be a questioning of rules and expectations of those in authority. Moodiness is common, and troubled teens are likely to "act out" their emotions, sometimes in harmful ways.

Typical and Atypical Cognitive Growth and Development

Cognitive development refers to development of a child's capacity for perception, thought, learning, information processing, and other mental processes. The *nature vs. nurture* debate questions whether cognitive development is primarily influenced by genetics or upbringing. Evidence indicates that the interaction between nature and nurture determines the path of development.

Some commonly recognized milestones in early cognitive development:

- One to three months: focuses on faces and moving objects, differentiates between different types of tastes, sees all colors in the spectrum

- Three to six months: recognizes familiar faces and sounds, imitates expressions

- Six to twelve months: begins to determine how far away something is, understands that things still exist when they are not seen (object permanence)

- One to two years: recognizes similar objects, understands and responds to some words

- Two to three years: sorts objects into appropriate categories, responds to directions, names objects

- Three to four years: Demonstrates increased attention span of five to fifteen minutes, shows curiosity and seeks answers to questions, organizes objects by characteristics

- Four to five years: Draws human shapes, counts to five or higher, uses rhyming words

The *Zone of proximal development* is the range of tasks that a child can carry out with assistance, but not independently. Parents and educators can advance a child's learning by providing opportunities within the zone of proximal development, allowing the child to develop the ability to accomplish those actions gradually without assistance.

Typical and Atypical Social Growth, Development, and the Socialization Process

Social development refers to the development of the skills that allow individuals to have effective interpersonal relationships and to contribute in a positive manner to the world around them.

Social learning is taught directly by caregivers and educators, but it is also learned indirectly by the experience of various social relationships.

Social development is commonly influenced by extended family, communities, religious institutions, schools, and sports teams or social groups. Positive social development is supported when caregivers engage in these behaviors:

- Attune to a child's needs and feelings
- Demonstrate respect for others
- Teach children how to handle conflict and solve problems encountered during social experiences
- Help children learn to take the perspective of another person and develop empathy
- Encourage discussion of morals and values and listen to the child's opinions on those topics
- Explain rules and encourage fair treatment of others
- Encourage cooperation, rather than competition

Social development begins from birth as a child learns to attach to their mother and other caregivers. During adolescence, social development focuses on peer relationships and self-identity. In adulthood, social relationships are also important, but the goal is to establish secure and long-term relationships with family and friends.

Another important contributor to social development are social institutions, such as family, church, and school, which assist people in realizing their full potential. Lev Vygotsky was a pioneer in this field with his concept of cultural mediation. This theory emphasizes that one's feelings, thoughts, and behaviors are significantly influenced by others in their environment.

Typical and Atypical Emotional Growth and Development

Emotional development encompasses the development of the following abilities:

- Identifying and understanding the feelings that one experiences
- Identifying and understanding the feelings of others
- Emotional and behavioral regulation
- Empathy
- Establishing relationships with others

Caregivers who are nurturing and responsive enable children to learn to regulate emotions and feel safe in the environment around them.

- By age two to three months, infants express delight and distress, begin smiling, and may be able to be soothed by rocking.

- By three to four months, infants communicate via crying and begin to express interest and surprise.

- Between four to nine months, infants respond differently to strangers in comparison to known individuals, solicit attention, show a particular attachment for a primary caregiver, and have an expanded range of expressed emotions that include anger, fear, and shyness.

- At ten to twelve months, babies show an increase in exploration and curiosity, demonstrate affection, and display a sense of humor.

- Children at age twelve to twenty-four months often demonstrate anger via aggression, laugh in social situations, recognize themselves in a mirror, engage in symbolic play, and have a complete range of emotional expression.

- Around age two, children begin using different facial expressions to show their emotions, begin to play cooperatively, and may transition from being calm and affectionate to temperamental and easily frustrated.

- At age three, children engage in more social and imaginative play, show interest in the feelings of others, begin to learn to manage frustration, and are often inconsistent and stubborn.

- Children at age four show improved cooperation, express sympathy, and may exhibit lying and/or guilty behavior.

- At age five, children can play rule-based games, often want to do what is expected of them, express emotion easily, and choose friends for themselves.

- Children at age six typically describe themselves in terms of their external attributes, have a difficult time coping with challenges and criticism, prefer routines, and show inconsistent self-control.

- Around age seven, children can typically describe causes and outcomes of emotions and show better regulation of emotions in most situations.

- From ages eight to ten, children have an increased need for independence, want to be viewed as intelligent, experience and better understand emotional subtleties, and may be defiant.

- During adolescence, children begin to master emotional skills to manage stress, increase self-awareness, develop identity, show increased ability for empathy, and learn to manage conflict.

Normal versus abnormal behavior is difficult to distinguish because each person is unique, so creating a standard of normal can be challenging. Though labeling behaviors as normal or abnormal can be problematic, it is important to have some standard by which it is possible to identify those behaviors that are indicative of an underlying psychological condition. Notwithstanding the challenges, it is possible and helpful to have general definitions of normal and abnormal behavior.

Normal behaviors are those that are common to the majority of the population, as related to emotional functioning, social interactions, and mental capacity. *Abnormal behavior* is generally considered that which is maladaptive, dysfunctional, and disruptive to life. These behaviors may be an exaggeration of a normal behavior or even an absence of a typical response. They do not conform to the accepted patterns or common behaviors of society. Sadness over the death of a loved one is considered normal, but disabling depression that interferes with school and work responsibilities is not. The *DSM-5* is the current standard for determining the diagnostic criteria that distinguishes abnormal behavior from normal.

Typical and Atypical Sexual Growth and Development

While not everyone develops sexually on exactly the same timeline, there are certain expectations that define healthy and unhealthy sexual development. These expectations differ based on age. During the early stage of life, from birth until age two, the child is focused on developing a relationship of trust with caregivers. Eventually, children become aware of their genitals and explore these through self-touch. By ages two to five, they begin to develop the ability to name and describe genitalia. They understand that male and female bodies are different. They have little inhibition about nudity.

As children enter middle childhood (ages six to eight or nine), they begin to understand the concept of puberty and what to expect about future body changes. They have a more sophisticated knowledge of reproduction, and may become more inhibited about nudity.

By the age of nine or ten, some children show signs of puberty, although the typical age of onset is eleven for girls and thirteen for boys. During puberty, there is a dramatic development in both primary and secondary sex characteristics. Children at this age show an increased interest in sex and may have questions about sexual orientation, sexual practices, or how the opposite sex behaves. By age twelve or thirteen, they begin to understand the consequences of sexual behavior, such as pregnancy or STDs. As they enter later adolescence, they may form longer relationships with their love interests, but many prefer casual dating. They are beginning to form an identity in terms of sexual orientation, preferences, and values.

It is important to understand red flags that may be signs of unhealthy sexual development. These may be brought on by abuse or by exposure to sexually explicit scenes. Children who are pre-occupied with sexuality at an early age and whose behaviors differ from peers their own age may be at risk. Other indicators include attempting adult-like sexual interactions. These behaviors may include oral to genital contact or some form of penetration of another person's body.

These issues should raise concerns:

- A child overly pre-occupied with sexual thoughts, language, or behaviors, rather than in more age-appropriate play
- Child engaging in sex play with children who are much older or much younger
- Child using sexual behavior to harm others
- Child involved in sexual play with animals
- Child uses explicit sexual language that is not age appropriate

A sexually-reactive child refers to one who is exposed to sexual stimuli prior to being sexually mature enough to understand the implications. The child becomes overly pre-occupied with sexual matters and often acts out what they witnessed or experienced.

Sexual Development Throughout the Lifespan

Sigmund Freud's Psychosexual Stages of Development

Sigmund Freud was an Austrian neurologist who is considered the father of psychoanalysis. Freud developed important concepts in Western psychology such as the id, ego, and super ego, and wrote literature focusing on what he called the *unconscious* and the repression and expression that stems from it.

Freud also focused on human development, especially relating to sexuality. Freud theorized that each stage of human development is characterized by a sexual focus on a different bodily area (*erogenous zone*), which can serve as a source of either pleasure or frustration. He believed that *libido* (psychosexual energy) is the determinant of behavior during each of five fixed stages, and that if a developing child experiences frustration during one of these stages, a resulting fixation (or lingering focus) on that stage will occur.

To understand Freud's developmental stages fully, one must also understand his conceptualization of the human personality.

Freud describes three levels of the mind as follows:

- Consciousness: the part of the mind that holds accessible and current thoughts
- Pre-consciousness: the area that holds thoughts that can be accessed by memory
- Unconscious: where the mind motivates behavior and contains thoughts, feelings, and impulses not easily accessible

Freud believed that the personality, or psyche, consists of three parts called the Psychic Apparatus, each of which develops at a different time.

Id

The id is the most basic and primitive part of the human psyche, based on instincts and all of the biological aspects of a person's being. An infant's personality consists only of the id, as the other aspects have not yet developed. The id is entirely unconscious and operates on the pleasure principle, seeking immediate gratification of every urge. It has two instincts: a death instinct called *thanatos* and a survival instinct called *eros*. The energy from eros is called the libido.

Ego

The ego is the second personality component that begins to develop over the first few years of life. The ego is responsible for meeting the needs of id in a socially acceptable, realistic manner. Unlike the id, the ego operates on the reality principle, which allows it to consider pros and cons, to have awareness that other people have feelings, and to delay gratification when necessary.

Super Ego

The super ego is the final personality component, developed by about age five. The super ego is essentially a person's internal moral system or sense of right and wrong. The super ego suppresses the instincts and urges of the id, but also attempts to convince the ego to act idealistically, rather than realistically.

In a healthy personality, there is balance between the three personality components. The individual has *ego strength*—the ability to function well in the world despite the conflicting pressures that the id and super ego place upon the ego.

Five Stages of Psychosexual Development

Oral Stage (Birth to Eighteen Months)

The infant satisfies its libido by feeding and by exploring the environment, primarily by putting objects in its mouth. The id dominates the oral stage of development, and every action an infant undertakes is guided by the pleasure principle. The key task of this phase is weaning from the breast, which also results in the infant's first experience of loss. Too much or too little focus on oral gratification at this stage was theorized to lead to an oral fixation and an immature personality. Examples of an oral fixation were believed to be excessive eating, drinking, or smoking.

Anal Stage (Eighteen Months to Three Years)

The key task of this stage is toilet training, which causes a conflict between the id (which wants immediate gratification of the urge to eliminate waste) and the ego (which requires delay of gratification necessary to use the toilet). A positive experience with toilet training was believed to lead to a sense of competence that continues into adulthood. Anal-retentive personality results from overly-strict toilet training, characterized by rigid and obsessive thinking. Likewise, anal-expulsive personality results from a lax approach to toilet training, characterized by disorganization and messiness.

Phallic Stage (Three to Six Years)

The libidinal focus during this stage is on the genital area, and it is during this stage that children learn to differentiate between males and females. The Oedipus Complex develops during this stage; Freud believed that a young boy views his father as a rival for his mother's attention and wants to eliminate his father in order to take his place. Similar to the Oedipus Complex, the Electra Complex says that a young may view her mother as her rival. Freud also believed that girls experience penis envy. The key task of this stage is identification with the same-sex parent.

Latency (Six years to Puberty)

During this period, libidinal energy is still present, but the child is able to direct that energy toward school, friendships, and activities.

Genital Stage (Puberty to Adulthood)

The libidinal focus is once again on the genital area (as it is during the phallic stage), but at this point, the psyche is more developed. During the genital stage, an individual achieves sexual maturation, becomes independent of his or her parents, resolves any remaining conflict from the earlier stages, and is able to function as a responsible adult in terms of both work and relationships.

Spiritual Development Throughout the Lifespan

Spiritual development refers to the way a person grows and changes spiritually over the course of their life, and particularly toward a sense of the purpose of their existence. This process may have conscious or unconscious origins, and it may be affected by other factors of their growth and development. Spiritual development is often linked to the stages of cognitive development, but evidence-based research pertaining strictly to spiritual development is limited. Theories often focus on the influence of psychosocial constructs (such as morality), cognitive beliefs, and religious or faith-based influences.

Jean Piaget (1896–1980) is renowned for his work in the field of cognitive development. He examined social, biological, and psychological constructs that influence cognitive development and intellect. He theorized four stages of cognitive development, from birth through adulthood. He believed that a multitude of constructs influences a person's moral beliefs and values, and this leads to their ultimate perspective on themselves and the environment.

Lawrence Kohlberg (1927–1987) studied moral psychology and development, and he developed a theory of the stages of moral reasoning. He theorized that individuals model behavior around them and behavior patterns to develop concepts of right and wrong as they progress through life. The more aware a person becomes of the effects of their thoughts, actions, and decisions, the more capacity they have for moral decision making. This may be connected to what shapes an individual's spiritual beliefs.

James Fowler (1940–2015), a theologian and university professor, contributed his "stages of faith" development, which breaks spiritual evolution down into six stages. He believed in the importance of safety and nurturing in the early years, which lead individuals to feel they are in touch with a greater good. Comparatively, individuals who feel unsafe or do not feel nurtured in their younger years are less likely to focus on spiritual aspects of life. Fowler made connections between his stages of faith and the developmental stages of Piaget and Kohlberg.

Racial, Ethnic, and Cultural Development Throughout the Lifespan

Racial, ethnic, and cultural identities are developed over the course of a lifespan and influenced by a number of factors. Atkinson, Morten, and Sue's racial and culture identity development model is accepted as one of the fundamental theories of racial and cultural development. This theory states that most individuals try to conform to the primary culture with which they're surrounded or which they believe is considered superior by peers. However, as the individual develops, they begin to seek out and reflect upon any underlying differences. Ideally, the developed individual ultimately becomes comfortable identifying in the way that feels best to him or her while respecting others' differences. Theorists have also focused on how specific minority groups develop racial, ethnic, and cultural identities. For example, Jean Kim's theory of Asian racial identity development focuses on Eastern populations. Minorities from Asian countries such as India, China, or Japan who grow up in the United States may act in traditional ways at home with their family unit, but they may struggle immensely to identify and assimilate with peers at school. This may be due to the fact that Asian culture is largely rooted in a collective, community identity (as opposed to the more individualistic Western culture). Additionally, Eastern and Western languages, traditions, and foods are different. While younger individuals may try to assimilate, older Asian individuals may tend to group together as they age. Bernardo Ferdman and Placida Gallegos's model of Latino identity development states that for Latino groups, ethnicity plays a larger role than race in self-identification. Finally, a number of researchers have theorized constructs and influences of white and black racial identity and culture. Often, these two racial identities are interrelated. Researchers have focused on the two races co-exist, based on historical interactions and contemporary narratives.

Physical, Mental, and Cognitive Disabilities Throughout the Lifespan

Approximately 7 percent of U.S. children have some type of disability. The most common physical disabilities that impact development are cerebral palsy, hearing issues, and visual issues. Learning disabilities are also common—these could be Down's syndrome or other developmental delays. Common psychiatric disabilities are ADHD and autism spectrum disorders. Others include mood disorders, oppositional disorders, anxiety disorders, and, in rare cases, schizophrenia. The impact upon the child and family corresponds to the family's ability to adapt to the condition, and their ability to connect to community resources.

How the individual develops and copes with the disability depends greatly upon the social context and the child's own personal attributes. Raising a disabled child puts tremendous stress on parents and siblings. There are issues of stigma, financial burden, missed days of work for parents, and the time and energy needed to seek useful resources. Siblings may be called upon to take roles of parenting to help out. These siblings may be bullied by peers who make fun of their disabled family member. They may feel neglected by parents. Additionally, there may be a need for special housing and special schools. Low-income families may face barriers to accessing services such as transportation, medical specialists, or assistance with childcare.

The impact of disabilities on development depends largely on (1) the extent of the disability and (2) whether that disability is experienced across the lifespan or for a limited amount of time. Positive coping skills and sufficient social support may lessen the impact of a disability. Although the tendency is to focus on negative impact, disabilities may also leave a positive impact in terms of the strengthening of relationships or the development of skills that an individual may not have otherwise acquired.

Interplay of Biological, Psychological, Social, and Spiritual Factors

The interplay of an individual's biological, psychological, social, and spiritual factors is an indicator of overall health and happiness. If one or more of these factors are imbalanced, the individual is unlikely to feel as though they are at their highest level of well-being or personal fulfillment (even if a clinically diagnosed disease is not present). This framework is often utilized in social work settings where mental or emotional health appears to be compromised. Practitioners address the issue in the client's life by examining their physical and physiological health, medical history, personal history, moods, reactions to events, environment, family life, home life, cultural beliefs, personal relationships, faith or belief system, spirituality, personal desires, and other factors to provide holistic drivers for any necessary interventions.

A number of these factors strongly influence each other. For example, a client who feels tremendous stress daily at work may find themselves constantly falling sick with colds, as stress negatively affects the immune system's ability to perform. Clients with clinically diagnosed mood disorders may have a more difficult time coping with major stressors, such as a divorce. Clients who report having some level of faith or spiritual belief system often appear to have higher levels of positivity and healthier coping mechanisms in the face of adverse personal events. As practitioners intervene in such scenarios, they must address not only the individual client, but all the systems in which the client exists and interacts. Practitioners may also need to work with the client's families, in communities, or in other group settings in order to effectively create balance between biological, psychological, social, and spiritual factors.

Basic Human Needs

Abraham Maslow is the most notable researcher in the area of basic human needs. Maslow theorized that human needs could be described in the form of a pyramid, with the base of the pyramid representing the most basic needs and the higher layers representing loftier goals and needs. Unless the basic needs are met, a person cannot move on to higher needs. For example, a homeless woman living under a bridge will need food, shelter and safety before she can consider dealing with her alcoholism.

The foundational layer in Maslow's hierarchy is physiological needs, and the final layer at the pinnacle of the pyramid is self-transcendence.

Maslow's Hierarchy of Needs

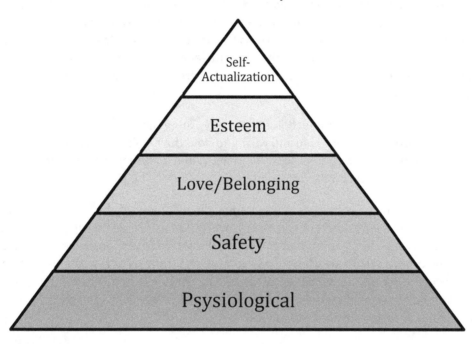

Maslow's Hierarchy of Needs

Physiological Needs: These needs must be met first and pertain to what humans need to survive. This includes basics, such as food, water, clothing, and housing.

Safety Needs: Once primary needs are met, the person may now focus on safety issues. This would include safety from abuse and neglect, natural disaster, or war.

Love and Belonging: Once the first levels of need have been satisfied, people are next driven to find a sense of acceptance and belonging within social groups, such as family, community, or religious organizations. Maslow suggests that humans have a basic need for love, affection, and sexual intimacy. Failure to achieve this level can lead to difficulty in forming and maintaining close relationships with others.

Esteem: The need for esteem is driven by a desire for recognition, respect, and acceptance within a social context.

Self-Actualization: The U.S. Army slogan, "Be All You Can Be," expresses this layer of need. Reaching one's highest potential is the focus. According to Maslow, this cannot be achieved until all the others are mastered.

Self-Transcendence: Devised by Maslow in his later years, he felt self-actualization did not completely satisfy his image of a person reaching their highest potential. To achieve self-transcendence, one must commit to a goal that is outside of one's self, such as practicing altruism or finding deeper level of spirituality.

Attachment and Bonding

Understanding attachment and bonding has become more important than ever, especially in relation to changes within the U.S. culture's attitudes about child welfare over the last fifty years. Child Protective Service Teams have become more active in every city. The medical profession, the educational system, and the mental health profession are more informed about children at risk. As a result, more children are being taken from parents, sometimes as early as the day of birth. An older child victim may travel from relative to relative, back to the mother, then into foster or group homes. These children do not have an opportunity to form attachments with their caregivers, nor do caregivers have the opportunity to bond with the children.

Bonding refers to a mother's initial connection to her baby. This generally occurs within the first hours or days of the birth. Mothers who are able and willing to hold their child close to them shortly after birth generally have more positive relationships with the child. When a mother fails to bond, the child is at greater risk for having behavioral problems.

Attachment, on the other hand, refers to a more gradual development of the baby's relationship with his or her caretaker. A secure attachment naturally grows out of a positive, loving relationship in which there is soothing physical contact, emotional and physical safety, and responsiveness to the child's needs. The baby who has a secure attachment will venture out from his or her safe base, but immediately seek his or her mother when fearful or anxious, having learned that mommy will be there to protect him or her. This type of secure relationship becomes impossible if the child is moved from home to home or has experienced abuse or neglect.

A child whose needs have not been met or who has learned through mistreatment that the world is unfriendly and hostile may develop an avoidant attachment or ambivalent attachment. An *avoidant attachment* is characterized by a detached relationship in which the child does not seek out the caregiver when distressed, but acts independently. A child with *ambivalent attachment* shows inconsistency toward the caregiver; sometimes the child clings to him or her, and at other times, resists his or her comfort. Establishing a secure, positive attachment with a caregiver is crucial to a child's life-long emotional and social success. The development of attachment disorder is often present in foster children or those adopted later in life and can create much frustration and heartache as the more stable parents step in and attempt to bond with them.

Effect of Aging on Biopsychosocial Functioning

Biological Aging
Biological aging is based on physical changes that have an impact on the performance of the body's organs and systems.

Psychological Aging
Psychological aging is based on changes in personality, cognitive ability, adaptive ability, and perception. Basic personality traits appear to be relatively stable through the lifespan, as does an individual's self-image. One aspect that does tend to change, however, is the tendency to become more inwardly focused, which may also result in reduced impulsivity and increased caution.

Studies have shown that a pattern of age-related changes in intelligence can typically be observed after age sixty, although changes vary widely across individuals. Furthermore, the somewhat poorer testing results are reflected in fluid intelligence (i.e., reasoning, problem-solving, and abstract thinking

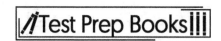

unrelated to experience or learned information), but not in crystallized intelligence (i.e., knowledge based on skills, learning, and experience). Normal age-related changes in memory typically involve acquisition of new information and retrieval of information from memory storage. *Sensory decline* is also a common experience for aging individuals.

Social Aging

Social aging is based on changes in one's relationships with family, friends, acquaintances, systems, and organizations. Most older persons experience a narrowing of their social networks. However, they are more likely to have more positive interactions within those networks, and they are more likely to experience more positive feelings about family members than younger persons do.

Disengagement theory states that it is natural and inevitable for older adults to withdraw from their social systems and to reduce interactions with others. This theory has been highly criticized and is incompatible with other well-known psychosocial aging theories. *Activity theory* proposes that social activity serves as a buffer to aging; successful aging occurs among those who maintain their social connections and activity levels. *Continuity theory* proposes that with age, individuals attempt to maintain activities and relationships that were typical for them as younger adults.

Impact of Aging Parents on Adult Children

There are about 10 million Americans over the age of fifty who are caring for aging parents. In the last fifteen years, thanks to modern medicine, the adult population has begun living longer. As a result, the number of adult children between the ages of fifty and seventy who provide care to aging parents has tripled. This amounts to about 25 percent of adult children who provide either personal or economic assistance.

Research indicates that becoming a personal caregiver to a parent increases the rates of depression, substance abuse, and heart disease. These adult children sometimes take significant financial blows in the form of lost income, earlier than planned retirement, and reduced pension plans, due to leaving the workforce earlier. At the same time, these adult children are assisting their own children as they move towards independence. Those in the youngest generation may still be in college or in the early stages of starting a career and still look to parents for some financial assistance. From a different perspective, the positives of this situation are that children are able to form deeper bonds with grandparents, and the longevity of life in loved ones can have very positive impact on all involved.

Gerontology

Gerontology is the study of biological, cognitive, and psychological features of the aging process. It includes the study of the impact of an aging population on social and economic trends. Gerontologists practice in the fields of medicine, psychology, physical and occupational therapy, as well as social work. Geriatric social work practice refers to a range of services provided to the population of those over age 60. Geriatric social workers are found in nursing homes, counseling programs, advocacy centers, and other programs serving seniors. Aging adults must deal with the very real issues of palliative care, hospice, and other end of life issues. The job of social workers is to support them through difficult decision-making processes and to counsel them as they deal with the complicated emotional and spiritual concerns of aging.

Personality Theories

There are several noted theories as to how personality is formed. In 400 B.C.E., Hippocrates attempted to identify personalities based on four temperaments. He called these *humors*, and these were associated with body fluid presence, such as phlegm or bile.

In the 1940s, William Sheldon came up with his body type theories that included the *endomorph*—an overweight individual, with an easy-going personality, the *mesomorph*—a muscular person, with an aggressive personality—and the *ectomorph*—a thin individual, with an artistic or intellectual personality.

Gordon Allport developed the trait theory of personality development. He believed that certain personalities were comprised of clusters of traits and that these traits could be categorized into cardinal, central, and secondary traits.

Freud believed the personality was composed of the id, the ego and superego. The *id* refers to a person's unconscious, with its suppressed desires and unresolved conflicts, whereas the *ego* and *superego* are more influenced by the conscious mind. He believed that these three components were often in conflict with one another and that how one resolved these conflicts determined personality. He also stressed the importance of childhood experience in personality development.

Carl Rogers was a proponent of the humanistic theory of personality development. This approach emphasized self-perception and a desire for striving to become the best person one can become. His theory was based on the basic goodness and potential of each person.

The behavioral theories of B.F. Skinner and others related to personality development implies that one's persona is developed as a result of classical or operant conditioning. Reinforcement and punishment guide behavioral choices.

Theories of Conflict

Conflict theories center on the premise that all human interactions involve some degree of power struggle, and this struggle may be exacerbated by differences in ideologies, acquisition of resources, culture and class differences, or other variables. Eventually, some groups end up controlling resources and decision making, therefore limiting opportunities for more submissive or resource-constrained groups. These dynamics eventually shape the culture and interpersonal relationships of a group, whether it is a small team or a country's entire society.

Karl Marx (1818–1883) contributed one of the most widely recognized social conflict theories, Marxism, which sees conflict between socio-economic classes as the driver of history. Marx saw capitalist societies as necessarily entangled in conflicts between the working class and the ruling class over resources and opportunities. As privileged groups leave wealth and other resources to their descendants, those descendants have more opportunities, compared to groups who possess lesser quantities and quality of resources. Marx also believed these class conflicts would eventually unseat the ruling class.

Ludwig Gumplowicz (1838–1909) focused on conflicts that arise between different cultures. They arise as one group's desired way of living is threatened by a group with vastly different ideals, especially if one group tries to force its cultural and ethnic norms, beliefs, and systems on another group. These norms may encompass religious views, social views, financial views, family views, and racial views.

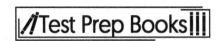

C. Wright Mills (1916–1952) developed conflict theories that focus on class structures and political parties. Inspired by Karl Marx, Mills focused his theories on ruling classes in societies and how their behaviors influence the larger group. He states that those in authority shape a society's culture and beliefs; however, the majority of the society does not have the same resources to uphold these behaviors. This is likely to eventually lead to conflict.

Factors Influencing Self-Image

Self-image has to do with how people view themselves. This concept includes *self-esteem*, whether a person has feelings of high or low worth. The concept of self evolves throughout the life span, but it always plays a significant role in a how a person functions in life.

Impact of Cultural Heritage on Self-Image

Although personal factors play a large role, self-esteem is also based on how closely a person matches the dominant values of his or her culture. For example, Western society tends to value assertiveness, independence, and individuality. Living up to these values is seen as an important accomplishment, and thus, children receive messages about their personal competence and success based on whether or not they are living up to these ideals.

Children who are able to exhibit behaviors that are valued within their home and family, as well as those valued by their culture, are more likely to develop a positive self-concept.

One study suggests that across culture, self-esteem is based on one's control of life and choices, living up to one's "duties," benefiting others or society, and one's achievement. However, the degree to which one's culture values each of those factors has an impact on how the individual derives his or her self-esteem.

A widely cited example of the way that a culture can affect a person's self-image is in the portrayal of women's bodies in the media. In the United States, young women are exposed to underweight models and unrealistically drawn cartoon "heroines," which can lead to the development of unachievable expectations and significant negative perceptions about their bodies.

Impact of Race and Ethnicity on Self-Image

Culture, race, and ethnicity can greatly impact one's self-image, whether one is part of a privileged population or a minority population. One's ethnic and racial background provides a sense of belonging and identity. Depending on a country's treatment of a particular group, self-image can be negatively impacted through racism and discrimination. As mentioned, non-whites are more likely to be arrested than whites and often receive harsher sentences for similar offenses. Racial jokes and racial slurs are common. Stereotypes abound, and some people judge entire racial groups based on the behavior of a few. Such treatment consistently impacts the self-esteem of minority groups. As children become aware of the environment and the culture in which they live, they inevitably notice a lack of prominent nonwhite politicians, entertainers, CEOs, or multi-millionaires. Non-white Americans—who grew up in the fifties or earlier—were denied access to restaurants, theaters, high schools, professions, universities, and recreational activities. Even within the last fifty to sixty years, African Americans who had achieved great status in the fields of music, sports and entertainment were still denied access to certain clubs, hotels, or restaurants.

Every person must explore and come to terms with his or her own culture, ethnicity, and race. Sometimes, this even means rejecting cultural aspects with which he or she disagrees and embracing new and evolving cultural norms. This is a significant part of self-identity development among teenagers and young adults as they are part of a new generation that may be culturally different from their parents. Those that have more exposure to other cultures and backgrounds will have a more open perspective and are better able to evaluate their own culture and ethnicity objectively.

Effects of Spirituality

Spirituality is sometimes mistaken for religion, but in fact, they are quite different terms. Religion is an organized system of beliefs that generally contain a code of conduct and often involve specific devotional or ritual observations. Spirituality is more abstract and includes participation in spiritual activities such as meditation, chanting, prayer, or unselfishly serving others. A spiritual person may or may not belong to a religious organization. Spirituality places emphasis on the growth and well-being of the mind, body and spirit.

Studies have shown that persons who embrace spirituality tend to live both longer and happier lives. Several benefits of being a spiritual person include the following:

- Encourages individual to strive towards being a better person
- Increases likelihood of connections with others
- Offers hope to the hopeless through strong faith
- Provides a path to heal from emotional pain
- Helps reduce anxiety through meditation and other spiritual activities
- Leads to greater life commitment via the optimism spiritual persons tend to have

Impact of Age on Self-Image

Aging is an inevitable phase of human development, and the impact is physical, psychological, social, and economic. Self-image is the perception of how one views oneself, but the perception is influenced by societal values. Some cultures revere the elderly and look to them for wisdom and strength. These cultures include the Native Americans, Chinese, Koreans, and Indians. In the United States, there is a different perception of aging. Many elderly Americans feel less valuable or important once they enter retirement. At the same time, they are coping with undesirable body changes and learning to accept that, physically, they can no longer do what they once did. In the U.S., youth and physical attractiveness are highly valued. The elderly are seldom seen as important social figures. They are also less connected with families today with only 3.7% of homes reporting multigenerational households, per Census Bureau reports. Family support and family contact is less available, currently. For some segments of the population, though, technology has allowed relatives to visit regularly with grandchildren and even participate in family meals or get-togethers.

Infancy: The ego is in charge. The baby thinks primarily of basic needs, such as food or warmth.

Childhood: In early to middle childhood, children tend to rate themselves higher than peers in terms of talents and intellect. As middle school approaches, there is a decline in self-evaluations. This could be related to feeling unattractive due to physical changes or being teased or bullied by peers in that age group.

Adolescence: In the early stage of adolescence (ages 9 to 13), another drop in self-esteem occurs. This is thought to be related to the need to let go of childish pleasures, such as a beloved toy or previous interests and step up to the plate of becoming a more responsible person. This can be a painful sacrifice for some youth. The next drop in self-worth occurs at the end of adolescence and beginning of young adulthood (ages 18 to 23). It is during this period that the young adults realize that they truly are

responsible for their own lives, yet they have not yet achieved a sense of mastery in the academic or vocational world. They are fearful and full of doubt about the ability to be successful as an independent adult.

Adulthood: Studies indicate a small but steady increase in self-image by mid-twenties. In general, during this period, men tend to have higher self-esteem than women. Persons who live in poor socioeconomic conditions tend to have lower self-esteem than their more financially stable peers. As later adulthood nears (the 70s), women tend to catch up with men in terms of how they evaluate themselves. Women in their eighties tend to have a more positive self-image than male counterparts. As a general rule, for both genders, there is a gradual increase in one's sense of self-worth throughout the life span until late middle age. Research shows that most adults' self-image peaks at around age 60.

Impacts of Disability on Self-Image
Disabilities impact self-image regardless of age; however, an individual who is born with a disability tends to fare better than one who acquires one later in life. Responses vary based upon severity of impairments. Some later life medical conditions cause the individual to give up independence as the person is forced to retire the car keys or move to an institutional setting. Less severe acquired disabilities, which still allow the person to maintain much of his or her previous lifestyle, are painful, but easier to accept. An individual's personality make-up and resilience to coping with change are also important factors. It is not uncommon for older adults to lapse into depression. This is often generated by a combination of losses. As one enters the later stages of life, loss of friends and family members is common. There may be declines in status, earning capacity, or physical abilities, all of which contribute to depression and negatively impact self-image.

Effects of Trauma on Self-image
Trauma can have a significant impact on self-image as a person's entire identity becomes intertwined with the traumatic event and the subsequent emotions. Some victims of trauma report a sense of isolation from others, feeling that they are not good enough or that they are less competent or less attractive than their peers. This generates feelings of shame and unworthiness, which, in turn, can lead to depression or anxiety. Some trauma survivors—especially victims of child or domestic abuse—feel a deep sense of betrayal and label the world and people as unsafe. They have trouble trusting others, and they may perform poorly in major areas of functioning, such as work or relationships. Some abuse survivors describe themselves as "damaged goods." Some individuals may engage in self-harm behaviors or may feel so depressed that suicide is seen as the only solution. These persons are prone to substance abuse as a means to numb the emotional pain. Addictive behavior can also negatively impact one's self-esteem. The more resilient will use their painful experiences as a tool for self-growth and may eventually learn to help others who have been through similar experiences.

Body Image

Body image refers to the thoughts and feelings about the appearance of one's body, as well as thoughts and feelings about how one's body is perceived by others. Body image is shaped by the messages that we receive from the people around us, the culture we live in, and the media.

Persistent negative body image can be associated with these factors:

- Low self-esteem
- Depression and/or anxiety
- Sexual risk-taking

- Impaired relationship satisfaction
- Withdrawal from activities where one's body may be visible to others (e.g., exercise, sexual activity, swimming, seeking medical care)
- Development of eating disorders

Parenting Skills and Capacities

Good parenting practices are essential for raising emotionally healthy children. Child psychologists vary on what types of parenting styles are most effective, but there are four generally recognized styles of parenting.

Authoritarian parenting style: This style of parenting reinforces the role of parent as controller and decision maker. Children are rarely given input into decisions impacting their lives, and the parent takes on a dictatorial role. Children raised by this kind of parent are often obedient and tend to be proficient. The drawback is that they do not rank high on the happiness scale.

Authoritative parenting style: This style of parenting allows for a greater sense of democracy in which children are given some degree of input into issues that impact their lives. There is a healthy balance between firmness and affection. Children raised in this environment tend to be capable, successful, and happy individuals.

Permissive parenting style: This type of parenting allows children to be more expressive and freer with both feelings and actions; they are allowed to behave in whatever manner they please. There are very few rules, and no consequences will be given, even if a rule is violated. These children are more likely to experience problems in school and relationships with others. In the long run, they are often unhappy with their lives.

Uninvolved parenting style: This form of parenting often occurs in dysfunctional families in which parents are emotionally or physically unavailable. They may be remiss in setting clear expectations, yet they may overreact when the child misbehaves or fails to understand what is expected. This is often seen in families where poverty is extreme or addictions or mental illnesses are present.

The authoritative style of parenting is considered to be the most effective form of parenting, yet much depends on the individual child or parent and the economic situation or cultural setting. One rule of thumb is that whatever style one chooses, it is helpful to remain consistent. A parent who is permissive one day and authoritarian the next sends mixed and confusing messages to the child. It is also important that the child is completely aware of rules, expectations, and what consequences may follow if the rules are broken. Communicating a sense that children are loved, wanted, and accepted is one of the most important parts of parenting.

Addiction and Substance Abuse

The repercussions of the addict's behavior can affect many significant aspects of life. The impact of addictions is felt not only by the addict, but everyone in that person's family and circle of social support. Those most powerfully affected are the immediate family members—particularly those who live under the same roof as the addict. Friends, extended family, co-workers, and employers also experience fallout from the addict's behaviors.

The spouses or partners of parents who struggle with addiction often feel depressed, anxious, and angry. Persons in the throes of addiction often lie and steal to to maintain their habit. It is not

uncommon for parents who struggle with addiction to steal from friends, family, or employers. Families must deal with the anxiety of not knowing when their loved one will come home or what mood or condition the person may demonstrate upon arriving home. Some families must deal with the shame of seeing their loved one arrested or knowing that this person harmed others while under the influence. Others simply become embarrassed by behaviors loved ones exhibit in public or their failure to show up for an important event, such as a graduation.

Children of parents who struggle with addiction experience embarrassment, fear, anxiety, and sadness. They are more likely to be abused or neglected, especially in single parent homes. Children may suffer when money intended for basic needs is spent on drugs or alcohol instead. When abuse and/or neglect are reported to CPS, these children may be taken from parents and placed in a series of group or foster homes. In some cases, custody is completely severed. Such experiences may lead to deep psychological scars for those closest to the addict.

Feminist Theory

Feminist theory is the study of relations between the sexes, especially in the context of inequality. Discussions often include the topics of gender roles, gender in work-life contexts, societal norms for the genders, and cultural perceptions of gender. Feminist theory also focuses gender relations and certain power relationships. Feminist pioneers have fought for equal political and social rights for men and women (such as the right to vote or the ability to work outside the home), for making previously male-oriented terms gender neutral (such as using "firefighter" instead of "fireman), for female body positivity and acceptance, for sexual and reproductive rights and protection, and for encouraging supportive relationships between the genders. Feminist theories also support equality for men in such areas as paternity leave, stay at home parenting for fathers, and a redefined masculinity that includes heightened emotional intelligence, awareness, and expression. Feminist theory researchers have been striving to reinvigorate feminist studies, believing that prior theories formed by primarily male researchers should be reexamined.

Influential Feminist Theorists

A number of American female psychologists, psychiatrists, and psychoanalysts have been influential in shaping psychological research that pertains to development in women and in serving as leaders in feminist theory.

Anna Freud (1895–1982) made significant contributions to the field of psychoanalysis, especially regarding the ego and child development. She was the youngest daughter of Sigmund Freud. Some of her works include *Introduction to Psychoanalysis: Lectures for Child Analysts and Teachers* and *Ego and the Mechanisms of Defense*.

Jean Baker Miller (1927–2006) is best known for authoring the revered text *Toward a New Psychology of Women* (1976). She is also known for her work with relational-cultural theory, which focuses on how culture affects relationships and how healthy connections with others are an integral part of psychological health and personal growth. These ideas often played a role in diagnosing and treating depression in women.

Carol Tavris (1944–) promotes critical thinking and evidence-based research in psychology, focusing on cognitive dissonance. She believes many of women's so-called psychological issues are actually social beliefs about women's limitations, and that these social beliefs are not backed by science.

Nancy Chodorow (1944–) authored the renowned text *Psychoanalysis and the Sociology of Gender* (1978). Her research focuses on mothering, gender systems, how the family influences female roles in society, and gender identity formation.

Harriet Lerner (1944–) is best known for her work regarding gender roles in marriage, cultural gender norms, and how women can balance self-care with other competing priorities in their lives.

Carol Gilligan (1936–) was a research assistant to Lawrence Kohlberg. She argues that his theories of moral development are male-focused and do not apply to women. Her research focuses on the development of morals and ethics in women. She initially published her findings as *In a Different Voice* in 1982.

Gail Sheehy (1937–), an author and journalist, wrote *Passages* (1976), which supports many of the beliefs and ideas of feminist psychologists. This book covers the different periods of life that women progress through and the emotions they experience in each one. The Library of Congress honored *Passages* as one of the top ten most influential books of its time.

Out-of-Home Placement

Children and elderly or disabled persons are sometimes legally removed from homes when it is determined there is a safety concern such as abuse or neglect. In these situations, the goal of removal is to secure the health, safety, and well-being of the displaced individual. It is likely that many other interventions have been attempted and have not worked, with removal being a last resort. These individuals, particularly children, who have lived in chaotic, dysfunctional environments will already have psychological and behavioral problems, including anxiety, depression, acting out, and displays of aggression. Following removal, these behaviors will likely escalate. Additionally, the parents or other caregivers who have had dependents taken away will also experience anger, confusion, guilt, and an assortment of challenges. Social workers can assume many roles in out-of-home placement, including working with the family of origin, the individual who has been displaced, or the respite caregivers.

Human Genetics

Social workers will begin to see more work done in the area of human genetics in the coming years. Since social workers are often the first individuals to diagnose mental disorders, it's imperative for workers to understand the ethical and legal implications behind a genetic diagnosis. The following is a list of social work *practice skills* related to genetics:

- Biopsychosocial assessment of clients who may have genetic disorders
- Providing assistance to clients with genetic disorders by identifying and/or developing programs for them
- Providing risks-benefits counseling before a client undergoes genetic testing
- Providing post-test counseling following diagnosis of a disorder
- Providing counseling related to family planning
- Providing adoption-related counseling pertaining to implications of an adoptee's genetic information

The following is a list of social work values related to genetics:

- Accessibility: availability of genetic screening to those who need it

- Self-determination: protection of rights when individuals are asked to take part in population screening

- Autonomy: the right and ability for an individual to choose whether or not to undergo genetic testing

- Confidentiality: assurance and maintenance of the privacy of genetic testing results

- Research: data from screening used for the purpose of developing services that may benefit others

Ethical dilemmas may arise as the result of genetic testing. Social workers should refer to the NASW Code of Ethics (1996) for guidance, paying particular attention to the ethical standards of self-determination, informed consent, and social and political action.

Family Life Cycle

Family life cycle theories assume that, as members of a family unit, individuals pass through different stages of life. Although various theories will break down the stages somewhat differently, the following is a common conceptualization of the stages:

Unattached Young Adult
The primary tasks for this stage are selecting a life style and a life partner. Focus is on establishing independence as an adult and independence from one's family of origin.

Newly-Married Couple
The focus in this stage is on establishing the marital system. Two families are joined together, and relationships must be realigned.

Family with Young Children
The focus in this stage is on accepting new family members and transitioning from a marital system to a family system. The couple takes on a parenting role. Relationships must again be realigned with the extended family (e.g., grandparents).

Family with Adolescents
The focus here is on accommodating the emerging independence of the adolescents in the family. The parent-child relationship experiences changes, and the parents may also begin to take on caregiving roles with regard to their own parents.

Launching Family
The focus in this stage is on accepting the new independent role of an adult child and transitioning through the separation. Parents also must face their own transition into middle or older age.

Family in Later Years
In this stage, spousal roles must be re-examined and re-defined. One focus may be the development of interests and activities outside of work and family. Another focus is on navigation of the aging process and losses that may occur.

The basic family life cycle can vary significantly as a result of cultural influences, expectations, and particular family circumstances (e.g., single-parent family, blended family, multi-generational family).

Family Dynamics and Functioning

Family dynamics are the interactions between family members in a family system. As discussed previously, under "Family Theories," each family is a unique system; however, there are some common patterns of family dynamics.

Common influences on family dynamics:

- The type and quality of relationship that the parents have
- An absent parent
- A parent who is either extremely strict or extremely lenient
- The mix of personalities in the family
- A sick or disabled family member
- External events, particularly traumatic ones that have affected family members
- Family dynamics in previous generations or the current extended family

Common roles in the family that may result from particular family dynamics:

- The problem child: child with problematic behavior, which may serve as a distraction from other problems that the family, particularly the parents, do not want to face

- Scapegoat: the family member to whom others unjustly attribute problems, often viewed as "bad," while other family members are viewed as "good"

- Peacekeeper: a family member who serves to mediate relationships and reduce family stress

The Effects of Family Dynamics on Individuals
There are many ways in which the family influences the individual socially, emotionally, and psychologically. All family systems have their own unique characteristics, with both good and bad functional tendencies. The family interactions are among the earliest and most formative relationships that a person has, so they define the relational patterns that the individual develops and utilizes with all subsequent relationships. Parenting styles, conflict resolution methods, beliefs and values, and coping mechanisms are just a few things that a person learns from their family of origin. It is also within the family that a person first develops an image of self and identity, often having to do with the role that they are given within the family system and the messages communicated by parents. If a child has a secure and healthy relationship with the family members, this will likely lead to overall well-being and emotional stability as an adult.

When it comes to physical or mental illness, the role that the family plays is critical in lowering risk factors and minimizing symptoms. A strongly supportive family will help a person function at the highest level possible. Oftentimes, family members can serve as caregivers or play less formal—but still critical—roles in supporting a person's health.

Couples Development

Many couples enter treatment after experiencing long-standing problems and may seek help because all other options have failed. One of the goals of couples' therapy is to help clients develop effective communication and problem-solving skills so they can solve problems throughout and after treatment. Other goals include helping the couple form a more objective view of their relationship, modifying dysfunctional behavior/patterns, increasing emotional expression, and recognizing strengths. Workers should create an environment to help the couple understand treatment goals, feel safe in expressing their feelings, and reconnect by developing trust in each other. Interventions for couples are often centered on goals geared toward preventing conflicting verbal communication and improving empathy, respect, and intimacy in a relationship. Therapeutic interventions, along with exercises, are designed to help couples learn to treat each other as partners and not rivals. Cognitive Behavioral Therapy is also used in working with couples. It uses cognitive restructuring techniques to help change distorted thinking and modify behavior.

Physical and Mental Illness on Family Dynamics

In some ways, physical illness is easier for a family to understand and deal with than mental illness because the symptoms and diagnosis are usually more obvious. When a person is diagnosed with a mental illness, the family may have a hard time accepting its reality. They may deny the diagnosis or try to find alternative explanations. There may be feelings of confusion or embarrassment, especially when those outside the family become aware of the illness. Because of the stigma that comes with mental illness, family members may become judgmental toward the individual who has been diagnosed. Since symptoms of mental illness often manifest themselves as emotional or behavioral responses, the family members can be tempted to blame the person with the mental illness and become frustrated with the perceived lack of responsibility and willingness to change.

As with physical illness, mental illness may impact the responsibility structure of the family as well as the financial situation, since all family members must adjust to caring for the mentally ill person. Beyond this, there may be irritation or bitterness toward the person suffering, which may be exacerbated by every episode of anxiety, anger, depression, or psychosis on the part of the mentally ill individual. It may be helpful for the social worker to provide the family with education about the illness, as well as involve them in treatment, when possible. It also helps to engage the family in counseling. Support groups or services for the family are also critical in helping them deal with the stressors they face. While families need to acknowledge the reality and seriousness of the mental illness, they also must recognize that, with their help and support, the ill person can thrive and successfully cope with the illness.

Psychological Defense Mechanisms

Sigmund Freud's *psychoanalytic theory* focused on the conflicts, drives, and unacceptable desires in the unconscious mind and how they affect a person. One method of dealing with unconscious conflicts is through *defense mechanisms*, which are the mind's way of protecting a person from unacceptable thoughts.

Here are some of the most common defense mechanisms:

- *Repression* is when a person suppresses thoughts or memories that are too difficult to handle. They are pushed out of the conscious mind, and a person may experience memory loss or have psychogenic amnesia related to those memories.

- *Displacement* takes place when someone displaces the feelings they have toward one person, such as anger, and puts it on another person who may be less threatening. For example, someone may express anger toward a spouse, even if they are really angry with a boss.

- *Sublimation* is when the socially unacceptable thought is transformed into healthy, acceptable creativity in another direction. Pain may become poetry, for example.

- *Rationalization* is when unacceptable feelings or thoughts are rationally and logically explained and defended.

- *Reaction formation* occurs when the negative feeling is covered up by a false or exaggerated version of its opposite. In such a case, a person may display strong feelings of affection toward someone, though internally and unconsciously hate that person.

- *Denial* is refusing to accept painful facts or situations and instead acting as if they are not true or have not happened.

- *Projection* is putting one's own feelings onto someone else and acting as if they are the one who feels that way instead of oneself.

Addiction Theories and Concepts

Addiction is a complex process involving biological, social, cultural and genetic factors. There is some disagreement in the addiction treatment community about the causes and best treatments for substance abuse disorders. There are several models of addiction.

The earliest theory of addiction is called the *Moral Model*. This model implies that the person abuses substances because they are morally weak. The addict is viewed as a sinner or criminal and one who does not have the intestinal fortitude to change negative behaviors, therefore choosing to wallow in the misery of their sins.

The *disease model* or *medical model* of addiction, upon which the twelve-step program of Alcoholics Anonymous (AA) is based, specifies that the addict suffers from an illness that will never be cured and is progressive in its development. Even if the individual ceases alcohol intake, the disease remains. AA literature indicates that when one relapses, even after years of sobriety, the addict picks up, not where he left off, but where the disease would have taken him if the drinking had continued. It is seen as a medical disorder and, at times, referred to in the Big Book of AA as having an allergy, with alcohol as the identified allergen. This theory is accepted and understood by many successful AA participants who have maintained sobriety throughout this program for years and who have shared their experience of strength and hope to help others struggling with addiction.

The *bio-psychosocial model* of addiction focuses on the role of the environment. Cultural and social factors influence one's beliefs and attitudes about substance use. In certain religions, it is unacceptable to use alcohol. In others, it may be encouraged—such as the huge sale and consumption of beer at

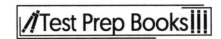

Catholic picnics and fish fries. An addict's observation of others and their patterns of alcohol ingestion influences their attraction to drug or alcohol use as a means for tension relief or a form of celebration. Exposure to family or community members who use large quantities of intoxicants may serve to normalize dysfunctional patterns of use. Some youth observing parents consuming a quart of vodka each night may believe their family members are just normal drinkers, whereas other youth are raised in environments where alcohol is unacceptable or served only on rare occasions.

The *learning theory* of addiction is based on concepts related to positive reinforcement. The assumption underpinning this model is that addiction is a learned behavior through operant conditioning, classical conditioning, and social learning. Social learning takes place through observation. Learning theory posits that the interplay between these three factors contribute to the initiation, maintenance, and relapse of addictive behaviors. The intoxicant serves as an immediate reinforcement in the form of increased euphoria or relaxation. In some cases, it also deters withdrawal symptoms. Both of these forms of reinforcement increase the likelihood that the behavior will be repeated in an effort to recreate the sensation of feeling better.

Genetic theory is based on research indicating that biological children of parents who struggle with addiction or alcoholics are more prone to addiction than children of non-alcoholics. According to genetic therapy, this genetic predisposition towards addiction accounts for about half of one's susceptibility to becoming an addict. Theorists of this model agree that other factors, such as social experiences, have an impact upon the formation of an addiction.

Systems and Ecological Perspectives and Theories

Systems Theory in social work refers to the view that human behavior is explained by the influences of the various systems to which individuals belong. When evaluating and conceptualizing an individual's behavior, that behavior must be considered in the context of the individual's family, society, and other systems.

All systems are seen as possessing interrelated parts and exerting influence on each other. There are many iterations of the premise of the basic systems theory. In practice, systems theory allows a social worker to understand the dynamics of a client's systems better, while also creating an appropriate intervention approach. The originator of systems theory in social work was Ludwig von Bertalanffy, a biologist, who was influenced by sociologists Max Weber and Emile Durkheim.

Talcott Parsons expanded on earlier work with his framework of structural functionalism, which proposes that a system is defined by its function in its social environment.

The four states of social systems are adaptation to the social environment, goal attainment, integration with other systems, and latency or homeostasis (social patterns and norms are maintained). It's also important to note the designations of social systems in social work. Microsystems are small systems, like an individual or a couple. Mezzosystems are medium-sized systems made up of extended families or groups to which the individual belongs. Macrosystems are large systems made up of organizations or communities.

The *ecological systems perspective* is concerned with the transactions between systems. It says that people and families must be considered within cultural and societal contexts, which also necessitates examining the events that have occurred in an individual's life. Changes made by the individual that cause the entire system to shift must also be considered.

The following lists common interventions based on systems theory:

- Strengthening a part of the system in order to improve the whole system

- Creating a genogram: a family tree constructed with a client in order to improve understanding of the familial relationships and to identify recurring patterns

- Connecting clients to organizations or individuals who can help them to function better within and between their systems

- Developing an ecomap: an Illustration of client's systems, such as family and community and how it changes over time

Role Theories

Different role theories have culminated in the social role theory, which emphasizes that people's behaviors are motivated by the roles they are given within society. These roles can include aspects of race, gender, employment, position in the family, etc. When a person assumes a particular role, they tend to adopt the expectations of that role as governed by social norms and conventions. Some roles, such as gender, may affect many domains of life, while others—like being a student—may be confined to a particular situation or environment. The roles that a person adopts can strongly impact self-image and behaviors. Philip Zimbardo illustrated this role dynamic when he conducted the Stanford Prison Experiment, in which individuals given the roles of prisoners and guards assumed their positions so completely that the experiment became dangerous. The guards became violent and aggressive, and the prisoners became overly submissive and afraid.

Social roles can both negatively and positively impact the individual. While the smooth functioning of society is dependent on different people fulfilling different roles and responsibilities, certain role expectations can limit a person's individuality and self-determination. For example, typical gender roles may cause a woman to feel that her role in society is restricted by the expectations placed upon her.

Theories of Group Development and Functioning

Some aspects of planning interventions for a group will be similar to planning for an individual. Other aspects are unique to groups. Methods for planning interventions with a group may include:

- Conducting a needs assessment for the group to determine issues
- Ensuring that key stakeholders are involved in data collection and planning
- Continuously involving and updating all stakeholders
- Delegating components of the intervention appropriately by individuals' strengths and resources
- Establishing SMART objectives for changes (specific, measurable, achievable, relevant, time-based)
- Setting goals
- Developing an evaluation plan to assess progress

Techniques for Managing Group Process and Maintaining Group Functioning

Group therapy process involves members becoming familiar with each other before getting to work on issues. There should be group rules that the entire group agrees upon before entering therapy. The social worker acts as a guide and mediator for the group, and may also act as an instructor for the

group. There are phases of group therapy process and functioning that include forming, norming, and storming elements. Groups may be open and allow members in at any time, or closed, which means that a group is specifically formed and only select participants are allowed entrance. Both the social worker and the group members are responsible for managing group dynamics.

The group and the social worker are involved in managing group process and maintaining group functioning. Group participants may be invested in maintaining group coherence and functioning, and someone may take the role of gatekeeper in maintaining the group. The social worker may assume the role of leader concerning group process and functioning and may be responsible for group growth and termination. Sometimes group members take specific roles within the group, such as helper, peacemaker, or gatekeeper. At times, group members may also take negative roles within the group setting. These should be ameliorated by the social worker.

Theories of Social Change and Community Development

Community development theory focuses on oppressed people who are in the process of overcoming social problems that were imposed upon them by external forces. In the process of community development, members of a community learn how to improve that community and gain control of their local environment. *Community-level change* brings people together and demonstrates the power of solidarity. This theory also acknowledges the reality that many problems are at the social, rather than individual, level. An implication of the theory is that therapy addresses only the symptoms of a problem and not the underlying causes.

Interpersonal Relationships

Interpersonal relationships refer to interactions (often of a close, friendly, romantic, or intimate nature) between people. They can form due to shared personal, professional, social, charitable, or political interests. Strong interpersonal relationships are built over time as participants are willing to honestly communicate on a regular basis, support one another's well-being, and develop a shared history. Psychological, evolutionary, and anthropological contexts suggest that humans are an inherently altruistic, community-oriented species that relies on interpersonal relationships to survive and thrive. These types of relationships (when healthy) provide security, a sense of belonging, an exchange of benefits and rewards, and a sense of self-esteem. Healthy interpersonal relationships are characterized by mutual respect, care, and consideration between members. Almost all groups assemble into a power structure of some kind, with natural leaders taking over decision making, resource sharing, and other tasks that affect the group as a whole. Dysfunctional interpersonal relationships may be characterized by an extreme power imbalance and dominance by one or more involved members, often leading to submissiveness, learned helplessness, and feelings of low self-esteem in the relationship's less powerful members. Submissive members of a group may find themselves without material resources or respect from the rest of the group.

Family Life Education in Social Work Practice

Family life education is an important aspect of social work practice in the psychoeducational realm of treatment. Families sometimes need to be educated concerning their biopsychosocial structure and other kinds of family structures. Family life models have changed in recent years and continue to change at a rapid pace with the advent of the legalization of gay marriage and the increase in extended and blended families. Family life has become very diverse, and social workers need to be educated on these models so they can further educate clients.

Strengths-Based and Resilience Theories

Rather than focusing on problems and pathology, the strengths perspective (or *strengths-based approach*) in social work encourages social workers to focus on a client's strengths or assets and to build upon the client's inherent resiliency and positive characteristics. Outcome studies regarding use of the strengths perspective are limited; however, it is posited that a strengths-based approach could help to remove some of the stigma attached to groups or conditions (e.g., mental illness, poverty).

Resilience theories account for risk factors that may threaten an individual's ability to cope with adverse events. Risk factors include lack of support, diagnosis of mental health disorders, and resource constraints. Protective factors that support high levels of resiliency include the ability to think positively about situations, the ability to feel hope, strong confidence in one's self-reliance, problem-solving abilities, and competence. Developing resilience should be treated as a preventative approach, rather than a reactive approach.

Strengths- and resilience-based approaches allow individuals to feel empowered and maintain a sense of self-efficacy, both of which are crucial components for lasting behavior change and resolution. Additionally, they minimize client's self-identification with a problem or issue, which can cause the client to fall into a self-fulfilling prophecy. It is important to note that clients can build the capacity to be resilient as a healthy method of coping. This type of skill building can often serve as a crucial component of an intervention. Exercises may include reframing perspectives, journaling, learning new abilities (such as problem-solving skills), practicing flexibility when unexpected changes arise, and examining public stories of strength and resiliency with the client. Finally, practitioners can support clients by providing positive reinforcement and feedback when the client displays strong and resilient behaviors.

Impact of Stress, Trauma, and Violence

Trauma affects everyone differently. The reaction depends on the person's emotional resiliency, history of past trauma, and other factors. Some trauma survivors exhibit symptoms that clearly meet the criteria for PTSD, while others exhibit smaller clusters of symptoms, such as anxiety or depression. Others show little or no symptoms. Below is an overview of common responses:

- Foreshortened future: This refers to the sense that one's life is shortened or forever altered and that a normal life may never be experienced again.

- Emotional responses: These may be fear, sadness, shame, anger, guilt, and/or anxiety.

- Physical reactions: Survivors of trauma often have multiple somatic issues, including gastrointestinal complaints, neurological problems, poor sleep, and muscle pain.

- Hyperarousal: Trauma survivors often become hypervigilant. They are frightened by neutral stimuli, such as a dog barking or a child screaming. They may experience a continual feeling that something terrible is going to happen.

- Intrusive thoughts: Survivors can become flooded with unwanted thoughts and memories about the trauma.

- Trigger/flashbacks: Triggers are stimuli that set off memories and provide a sensory reminder of the traumatic event.

- Dissociation: This coping mechanism allows the person to "check out" temporarily. This process severs connections to the painful memories.

- Self-harm: Some survivors use self harm as a means of distraction from emotional pain. This could transition into more serious self harm and can result in suicidal behaviors if not treated.

- Substance abuse: Many survivors use substances to medicate unpleasant emotions, such as fear or shame.

Common Effects of Stress, Trauma, and Violence

Many people equate stress with an emotional experience, but stress can actually have a profound effect on the body, cognition, and behavior as well.

Common Effects of Stress		
Body	Mood	Behavior
Headache	Anxiety	Overeating or under eating
Muscle tension or pain	Restlessness	Angry outbursts
Chest pain	Lack of motivation or focus	Drug or alcohol abuse
Fatigue	Irritability or anger	Tobacco use
Change in sex drive	Sadness or depression	Social withdrawal
Stomach upset		
Sleep problems		

Although everyone experiences some degree of stress, stress becomes trauma when the intensity of the stress causes a person to feel helpless and seriously threatened, either physically or psychologically. Unfortunately, trauma and violence are common experiences for both adults and children, and the risk for traumatic and/or violent events is particularly high for individuals suffering from mental illness. Some people will experience a trauma with little to no lasting impact, while others may struggle with the aftermath of the trauma for the rest of their lives.

Many variables can either exacerbate or ameliorate the impact of trauma:

- Whether the event occurred once or was ongoing
- Whether the event occurred during childhood or adulthood
- Intensity of the traumatic event
- Personal experience vs. observation
- Ability to access supportive resources
- The way in which people and systems respond to the individual who has been traumatized

Potential effects of trauma and violence:

- Substance use and abuse
- Mental health problems
- Risk-taking behavior
- Self-injurious behavior
- Increased likelihood or exacerbation of chronic illnesses, including cardiovascular disease
- Difficulties with daily functioning, including navigating careers and relationships

Post-Traumatic Stress Disorder (PTSD)

Some people who have experienced trauma or violence will experience an impact significant enough to be diagnosed with PTSD. Symptoms must last for more than one month before the diagnosis of PTSD is considered and must include the following:

- One or more *re-experiencing symptoms* (flashbacks, disturbing dreams, frightening thoughts)

- One or more *avoidance symptoms* (avoiding reminders of the trauma, experiencing emotional "numbing," losing interest in activities that one previously enjoyed)

- Two or more *arousal and reactivity symptoms* (startling easily, experiencing tension, hypervigilance, difficulty falling or staying asleep, eruptions of anger)

- Two or more *cognition and mood symptoms* (difficulty remembering the traumatic event, persistent negative thoughts, excessive feelings of blame or guilt)

Crisis Intervention Theories

Crisis intervention is typically a short-term treatment usually lasting four to six weeks and is implemented when a client enters treatment following some type of traumatic event that causes significant distress. This event causes a state of disequilibrium when a client is out of balance and can no longer function effectively.

Gerald Caplan's Stages of Crises

Caplan theorized that individuals need to maintain homeostasis or remain in balance with their environment. A crisis is caused by an individual's reaction to a situation, not by an actual incident. Following a crisis event, an individual experiences the following stages:

Stage 1
Increase in feelings of stress immediately following the event. Client may experience denial and typically tries to resolve the stressful reactions using past problem-solving and coping skills.

Stage 2
Client experiences higher levels of stress as the usual coping mechanisms fail. Client may employ higher-level coping skills to alleviate the increasing stress levels.

Stage 3
As stressful feelings continue to escalate, client experiences major emotional turmoil, possible feelings of hopelessness, depression, and anxiety.

Stage 4
The final stage is marked by complete psychological and emotional collapse, or the individual finds a method to resolve the situation; however, there may be remaining emotional and psychological dysfunction or impairment if the coping mechanisms used were maladaptive.

Social workers can either use generic crisis intervention models for varied types of crises or can create an individualized plan for assisting the client. The main goal of crisis intervention should be to help clients develop and use adaptive coping skills to return to the level of functioning prior to the crisis.

The Crisis Intervention Process

Engage and Assess

Social workers participate in client engagement by helping to de-escalate volatile emotional states through establishing rapport, using empathy, employing emotional management techniques, and accessing outside systems (family, friends, and support groups). Additionally, the social worker assesses the crisis situation to determine the level of care required (general triage may include intensities ranging from one to three) and how the client has been impacted.

Set Goals and Implement Treatment

Goal setting should occur in collaboration with a client's treatment plan. Intervention strategies, tasks, and timeframes should correspond with the desired goal and objectives. The primary goal should be to assist clients in returning to pre-crisis functioning. However, there will likely be additional and related goals and tasks as the plan of action is implemented.

Evaluate and Terminate

Worker concludes treatment and evaluates completion of goals. It is important to discuss with the client what coping skills have been developed and how they might be able to use those skills for future crises and challenges.

Theories of Trauma-Informed Care

Trauma-informed care refers to providing interventions in a way that accounts for the possibility that a client has had traumatic experiences. The definition of trauma will be relative to the client, but common experiences include major loss, assault, abuse, manipulation, neglect, major injury or accident, and major life change. If these events occur during vulnerable periods in a client's life (such as early childhood), symptoms associated with trauma may be more pervasive or exacerbated. Personal trauma often drives mental health and behavioral conditions, so understanding a client's history and the influence of any experienced trauma is a critical component of providing effective care. Experiences of multiple or repeated trauma are associated with higher rates of substance abuse and other health problems. These can present with additional coinciding and related risk factors, such as poverty, infectious disease, homelessness, or lack of personal support.

The trauma-informed model of care encourages all practitioners who work with clients experiencing mental or physical health issues to recognize the influence of traumatic experiences. This model helps practitioners assess the level of risk assumed by clients, and provides preventative interventions to help mitigate risks at different trauma levels. The client's perspective of how the traumatic event occurred (i.e., unexpectedly or expectedly, from a stranger or loved one), the time during the lifespan in which the event occurred, and other cultural, social, or personal factors determine the level of risk faced by the client. Reactions to traumatic events may manifest less subtly than obvious problems such as substance abuse. They can present as anxiety, pain, muscular tension, elevated heart rates or cortisol levels, depression, headaches, and so on. Therefore, allowing room for the consideration of prior trauma when working with all clients broadens the scope of interventions that practitioners choose to employ.

Impact of the Environment

The Impact of the Physical Environment on Client Systems

The ecological perspective focuses on the *person in environment,* or the interaction between the individual and the environment around them (including physical environment and family). Privilege, or lack thereof, may also have a large impact on the development of individuals.

As mentioned, the *person-in-environment (PIE) theory* emphasizes the importance of viewing and treating a person within the context of their environment, rather than as a completely independent entity. In order to understand and effectively treat a person, it is critical to evaluate the environment they are in and the physical, emotional, and psychological impact that it has had as related to individual strengths and needs. The environment includes the dynamics of family, school, work place, culture, and social relationships. Rather than being exclusively person-focused or environment-focused, the PIE theory looks at the interplay between the two. If a person is displaying anxiety or depression, for example, the goal would be to determine what cultural, social, or familial factors may be playing a role. PIE seeks to have a holistic view, which then leads to broader and more comprehensive treatment options.

The importance of the PIE theory can be seen when working with children. Often children are identified as the primary problem, with behavioral or emotional issues. However, when the situation is explored more closely, there are almost always other factors that are contributing to the child's behaviors, including parental conflict, abuse and neglect, or some traumatic experience. Without evaluating the context the child is in, but instead focusing exclusively on that child's behaviors, it is impossible to determine the root cause of the presenting problem or the most appropriate steps to take. Similarly, it would be futile to merely change or address the child's environment without also dealing directly with the child's emotional and behavioral needs. The person, their emotions and behaviors, as well as their environment and the context in which they live, are all significant when it comes to planning a treatment.

The Impact of the Political Environment on Policy-Making and Client Systems

Social welfare legislation can have a dramatic effect on social work practice. Some legislation may help solve social problems that social workers encounter and other legislation may create more problems, challenges, and barriers through which social workers must help clients navigate. To be effective, social workers must be knowledgeable about legislative measures that affect clients. Another possible role of a social worker is that of legislative advocate, which is working to change, modify, or create legislation for the benefit of a group of people.

Significant Social Welfare Legislation:

- Civil Rights Act of 1964
- Older Americans Act of 1965
- The Child Abuse and Prevention Act of 1974
- Adoption Assistance and Child Welfare Act of 1980
- Americans with Disabilities Act of 1990
- The Family Medical Leave Act of 1993
- The Health Insurance Portability and Accountability Act of 1996 (HIPAA)
- The Patient Protection and Affordable Care Act of 2010

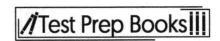

Impact of Social Environment on Client Systems

Social institutions exist to meet the needs of individuals, promote pro-social behavior, define social norms, and create order.

There are five major social institutions:

Family
- Regulates sexual behavior (monogamy)
- Creates and provides for new society members
- Socializes new society members

Religion
- Provides explanations for the unexplainable
- Supports societal norms and values
- Provides a means of coping with life situations

Government
- Institutionalizes norms (by creating laws)
- Enforces laws
- Protects members of society
- Provides a means of resolving conflict

Education
- Prepares society members to contribute to the society in specified roles
- Teaches skills necessary to function within the society

Economics
- Produces and distributes goods needed by society members
- Provides services necessary to the society

Impact of Economic Changes on Client Systems

Economic changes, particularly negative ones, can have a substantial impact on client systems.

- In times of economic turmoil, people tend to cut back on spending and stop seeking services in order to conserve money. Over time, this can lead to a backlog of individuals with major problems that need to be addressed, burdening many components of society.

- A poor economic climate can also exacerbate pre-existing problems, such as depression or substance abuse, and can create significantly more stress on the family unit, which may spill over into work or school.

- Unemployment has been linked to a withdrawal from social activity, low self-esteem, an increased sense of hopelessness, poorer mental health, and an increase in substance use.

- Such change has an impact within a family, and when enough families are affected, entire communities can experience shifts in attitude and behaviors.

- The experience of living in poverty for many years or at crucial points in time is linked to certain individual outcomes. Children living at the poverty level during preschool and elementary school years are less likely to finish their schooling than are those who experience poverty during later childhood or adolescence only.

- When economic factors are at play with regard to a client's well-being, social workers must be prepared to assist with the development of appropriate coping skills and identification of resources for the client and family system.

The Impact of the Cultural Environment on Client Systems

As mentioned, it is important not to use information about culture, race, and ethnicity in a stereotypical or overgeneralized manner. There are vast differences within groups. For example, group members holding a traditional viewpoint are likely to identify very strongly with their group and to reject the practices of other groups. In contrast, other individuals may be acculturated into a dominant group culture and may not identify with their culture of origin.

Race refers to biologically distinct populations within the human species. *Ethnicity* is a cultural term referring to the common customs, language, and heritage of a category of people. *Ethnic identity* is the identification with a particular group of people who share one's culture and heritage.

William Cross's Stages of Identity Development

William Cross is a theorist and researcher in the field of ethnicity identity development. He is known for his Nigrescence model and for his novel *Shades of Black*. The following depicts William Cross's Stages of Identity Development for people of color:

- Pre-encounter: Unless prompted to do so, children do not critically evaluate the race-related messages that they receive from the world around them.

- Encounter: Often experienced in early adolescence, the individual has one or more experiences that are related to race. Though it is possible for the experiences to be positive, this is often when an individual first experiences racism or discrimination and begins to understand the personal impact of their race.

- Immersion-Emersion: After experiencing a race-related incident, the individual strongly identifies with their racial group and may seek out information about history and culture.

- Internalization: Racial identity is solidified, and the individual experiences a sense of security in identifying with their race.

- Internalization-Commitment: Racial identity is taken one step further into activism pertaining to issues related to the experiences of the individual's racial group.

Sue & Sue's Stages of Racial/Cultural Identity Development

Derald Sue and David Sue developed *Stages of Racial/Cultural Identity Development*. Derald Sue is a professor of counseling psychology at Colombia University. David Sue is a professor emeritus of psychology at Western Washington University. Their works revolve around multicultural issues in

counseling and multicultural therapy. The following are the stages of racial-cultural identity development:

- Conformity: The individual displays a distinct preference for the dominant culture and holds negative views of their own racial and/or cultural groups. They may also experience shame or embarrassment.

- Dissonance: The individual undergoes a period of re-thinking or challenging their beliefs. For the first time, the individual examines and appreciates positive aspects of their own racial/cultural group.

- Resistance and Immersion: The individual shows preference for minority views and actively rejects the views of the dominant culture, experiencing pride about and connection to their racial or cultural group.

- Introspection: The individual becomes aware of the negative impact of the resistance and immersion stage and may realize that they do not actually disagree with all majority views or endorse all minority views.

- Integrative Awareness: The individual is able to appreciate both their own culture and differing cultures.

Life Events, Stressors, and Crises on Individuals, Families, Groups, Organizations, and Communities

Life events are experienced by all families and can be both positive and negative—everything from marriage or childbirth to death or divorce. If the life event is more negative and sudden, it may be considered a crisis, such as the unexpected loss of a family member, diagnosis of a major illness, a car crash, financial trouble, or something even more intense like a natural disaster or terrorist attack. Even positive life events can become crises for families if they have difficulty adjusting to the changes. Crises often involve both hard decisions and emotional turmoil.

The *ABCX Model*, introduced by Reuben Hill, seeks to explain how families deal with stressful situations that arise. A is the event that occurs, B is the family resources, C is the family perception, and X stands for a crisis. It claims that the event, plus the family resources and plus the family's perception, all combine to determine whether the event is viewed as a crisis and whether the family is able to cope with it. Depending on the family's ability to adapt their normal functioning patterns, a life event or crisis can either strengthen their relationships and the family unit or tear them apart. A family can effectively deal with the crisis if they utilize *positive coping mechanisms*, such as pursuing practical solutions to deal with the issues that arise, seeking counseling from a therapist or clergy, engaging social supports, and communicating openly with each other. *Negative coping strategies* could involve drug or alcohol use, isolation, or displacement of anger and frustration onto family members. Though all families will face a period of disordered chaos in trying to deal with a crisis, the families that are successful are those that can engage in new and positive coping methods.

Person-In-Environment (PIE) Theory

Carel Germain described person-in environment interaction, based upon earlier work in systems theory. This perspective takes into consideration an individual's environmental and systemic influences. It is specific to social work, which differentiates it from other like professions.

- Life stress: the normal tension that occurs as the result of both external demands and internal experiences

  ○ What is experienced as stressful varies across people and their perceptions. For example, two people placed in the same environment may have completely different experiences due to the ways in which they experience and perceive the situation.

- Adaptation: when the environment and the individual change in response to the interaction with each other

- Coping: individual use of one's own strengths and problem-solving abilities to navigate life stress and develop self-esteem and hope

- Power: a source of stress to the individual and the larger system misused by groups

- Human Relatedness: the ability of individuals to cultivate relationships

- Three related concepts are *self-direction*, *competence*, and *self-esteem*. These attributes are interdependent and occur cross-culturally.

Communication Theories and Styles

One of the main names associated with communication theory is Niklas Luhmann, a sociologist and systems theorist. In Luhmann's theory, it is the communication *between* people and not the people themselves that makes up a social system.

Luhmann uses the term *autopoiesis* to define social systems as self-creating. By this he means the social system has the ability to produce itself and maintain itself. Luhmann believed that communications make up the system, and communications create other communications. The meaning of a communication is the response it generates.

The Shannon and Weaver model of communication, though its origins are mathematical and technical, is cited as one of the primary communication models. This model was the first to conceptualize the activity of the sender and the receiver. For communication to occur in this model, the sending entity has to prepare and actively deliver information, and the receiver has to wait and actively accept information. The Berlo model of communication added that all communication also needed a channel over which to travel.

There are four primary communication styles. Passive communication refers to senders who avoid full, direct, and clear verbal or written expression to send a message. Rather, their body language and behaviors may provide a large chunk of the intended message. Passive communicators tend to avoid direct communication; they are unassertive, quiet, and anxious. Aggressive communicators are overly direct senders, so much so that their communications may harm those who are listening to them. Aggressive communicators are characterized as dominating, impulsive, and critical. Passive-aggressive

communication refers to senders who outwardly show mildly expressive communication but inwardly feel aggression that is manifested in body language or behavior. Passive-aggressive communicators often have a difficult time with confrontation, expressing powerful feelings, and understanding anger. Assertive communication refers to senders who are clear and firm yet considerate when stating their message. Assertive communicators tend to speak clearly, feel in control, and respect themselves and others.

Psychoanalytic and Psychodynamic Approaches

Psychodynamic approaches engage clients in discovering how their unconscious drives affect their conscious lives. Unconscious drives include sexual and aggression drives that may be unknown to the client on a conscious level. Clients engage in stream of consciousness discussion with the therapist, and the therapist acts mostly as a listener. There is also a focus on dream interpretation in psychodynamic approaches, in which clients are encouraged to discuss their dream states with the social worker. Psychodynamic approaches originate with Freud's "talking cure," in which Freud encouraged clients to attend sessions several times a week.

There are several psychoanalytic organizations in the United States devoted to psychodynamic training. These schools usually have multiyear programs to train new psychoanalysts. While psychodynamic approaches may not encompass the entirety of a client's experience, they are a useful approach for certain clients and may be integrated into psychotherapeutic treatment along with other approaches.

Carl Jung's Psychoanalytic Theory

Jung's theory is similar to Freud's psychoanalytic theory, with differences related to the purpose of the libido, the unconscious, and behavioral motives. Libido is a psychic energy that motivates individuals.

Jung theorized two parts to the unconscious:

- Personal unconscious: contains information not accessible to the conscious mind
- Collective unconscious (transpersonal): the memories from a person's ancestors that the individual has from birth

Jung identified this collective unconscious into four main archetypes.

- Persona: the artificial self that an individual shows to the world to hide who they really are
- Anima/Animas: the masculine qualities that women express to society and the feminine qualities that men express to society
- Shadow: similar to Freud's id, signifies raw needs and desires
- Self: the unconscious and conscious mind come together to form a unified whole, occurs as a consequence of individuation

Impact of Caregiving on Families

There are about 10 million Americans over the age of fifty who are caring for aging parents. In the last fifteen years, thanks to modern medicine, the adult population has begun living longer. As a result, the number of adult children between the ages of fifty and seventy who provide care to aging parents has tripled. This amounts to about 25 percent of adult children who provide either personal or economic assistance.

Research indicates that becoming a personal caregiver to a parent increases the rates of depression, substance abuse, and heart disease. These adult children sometimes take significant financial blows in the form of lost income, earlier than planned retirement, and reduced pension plans, due to leaving the workforce earlier. At the same time, these adult children are assisting their own children as they move towards independence. Those in the youngest generation may still be in college or in the early stages of starting a career and still look to parents for some financial assistance. From a different perspective, the positives of this situation are that children are able to form deeper bonds with grandparents, and the longevity of life in loved ones can have very positive impact on all involved.

Loss, Separation, and Grief

The concept of loss is at the root of many depressive episodes. Losses can include anything one holds dearly. Losing a loved one, a pet, a job, housing, or financial or social status can all bring emotional pain. Other losses include the loss of physical or mental health. Separation is a form of loss that can occur in many forms, including divorce, military deployment, a job that requires one to move far away, or the loss of custody of a child. Grief is the emotional response to loss. Grief includes the main emotion of sadness, but other strong emotions may be present as well. Other feelings include confusion, anger, frustration, anxiety, or guilt.

The five stages of grief is a concept developed by Elisabeth Kubler-Ross in her book *On Death and Dying* in 1969. The five stages model originally pertained to those experiencing the dying process as the result of a terminal illness, but the model has been widely used to understand the grief reactions that people have in response to a number of situations, including loss of a loved one. The stages were first posited to be linear, but Kubler-Ross later stated that they are five common experiences that may or may not be experienced during grieving.

Denial
This is the first stage. It occurs at the point that the person on some level becomes aware that they have lost someone or something dear, but on another level, they refuse to accept the truth. This stage is generally brief as the person begins to process irrefutable evidence.

Anger
This is a period of venting anger at anyone who the person feels contributed to the loss occurring. It may be towards God, the drunk driver who caused an accident, or the CPS worker who takes a child from the home. In the case of a suicide, there could be anger at the deceased for choosing to leave.

Bargaining
This stage is almost a form of magical thinking. A person may think that if they promise to do better, work harder, or pray harder, the loss process can be reversed. This again is generally a short-lived phase as one realizes that promises made will still not bring back that which has been lost.

Depression
During the fourth stage, a person allows themself to feel the sadness, and they may experience an even deeper emotional pain while learning to accept the loss and move forward. It may be a time of crying, despondency, and anguish. It must be experienced in order to move to the next stage.

Acceptance

The last stage is the point at which the grieving person recognizes that, while the pain is tremendous, they will be able to handle it. Those at this stage understand that time will ease some of the suffering. They are learning to make peace with the experience and move forward with their lives.

Concepts of Abuse and Neglect

Physical abuse is the intentional act of physical force that may result in pain, injury, or impairment to a child or other dependent. Physical abuse is typically thought of as violent acts such as hitting, kicking, burning, etc., but it may also include extreme physical discipline, force-feeding, and some uses of drugs or restraints. Physical indicators of physical abuse are multiple physical injuries in various stages of healing; physical injuries that are inconsistent with an individual's account of how the injuries occurred; multiple injuries, accidents, or unexplained illnesses occurring over a period of time; and injuries reflecting the object used to inflict the injury (e.g., cigarette burns, tooth marks, bruising in the shape of finger/hand marks). Behavioral indicators of physical abuse are flinching; offering inconsistent explanations of injuries or being unable to remember how injuries occurred; exhibiting wariness around adults or authority figures; aggression or abusive behavior toward others; and withdrawn, sad, depressed, or even suicidal behavior.

Neglect is failure by a parent or other responsible party to provide basic needs for a child or other dependent, resulting in endangerment of the dependent. Basic needs of a dependent are food, adequate supervision, medical care, shelter, or clothing. Some indicators of neglect are not registering for school or not attending school (if a school-aged child), abandonment, inappropriately dressing for the weather or season, poor hygiene, lack of shelter, ingestion of dangerous substances, recurrent hunger and/or malnourishment, and untreated medical conditions.

Abuse and Neglect Throughout the Lifespan

Indicators and Dynamics of Sexual Abuse

Sexual abuse is forced or coerced sexual contact or exposure, usually by someone older or in a position of authority over the victim. Sexual abuse can also include forcing someone to watch sexual acts or receive messages involving unwanted sexual content. The impact of sexual abuse is complex, and the emotional and psychological response to the trauma may evolve as the victim gets older and understands more fully what happened to them. Children who suffer sexual abuse may struggle from confusion about the abuse, especially if they are told by the perpetrator that it is right and good and if that person is someone with whom they have a relationship of trust. They may be blamed by the perpetrator for the abuse, which leads to further feelings of confusion and guilt. If they report the abuse to someone who does not believe it, the long term effects of the abuse may be even greater, as well as the guilt, self-doubt, and shame. A history of sexual abuse will normally impact a person's relationships with others throughout life, and there may be issues of trust as well as confused feelings toward sex.

Indicators of Sexual Abuse (Child)
- The statement that one has been sexually assaulted
- Mistrust or fear of those who bear resemblance to the abuser, potentially due to gender or size (children may be mistrustful of all adults)
- Changes in behavior
- Depression
- Anxiety with presenting symptoms (hair loss, fluctuations in weight)

- Increased fearfulness (possible night terrors and enuresis/bed wetting from children)
- Withdrawal from preferred activities/social isolation
- Compulsive masturbation
- Substance abuse
- Overly-sexualized behavior
- Parent, spouse, or caregiver demonstrating inappropriate behaviors
- Role confusion, distortion of child's role in the family
- Jealousness or over-protection of the victim
- Excessive, abnormal alone time with the child
- Lack of appropriate social and emotional contacts outside the home
- Substance and/or alcohol abuse
- Parent or caregiver reports being sexually abused previously (possible normalization or continuation of the cyclic behavior)

Indicators and Dynamics of Psychological Abuse and Neglect

Psychological abuse—or emotional abuse—is more difficult to define than sexual or physical abuse, but it can be just as damaging to the victim. Psychological neglect, especially as a child, involves withholding the love, affection, and emotional security that a child needs in order to grow and thrive. Psychological abuse involves emotional manipulation that uses strategies of shame, fear, and guilt to control someone's behaviors. Another aspect of psychological abuse can be verbal abuse which takes the form of yelling, constant criticisms or belittling, threats, or name-calling. Alternatively, the child may be ignored, be made the witness of violence, or isolated as a punishment. These are all forms of psychological abuse and neglect. Because of the often vague or indefinable aspects of psychological abuse, it may be difficult for victims to understand or believe that they are being mistreated. Even if they do, they may be convinced that no one will believe them because of the manipulation of the perpetrator, who may either threaten or undermine the victim to such an extent that they are unwilling to take any action. Long-term, a victim of psychological abuse is more likely to be fearful and withdrawn as a result of the many insecurities that have developed because of the abuse.

Indicators and Dynamics of Physical Abuse and Neglect

Physical abuse can be defined as bodily mistreatment, including hitting, slapping, kicking, burning, unnecessary constraints, strangling, or other acts of physical violence. Physical abuse is often perpetrated out of anger or frustration, as is the case with parents who use physical abuse to inappropriately discipline their children. In cases where there is a higher level of family stress or conflict or when parents have not received adequate training in parenting strategies, the levels of physical abuse may be higher. Physical abuse can also take place in adult relationships, most usually in an intimate relationship where one person struggles with anger management. Victims of physical abuse may show obvious signs of the abuse, such as injuries or multiple trips to the emergency room. However, there are other less obvious signs of physical abuse, such as fearful withdrawal, aggression, or other acting-out.

Physical neglect is withholding anything that is necessary for physical health and safety, as well as educational and medical needs. If a parent, for example, does not provide a child with enough food or with warm clothes in the winter, this would be considered neglect. This type of neglect can sometimes be deliberate, but may also be the result of ignorance or a lack of resources.

Effects of Physical, Sexual, and Psychological Abuse

People may experience abuse at the hands of strangers, caretakers, or close friends and family. The effects of abuse are traumatic, pervasive, and long lasting. Beyond affecting the abused parties, abuse often impacts those who are close to the victims. Physical, sexual, and psychological child abuse can lead to impaired intellect, learning abilities, deficits in trust and language skills, and long-term inappropriate behaviors or lack of coping mechanisms. As abused children grow, they may be unable to make healthy friendships or desire or maintain intimate relationships. They may have failed marriages, or they may perpetuate the cycle of abuse when they become parents. They may often feel unworthy or that they did something to cause the abuse. This often has an impact on their attachment styles and how they relate to others.

In adults, abuse may cause permanent or temporary physical damage, low self-esteem, shame, despair, or feelings of helplessness. Victims of abuse as an adult may experience mental health disorders such anxiety and depression. If children witness their loved ones experiencing abuse, it may be traumatic for them, or they may normalize the behavior and perpetuate abuse themselves. Elder abuse, especially in nursing homes, often goes undetected as victims may be weak or losing mental faculties. Elders are especially vulnerable to physical and financial abuse. Effects may include rapid physical or mental deterioration, submissiveness, bedsores, increased rate of illness, or premature death.

In traumatic cases, both children and adults may become severely depressed or anxious. They may abuse substances or commit suicide.

Exploitation Across the Lifespan

Exploitation is taking advantage of someone in a vulnerable position for personal gain.

Financial exploitation of older adults occurs when caretakers, family members, or other individuals take advantage of the elderly member's finances. Indicators of financial exploitation are missing identification, money, credit cards, documents, or valuable possessions; large or frequent checks made out to cash; frequent or expensive gifts for caregiver; older adult's unawareness of income or bills; and blank checks, cash withdrawals, or money wires/transfers.

Sexual exploitation of children occurs when an individual takes advantage of a minor by trading sexual acts or pornography for basic needs. Indication of sexual exploitation are spending time with older individuals or an older "boyfriend" or "girlfriend"; spending time in inappropriate locations such as hotels or bars; signs of emotional or physical abuse or neglect; uncertainty of where one's self is (as they have moved around to various geographic locations); missing from home or not attending school; fearful or anxious around others; signs of being groomed (someone building a connection with the child, either online or in-person, in order to gain trust and ultimately abuse and/or exploit the child). Individuals who are being groomed might be secretive about their behavior, might possess unexplained money or items, and may have access to alcohol and/or drugs.

Girls are disproportionately affected by sexual exploitation and trafficking. The majority of children and adolescents are exploited by someone they know.

Perpetrators of Abuse, Neglect and Exploitation

Abuse perpetrators are individuals who cause or allow mistreatment of a child or other dependent. Common characteristics of abuse perpetrators are having experienced or witnessed abuse during childhood; lack of coping skills to manage anger and frustration; isolation or lack of a substantial support system; immaturity with poor regulation of emotions; abuse of alcohol or other substances; inappropriate expectations for the behavior of others; and poor social skills.

Diversity, Social/Economic Justice, and Oppression

Effect of Disability on Biopsychosocial Functioning Throughout the Lifespan

Disability can be a difficult adjustment, especially when it comes on acutely. People may experience disability from a traumatic incident, or it may come on gradually from a chronic disease. Some individuals are born with disabilities; they and their families and caregivers must adjust traditional ways of living. The biopsychosocial model is a view that accounts for biological factors, psychological factors, social factors, and their interplay within certain contexts. With regard to disability, an individual who experiences a disability is likely to feel biological changes, psychological adjustments, and social issues. From a biological perspective, an individual with a disability may have a body part that does not function typically. This in turn may affect adjacent body parts or other biological functions. For example, a patient with a heart disability is also likely to have certain vascular dysfunctions. From a psychological standpoint, an individual with a disability may have trouble adjusting if the disability is sudden (i.e., an unanticipated amputation).

This individual may struggle with feelings of depression or low self-worth, or they may simply feel a general sense of limitation. Socially, people with disabilities may feel it is more difficult for them to do things that other people can do easily. They may worry about making friends or finding romantic relationships, or they may worry that they will be unfairly discriminated against in public or in the workplace. Children, especially, may experience teasing or exclusion from peers who are not developmentally mature enough to regularly exhibit sensitivity and compassion. Adults and elders with disabilities may mourn losses of freedom or changes in their lifestyles more than children who were born with disabilities and therefore have not experienced any other way of living. Practitioners who work with individuals experiencing disability should use strengths-based approaches to empower the client to live as well as they can with a disability. Acceptance, positive reinforcement, positive perspective and mindsets, and fostering a sense of community among individuals who are facing similar struggles are ways to support individuals with disabilities.

Effect of Culture, Race, and Ethnicity on Behaviors, Attitudes, and Identity

Societally, culture, race, and ethnicity appear to be distinguished by certain behaviors, attitudes, and identities. These may be misinterpreted, rejected, or stereotyped by other groups. Data show that minority groups tend to have less access to and receive fewer health care services; minority groups also tend to have higher rates of chronic disease. Additionally, these groups are more likely to be punished or incarcerated than are majority groups for the same crimes. This may lead to sense of learned helplessness, in which minority groups believe they cannot eliminate these risks and tendencies from their lives and that these patterns of societal activity are normal. The theory of learned helplessness also states that those who experience the phenomenon are also more likely to suffer from mental illness, such as depression and anxiety. These individuals may also become more defensive and aggressive as a result.

Additionally, the misunderstanding of certain cultural beliefs may promote rejection or outward hatred of some groups. This can lead to behaviors of microaggression, which are daily, relatively ingrained acts performed by society to marginalize some groups. It can also lead to large-scale instances of violence

and rejection, including bullying and homicide of minority group members due to their perceived differences.

Effects of Discrimination and Stereotypes on Behaviors, Attitudes, and Identity

Discrimination is the unfair or unequal treatment of a person or group, based upon a characteristic, such as race, ethnicity, religion, age, sex, or sexual orientation. There are several forms of discrimination that minorities experience.

Direct discrimination refers to unfair treatment based on someone's characteristics. An example would be refusing to hire someone because of their ethnicity.

Indirect discrimination refers to situations in which a policy applies the same to everyone, but a person or group of people are negatively impacted due to certain characteristics. For example, a company might require that everyone help unload shipments that come to the office. The policy is the same for everyone, but it's discriminatory towards any disabled employees. In a workplace environment, indirect discrimination can sometimes be allowed if there's a compelling reason for the requirement. For example, firefighters have to meet certain physical criteria due to the nature of their work.

Another form of discrimination is *harassment*. This involves unwanted bullying or humiliation intentionally directed to a person of minority status. *Victimization* refers to the unfair treatment received when a person reports discrimination and is not supported by authorities.

Effects of discrimination on the individual may include depression, anxiety, and other mental health issues; and medical/health-related problems caused by lack of access to health resources. Effects of discrimination on society include diminished resources (e.g. employment, educational opportunities, healthcare) and a culture characterized by fear, anger, or apathy.

Influence of Sexual Orientation on Behaviors, Attitudes, and Identity

Even with today's advances in technology, medicine, and genetics, scientists have not clearly established how sexual orientation develops. It is believed that sexual orientation is a complex interplay of environmental, hormonal, and genetic influences. According to the American Psychological Association, *sexual orientation* refers to an innate attraction. As such, the Association opposes psychiatric treatments such as *conversion therapy*—a form of treatment designed to help homosexuals become heterosexuals through therapy and, sometimes, medical interventions.

Research indicates that family composition may play a role in sexual orientation. For example, homosexual males are more likely to have older male siblings than homosexual women. For men, other factors include being the youngest child, having older mothers, absent fathers, or divorced parents. In women, examples include being an only child, youngest child, being the only girl in the sibling group, or the death of a mother during adolescence. Setting and culture also influence homosexual behavior, i.e., urban areas vs. rural areas.

Impact of Transgender and Transitioning Process on Behaviors, Attitudes, Identity, and Relationships

Being transgender can be defined as identifying as a gender other than they the gender one was assigned at birth. Publicly sharing that one is transgender can be difficult for some individuals. Transgender individuals may live in a community where their identity is not positively accepted or is misunderstood, and they may feel shamed or ridiculed. It may be a difficult experience for close family members to understand the perspective of a transgender individual, which can affect the cohesiveness of family relationships and the family unit. Transgender individuals may also feel a lack of acknowledgement when others fail to use the correct pronouns or respect other identity wishes.

Some transgender individuals choose to medically transition to the gender they identify as. This is a procedure that requires physical, emotional, and psychological support. Individuals not receiving support during their transition can experience extreme feelings of sadness, isolation, and lack of belonging. Medically transitioning individuals also undergo hormonal changes in addition to surgical procedures, and these can cause unexpected feelings and reactions in the individual. There are also medical risks that go along with both the surgical and hormonal procedures of transitioning that the individual has to be aware of and manage. Finally, after the transition is complete, individuals may struggle with living as someone who is relatively unfamiliar to their friends, family members, and colleagues. The transgender person may or may not experience support and acceptance in these groups and relationships, and some group members may even act aggressively toward the transgender person. If this is the case, it may be helpful to find support groups where transgender individuals can find not only friendship and community, but also guidance on how to navigate their new life, society, friends and relationships, and medical recovery.

Systemic Discrimination

Systemic (institutionalized) discrimination refers to discrimination taking place within a society or other institution (e.g., a religion or educational system). Such discrimination can be either intentional or unintentional and results from the majority of people within the institution holding stereotypical beliefs and engaging in discriminatory practices.

Systemic discrimination is often reflected in the laws, policies, or practices of the institution. Systemic discrimination creates or maintains a disadvantage to a group of people by way of patterns of behavior; it can have wide-reaching effects within a region, profession, or specific institution.

The following are example of systemic discrimination:

- Hiring practices that create barriers or result in lower wages for certain groups

- U.S. Supreme Court case, *Plessy vs. Ferguson* (1896) – "separate but equal" public facilities for African-Americans

- Oppression of women in certain countries (e.g., being unable to vote, obtain education, or hold jobs)

Culturally Competent Social Work Practice

Social workers must be culturally competent to meet the needs of all clients. One way to do this is to have the staff demographics reflective of the community served. Workers must also recognize the differences in individuals of the same culture and not use a cookie-cutter approach to deal with people of the same demographic group. Social workers must also work to create agency policies that encourage culturally sensitive treatment and do not allow discriminatory practices. When choosing interventions, treatment methods, and evaluation techniques, workers must also consider the appropriateness of the

selection for the client's cultural background. According to the NASW Code of Ethics, social workers must:

- Understand and be knowledgeable of their clients' culture and demonstrate sensitivity in providing services.

- Become educated as it relates to oppression and diversity regarding race, ethnicity, nationality, gender, disability, sexual orientation, age, and religion.

- Be aware of their own biases and prejudices and use culturally sensitive language in communications with clients.

Gender, Gender Identity, and Sexual Orientation Concepts

The term *gender* refers to a range of physical, behavioral, psychological, or cultural characteristics that create the difference between masculinity and femininity. *Gender identity* is a person's understanding of his or her own gender, especially as it relates to being male or female. *Sexual orientation* is a more complex concept as it refers to the type of sexual attraction one feels for others. This is not to be confused with *sexual preference*, which refers to the specific types of sexual stimulation one most enjoys.

Types of Sexual Orientation
- Heterosexual: An individual who is sexually and emotionally attracted to members of the opposite gender, also known as "straight"

- Homosexual: An individual who is sexually and emotionally attracted to members of the same gender, sometimes referred to as "gay" or "lesbian"

- Bisexual: A male or female who is sexually attracted to both same and opposite gender sex partners

- Asexual: An individual who has a low level of interest in sexual interactions with others

Types of Gender Identity
- Bi-gender: An individual who fluctuates between the self-image of traditionally male and female stereotypes and identifies with both genders

- Transgender: A generalized term referring to a variety of sexual identities that do not fit under more traditional categories, a person who feels to be of a different gender than the one he or she is born with

- Transsexual: A person who identifies emotionally and psychologically with the gender other than that assigned at birth, lives as a person of the opposite gender

Those who are transgender or transsexual may be homosexual, heterosexual, or asexual.

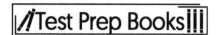

Social and Economic Justice

Professional Commitment to Promoting Social Justice

Social justice is defined as equal rights, opportunities, and privileges for all members of society. The Code of Ethics of the National Association of Social Workers (revised 2008) specifically lists social justice as a core value. The NASW Code of Ethics states, "Social workers pursue social change, particularly with and on behalf of vulnerable and oppressed individuals and groups of people. Social workers' social change efforts are focused primarily on issues of poverty, unemployment, discrimination, and other forms of social injustice. These activities seek to promote sensitivity to and knowledge about oppression and cultural and ethnic diversity. Social workers strive to ensure access to needed information, services, and resources; equality of opportunity; and meaningful participation in decision making for all people."

The Effect of Poverty

Poverty is often the foundation of a number of other socioeconomic and health problems faced by individuals, families, and communities. Without resources such as money, transportation, or housing, it becomes difficult to buy healthy food, access medical care, drive to work, have quality childcare, or live in a safe area. For adults in poverty, the extreme level of stress that arises from trying to pay bills, provide basic necessities for themselves and their families, and manage multiple jobs often leads to a number of mental, physical, and emotional problems. These can include substance abuse, domestic violence, inability to maintain family units and romantic relationships, hopelessness, depression, and desperation. Children who live and grow up in poverty are prone to traumatic and catastrophic health risk factors, such as experiencing or witnessing violence, chronic malnutrition, higher rates of illness, and mood disorders. Experiencing such adverse events in childhood is associated with high levels of stress, impaired functioning, and impaired cognitive ability that can be irreparable. Individuals experiencing poverty are more likely to visit the emergency room for health problems (and often be unable to pay), require government assistance, and commit crimes (often in order to obtain necessary resources). These outcomes create a financial burden on the community and local economy.

Impact of Social Institutions on Society

Social institutions exist to meet the needs of individuals, promote pro-social behavior, define social norms, and create order.

There are five major social institutions:

Family
- Regulates sexual behavior (monogamy)
- Creates and provides for new society members
- Socializes new society members

Religion
- Provides explanations for the unexplainable
- Supports societal norms and values
- Provides a means of coping with life situations

Government
- Institutionalizes norms (by creating laws)
- Enforces laws
- Protects members of society
- Provides a means of resolving conflict

Education
- Prepares society members to contribute to the society in specified roles
- Teaches skills necessary to function within the society

Economics
- Produces and distributes goods needed by society members
- Provides services necessary to the society

Criminal Justice Systems

Social workers can have an important role in the criminal justice system. Prison and jail systems are full, and less than a third of incarcerated individuals who are released remain free. Most end up back in the criminal justice system. Additionally, a number of incarcerated individuals have mental and emotional disorders that often contribute to unlawful behavior. These can include substance abuse problems or high levels of personal stress. Social workers are trained to understand these contexts, and therefore they can provide valuable insight and counsel before, during, and after legal cases. Therefore, social workers can intervene and offer support during all phases of the justice system. Social workers can work with individuals who were the victims of criminal activities. They are also able to work with perpetrators who have been released, thereby helping to prevent re-incarceration. Social workers can also provide support to the families of both victims and perpetrators, assist with the transition of having family member in jail, assist with the transition of having a family member released, and support in educational and professional activities after release. Finally, social workers can have a meaningful impact in the lives of children who may be at risk of ending up in the criminal justice system. By focusing interventions on vulnerable youth, such as education, positive recreational activities, mentoring programs, support for parents, and so on, social workers potentially have the ability to prevent youth and families from ever entering the criminal justice system. This is much more powerful approach for positive behavior and social change, rather than addressing individual, family, and community issues after crimes have already been committed. Social workers will need to remember to show compassion and withhold judgment when working with criminal offenders; however, they must also be mindful to protect their personal safety in these situations.

Impact of Globalization on Clients

Globalization, or the process of working and operating in a hyper-connected, international capacity, has affected nearly every industry, including social work. Social workers are no longer limited to working with clients who are in close geographical proximity. They now have the ability to connect with audiences and clients all over the world through social media, email, virtual consultation, and web platforms. This expanded level of outreach can be positive, in that mental health and behavioral interventions, support, and awareness are more easily accessible. However, connecting online with clients can sometimes hinder the quality of personal interaction that practitioners cultivate with their clients. Additionally, it can be tricky to navigate the financial, legal, and security aspects of working with clients online, as these standards vary by geographical location.

Globalization has also opened new topics of interest for social workers. Globalization has led to increased working time, increased use of technology, and increased interactions across cultural, socioeconomic, and gender lines. In many ways, these changes have been associated with higher levels of work-related stress, health problems such poor sleep, increased rates of mood disorders such as depression and anxiety, and higher awareness of harassment against women and subordinate employees. These are all issues that social workers may not have typically handled with clients in previous decades. They must now become skilled in addressing these issues. Finally, the use of technology, screens, and social media in children has been potentially linked with addictive behaviors, cyberbullying, and increased depression and anxiety rates. This is yet another avenue in which social workers must develop interventions that work in a relatively new context with variables about which research is still emerging.

Practice Questions

1. What is the last stage of Freud's model of the five stages of human development?
    a. Latent stage
    b. Adult stage
    c. Genital stage
    d. Self-Actualization stage

2. In Erikson's eight stages of development, Identity Versus Role confusion begins at age twelve and contains all but which of the following challenges?
    a. Working through and understanding multiple changes and demands placed upon the child as he or she moves towards adulthood.
    b. Increasing understanding of sexual, hormonal, and other physical changes that are occurring.
    c. Finding a long-term partner and starting a family.
    d. Assessment of one's talents, sexual preferences, and vocational interests.

3. According to Piaget, what is the process by which old ideas or beliefs must be replaced with new ones due to obtaining new and more factual information?
    a. Schemas
    b. Assimilation
    c. Object permanence
    d. Accommodation

4. Ivan Pavlov is best known in the field of psychology for his concepts regarding which of the following?
    a. Classical conditioning
    b. Training dogs to behave obediently
    c. Development of sexual identity and orientation
    d. How positive reinforcement helps developmentally developed children.

5. According to B.F. Skinner, providing positive reinforcement increases the likelihood that a desired behavior will be repeated. Which of the following is NOT a form of positive reinforcement when working with children?
    a. A trip to the park with Mom following a week of good behavior
    b. Praise in response to a task well done
    c. Taking TV and computer privileges for a week
    d. Putting a colorful sticker on a poster each time the child goes to bed on time

6. As an elementary school social worker, you are interacting with an eight-year-old child who is unable to speak clearly or coherently, who sometimes has issues with bladder control, and who cannot yet tie his own shoes. The child should receive further assessment for which of the following?
    a. Developmental Delays
    b. Conduct Disorder
    c. Genetic Deficiencies
    d. Oppositional Defiant Disorder

7. Most researchers divide adult development into three sections of life following the end of adolescence. What are these three sections called?

a. Early adulthood (ages eighteen to forty), middle adulthood (ages forty to sixty-five), and late adulthood (age sixty-five until death)

b. Post adolescence (ages eighteen to twenty-four), middle adulthood (ages twenty-five to forty), and mature adulthood (age forty until death)

c. Initial adulthood (ages eighteen to thirty-five), middle adulthood (ages thirty-six to sixty) and later life stage (age sixty until death)

d. Stage one adulthood (ages eighteen to twenty-eight), stage two adulthood (ages twenty-nine to fifty-eight), and stage three adulthood (age fifty-nine until death)

8. Biological, psychological, and social factors all interact together as an individual transitions through various life stages. As a clinician evaluating biological factors that may contribute to the person's current psychological issues, the areas to review should include which of the following?

a. A parental history of psychiatric illness and/or addiction

b. Family income and social status

c. Years of education completed

d. Employment history

9. For therapists working primarily with adolescents, it is helpful to share which of the following with clients?

a. Sexual Identity and preferences will probably never change throughout one's lifetime.

b. It is important to offer a diagnosis to the adolescent of their sexual orientation so that they can be reassured of where they stand.

c. Disclosure of oneself or others' sexual orientation to help the client feel empowered to share their own experience.

d. Sexual development is a unique and individual process, and not everyone reaches sexual milestones at the same time.

10. Gerontology is the study of what?

a. The biological aspects of aging, economic trends of the aging, population, and the impact of aging on social trends.

b. Economic trends of youth, consumer spending as it pertains to children, and the focus on youth in the media.

c. The impact of social trends on schools, how schools function in the technology age, and the evolution of administration within schools.

d. The biological aspects of mental illness, and how substance abuse is viewed within social trends.

11. An autopoietic social system has which of the following qualities?

a. A clear hierarchy within itself

b. The ability to produce and maintain itself

c. The ability to expand and regrow itself

d. A definitive start and end point innate in the design

12. For many years, Abraham Maslow, who developed the hierarchy of human needs, described self-actualization as the highest level of achievement. In later years, he adjusted the model in order to add another level, which is referred to as what?
   a. Peace and Serenity
   b. Spiritual Attainment
   c. Self Determination
   d. Self-Transcendence

13. Those who research self-image throughout the life cycle report which of the following?
   a. Most people's self-image tends to peak around the age of sixty.
   b. Adolescents have the highest likelihood of a positive self-image than other age groups.
   c. There is very little change in self-image once middle school is completed.
   d. Young adults who are completing high school and entering the work force or college show an increase in self-image.

14. According to Elizabeth Kubler-Ross, there are five stages of grief. They occur in what order?
   a. Denial, anger, bargaining, acceptance, depression
   b. Anger, depression, denial, isolation, and bargaining
   c. Refusal, denial, isolation, anger, acceptance
   d. Denial, anger, bargaining, depression, acceptance

15. Receiving a diagnosis of a serious pulmonary illness can have many biopsychosocial impacts. Some things a therapist will want to address with a client who has just received a diagnosis of this nature may include which of the following?
   a. Asking why he or she continued to smoke, even after being told by a doctor it was affecting the respiratory system.
   b. Insisting that the client discuss the diagnosis with all immediate family members within twenty-four hours.
   c. Providing support and encouraging ventilation of emotions, especially grief and anger.
   d. Accompanying the client to his next medical appointment to make sure the information is accurate.

16. Changes that occur in a normal family life cycle tend to cause a re-alignment of relationships and roles within the family unit. This is because of what?
   a. At some point, the adult child is expected to provide more care and support to the parent than the parent can provide to the child.
   b. Families often split apart due to disagreements over money and relationships.
   c. Most parents view their adult children as being incapable of properly raising children and feel they must intervene.
   d. Some elderly people are constantly critical when their adult children are having a more successful career than the parents had.

17. Hypervigilance, disturbing dreams, and eruptions of anger are symptoms of what psychiatric disorder?
   a. Claustrophobia
   b. PTSD
   c. Borderline personality disorder
   d. Severe anxiety with panic attacks

18. Sigmund Freud and his daughter Anna developed a lengthy list of defense mechanisms, including denial, projection, rationalization, and sublimation. They proposed that the need for people to employ defense mechanisms was for which of the following reasons?
    a. Because they were dishonest and did not want others to see the real person.
    b. Because if they admitted the truth about themselves others would no longer accept them.
    c. Because the defense mechanism allows one to avoid perceiving or accepting something very unacceptable about themselves, which they are not yet ready to address.
    d. Because using defense mechanisms gives one an emotional advantage over others and makes it easier to exploit them.

19. Which of the following is NOT true?
    a. Social context refers to one's environment and how this influences behavior.
    b. What appears normal in one culture may appear bizarre or disgusting in another.
    c. The neighborhood where one resides has no bearing on behavior.
    d. Certain behaviors are acceptable in some social contexts, but the exact same behavior in a different social context might cause a person to be shunned or excluded from certain circles.

20. According to Erikson's stages of development, what is the dichotomy experienced during maturity (sixty-five years or older)?
    a. Intimacy vs. isolation
    b. Industry vs. inferiority
    c. Ego integrity vs. despair
    d. Generativity vs. stagnation

21. According to Sue & Sue's Stages of Racial/Cultural Identity Development, which stage is characterized by a period of re-thinking or challenging one's beliefs where the individual examines and appreciates positive aspects of his or her own racial/cultural group for the first time?
    a. Dissonance
    b. Conformity
    c. Introspection
    d. Resistance and immersion

22. Studies have shown that those who embrace spirituality tend to live longer and happier lives. The benefits of being a spiritual person include all of the following EXCEPT?
    a. It increases the likelihood of connection with others.
    b. It increases the likelihood of being artistic.
    c. It increases the likelihood that the client will find purpose in their lives.
    d. It increases the likelihood of self-actualization.

23. When people experience a major life-changing crisis, such as an earthquake or a terrorist attack, which of the following is NOT true?
    a. Children are more resilient and, therefore, less likely to experience the negative impact as severely as adults.
    b. Some immediate reactions may include disorientation, disbelief, or a sense of helplessness.
    c. As the event and its aftermath is processed, more symptoms, such as insomnia or withdrawal, may begin to surface.
    d. Most events of this nature are sudden and unexpected, and there is no way to prepare for them emotionally.

24. One's cultural background is based primarily upon all of the following EXCEPT?
    a. Where one was born
    b. At what point in time one was born
    c. Sociological practices and standards in which one was raised.
    d. Genetic predispositions inherited at birth

25. You are running a therapy group for teenage girls who have been sexually abused by a family member, and one common thread you have noted is that most of the girls experience feelings of shame and unworthiness, as well as a sense that they are different from most of their peers. Which of the following is NOT a learning goal of therapy within this group?
    a. They have been deeply betrayed by someone who was supposed to love and protect them.
    b. These feelings are normal and are experienced by most people who have been sexual assault victims.
    c. Most people who engage in therapy eventually feel better about themselves and can learn to make peace with what happened.
    d. Assessing why self-defense did not come into play so that next time they will be better prepared to fight back.

26. Which of the following is an example of indirect discrimination?
    a. An employer who tosses a resume in the trash because the name on it is commonly held by persons of the Muslim religion.
    b. A school requiring all students to come to school on Saturday for a make-up day despite having Jewish students who observe Saturday as a day of rest.
    c. A restaurant owner who refuses to serve a customer because the customer is black.
    d. A landlord who tells an interracial couple seeking an apartment that there are no vacancies, even though there are several empty units ready to be rented.

27. You are a psychiatric social worker completing a psychosocial history on a new patient admitted to the psych unit. As part of the assessment, you ask questions about sexual practices. This person indicates that she tends to fluctuate between a self-image of traditional male and female stereotypes and identifies feeling comfortable with both genders. This would be an example of which of the following?
    a. Sexual identity confusion
    b. Bi-gender sexual orientation
    c. Bi-sexual sexual orientation
    d. Transvestite sexual behavior

28. Risk-taking behavior often increases in adolescence. Which of the following is not a common theory to explain the prevalence of risk-taking behaviors among adolescents?
    a. The need for excitement and thrill outweighs any potential consequences or dangers.
    b. Risk-taking often occurs within groups to gain status and acceptance among peers.
    c. Adolescents are modeling adult behavior that has been romanticized.
    d. Adolescents engage in risk-taking behavior as a healthy outlet to channel their talents.

29. In your job as a social worker at a community senior center, you are facilitating a group on wellness in later life. One area of group focus is on spirituality. You introduce this topic because of which of the following reasons?

    a. It is important that older people all have a religious community for a sense of support and belonging.

    b. You believe that persons who go to church are more likely to enter the kingdom of heaven.

    c. Spiritual persons tend to be more optimistic, which leads to a greater quality of life.

    d. Persons who prefer not to attend church regularly tend to be angry and egocentric.

30. The learning theory of addictions is based on the premise that addictions are developed due to which of the following?

    a. A need to reduce feelings of shame and poor self-esteem

    b. Operant conditioning, classical conditioning, and social learning

    c. An inability to be morally strong or to use will power to overcome the addiction

    d. The interplay of social and cultural factors and one's genetic makeup

31. What defense mechanism occurs when a negative feeling is covered up by a false or exaggerated version of its opposite?

    a. Reaction Formation

    b. Displacement

    c. Projection

    d. Denial

32. Which of the following may be a dysfunctional family pattern?

    a. Scapegoating a child

    b. Affirming a child

    c. Undermining a child

    d. Disavowing a child

33. Which type of abuse involves the use of shame and manipulation to control a person, such as yelling, constant criticizing, or belittling, threatening, or name-calling?

    a. Physical Abuse

    b. Vocal Abuse

    c. Psychological Abuse

    d. Critical Abuse

34. What factor can cause family members or those outside the family to be judgmental toward a person suffering from mental illness?

    a. Ease

    b. Confusion

    c. Ambiguity

    d. Stigma

35. Which of the following is NOT a characteristic of a perpetrator of abuse?

    a. Uses/abuses drugs or alcohol

    b. Has a learning disorder

    c. Tends to be controlling toward others

    d. Has a history of mental illness

36. A social worker who is working to encourage her client to acknowledge and focus on his determination, ingenuity, and resiliency rather than his perceived "failures" he harbors for the financial strife he is in, is using which of the following approaches?
    a. The strengths perspective
    b. The re-centering method
    c. The bio-psychosocial perspective
    d. The learning theory

37. What is the general focus on the "launching family" stage in the basic family life cycle?
    a. Accepting new family members and transitioning from a marital system to a family system
    b. Selecting a life style and a life partner
    c. Establishing independence as an adult and independence from one's family of origin
    d. Accepting the new independent role of an adult child and transitioning through the separation

38. In Skinner's theory of operant conditioning, the term *shaping* refers to which of the following?
    a. The term *shaping* refers to placing a neutral stimuli before a reflex that occurs naturally.
    b. Changing behavior through rewarding the person each time an approximation of desired behavior occurs
    c. Exploring superstitions that might impact willingness to make behavioral changes
    d. Giving a person a reward when the desired behavior is perfected

39. In the field of personality theories, which researcher proposed that personality develops as a result of striving to become the best one can be, combined with the importance of self-perception?
    a. Eric Ericson
    b. Sigmund Freud
    c. Carl Rogers
    d. Gordon Allport

40. The process of social development as defined by Lev Vygotsky suggests that one's development in life is deeply impacted by:
    a. Income Status
    b. Birth order and gender
    c. The variety of social institutions, such as family, school, or church, to which one is exposed throughout life
    d. Physical stamina and overall health

Answer Explanations

1. C: The Genital stage starts in adolescence and lays the groundwork for future life relationships. As one enters adolescence, sexual identity and orientation begin to develop. Values regarding sexuality, views about the opposite sex, and the process of interacting with others on a more intimate level occur. These more mature elements of relationship building lay the foundation for future relationships, but not only from a sexual standpoint. Choice A, the Latent Stage, occurs from age six to puberty, and it is a time when the child's sexual energy becomes somewhat dormant. Choices B and D are not included in Freud's model of human development.

2. C: Developing a long-term relationship and starting a family are concepts more closely associated with stage six of Erikson's Model. This is Intimacy Versus Isolation, occurring from age eighteen through age forty. During this period, one is faced with the challenge of coming to terms with sexual preference, choosing a career path, and determining where, with whom, and how one plans to live. Long-term, future-oriented thinking is required. This phase is important, in that if not successfully mastered, the following phases—Generativity versus Stagnation and Ego Identity Versus Despair—could lead to emotional pain and anxiety in later life.

3. D: Accommodation occurs when one recognizes that previous beliefs were incorrect or no longer beneficial, based upon learning and integrating new information. Accommodation should occur throughout one's life as new information enters the consciousness and the process of assimilation occurs. If one is unable to accommodate new ideas, then it is difficult to grow emotionally and intellectually. If an individual continues to insist that a yellow legal pad and an encyclopedia is just as efficient as using a computer to complete a complex research project, accommodation has failed to occur. This forces the person to work at a snail's pace in comparison to using technology to more quickly and accurately complete the task. Choice A is incorrect in that schemas are a set of thoughts and ideas that fit together and present the person with a belief, or even a script, for life. Choice B is incorrect because assimilation refers to the process of integrating the new information gained through accommodation. Choice C refers to object permanence, a process in which an infant learns that even though a person or object leaves the room, that person still exists, and this understanding reduces anxiety and fear of abandonment.

4. A: Pavlov developed the theory of classical conditioning in which it has been demonstrated that pairing one stimuli with another produces specific responses in animals and humans. In his famous experiment, he noted that when feeding a dog—simultaneously pairing that feeding with the sound of a bell—the ringing of the bell eventually became associated with feeding time. Soon, a behavioral change was noted. The dog salivated to the sound of the bell, even when no food was provided. This demonstrated that people and animals can learn things though pairing one stimulus with another. Although dog training was part of his research, Choice B is wrong as it was not the focus of his research. Choice C reflects one of Erikson's stages of development, and D relates more to the function of behavioral theory devised by B.F. Skinner.

5. C: Taking privileges for a week is a form of punishment for negative behavior, versus a reward for positive behavior. While punishment can be an effective means for changing behavior, research indicates it is less desirable than positive reinforcement. Choices A, B, and D are all forms of positive reinforcement in which a person is rewarded for performing a specific behavior.

6. A: While some children who are oppositional and defiant may refuse to conform to certain standards as a means to establish control, the child described in this scenario is more likely experiencing developmental delays due to the deficits in a number of areas. At one time, the state of Illinois required children to be able to tie their own shoes before being admitted to kindergarten. Although this is a crude measure of academic readiness, it probably served as a red flag, based on the fact that the vast majority of children can perform this task by age 5. Pre-schools generally require that a three-year-old must be fully potty-trained before they will admit him or her to their program, again using a standard that the majority of children can achieve by that age. Language issues may have other causes, such as physiological symptoms, but being unable to meet these three standards is an indicator that the child is lagging behind others in attaining developmental milestones. Choices *B* and *D* refer to behavioral disorders of childhood that include symptoms of disregard/disrespect for others and sometimes include criminal behavior. Genetic deficiencies, Choice *C*, may contribute to a developmental delay, yet they could also be associated with physical issues passed genetically, such as deafness or dwarfism.

7. A: This description of states of adulthood is most commonly used in psychology and medicine. While some may question that early adulthood extends until age forty, with life spans increasing, this is a reasonable standard and is generally an acceptable conception in the fields of psychology and medicine as to how a lifetime is divided.

8. A: Parental history of mental illness is a biological feature and should serve as a red flag because some psychiatric conditions do have a genetic link, including—but not limited to—addictions and mood disorders. In addition, being raised by a parent impaired by mental illness or addictions often causes deep emotional scars that should be addressed in therapy. Income, education, and employment history are not considered biological factors; therefore, they are incorrect responses. The issues mentioned in *B*, *C*, and *D* can certainly have a biological impact, such as a scenario in which the child is deprived of good nutrition or medical care.

9. D: Sexual development is different for each person, and there is a wide range of variations in terms of achieving physical and emotional maturation. Sexuality is a very fluid and continuously changing process for most. The sexual practices one finds gratifying at age 16 may no longer be pursued at age 40. Some people do not seem to access their true sense of sexuality until mid-life. Others switch gears frequently throughout life when it comes to sexual preferences. This explains why *A* and *B* are incorrect. Choice *C* is also incorrect; in some cases it may be helpful to share one's own experience with sexual orientation, but disclosing others' sexual orientation is inappropriate.

10. A: Gerontology covers a wide range of issues related to biological, social, and psychiatric features of aging. The study of gerontology is essential as the population ages and lives longer, healthier lives. How a population ages impacts the field of economics, psychology, medicine, even architecture. For example, a two-story apartment complex in the middle of Iowa will probably not have an elevator. In Florida, where there is a large senior population, almost every apartment complex has an elevator to accommodate those in wheelchairs or those who have difficulty climbing steps.

11. B: Niklas Luhmann, a sociologist associated with communication theory, uses the term autopoiesis to describe social systems that are self-creating, which means they have the innate ability to produce and maintain themselves. Communications make up these systems, and in turn, generate other communications.

12. D: Maslow devised his last level during his later years and referred to it as Self-Transcendence. Achievement of this goal relies on experiencing a greater sense of spiritual growth and practicing one's beliefs on a deeper level. Previously, self-actualization, Choice *C*, was the ultimate achievement in Maslow's hierarchy of needs. In later life, as he worked on his own spiritual evolution, he believed this went beyond the process of self-actualization and deserved to be added to his original model of human needs. Self-transcendence refers to elevating one's self to a state of spiritual enlightenment in which there is greater clarity and understanding of certain spiritual truths. Choices *A* and *B* are factors that contribute to the Self Transcendence Level, but these are not listed in Maslow's hierarchy of needs theory.

13. A: Self-image does change throughout the life cycle, and while this varies from individual to individual, age sixty represents a change in roles from being an actively engaged parent and successful member of the work force to an empty nester who will soon face retirement. In our society where youth, beauty, and wealth are revered, there is often a shortage of several of these when one enters the sixties. Even those who are financially fit will begin to experience physical changes, such as less energy, more body fat, and the onset of a variety of medical conditions that prevent one from doing some of the things that were once simple, such as lifting a three-year-old grandchild. Gracefully accepting these changes is difficult and painful. Choices *B*, *C*, and *D* all represent stages that consist of great change and challenging transition and often fail to correlate with a positive self-image.

14. D: Denial is first so that the person has a moment to process the loss, followed by anger at others or self for causing the loss to occur. The grieving person in desperation tries to bargain with his or her God or others in hopes of bringing back that which was lost. As reality sets in, the person grieves the loss and experiences sadness and depression. Resolution occurs when the person accepts the loss and is ready to move on, with an understanding that in spite of that which is gone, they will be all right in the long run. The other responses do not outline the order correctly.

15. C: Providing support and encouraging talking about the issue, but only at the chosen pace of the client, is the correct response. The person receiving a frightening diagnosis needs time to process thoughts and feelings. Choice *A* would be a form of shaming the client about the smoking addiction and does nothing to help the individual make peace with the diagnosis. Choice *B* is inappropriate because family is not always the client's first choice for support, and the client should decide when and with whom to share this news. Choice *D* puts the therapist in a sticky situation in terms of boundaries. There may be some settings in which this could be helpful, but generally this is not an expectation of either client or therapist.

16. A: At some point, the adult child is expected to provide more care and support to the parent than the parent can provide to the adult child. This is a painful process for both parent and adult child. While most adult children are willing to lend a helping hand to parents, parents sometimes feel diminished and awkward as the roles shift. When assistance is in the form of direct care, such as bathing and dressing, it can be even more difficult for the parent to accept care from their child. Choices *B*, *C*, and *D* may each be true in terms of causing realignments of roles, but the process of caring for aging parents, who sometimes become quite childlike and difficult in later years, is at the core of relationship realignment.

17. B: The three symptoms noted are common experiences for persons diagnosed with Post Traumatic Stress Disorder (PTSD). Along with these, PTSD survivors can be triggered into a state of anxiety or panic when exposed to stimuli associated with the trauma such as smells, sensations, or sights. Those diagnosed with PTSD may be easily started, and they can even have periods in which they feel they are re-experiencing the traumatic event. Choice *A*, claustrophobia, is a fear of small spaces. Choice *C* is incorrect, although persons with borderline personality may have a history of PTSD. Choice *D* can be a symptom of PTSD, but it is generally seen as a completely different diagnosis with a different set of criteria.

18. C: Defense mechanisms protect the ego from absorbing information it does not want to see, feel, or experience. This protective shield—which comes in many forms, such as rationalization, sublimation, or projection—helps reduce anxiety and guards against unwanted emotions like shame or guilt. Defense mechanisms can be helpful in reducing anxiety or can sometimes help one become immune to reality. Choices *A* and *B* imply that defense mechanisms are used to protect others from the truth about themselves, when this is not entirely accurate. Choice *D* suggests that defense mechanisms better allow one to exploit others. In some instances, this could apply, but for the most part, these mechanisms are acts of self-defense that keep the ego from accepting an unwanted truth.

19. C: The neighborhood in which one lives has great impact on things, such as education quality, exposure to crime, access to drugs or alcohol, and the type of role models one is exposed to. Social context shapes behavior, expectations and morals. Choices *A*, *B*, and *D* are all true and reflect various aspects of social context that can significantly influence behavioral choices, such as differences from one culture to another and how these can be impacted by different social contexts.

20. C: Erikson devised eight stages of psychosocial development. He emphasized the importance of social context, asserting that family and environment are major contributors to child development. During maturation (aged sixty-five and above), ego identity vs. isolation is the struggle. Important life tasks, such as child rearing and career, are being completed. Reviewing and evaluating how one's life was spent and success over the course of one's life provides a sense of fulfillment, while failure emerges if one is dissatisfied with accomplishments, which leads to depression or despair.

21. A: Sue & Sue's Stages of Racial/Cultural Identity Development include the following: conformity, dissonance, resistance and immersion, introspection, and integrative awareness. In the conformity stage, individuals hold a strong preference for the dominant culture and display negative views, shame, or embarrassment regarding their own racial and/or cultural groups. In the dissonance stage, individuals reconsider or challenge their beliefs. For the first time, they appreciate positive aspects of their own racial/cultural group. During the resistance and immersion stage, individuals have a pride of their racial and cultural group along with a preference for minority views and instead actively reject the views of the dominant culture. In the introspection stage, individuals become aware of the negative impact of the earlier resistance and immersion stage. At this point, they may realize that they do not actually disagree with all majority views or endorse all minority views, but find some sort of balance. Lastly, in the integrative awareness stage, individuals are able to appreciate both their own culture and differing cultures.

22. B: Spirituality tends to increase the likelihood of someone being connected to other people, the likelihood that the client might have a greater sense of purpose, and the likelihood of self-actualization. It also can provide hope to the hopeless, help reduce anxiety, aid in healing from emotional pain, and contribute toward a greater optimism. Being more artistic is not a factor connected to levels of spirituality.

23. A: Children have fewer resources for processing events of this nature because they have limited life experience and, therefore, fewer tools to help them adapt. Children are also less equipped to identify and share the emotions, memories, or thoughts they are experiencing than adults. The other responses are correct in that disorientation and disbelief are common in the beginning, and in the aftermath of disaster, other symptoms begin to emerge. Such events are indeed difficult to predict; therefore, one cannot easily prepare for trauma of this nature.

24. D: Culture is a complex and multi-faceted concept and is related to when, where, and with whom one was raised. Those in the mental health field should be constantly vigilant about a client's cultural practices because these strongly impact beliefs, ethics, and behavior. Choice *D* is the best answer because it does not constitute an aspect of cultural identity as easily as where, where, and how one was raised.

25. D: It is important to acknowledge the girl is not in any way at fault and that the act of sexual assault upon a minor is a felony. Choices *A, B,* and *C* plant a seed of hope that through sharing feelings in a safe setting. One can begin to move down the path to healing the emotional pain. It is helpful to normalize the experience to some extent so that the child realizes one in four girls are victims of some form of sexual abuse. The therapist should never blame the victim for abuse, regardless of the circumstances.

26. B: Indirect discrimination relates to laws and policies that are applied equally but have negative consequences for certain groups. The other three answers are examples of direct discrimination since the actions are based on individual biases rather than organizational decisions. In those three scenarios, people are purposefully discriminating against others. In Choice *B*, the school administrators may not have even considered the negative consequence for Jewish students.

27. B: This person's sexual orientation is bi-gender due to comfort in identification with both genders. Choice *A* is wrong because the person does not appear confused about her sexual identity. Choice *C* is incorrect as bi-sexual refers to being attracted to both genders, and that information was not really provided. Choice *D* is also incorrect. Transvestites enjoy dressing in attire of the opposite gender and engaging in stereotyped versions of the opposite gender.

28. D: Risk-taking behavior is purported to increase during adolescence by several theories including the need for excitement outweighing perceived consequences, the desire to gain status and acceptance among peers, and modeling adult behavior that may have been romanticized.

Social workers should work with adolescents who engage in risk-taking behavior to find healthy outlets to channel their talents or get them involved in more positive activities.

29. C: Spirituality and religion are different concepts. Religion can be defined as an organized system of beliefs that others are expected to follow. Spirituality is a more personal process of self-growth and self-actualization. Spirituality in its purest form does not rely on an institution, religious leader, or set of rules to guide beliefs, making Choice *A* incorrect. Choice *B* is an example of a therapist overstepping boundaries and attempting to encourage others to accept his or her personal spiritual beliefs. There is no evidence to back up the statement that persons who do not attend church tend to be any angrier than anyone else.

30. B: This theory of addiction is based on the interplay of classical conditioning, operant conditioning, and social learning (observation). Choice *A* is not specifically a model of addiction, but rather a supposition as to why people abuse substances. *C* refers to the Moral Model of addictions in which the person addicted to drugs or alcohol is viewed as weak-willed. Choice *D* refers to a hybrid of the *bio-psychosocial model* of addiction, which focuses on the role of the environment, such as cultural and social factors, and *genetic theory*.

31. A: Reaction formation is when a person displays an exaggerated version of the opposite emotion to what he or she is really feeling. For example, a person may display strong feelings of love toward someone, though internally and unconsciously he or she detests that person. Displacement is when the feeling someone has toward one person is displaced to another object or person, such as the dog or spouse. Projection happens when one's own feelings are viewed as actually being someone else's. Denial is the refusal to admit something exists, such as painful facts or situations.

32. A: Scapegoating a child occurs when a child is blamed for family problems and for things that are not his or her fault. This pattern of family dysfunction may happen in families where the problems are not being properly recognized or addressed, and members of the family seek to shift the blame. Affirming, undermining, or disavowing the child are not concepts connected to family dysfunction.

33. C: Psychological or emotional abuse is when the abuser uses strategies of manipulation through shame, fear, and guilt to control the other's behaviors. It also involves verbal abuse, which takes the form of yelling, constant criticisms, or belittling, threats, or name-calling. Physical abuse involves some type of physical harm. Vocal abuse is when a person damages their vocal chords. Critical abuse does not exist.

34. D: The stigma of mental illness can cause family members to become judgmental toward the individual who has been diagnosed, or he or she may have to deal with the misunderstandings of people outside the family. This is one of the reasons that dealing with a diagnosis of mental illness can be more complicated for a family than dealing with a diagnosis of physical illness. There is no ease associated with mental illness. Even though mental illness may involve some level of confusion or ambiguity, those are not terms that best answer the question.

35. B: While the use/abuse of alcohol, a history of mental illness, and a tendency to control others are all risk factors for abuse, the presence of a learning disorder is not associated with this. There are many factors that may indicate a potential abuser, but there are no foolproof ways to identify one apart from the evidence of abuse.

36. A: Rather than focusing on problems and pathology, The strengths perspective, or strengths-based approach, in social work shifts the focus away from the traditional topics (problems and pathology), and instead, encourages social workers to focus on a client's strengths or assets and to build upon the client's inherent positive characteristics. In this example, the social worker is helping the client recognize his strengths, such as his determination, ingenuity, and resiliency, despite his financial challenges.

37. D: Family life cycle theories assume that, as members of a family unit, individuals pass through different stages of life. The main focus in the launching family stage is of accepting the new independent role of an adult child and transitioning through the inevitable separation that comes with those changes. Also in this stage is the need for parents to face their own transition into middle or older age. Choice *A* describes a family with young children stage wherein couples must accept the new family member and shift from a marital system to a family system. Choices *B* and *C* describe the unattached young adult stage.

38. B: Changing behavior through rewards for approximation of desired behavior is the correct answer. Skinner demonstrated that behavior could be learned by rewarding actions that are similar to the desired behavior. If one wants to teach a dog to chase and catch a Frisbee thrown to the end of a field, the dog must first be rewarded for sniffing the Frisbee, then grasping the Frisbee, and then catching it when thrown four feet, then six, then ten. This process is called successive approximation. Choice *A* refers to a classical conditioning. Choice *C* refers to superstitions, meaning that one can sometimes be confused as to which behavior is soliciting the reward. Some athletes wear the same pair of "lucky" socks each game, thinking this behavior leads to the reward of winning. In reality, the behavior that leads to the win can be anything from practicing harder to playing a team that is not highly skilled; therefore, the behavior is superstitious. Choice *D* is a poor form of teaching a person to learn a new behavior because it may take much trial and error before perfection is achieved.

39. C: Carl Rogers placed much emphasis on reaching one's greatest potential and the interplay between this potential and one's perception of self. Erikson and Freud theorized that one must achieve certain developmental challenges before moving to the next level of human growth. Allport, on the other hand, believed one's destiny depended on the possession of certain clusters of personality traits. Therefore, *A*, *B*, and *D* are wrong. Rogers focused on the concept that humans are driven by their own need to develop into the best person they are capable of becoming.

40. C: Vygotsky believed individuals are significantly shaped by the formal and informal social groups in which they interact. These institutions teach values, how to behave in relationships, how closely one must follow rules and laws, and, in general, what is important in life. A child growing up hungry and neglected will have a very different view of life than one who is cherished and provided with love, support, and material needs. Choices *A*, *B*, and *D* all impact the quality of one's life, but Vygotsky leaned toward a more global explanation of social development that encompasses multiple social factors.

Assessment and Intervention Planning

Biopsychosocial History and Collateral Data

Biopsychosocial Assessment

In order for an assessment to be comprehensive, the practitioner must gather information and assess the individual *holistically*, which includes examining systems related to the biological, psychological, and social or sociocultural factors of functioning. In some cases, a spiritual component may be included. This process is based off of the *biopsychosocial framework* that describes the interaction between biological, psychological, and social factors. The key components of the biopsychosocial assessment can be broken down into five parts: Identification, Chief Complaint, Social/Environmental Issues, History, and Mental Status Exam.

Identification
Identification consists of the details or demographic information about the client that can be seen with the eye and documented accordingly. Some examples of identification information are age, gender, height, weight, and clothing.

Chief Complaint
Chief complaint is the client's version of what the over-arching problem is, in his/her own words. The client's description of the chief complaint may include factors from the past that the client views as an obstacle to optimal functioning. It could also be an issue that was previously resolved but reoccurs, thus requiring the client to develop additional coping skills.

Social/Environmental Issues
This is the evaluation of social development and physical settings. *Social development* is critical to understanding the types of support systems the client has and includes information about the client's primary family group, including parents, siblings, and extended family members.

The client's peers and social networks should also be examined. There should be a clear distinction between peers available *online* (such as through online social networks) and peers the client interacts with *face-to-face,* as online systems may provide different forms of support than in-person systems.

The client's work environment and school or vocational settings should also be noted in this portion of the assessment. The client's current housing situation and view of financial status is also included to determine the type of resources the client has. Legal issues may also be included.

History
History includes all of the events in the client's past. Clients may need to be interviewed several times in order to get a thorough picture of their history. Some information in a client's history, such as events that occurred during the stages of infancy and early childhood, may need to be gathered from collateral sources. Obtaining the client's historical information is usually a multi-stage process and can involve the following methods of data collection:

Presenting Problem
Clients should be asked to describe what brings them in for treatment. Although a client may attempt to delve into information that is well in the past, the practitioner should redirect the client to emphasize the past week or two. Emphasis is placed on the client's current situation when assessing the presenting problem.

Past Personal
When reviewing a client's history, noting biological development may determine whether or not the client hit milestones and the ensuing impact it had on his/her health. In reviewing biological development, other physical factors should also be assessed for impact on current emotional well-being, including those that may no longer persist, like a childhood illness. As much information regarding the client's entire *lifespan* (birth to present) should be gathered, with attention paid to sexual development.

Medical
During the medical component of the assessment process, information should be obtained on the client's previous or current physiological diagnoses. These diagnoses can contribute to the client's current situation.

For example, a client with frequent headaches and back pain may be unable to sleep well and therefore be experiencing the physical and psychosocial effects of sleep deprivation. Additional information on other conditions, such as pregnancy, surgeries, or disabilities, should also be explored during this time.

Mental Health
Previous mental health diagnoses, symptoms, and/or evaluations should be discussed. If a client discloses prior diagnoses or evaluations, the practitioner should determine the following:

- Whether or not the client has been hospitalized (inpatient)
- If the client has received supervised treatment in an outpatient setting (to include psychotherapeutic intervention)
- Whether the client has been prescribed medications
- If the client has undertaken other treatments related to mental health diagnoses

The client's psychological development should also be reviewed. It is important to gather details on how clients view their emotional development, including their general affect.

The client's cognitive development, in relation to information previously obtained regarding the biological development, should also be reviewed.

Substance Use
Without demonstrating judgment, practitioners should encourage clients to disclose whether or not they have used controlled substances. It is important that thorough information is gathered and symptoms related to substance abuse are assessed BEFORE rendering a primary mental health disorder diagnosis.

Should a client disclose that he or she has engaged in the use of substances, information as to the type of substance, frequency of use, and duration of exposure to the lifestyle, should be gathered. Additionally, information on what the client perceives as the positive and negative aspects of substance use should be gathered, noting whether or not the client perceives any consequences of substance abuse, such as job loss, decreased contact with family and friends, and physical appearance.

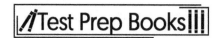

Mental Status Examination

A mental status exam is a concise, complete evaluation of the client's current mental functioning level in regard to *cognitive and behavioral aspects* (rapport-building, mood, thought content, hygiene). There are mini-mental status examinations available that allow practitioners to provide a snapshot of the client's overall level of functioning with limited resources and time available. Mental status examinations are usually conducted regularly and discreetly through questioning and noting non-verbal indicators (such as appearance), in order for the practitioner to best guide the session.

Practitioners should document a mental status examination as part of the individual's personal file in order to complete an accurate assessment with all client information. This examination also serves as a baseline for the development and implementation of ensuing therapies, treatments, and interventions. The mental status typically includes details about the individual, such as appearance, grooming, facial expressions and general body language, cognition, orientation, manner of speech, indicators of the influence of any controlled substances, mood, impulse control, judgment, thinking style, memory, intellectual functioning, perception of reality, presence of hallucinations or delusions, and interest in the session.

Biopsychosocial Responses to Illness and Disability

Receiving a diagnosis of a serious physical illness is life changing in many ways. Along with the many physiological impacts of the illness, such as pain and tiredness, there are many psychological and social factors that influence a person's ability to cope with the new diagnosis. Parenting, careers, and intimate relationships are just a few areas that may be impacted.

One's lifelong aspirations are challenged and may have to be adjusted with the reality of a foreshortened future. Some illnesses may bring feelings of guilt or shame, if related to unsafe sexual behaviors, drug use, smoking, overeating, or other unhealthy behaviors. Depression is a common response to a diagnosis of illness, which may reduce motivation to comply with treatment. It could also cause the person to withdraw at a time when support is important or reduce one's confidence in asking others for needed assistance.

Many illnesses have an emotional component and symptoms can be triggered or exacerbated by stress. In addition to counseling or the use of anti-depressant medication, taking an active role in treatment and finding a support group of others dealing with the same illness has been proven helpful. Marriage and family therapy may be useful as well since serious illness impacts all the people who are close to the patient.

Biopsychosocial Factors Related to Mental Health

The *biopsychosocial model* proposes multiple causes from three main groups (biological, psychological, and social/environmental) that can contribute to mental health disorders. *Biological factors* are related to the body's physiological response and may present in the form of fluctuations in heartbeat, sweating, shortness of breath, digestive issues, or issues with brain function.

Biological factors are also linked to genetics. One may have pre-disposed vulnerabilities to mental health disorders, based on inherited traits or a history of mental health disorders within one's family. Although biological factors may heighten one's vulnerability to mental health issues such as stress and anxiety, they are not enough to substantiate a mental health diagnosis.

Psychological factors refer to cognitive processes, such as thoughts, beliefs, one's view of an experience, and one's view of self. Thought process and shape the view of self, which, in turn, shapes the sense of stability and control across environments and has a direct impact on how a person functions. Specifically, cognitive process or psychological factors determine whether a person perceives a situation as threatening or non-threatening and reacts accordingly.

Social or *environmental factors* are present in one's immediate physical surroundings and social systems such as work, school, home, and peer group. A person's social environment is significantly influenced by the aforementioned biological and psychological environments. For example, his or her level of stress may be directly and simultaneously affected by conditions in the workplace and by a peer group. The stress may present with physiological symptoms (such as muscle pain), negatively contributing to one's overall health and wellness.

Psychosocial Stress

Psychosocial stress occurs when an individual perceives a real or imagined threat and feels unable to cope with it. Unchecked, stress can lead to physiological and mental health problems such as heart disease, depression, and anxiety. Indicators of psychosocial stress include:

- High blood pressure
- Regular feelings of sadness, irritability, or anxiousness
- Withdrawal from social events
- Sweating
- Feeling faint or dizzy
- Feeling jittery or antsy
- Muscle and joint pain and stiffness
- Teeth clenching and grinding; chronic jaw pain
- Headaches
- Feeling constantly overwhelmed or unable to complete routine tasks
- Chronic fatigue or sleep problems
- Inability to concentrate

Basic Medical Terminology

Basic medical terminology can help the practitioner determine the relationship between an individual's physiological and psychological health. It can also help practitioners work seamlessly in multidisciplinary teams with health care professionals such as psychiatrists and nurses. There are ten primary biological systems in the human body, and learning certain prefixes and suffixes can help one understand which systems are related to common medical conditions and terminology.

Cardiovascular System

The cardiovascular system circulates blood through the body via the heart. It uses arteries to bring oxygen and nutrients to the organs of the body and veins to take away waste from the organs. Related terms include:

- Cardi-/Cardio-: heart
- Angi-: vessel
- Veno-: vein
- Hem-/Hemo-: blood

- Thromb-: clot
- Atherosclerosis: hardening of the blood vessels
- Angina pectoris: chest pain
- Arrhythmia/dysrhythmia: abnormal heart rhythms (e.g., too fast or too slow)
- Ischemia: insufficient blood flow to the heart, which can lead to angina or heart attack

Digestive System

The digestive system removes nutrients from consumable energy sources through the mouth, esophagus, stomach, and intestines. It removes wastes from the body through the intestines and bladder. Related terms include:

- Gastr-/Gastro: stomach
- Hep-/Hepato-: liver
- Chol-: gall
- Cyst-/Cysto-: bladder, sac
- Emes-: vomit
- Gastroesophageal Reflux Disease (GERD): a condition where stomach acid reverses into the esophagus and causes severe burning and inflammation
- Cirrhosis: progressive liver disease, often caused by alcoholism
- Crohn's Disease: a chronic, painful bowel or intestinal disease marked by constant inflammation
- Peritonitis: inflammation of the abdomen

Endocrine System

The endocrine system uses hormones to regulate complex functions like growth, reproduction, and metabolism. Related terms include:

- Thyro-: thyroid
- Aden-: gland
- Hypo/hyperthyroidism: a condition where the thyroid makes too little or too much thyroid hormone, resulting in metabolic and energy issues

Integumentary System

The integumentary system consists of skin, hair, and nails to protect the internal organs from external damage. Related terms include:

- Adip-: fat
- Lip-: fat
- Cutaneo-: skin
- Derm-: skin
- Melan-: black, dark
- Seb-: sebum, oily
- Melanoma: a type of skin cancer
- Dermatitis: inflammation of the skin
- Kaposi Sarcoma: usually fatal skin tumor

Lymphatic System

The lymphatic system is a network of vessels that promote the body's ability to fight infection and disease. Related terms include:

- Blast-/-blast: bud or germ
- Lymph-: clear fluid
- Phag-: eat
- Lymphoma: a malignant condition of lymph tissue
- Metastasis: the spreading of cancerous cells, usually through lymph

Muscular/Skeletal System

The muscular/skeletal system enables the body's physical structure and movement. Related terms include:

- Oste-: bone
- Chondr-: cartilage
- Arth-: joint
- Myel-: bone marrow
- Ten-: tendon
- Burs-: bursa
- Myo-: muscle
- Arthritis: loss of mobility and cartilage in joints
- Osteoporosis: loss of calcium in bones resulting in structural weakness

Nervous System

The nervous system is responsible for communication between the brain and the muscles, resulting in physiological action and tangible sensation. Related terms include:

- Ceph-: head
- Myel-/Myelo-: spinal cord
- Neur-/Neuro-: nerve
- Multiple Sclerosis: a disease where nerve fibers lose their insulation and ability to communicate with muscles, often leading to paralysis or other sensory problems
- Epilepsy: seizures or convulsions
- Aphasia: loss of speech

Renal System

The renal system comprises primarily the kidneys, which filter waste from the blood. Related terms include:

- Neph-: kidney
- Ren-: kidney
- Ur-/-uria: urine
- Pyel-: renal ducts
- Nephrosis: diseased kidneys
- Nephrolith: kidney stone
- Urethritis: inflamed urethra, which affects the expulsion of urine
- Enuresis: uncontrollable bladder and urine expulsion

Reproductive System

The reproductive system includes sexual organs responsible for conception and maturation of a fetus. Related terms include:

- Orchid-: testes
- Test-: testes
- Andr-: male
- Hyst-: uterus
- Colp-: vagina
- Men-: menstruation
- Mammo-: breast
- Masto-: breast
- -pareunia: intercourse
- Prostate-Specific Antigen: a protein which, in high levels, may indicate prostate cancer in males
- Endometriosis: excessive, hardened uterine tissue that can cause abdominal bleeding and painful menstruation in females
- Pelvic inflammatory disease: inflamed uterine tubes in females
- Dyspareunia: painful sexual intercourse

Respiratory System

The respiratory system brings oxygen into the body and releases carbon dioxide out of the body through the lungs. Related terms include:

- Rhin-/Rhino-: nose
- Laryn-: larynx
- Trach-: trachea
- Bronch-: lung
- Pne-/Pneu-: breathing, lungs
- Pulmo-: lung
- Ephysema/Chronic Obstructive Pulmonary Disease (COPD): a lung condition where the progressive deterioration of the membranes results in the inability to exchange oxygen
- Cystic fibrosis: a genetic disease resulting in abnormal mucous production, lung infections, and lung scarring
- Pneumoconiosis: any lung disease in which pollutants become trapped or lodged in the lungs

Mental and Emotional Illness Throughout the Lifespan

Mental and emotional illness can present in a number of ways and vary depending on the illness, the person, and the circumstances. Some symptoms of mental and emotional illness include:

- Chronic feelings of sadness
- Inability to focus
- Extreme mood variation
- Loss of interest in activities one used to enjoy
- Lack of sexual interest or desire
- Intense, and sometimes unexplainable, feelings of guilt, shame, regret, fear, or worry
- Chronic fatigue

- Sleep problems, such as insomnia or sleeping too much
- Feeling overwhelmed by daily routines or tasks
- Substance abuse
- Compulsive or obsessive thoughts or behaviors
- Hallucination
- Thoughts of suicide
- Thoughts of harming oneself or others
- Excessive weight gain or weight loss
- Unexplained anger or irritability
- Detachment from loved ones
- Medically unexplained physical symptoms (psychosomatic) such as headaches, jaw pain, stomach pain, or joint stiffness.

Information Available from Other Sources

When working with clients, social workers need to compile a complete and accurate assessment of the client's background. Assessments may include information from a variety of sources. Primary sources of information are those provided directly by the client. This may include the intake form they complete, direct responses to questions asked by the social worker (such as during an interview or counseling session), documented medical history provided straight from the client, journal entries or other personal communications of the client, or body language exhibited in person. Secondary sources of information are taken from a source other than the client. A medical history provided by the client's doctor, rather than by the client, is considered a secondary source. Records from the client's place of employment, schools, and public data such as home ownership or jail information are also examples of secondary sources of information. Social workers may choose to interview or provide group services to a client's family and friends. Any information that is shared about the client by people close to him or her is considered secondary information. Additionally, if the social worker chooses to conduct literature reviews or searches of evidence-based research to shape an intervention, they are seeking secondary sources.

When requesting or seeking secondary information, such as from employment records or from interviews with family members, social workers must carefully consider the legal, ethical, and moral consequences of their actions. Whenever applicable, consent to seek and use secondary source information should be provided by the client. When this is not possible, such as with a client who is physically or mentally unable to provide valid consent, social workers should use empathy, compassion, a high standard of ethics, and discretion when searching for information about the client. The client should be treated with dignity and respect during this process. All information should be gathered with the sole intention of providing help and support in the client's best interest.

Obtaining Sensitive Information

Interviews are a critical component of social work practice wherein clients provide verbal reports, accounts, or narratives that serve as the main source of information and data collected during the assessment process.

The basis of the interview is a verbal report that involves introductions between the practitioner and client. In some practice settings, the verbal report may be supplemented by an *information sheet* that provides client demographics and a brief overview of the *presenting problem*. Presenting problems are

prevailing circumstances, symptoms, or difficulties that the client believes is a problem requiring psychotherapeutic assistance.

Principle: Practitioners Need to Establish Rapport with the Client

Providing a description of the services provided and what the client can expect during sessions is the practitioner's first opportunity to build rapport with the client. Rapport development impacts the thoroughness of the information provided from the client. If the level of rapport is limited, the client may not feel comfortable enough to provide sufficient information. The level of rapport also affects the type of impression the client wishes to make on the practitioner. Consequently, it is linked to the client's perception of self-awareness. Some key points to remember are as follows:

- The social worker's own personal characteristics (gender, race, age, etc.) may affect the level of client interaction, based on the client's cultural background.

- Clients may adjust their responses to questions based on how they perceive the social worker's characteristics.

- The social worker's demographics may also have an impact on how the client feels about disclosing sensitive information, such as domestic violence, sexual conduct, or child abuse.

Principle: The Basics of Social Work Practice Should be Used When an Interview is Conducted

Once the introductions have been made and an overview of services and interview processes provided, the client should be asked to explain why they came in for treatment.

Empowering clients to share their concerns and emphasizing the point of hearing things from their perspective provides the practitioner with an opportunity to gauge a client and start "where the client is" in the initial phases of the assessment process.

Technique

The use of encouraging, neutral phrases will help move the conversation forward and encourage the client to share, e.g., "What brings you in to see me today?"

While being encouraging to the client, it is important that practitioners are genuine and not phony. Practitioners should avoid overly complimentary statements, such as "I'm so glad you came in today!" If the client senses the interest is insincere, they may not wish to share.

Principle: The Practitioner Should Start Where the Client is.

After engaging the client, they should be allowed to open up, "vent," or speak freely for approximately fifteen minutes.

Technique

While the client is delving into any emotions, the practitioner should utilize active listening to keep the client engaged. Additionally, it is important to observe the client's *non-verbal cues* (posture, gestures, voice tone and pitch, and facial expressions) that lend to the emotional state. Once the client shares primary concerns, the practitioner can focus on what is important to the client.

The practitioner should observe the client's emotional state, allowing them to feel those emotions freely while providing the account of the problem. Demonstrating empathy is important when responding to the client's emotions. The emotion observed should be acknowledged. For example, if a client is crying, the practitioner can state, "You seem saddened about this," to demonstrate empathy. This practice can also hone in on an important area of the client's life that may be addressed later.

Once the client has been allowed to speak freely, the practitioner should utilize exploratory interviewing skills to delve into the specifics of topics that seemed particularly troubling for the client during the disclosure of the presenting problem.

After the client has revealed the presenting problem and the emotional state has been observed, the client should be asked to delve further into details about current life circumstances. This will provide an opportunity for the practitioner to gain additional information related to the context of the client's problem. It also allows the practitioner to uncover particularly troubling areas that can be explored later. Moreover, it may reveal certain boundaries for the client who is unwilling or unready to discuss certain details of their life.

Principle: It is Important to Engage the Client Verbally While Simultaneously Observing Non-Verbal Cues

The practitioner should ask questions to provide clarification and deeper insight into the client's problems and level of functioning.

Question Techniques

Open-ended questions may provide more detail and allow the client to expand into other areas that can be explored later.

Closed-ended questions are ideal for fact-finding from a client.

Clarification questions should be asked whenever necessary. This may be done through active listening and reflective sharing on the social worker's part, to foster comprehensive communication and further build rapport.

Note Taking Techniques

If the client has questions as to why notes are taken, the reasoning behind it should be explained, and a copy should be offered to provide the client to make them feel more comfortable and involved in the interview process.

Observation of client behaviors during the interview may be indicative of how the client behaves or reacts in settings outside of the session. Conversely, clients may act outside of their norm, due to the perceived pressure from the interview process. The aforementioned questions and non-verbal observations are essential to determine factors of the client's personality and the context of presenting issues.

Practitioners should also be aware that their interactions affect client behaviors and responses during the interview process. For example, the client may mimic rigid body language (folded arms, crossed legs, minimal eye contact) from the practitioner and become defensive in speech pattern, pitch, or tone.

Indicators of Addiction and Substance Abuse

Substance abuse and addiction problems come in many forms. These problems are often undetected or incorrectly attributed to other causes. Indicators include:

- Problems at work or school
- Friction with romantic partners, friends, or colleagues
- Neglect of household responsibilities, self-care, or hygiene
- Reckless behavior leading to legal trouble or financial problems
- Violence
- Tolerance of the substance/behavior over time
- Inability to stop using the substance/engaging in the behavior
- No longer engaging in normal activities in order to spend time/resources on the substance or behavior

The Indicators of Somatization

Somatization refers to physical and physiological manifestations of mental, emotional, and psychological conditions. Somatization most commonly occurs when a client does not have coping tools or capacity to manage mental, emotional, or psychological stressors. There may or may not be physical or physiological indicators of the symptoms that the client says they feel; however, the symptoms feel extremely real to the client. If a client visits a medical doctor reporting physical or physiological symptoms for which the doctor can find no tangible cause, this may be an indicator that the client is experiencing a somatoform disorder. Common somatoform symptoms include pain, muscle stiffness, nausea, fatigue, gastrointestinal disorders and discomfort, the experience of losing a function or sense, and hypochondriasis. When investigated from a biopsychosocial perspective, these symptoms often correspond with anxiety, stress, or trauma. Pediatric patients often report somatoform symptoms if they feel neglected, scared, or in need of attention. Therapeutic interventions often involve cognitive behavioral therapy, including introspective practices, the development of healthy coping mechanisms, and the development of problem solving skills. Therapy may extend to the family unit in pediatric cases, as a shift in parenting style or the provision of parenting support can often help alleviate the pediatric patient's symptoms.

Co-Occurring Disorders and Conditions

Co-occurring disorders may also be known as *dual disorders* or *dual diagnoses*. Co-occurring disorders are more prevalent in clients who have substance use history (or presently use substances). Substance use is diagnosed when the use of the substance interferes with normal functioning at work, school, home, in relationships, or exacerbates a medical condition. A substance use diagnosis is often made in conjunction with a mood or anxiety related disorder, resulting in a dual diagnosis.

Co-occurring disorders or dual diagnoses may be difficult to diagnose due to the nature of symptom presentation. Some symptoms of addiction or substance abuse may appear to be related to another mental health disorder; conversely, some symptoms of mental health disorder may appear to be related to substance use. On the contrary, there are some signs that a co-occurring disorder is present:

Mental health symptoms worsening while undergoing treatment: For example, a client suffering from depression may be prescribed anti-depressants to address depressive symptoms. However, if the client is using substances, he or she may mix other medications with anti-depressants. This can be dangerous in itself, but may also create a prolonged false sense of well-being while under the influence. Once this feeling fades, it can be confusing for the client to realize whether the prescribed medications are working. Even worse, the client may increase recreational substance use, leading to worse overall mental health symptoms over time.

Persistent substance use problems with treatment: There are some substance use treatment centers that transition clients off of one medication and place them on another, for example, methadone. This may result in a transfer of dependence and ongoing substance use while the client is receiving treatment for mental health disorders.

Another scenario is that a client may seek treatment from a substance use treatment center with clinicians that are not equipped to provide adequate mental health treatment for the client. As the mental health problems persist or worsen while undergoing withdrawal, the client may continue to engage in substance use as a coping skill, therefore making the substance use problem appear resistant to treatment.

It is important for co-occurring disorders or dual diagnoses to be treated together because they occur simultaneously. This may be done utilizing a multidisciplinary team approach in an outpatient or inpatient setting. Treatment of dual diagnoses or co-occurring disorders at the same time in the same setting by the same treatment team is also known as an *integrated treatment* approach.

Symptoms of Neurologic and Organic Disorders

Neurological and organic processes control the nervous system, and, consequently, all of the physical sensations, muscle contractions, perceptions, sensory experiences, and other biological mechanisms. Therefore, if something goes wrong in these processes, the symptoms that present can vary vastly. These symptoms include:

- Pain: muscle pain, joint pain, nerve pain, tingling or burning in an area

- Physical dysfunction: muscle paralysis, muscle tremors, muscle spasms, involuntary muscle tics, imbalance, fainting, vertigo, slurred speech, loss of tongue control

- Abnormal sensations: tingling, burning, hot or cold bursts on the skin, inability to feel cold or heat, incorrect indicators for cold and heat (i.e., touching something warm only to have it feel cool), numbness, "creepy-crawly" feelings on the skin

- Sensory dysfunction: sudden partial or complete blindness, abnormal smell and taste perception, hallucination, ringing in the ears

- Cognitive changes: loss of memory, difficulty in comprehending language or speech, inability to form sentences, difficulty recognizing familiar objects or faces

Indicators of Sexual Dysfunction

Sexual dysfunction can be related to physical or psychological causes and symptoms—or both. A medical examination can determine if the cause is physical and can usually provide treatment options that include medication or lifestyle changes. If the cause is psychological, such as a result of abuse, depression, or stress, then psychotherapeutic intervention may also be needed. Indicators of sexual dysfunction include:

- Erectile dysfunction in men
- Vaginal dryness or pain in women
- Pain during intercourse or arousal
- Lack of interest in sexual behavior (physically, mentally, or emotionally)
- Fear of sexual interaction
- Inability or difficulty reaching orgasm
- Inability to become aroused or difficulty maintaining arousal
- Negative emotions associated with sexual behavior (i.e. guilt, fear, shame, regret)

Methods Used to Assess Trauma

Trauma occurs when a client experiences a deeply disturbing experience that yields an intense emotional response. Traumatic events may interfere with a client's baseline level of functioning. It is important for the social work practitioner to have an understanding of the detrimental effects, both visible and invisible, that traumatization can have on a client.

The practitioner should have an understanding of the client's baseline level of functioning. This information may be gathered first-hand from the client or through collateral sources, if the client is unable or unwilling to provide that information.

The practitioner should have an understanding of how to guide the client gently through describing the traumatic experience and the emotions related to it. In doing so, the practitioner should have an understanding of the widespread, lasting, effects that trauma can have, as well as the multiple recovery and treatment options. This knowledge also helps prevent re-traumatizing the client.

An adult client may present with traumatic stressors due to one or more events that occurred during childhood. Symptoms of anxiety, depression, or other mood disorders that are actually related to the traumatic event(s) may present in session and daily functioning. A practitioner should be aware that symptoms of trauma could manifest in places and interactions outside of the client, such as within the family system, with peers, and at work.

Traumatic Stress and Violence

In normal circumstances, an individual is typically able to return to a calm state after a stressor passes. Traumatic stress and violence, however, cause long-term effects, and the patient may not be able to recover to a normal state. Indicators of traumatic stress and violence include:

- Unexplained anger or outbursts
- Substance use and abuse
- Uncontrolled behaviors such as binge eating, compulsive shopping, gambling, hoarding, or sex addiction

- Attachment issues
- Chronic and intense feelings of shame, regret, guilt, and/or fear
- Obsessive thoughts or behaviors related to the traumatic event
- Eating disorders
- Self-harm, self-injury, or other self-destructive behaviors
- Sleep problems such as insomnia or sleeping too much
- Intense anxiety, especially in social or crowded situations
- Children may become fearful, clingy, aggressive, or withdrawn, or they may regress in developmental behavior

Psychotropic and Non-Psychotropic Prescriptions and Over-the-Counter Medications

Psychotropic prescription medications are used to treat disorders such as schizophrenia, psychosis, depression, anxiety, bipolar disorder, attention deficit disorder, and a variety of mood disorders. Common antipsychotics include the brand names Abilify, Risperdal, and Seroquel. Possible side effects of antipsychotic medications include fatigue, weight gain, nausea, vomiting, anxiety, and gastrointestinal discomfort. Common mood stabilizers include the brand name Depakote and a variety of lithium-based medications. Possible side effects of mood stabilizers include gastrointestinal discomfort, weight gain, and fatigue. Common antidepressants include brand names Celexa, Lexapro, Zoloft, Prozac, Elavil, Tofranil, and Parnate. Possible side effects of antidepressants include nausea, weight gain, sexual dysfunction, sleep disorders, and gastrointestinal discomfort. Common antianxiety medications include brand names Ativan, Xanax, Valium, Lexapro, and Buspar. Possible side effects of antianxiety medications include fatigue, nausea, and gastrointestinal discomfort. Other psychotropic prescription medications include Vyvanse, which manages attention deficit disorders and hyperactivity, and Lyrica, which prevents seizures.

Non-psychotropic prescription medications are used to treat non-psychological disorders, such as hormonal disorders. The most common non-psychotropic prescription medications include the brand names Lipitor and Crestor (which lower cholesterol levels), Synthroid (which manages hypothyroidism), Ventolin (which manages asthma), and Nexium (which manages acid reflux). The side effects of these medications vary based on pre-existing conditions, but can include appetite dysfunction, nausea and vomiting, gastrointestinal discomfort, sleep problems, jitters, dry mouth, and fatigue.

The most commonly used over-the-counter medications include cough, cold, pain relief, and fever-reducing medications. These include the brand names Tylenol, Motrin, Aleve, Advil, Mucinex, Sudafed, and Claritin. Major side effects are typically only associated with over-the-counter cough and cold medications and can include extreme drowsiness. Other commonly used over-the-counter medications include those that treat acid reflux, constipation, and diarrhea.

Assessment Methods and Techniques

Problem Formulation

The problem system refers to factors that are relevant to the client's presenting problem, which may include other people or environmental elements the client deems relevant to the situation. It is important that questions be asked to determine what the client's perception of the presenting problem is.

Additionally, the practitioner should determine if there are other legal, medical, or physical issues related to the problem. For a comprehensive assessment, the client should also be asked how long the problem has been present and if there are any triggers he/she believes contribute to the problem. Identification of external supports and access to resources is also key when examining and discussing the problem system.

The presenting problem is generally revealed in the client's statement about why he or she has come in for treatment. If collateral sources are used, information can also be gathered from one or more of the collateral sources who have insight as to why the client is in need of assistance.

Disclosure of the presenting problem allows the social worker to determine the prevailing concerns deemed important by the client.

Social workers can gain a sense of how distressed the client is about the problem or situation and what client expectations are for treatment.

The manner in which the client describes the presenting problem can also provide insight as to how emotionally tied the client is to the problem and whether or not the client came in under his/her own volition.

It is important to determine the true root causes of the presenting problem. Although a client may come in and voice a concern, it may not be the root cause of the issue. Rather, this concern may simply be an item the client feels comfortable discussing. For example, a client who is experiencing sexual issues may initially speak about anxiety before disclosing the actual problem. This may require an investment of time to allow the client to become comfortable trusting the practitioner.

The history of the problem is important to address because it clarifies any factors contributing to the presenting problem, as well as any deeper underlying issues. Gathering background information on the problem history is also helpful for developing interventions. There are three key areas to address when reviewing the problem history: onset, progression, and severity:

Onset
Problem onset addresses when the problem started. It usually includes triggers or events that led up to the start of the problem; these events may also be contributing factors.

Progression
Assessment of the progression of the problem requires determining the frequency of the problem. The practitioner should ask questions to determine if the problem is intermittent (how often and for how long), if it is acute or chronic, and if there are multiple problems that may or may not appear in a pattern or recurring cluster.

Severity

Practitioners should determine how severe the client feels the problem is, what factors contribute to making the problem more severe, and how the situation impacts the client's adaptive functioning. This may be determined by addressing the following questions:

- Does the problem affect the client at work?

- Is there difficulty performing personal care because of the problem?

- The practitioner should ascertain whether or not the client has access to resources that can provide adequate care (running water, shelter, and clothing).

- The client's living situation should be explored, if there are difficulties with personal care activities.

- The practitioner should also ask if there are others for whom the client is responsible, like children or elderly parents/relatives.

- Has the problem caused the client to withdraw from preferred activities?

- Has the client used alcohol or other controlled substances to alleviate or escape the problem? If so, for how long and to what degree?

Psychosocial Stressors

Psychosocial stressors related to the problem should also be addressed by examining what the stressors are and addressing how they may influence the presenting problem.

A Likert Scale can be designed to assess the client's perception of how certain stressors are influential.

A *Life Events Scale* can also be utilized to assess the impact of psychosocial stressors. This scale has more than 40 life changes including divorce, death of immediate family members, marriage, work termination, and retirement, and provides a quantitative level of stress associated with such major events.

Problem ABCs

The *ABCs of a problem* refer to the Antecedent, Behavior, and Consequences linked to a client's perceived problem. The discovery of these items allows the client to define the problem specifically and examine factors affecting emotional well-being.

Antecedents to a problem may be prefaced by the involvement of certain individuals in the client's life. It is important to gather understanding on how the client was involved with these individuals and how the client felt affected. Environmental antecedents may also be present.

The client may disclose interactions that lead to problematic *behaviors*, based on the aforementioned information in the evaluation of the antecedent. When addressing the behavior, it is important that practitioners gather information on what is said before, during, and after the maladaptive behavior takes place.

The *consequences* to a presenting problem are comprised of both cognitive, or personal (internal), and environmental (external) interactions or reactions to the behavior. The client and other identified participants linked to the problem will reveal their belief sets and values based on the role played in either sustaining the behavior or attempting to decrease it.

The client's coping skills should be evaluated to determine the type of mechanism that he or she implements when the problem is present and whether or not it is an appropriate coping mechanism for the situation.

If the client presents with a heightened emotional reaction, as a consequence to the problem, it could parlay into another problem and create more complex issues for the client.

At this juncture, the information previously gathered on the client's legal and medical history is beneficial for practitioners to incorporate into the assessment process as it may have a significant impact on the factors shaping the client's problem and the resulting consequences.

Involving Clients/Client Systems in Problem Identification

Accurately identifying an individual's problem helps the practitioner tailor an appropriate intervention. This process includes defining the issue and why it's an issue in the individual's life. It's important to note that the problem is separate from the individual in order to allow the individual to look at the issue objectively without directing blame or shame. Problem identification can be accomplished by administering written or verbal assessments, interviewing the individual's social system or support, and holistically examining the individual's personal situation.

Techniques and Instruments used to Assess Clients/Client Systems

Many psychometric instruments exist to assess and diagnose psychological functioning. Some of the most common tests include:

Beck Depression Inventory-II (BDI-II)
BDI-II is a twenty-one-question inventory used to measure presence and severity of depression symptoms in individuals aged thirteen years and older.

Bricklin Perceptual Scales (BPS)
BPS is a thirty-two-question inventory designed for children who are at least six years old. It examines the perception the child has of each parent or caregiver and is often used in custody cases.

Millon Instruments
- Millon Clinical Multiaxial Inventory III (MCMI-III): This 175-question inventory is used to determine indicators of specific psychiatric disorders in adults aged eighteen years and older.

- Millon Adolescent Clinical Inventory (MACI): This 160-question inventory is used to determine indicators of specific psychiatric disorders in adolescents aged thirteen to nineteen years.

- Millon Adolescent Personality Inventory (MAPI): This 150-question inventory is used to determine specific personality indicators in adolescents aged thirteen to eighteen years.

- Millon Behavioral Health Inventory (MBHI): This 165-question inventory is used to determine psychosocial factors that may help or hinder medical intervention in adults aged eighteen years and older.

Minnesota Multiphasic Personality Inventory (MMPI-2)
MMPI-2 is a 567-item inventory. It is one of the most widely administered objective personality tests. It is used to determine indicators of psychopathology in adults aged eighteen years and older.

Myers-Briggs Type Indicator

Myers-Briggs is a 93-question inventory widely used to help people aged fourteen years or older determine what personality traits influence their perception of the world and decision-making processes. A preference is identified within each of four different dimensions: extraverted (E) or introverted (I); sensing (S) or intuitive (I); thinking (T) or feeling (F); and judging (J) or perceiving (P).

Quality of Life Inventory (QOLI)

QOLI is a 32-question inventory that determines the perception of personal happiness and satisfaction in individuals aged seventeen years and older.

Thematic Apperception Test (TAT)

TAT is a narrative and visual test that typically requires the individual to create a story and allows the practitioner insight into the individual's underlying emotional state, desires, behavioral motives, and needs. It's used for individuals aged five years and older.

Rorschach Test

Rorschach test is a visual test that records an individual's perception and description of various inkblots. It's used to determine underlying personality or thought disorders in individuals aged five years and older.

Wechsler Adult Intelligence Scale – Fourth Edition (WAIS-IV)

WAIS-IV is a series of subtests that assesses cognitive ability in individuals aged sixteen years and older.

Incorporating Psychological and Educational Tests into Assessment

Psychological and educational tests play a critical role in understanding client backgrounds, belief systems, and perspectives as part of the overall assessment. They also indicate any current or potential psychological, social, or physical needs that the client may have. These pieces of information shape the way social workers develop and tailor interventions for a specific client; they also allow social workers to maintain the highest level of safety for the patient as well as themselves. Psychological testing usually includes an interview component, in which the social worker may conduct the initial intake assessment, ask the client personal and family-related questions, and notice body language and other physical behaviors. Answers to interview questions and body language observations are incorporated into assessments by indicating potential risk or protective factors, individual capacity to accept and receive services, and strengths and challenges that the social worker can incorporate into the client's treatment plan. Clients are also often tested for their communication, comprehension, reasoning, and logic skills in order to determine which methods of intervention will be best received. For example, a client that is unable to communicate verbally may not benefit from simply listening to the social worker providing counseling; a non-verbal, interactive approach will need to be developed for such a client. Clients may also take personality and behavior tests, which allow the social worker to incorporate aspects of the client's beliefs, attitudes, perspectives, and reactions into the assessment.

Risk Assessment Methods

The practitioner conducts risk assessment to determine any influence that could result in harm or increased risk of harm to the individual. Assessing risk can be an ongoing process, as it's important to always have updated, accurate information. Risk-assessment methods will also vary depending on the circumstance (i.e. criminal justice, child abuse or neglect, community care). Some common methodology themes in risk assessment include the following:

Universal Risk Screening

General screening for certain risky behaviors (e.g., violent behavior, substance abuse problems, self-harm) that may result in additional screenings, referral for treatment, or stronger outcomes such as institutionalization (in the instance of high suicide risk, for example). This screening often takes place in initial consultations or as part of the individual's intake forms and may be administered on an ongoing basis (e.g., at every session) to remain current.

Unstructured Methods

These typically include clinical assessments without any specific, prepared structure. While high-level professionals often make judgments during this process, outcomes can sometimes be considered biased and unreliable.

Actuarial Methods

These include highly logical, regimented tests and scales used to predict the likelihood of certain behavior patterns in a specified time frame. While scientific and evaluative in nature, some argue that these methods may place undue blame on individuals or be too inflexible to allow for the likely interplay of many influencing factors in an individual's presenting issue.

Structured Professional Judgment

This combination of the previous two methods is generally the most accepted. It uses structured tools appropriate for the scope of the case, but allows for the judgment and flexibility of the practitioner to decide what information is useful and to note any external information that may not be caught by standardized assessments.

Client's Danger to Self and Others

Practitioners should always be alert to indicators that individuals may pose a threat to themselves or others. These indicators may be obvious or discreet and may include:

- Substance use and abuse
- Sudden apathy towards others or society
- Sudden lack of personal care or grooming
- Isolation
- Apparent personality change
- Drastic mood shifts
- Marked change in mood. Both depressed mood and a positive change in mood can be associated with suicidal thoughts or plans. A sudden positive change may indicate that the individual has made a decision and is no longer experiencing personal turmoil.
- Verbalization of feelings such as extreme self-loathing, desire to be dead, being a burden to others, or volatility toward others.

Risk Factors for Danger to Self and Others

A client who presents as a danger to self or others should be assessed through a biopsychosocial lens. In addition, tailoring crisis management techniques to the immediate problem can help de-escalate the situation. Open-ended questions should be used to gather as much information from the client as possible. It is also important to consult collateral information from any nearby family members to document other pertinent information about the client.

- The client should be asked if there are plans to harm anyone. If the client states yes, the practitioner should determine what the plan entails.

- Any and all threats made should be taken seriously and reported to the proper authorities. Colleagues may be consulted to determine the validity of a threat, if the practitioner is unclear on the client's intent.

- Identifying the critical event and antecedent that preceded it is important. The client should be asked to provide as much information on this as they are willing, in order for the practitioner to gain a better perspective of the client's point of view.

- Determining whether or not the client has engaged in self-injurious behaviors (SIB) is also important. Here are a few examples of SIB:

  o Excessive use of alcohol or other substances

  o Cutting

  o Banging one's head against a hard object

  o Ignoring necessary medical advice (not taking prescribed pills, leaving a hospital against medical advice)

- The practitioner should also evaluate the social and cultural factors that contribute to how the client reacts to stressful situations, including the following:

  o History of violence

  o Stability of relationships (school, work, and home)

  o Social isolation or withdrawal from others

  o Limited access to social resources

- Any recent life stressors that would lead to the client carrying through with a plan to harm self or others

- Assessing the client's current thought process is important. Do they present with confusion, clarity of the situation, or irrational thinking?

- If the client has a clear, concrete plan of action, then the risk for harm to self or others should be considered high.

Risk Factors Related to Suicide

- Previous attempts at committing suicide
- History of cutting
- Multiple hospitalizations related to self-injurious or reckless behavior, such as those noted below:
- Drug overdose
- Alcohol poisoning
- Inhalation of carbon monoxide
- Statement of a plan to commit suicide/suicidal ideations and access to the means to complete it
- Ownership or access to a lethal firearm
- Stated plan to cut one's wrists "the right way"
- Warnings or statements that suicide is planned
- Other factors related to suicide risk
- Age—middle-aged adults present highest suicide risk over other age groups
- Gender—males more likely to commit suicide than females
- Adolescents—high suicide risk, especially those heavily-entrenched in social media groups as a means of support and socialization
- Presence of a mental health disorder
- Life stressors from work or school
- Family history of suicide
- Family discord or other relationship trauma (divorce, break-up, widowed)
- Excessive drug or alcohol use
- Chronic illness
- Job loss

Assessing the Client's/Client System's Strengths, Resources, and Challenges

Once the client has identified the existing problem and systems, the client's *internal support systems* should be assessed, which includes examining the client's strengths and coping abilities. As with other facets of the assessment process, the client can provide a verbal report answering an open-ended question about what they view as current strengths and weaknesses.

Additionally, the social work practitioner can ask the client to provide a narrative related to a recent experience (it does not necessarily have to be linked to the presenting problem), in order to showcase strengths and weaknesses. Using finding questions can guide the client to describe their reaction to events comprehensively, to identify what favorable actions were taken, and to research what alternative actions could be taken. The social work practitioner may then summarize back to the client the strengths they heard in the narrative. This ensures that the client feels heard and understood.

The social work practitioner may also use scales to assess the client's strengths and weaknesses. A *dual perspective worksheet* may be utilized to identify the supports and obstacles perceived by the client in current social interactions. The worksheet helps create a visual map of the areas of strength the client can rely on as a means of improving areas of functioning, while simultaneously allowing the client to see areas that could use additional improvement. The social work practitioner can create a treatment plan with the client to develop or enhance coping skills, focusing on strengthening weaker areas and utilizing stronger ones.

Assessing Motivation, Resistance, and Readiness to Change

Motivation and resistance pertain to the individual's readiness to acknowledge and change behaviors. The more the individual feels ready to make a change, the higher the motivation and the lower the resistance. Some indicators of high motivation and low resistance include:

- Awareness and open acknowledgment of the presenting issue
- Willingness to list pros and cons of behavior change
- Willingness to make small steps toward and document outcomes of behavior change
- Acknowledgment that changing behavior is in the individual's best interest

Some indicators of low motivation and high resistance include:

- Lack of recognition of a present problem
- Hostility or apathy towards the practitioner (which may be revealed by skipping sessions)
- Discussion of a presenting issue without openness to changing associated behaviors

Practitioners can increase the client's motivation by discussing changes positively in terms that demonstrate benefit to the client's life, allowing the client to set his or her own goals and providing assistance only for those specific goals, highlighting the tools the client possesses to make changes, and acknowledging and respecting the client's fears about change.

Assessing the Client's/Client System's Communication Skills

An individual can communicate verbally and non-verbally through body language or silence. Interviews, two-way casual conversations, and written or verbal standardized assessments can help the practitioner determine the individual's communication skills. Role-playing a specific situation can help the practitioner determine how an individual communicates in certain contexts. Assessing the individual's personal, family, social, or cultural context can also provide valuable insight to communication skills and help validate an assessment.

Assessing the Client's/Client System's Coping Abilities

Ego strength is the ability of the individual to be resilient in the face of stressors. Generally, individuals with high ego strength will be able to return to a normal emotional state after experiencing crisis. They will be able to appropriately process it and cope with the demand of doing so. Positive or high ego strength is marked by:

- The ability to acknowledge mood shifts without getting overwhelmed
- The ability to cope positively with loss and setbacks
- Realizing painful or sad feelings will decrease in intensity over time
- Taking personal responsibility for actions and reactions
- Self-discipline in the face of temptation or addictive urges
- Setting and respecting firm limits and boundaries
- Avoiding people who are negative influences
- Learning from mistakes rather than blaming oneself or someone else

Consequently, the absence of these indicators may reveal areas around which to tailor intervention or treatment. These indicators may be determined through verbal discussion or standardized assessments.

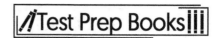

Strengths and Challenges of the Client

A client's personal and system strengths are aspects that support and promote an effective intervention and recovery. Individual client strengths may include a desire for positive change, willingness to collaborate with the social worker in developing an intervention, an interest in personal growth, resiliency, the presence of positive coping mechanisms, reliable transportation to and from counseling sessions, a way to pay for services, and any other physical, psychological, emotional, or financial behavior that promotes a continuous journey toward a positive resolution for the client. The client's system refers to their personal support system (such as family, friends, and professional colleagues) and the environment in which the client lives and works. Strengths in the client's system include aspects like close friends and family who support intervention procedures, employers that allow time off or sponsored insurance for receiving care, and colleagues that support the client's goals during the work day.

Client challenges include any personal aspect that may be a barrier to an effective intervention. Challenges may include a client who does not desire to change, who is not willingly attending social services, who feels their situation is hopeless, or who does not have the means to reliably attend intervention services (whether due to financial reasons, lack of child care, lack of transportation, and so on). Challenges in the client's system may include a non-supportive family unit (that does not support receiving social services, or that is unwilling to examine the family role in the client's issues), a lack of close friendships or relationships, the inability to leave work for sessions, or cultural norms or beliefs that stigmatize receiving counseling services.

Assessing Ego Strengths

Ego strength is the ability of the individual to be resilient in the face of stressors. Generally, individuals with high ego strength will be able to return to a normal emotional state after experiencing crisis. They will be able to appropriately process it and cope with the demand of doing so. Positive or high ego strength is marked by:

- The ability to acknowledge mood shifts without getting overwhelmed
- The ability to cope positively with loss and setbacks
- Realizing painful or sad feelings will decrease in intensity over time
- Taking personal responsibility for actions and reactions
- Self-discipline in the face of temptation or addictive urges
- Setting and respecting firm limits and boundaries
- Avoiding people who are negative influences
- Learning from mistakes rather than blaming oneself or someone else

Consequently, the absence of these indicators may reveal areas around which to tailor intervention or treatment. These indicators may be determined through verbal discussion or standardized assessments.

Placement Options Based on Assessed Level of Care

A client's need for care can fall on a wide spectrum. Some clients may comfortably live in their own residence but attend regularly scheduled meetings with a social worker to receive care. Other clients, after being appropriately assessed, may require institutional care where they can receive medical and therapeutic support as often as is needed. Institutional care may be a long-term or short-term solution for a client. The level of care required for a client is assessed by examining a number of self-sufficiency factors, such as the presence of any formally diagnosed developmental disabilities, physical disabilities, or mental disorders. Additionally, the client's ability to communicate needs, IQ level, ability to complete self-care tasks (such as dressing, toileting, grooming, et cetera) alone or with assistance, and risk of voluntary or involuntary harm to self or others will also be taken into consideration. Based on the client's health and caretaking needs, they may receive outpatient services (such as regular therapeutic appointments), inpatient services (such as a behavioral program that lasts for a predetermined period of time), assisted living in a facility such as a nursing home, or in-home support (such as a home health nurse). Regardless of where a client falls on the care spectrum, services for mental wellness and adjusting to this new context of life will likely be beneficial to care.

Diagnostic and Statistical Manual of the American Psychiatric Association

The current *Diagnostic and Statistical Manual of the American Psychiatric Association* (APA) utilized for the classification of mental disorders is the *DSM-5*. It is an update to the APA's previous classification and diagnostic tool from 2013, the *DSM-IV-TR*. The *DSM-5* serves as an authority for psychiatric/mental health diagnosis and functions as a tool for practitioners to make treatment recommendations. The *DSM-5* is organized in accordance with the developmental lifespan.

While the *DSM-5* provides classifications and symptoms of mental disorders, causation is not discussed. There are several notable changes to the *DSM-5*:

- the exclusion of Asperger syndrome as a distinct disorder on the autism spectrum
- the loss of some subtype variations for schizophrenia
- the renaming of gender identity disorder to gender dysphoria
- the restructuring of criterion for posttraumatic stress disorder (PTSD) to incorporate application to combat veterans and first responders
- the omission of the bereavement exclusion for depressive disorders

Complete Listing of DSM-5 Chapters
- Neurodevelopmental Disorders
- Schizophrenia Spectrum and other Psychotic Disorders
- Bipolar and Related Disorders
- Depressive Disorders
- Anxiety Disorders
- Obsessive Compulsive and Related Disorders
- Trauma and Stressor Related Disorders
- Dissociative Disorders
- Somatic Symptom Disorders
- Feeding and Eating Disorders
- Elimination Disorders
- Sleep-Wake Disorders
- Sexual Dysfunctions
- Gender Dysphoria
- Disruptive, Impulse Control and Conduct Disorders
- Substance Use and Addictive Disorders
- Neurocognitive Disorders
- Paraphilic Disorders
- Other Disorders

Indicators of Behavioral Dysfunction

Ideas about what is normal versus what is abnormal with regard to behavior are society-dependent. People tend to equate *normal* with "good" and *abnormal* with "bad," which means that any behavior labeled as abnormal can potentially be stigmatizing. Use of person-centered language is one way to reduce stigma attached to abnormal behavior or behavior health issues (e.g., saying "a person with schizophrenia," rather than "a schizophrenic.")

The "Four Ds" of Abnormality assist health practitioners when trying to identify a psychiatric condition in their clients. Deviance marks a withdrawal from society's concept of appropriate behavior. Deviant behavior is a departure from the "norm." The *DSM-5* contains some criteria for diagnosing deviance. The second "D" is dysfunction. Dysfunction is behavior that interferes with daily living. Dysfunction is a type a problem that may be serious enough to be considered a disorder. The third "D" is distress. Distress is related to a client's dysfunction. That is, to what degree does the dysfunction cause the client distress? A client can experience minor dysfunction and major distress, or major dysfunction and minor distress. The fourth "D" is danger. Danger is characterized by danger to self or to others. There are different degrees of danger specific to various types of disorders. *Duration* is sometimes considered a fifth "D," as it may be important to note whether the symptoms of a disorder are fleeting or permanent.

Crisis Plans

Any client who visits a social worker may experience a personal crisis at any time. A crisis is defined as any instance where the client is unable to cope with an event in a healthy, resolution-seeking manner. While all social workers should have a general plan for developing with unexpected client crises (such as calling for backup support or an emergency contact), a tailored plan should be developed during the initial sessions with the client based on what the client's needs are. The client should feel invited to collaborate in developing this plan to promote a sense of responsibility, accountability, empowerment, and engagement. Developing a crisis plan may include discussing what possible stress and crisis triggers are for the client, and discussing what the client feels like is the best solution for diffusing a crisis situation (such as employing trusted family members, utilizing a security item, managing therapeutic medications, and so on). This plan should be reviewed at regular intervals with the client to ensure it is still valid and does not need revisions to account for new triggers or resolved behaviors. Finally, should a crisis arise, social workers should be as transparent as possible about implementing the crisis plan. They should clearly communicate the steps they are taking as they take them, and invite the client to engage in the plan as well (if it is possible). Social workers should be mindful to note the context and present situation of the crisis, so that they can provide the best support in that moment. If the social worker tries to push the client too far in taking responsibility during a crisis or is too overbearing when the client would like to practice self-sufficiency, the crisis intervention may backfire and create a long-term barrier between the client and the social worker.

Objective and Subjective Data

Both objective and subjective data are used during the assessment and treatment processes. The client provides their perspective on what happened and the correlated feelings and experiences felt, which is the *subjective data*. Subsequently, the social work practitioner uses the information and may ask finding questions to better understand where the client is emotionally, while teasing out facts related to the client's situation. These facts are *objective data*.

The information from both the subjective and objective data is combined to formulate a concise, yet comprehensive, assessment for the client. In some note-taking practices, the identification of the subjective and objective data, along with assessment formation, is required. This style of documentation is known as the *SOAP method*, an acronym that stands for Subjective, Objective, Assessment, and Plan. Another note-taking style that focuses on the subjective and objective data is the BIRP documentation method. *BIRP* stands for Behavior, Intervention, Response, and Plan. It is not as commonly used as SOAP.

Methods to Interpret and Communicate Policies and Procedures

Social workers have direct contact with clients and are in strategically critical positions to develop, implement, evaluate, and communicate policies and procedures. Policies and procedures are necessary to allow clients and employees to be aware of treatment and agency goals, objectives, resources, and limitations. Policies can sometimes be a barrier to client services, so social workers must be aware of this possibility and point out these barriers when necessary.

Factors in policy and procedure development:

- Front line workers should be involved in policy and procedure development, since they are in the best position to determine and evaluate how clients are affected.

- Policies should be clearly written and communicated to clients/workers with copies available for distribution. Workers should receive periodic training on current policies and procedures.

- Polices should be in the best interest of clients, but also protect the agency and staff.

Factors to consider when evaluating the effectiveness of policies and procedures:

- The origins of the policy and/or procedure, including values and the related ideology
- Client reactions, thoughts, and feelings about the policy
- Alignment with social work ethics and values
- Intentional and unintentional consequences and benefits
- Regular re-evaluation to ensure policies and procedures are still relevant and in the best interests of clients, workers, and the agency

Research Designs and Methods

Basic and applied research are two separate categories of systematic investigation. Basic research aims to expand knowledge, although the new knowledge may not have any immediate application in the real world. Basic research can often lead to new ideas and theories. Basic research can explore, explain, or describe existing or potential ideas, with the end goal of simply understanding or creating new information. Applied research is conducted with the specific aim of answering a question or solving a problem. It is often used by business entities, scholars, and non-profit organizations to gather and analyze data relating to a very specific inquiry.

Basic and applied research designs can be qualitative (where qualities of interest are examined) or quantitative (where measurements of data are examined to statistically explain relationships between variables). Qualitative data methods include performing case studies on a specific entity, observation, interviews, and developing and confirming narratives about a phenomenon. These techniques are commonly employed in social work cases and interventions, where human behavior, family history, relationship history, environmental interactions, and other subjective variables are examined and

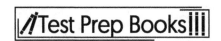

manipulated to support a client's health outcome. Quantitative methods measure two or more variables and concretely examine the relationship between them. Correlational design is a quantitative method that examines two or more variables to determine the influence one variable has on other variables (such as the relationship between age and IQ). Causal comparative design examines groups with similar features and differences to understand factors that may influence the similarities and differences. Experimental design establishes one control group as a baseline and conducts an experiment on another group to quantify the influence of the experimental factor. Control and experimental groups may be randomly assigned or assigned with a purpose (such as employing a sample of 21-year-olds in order to examine a specific behavior in this age range). Some designs use both quantitative and qualitative methods; these are called mixed research designs.

Data Collection and Analysis Methods

Qualitative data can be collected through interviews, observations, anecdotes, and surveys, and by reviewing literature and other relevant documents. Qualitative data collection methods are often subjective and cannot be generalized to larger samples or populations. Quantitative data can be collected from experiments, recordings of certain events and timed intervals, surveys in which an answer choice must be selected for each question, data management systems, and numerical reports. Quantitative data methods are often objective and abstract, and they can be generalized to explain relationships between variables in large populations.

To analyze data, researchers must ensure all collected data are relevant to the questions being posed, are accurate, come from a credible, unbiased source, and are complete. Often, all "cleaned" data sets are entered into a computer-based data management system software from which analyses and inferences can be calculated. Clean data sets can be accurately described for relationships between variables and to make simple observations. They can also be used to answer related hypotheses, or propose new ideas and inferences based on visible relationships. Often, these can be applied to explain behaviors, phenomenon, or other questions related to large population.

Reliability and Validity in Social Work Research

Reliability is used to describe whether a measurement method produces the same results over a long period of time and across different users. The reliability of a measurement method is analyzed through inter-rater reliability (if multiple researchers can use the method the same way), test-retest reliability (when measurements stay the same even when the method is used multiple times by the same person), parallel forms reliability (measuring the same results even when slight variations in the method exist), and internal consistency reliability (how consistent responses to the measure are). A strong measurement method performs well across all four of these reliability techniques.

Validity is used to describe how well a measurement method works to collect the data it is designed to collect. Face validity is used to describe how well a measurement method appears to be collecting desired information to the participant who is using the method. This is believed to influence participants into responding accurately. Construct validity is used to describe how well a specific variable is measured (as opposed to other measures that may be present). Criterion validity is used to infer performance. Formative validity is used to study outcomes and determine how to improve a measure or program. Sampling validity is used to describe how complete a sample is in order to eliminate bias.

Measurement methods can have high reliability and low validity, and vice versa. A strong research metric will be high in both reliability and validity.

Intervention Planning

Methods to Involve Clients in Intervention Planning

Practitioners should always treat the individual as the expert on the individual's life, and while practitioners should gather relevant external and collateral information, they should make all efforts not to allow these sources to supersede information provided by the individual. Practitioners should involve the individual as much as possible in problem identification and resolution planning by asking about details about the individual's life, any presenting issues and what might be causing them, what kinds of changes the individual would like to make, how these changes might enrich quality of life, and real and perceived fears.

All of these details should be acknowledged, respected, valued, and referred to when planning and implementing interventions. Practitioners should also tailor interventions to highlight and utilize established strengths and resources of the individual.

Indicators of Motivation, Resistance, and Readiness to Change

Motivation and resistance impact a client's readiness to change behavior. These are two crucial components to examine when developing an intervention plan. High motivation is indicated by self-confidence and self-efficacy, as the client believes they are capable of change. High motivation is also characterized by a client's desire to correct an identified problem, work toward a goal, and reliably show up for sessions. High motivation also shows in the client's belief that implementing a change will improve their overall quality of life.

Resistance can refer to any behavior that indicates the client does not want to work with the social worker or improve their personal situation. Resistance may be indicated by a client's refusal to show up on time, or at all, for sessions. A client involuntarily coming to sessions (such as by a court order) may state that there is no tangible problem to work on, or the client may state they feel no changes are occurring. Social workers should examine resistance holistically to ensure they are not contributing to it. For example, clients may exhibit resistance to counseling sessions if they do not feel comfortable with the social worker, if they do not understand the social worker, or if they are expected to work on issues they do not yet feel ready to address.

Readiness to change occurs in six stages: pre-contemplation (where an individual does not believe a need for change exists, or is not self-aware), contemplation (where an individual recognizes a problem but is not ready to address it), preparation (where an individual recognizes a problem and sets the stage for change), action (where an individual takes active, involved steps to stop a problem), maintenance (where the individual commits to the desired behaviors), and termination (where the individual is able to regularly sustain the desired behaviors without relapse).

Cultural Considerations in the Creation of an Intervention Plan

An intervention's success depends in part on whether the intervention plan is aligned with the individual's cultural experience. All individuals are part of cultures with specific traditions, habits, and norms. These can vary by race, ethnicity, immigration status, income level, geographical location, or social status. It's important to take culture into context in order to show respect for the individual's way of life, tailor interventions to be easily understood, create trust and cooperation, and avoid wasting time

or resources. Cultural contexts can be understood through researching the community, reading literature or periodicals from the area, and networking with people in the setting.

Intervention/Treatment Modalities

When utilizing a holistic approach for client assessment and treatment planning, practitioners should utilize evidence-based research to support the selected interventions and treatment modalities. The interventions and treatment modalities selected will be based on a number of things, including the client's current level of functioning (based on the biopsychosocial assessment), level of care needed, presenting symptoms, and the practitioner's background. Here are some things a practitioner will want to consider when constructing interventions or treatment modalities:

- Are the selected interventions evidence-based?
- Do the selected interventions arise from a strengths-based perspective specifically tailored around the client's strengths, interests, and needs?
- Do the associated risks with the selected interventions outweigh the possible positive outcomes?
- Is the selected intervention culturally-sensitive and culturally-appropriate?
- Did the client participate in the construction of the intervention selection and/or consent to it?
- Does the practitioner feel comfortable and well-versed in the selected intervention to increase the levels of intensity as needed and provide a continuity of care for the selected modalities?
- Does the selected intervention coincide with the client's financial ability to pay?

Intervention, Treatment, and Service Plans

Creating SMART objectives allows for data-driven and measurable intervention plans. When creating objectives, practitioners should be able to measure the desired behavior that is exhibited, the number of times the desired behavior is exhibited over a period of time, the conditions in which the desired behavior must be exhibited, and progress from the undesired behavior to the desired behavior through baseline evaluation and evaluation at pre-determined intervals.

Psychotherapies

Social workers need skills in a broad spectrum of areas, including case management, advocacy, and political change. Social workers need also be versed in psychotherapy modalities so as to enhance client engagement in the change process. Psychotherapy modalities originated with the "talk therapy" based on Sigmund Freud's work, and include, but are not limited to, cognitive behavioral, narrative, psychodynamic, solution focused, and behavioral therapies. It is up to social workers to decide which psychotherapies are most effective for their clients and should be pursued. Agencies may favor a particular type of psychotherapy that the social worker should learn. Insurers may favor psychotherapy modalities and social workers need to consider this in their work with clients.

Immigration, Refugee, or Undocumented Status on Service Delivery

Immigrants, refugees, and undocumented individuals often have the highest need for social services but also have the most barriers to effectively receiving support. Immigrants often face the stress of leaving their home country and assimilating into a completely new culture, economy, and lifestyle. While a social worker can help navigate these changes to set the foundation for a new life, immigrants often experience language barriers or simply may not realize such services exist for their use. Social workers may need to actively advertise their assistance and understand the background and culture of the immigrant in order to help.

Refugees often have the same stresses and barriers that immigrants have, but often they have also left violent or destructive situations in their home country. They may be happy to be safe, but they may also have deep feelings of sadness, especially if their families were affected (such as through death of a loved one or the necessity of leaving family members behind). While many immigrants come on work visas, refugees may have no means to make money and may need help navigating welfare benefits. There may also be feelings of discomfort in receiving these benefits. Social workers should be especially sympathetic to the diverse reasons behind an individual's refugee status.

Undocumented individuals may feel scared to seek out social services, fearing reprisal or deportation, even though social services can be an avenue to help undocumented families change their status to documented. Social workers who hope to help these groups should focus on building trust and creating spaces of security and safety.

Discharge, Aftercare, and Follow-Up Planning

An important part of treatment planning is discharge planning. There are numerous reasons that services for a client may end. Clients may feel that they no longer need the services, that they are not compatible with the social work practitioner providing the services, that an increased level of care is needed that is beyond the scope of the practitioner, or they may have successfully met goals for treatment.

Discharge planning should begin with the onset of the initial assessment for the client. The practitioner should not delay discharge planning, as discharge may occur at any time. Making the client aware of the choices for discharge and the discharge planning process empowers the client during treatment. It also provides continuity of care for the client.

The main purpose of discharge planning is to develop a plan of care that goes beyond the current treatment sessions to promote success once services have concluded. In the event the client is going to a higher level of care or to a different professional, effective discharge planning is useful in disseminating pertinent information about the client to assist in continuity of care and effective treatment. In this sense, the current practitioner should prepare to become a collateral resource linked to the client's level of care for the next professional.

In addition to benefitting the other practitioners the client may meet with, effective discharge planning is a benefit to the client as well. If services have been completed successfully and the client has met the stated goals, then discharge planning ensures the client has a plan to sustain a stable level of function and maintain the successes achieved. This is particularly useful with clients who suffer from substance use or other addictive behaviors, as effective discharge planning can prevent relapse.

Upon the conclusion of the client discharging from services, a discharge summary should be created and placed in the client's file. The *discharge summary* should include the following information:

- Reason for discharge
- Description of treatment goals and the degree to which they were met
- Client's response to the interventions
- Description of the client's levels of functioning
- Baseline

- Progress during treatment
- Functioning at discharge
- Recommendations for follow-up care
- Links to community resources
- Appointment dates for other providers (if available)
- Provision of additional contacts, client supports
- Description of potential risks post-discharge
- Contact information for post-discharge support and crisis intervention

Follow-Up Techniques in Social Work

At the final session, the social worker and client can schedule a follow-up session at a predetermined time to evaluate the client's continued progress after termination. Another option is to propose a time to meet and alert the client that the worker will contact the client to schedule a follow up. The follow-up session enables the social worker the opportunity to determine how well the client has progressed and to determine the effectiveness of the intervention(s) used during sessions.

Practice Questions

1. Which of the following is NOT a critical part of client interview?
    a. Building rapport
    b. Verifying payment
    c. Starting where the client is
    d. Use of encouraging, neutral questions

2. How many main sections make up the DSM-5?
    a. One
    b. Two
    c. Three
    d. Four

3. Jane wakes up every morning with a headache, jaw pain, and neck pain. She struggles to get out of bed, and even basic household tasks seem to take all of her energy. She has trouble getting to work on time, and even when she has an important deadline, she doesn't seem to care or be able to concentrate. She always feels cranky and sometimes finds herself crying over things that never used to bother her. At her office health fair, a vendor took Jane's blood pressure and found it to be 150/90. What might Jane's symptoms indicate?
    a. Psychosocial stress
    b. Gout
    c. Alzheimer's disease
    d. Generalized Anxiety Disorder

4. An individual with schizophrenia may be prescribed which of the following medications?
    a. Vyvanse
    b. Ritalin
    c. Nexium
    d. Abilify

5. What does a genogram visually depict?
    a. History of all prescribed medications and dosages
    b. Social interactions over a specific period of time
    c. Risk of carrying certain genetic diseases
    d. Stress triggers

6. Which of the examples listed depicts obtaining information from a collateral source?
    a. An initial verbal consultation conducted with a potential client
    b. A self-report assessment filled out by the client
    c. An official medical report brought by the client to their first session
    d. The client draws a picture illustrating their current mental state during a session

7. Which of these is NOT a commonly used psychometric in social work?
    a. Myers-Briggs Type Indicator
    b. Beck Depression Inventory
    c. Wechsler Adult Intelligence Scale – Fourth Edition
    d. Miller Analogies Test

8. Social workers typically examine a client's personal history holistically through what kind of lens?
    a. Clinical
    b. Biopsychosocial
    c. Psychosomatic
    d. Environmental

9. What are the components of a SMART objective?
    a. Sensitive, Makeshift, Attainable, Reliable, Time-Specific
    b. Sensitive, Measurable, Attentive, Retainable, Tolerable
    c. Specific, Measurable, Ability, Retention, Timing
    d. Specific, Measurable, Achievable, Relevant, Time-Specific

10. Joe is a fifteen-year-old white male. He and his family immigrated to the United States from Israel when Joe was five years old. His family celebrates traditional Jewish holidays like Hanukkah, Rosh Hashanah, and Yom Kippur with neighbors in their subdivision who are also of the Jewish faith. All of these qualities are examples of Joe's what?
    a. Upbringing
    b. Class
    c. Culture
    d. Friendships

11. Ella comes to her therapy session and is openly hostile towards her social worker. She remains quiet whenever a question is asked, and only speaks to say things like "This is a stupid idea"; "I don't need to change, they need to change"; "I hate doing this, and it's pointless." Ella is showing _____ motivation and _____ resistance.
    a. high, high
    b. low, low
    c. high, low
    d. low, high

12. Wellbutrin, Zoloft, and Prozac are all prescription medications classified as what?
    a. Atypical antipsychotics
    b. Typical antipsychotics
    c. Antidepressants
    d. Anti-inflammatory

13. Which of the following is a new class and new chapter of disorders in the DSM-5?
    a. Feeding and Eating Disorders
    b. Neurodevelopmental Disorders
    c. Anxiety Disorders
    d. Bipolar and Related Disorders

14. Which of these disorders is listed in Section III of the DSM-5 as a suggested topic for future research?
> I. Internet Gaming Disorder
> II. Caffeine Use Disorder
> III. Pica Consumption Disorder

a. I and II only
b. II and III only
c. I and III only
d. I, II, and III

15. An intervention plan should be which of the following?
a. Data-driven
b. Short, with details that can be expanded later as needed
c. Cumbersome
d. Mostly observational

16. To meet the client's needs and produce successful outcomes, intervention plans should be what?
a. Tightly structured
b. Flexible
c. Typed
d. Five-dimensional

17. During a mental status exam (MSE), assessing how well the client pays attention is an example of what main element of the MSE?
a. Psychomotor behavior
b. Mood and affect
c. Cognition
d. Thought patterns

18. It's essential that client information is always stored in what way?
a. In a filing cabinet
b. In an online database
c. Securely
d. At the end of the session

19. In the DSM-5, attention-deficit/hyperactivity disorder is classified as which of the following?
a. Neurocognitive Disorders
b. Neurodevelopmental Disorders
c. Neurological Disorders
d. Section III

20. When the client provides his or her perspective on what happened and the correlated feelings and experiences felt, it is known as what?
a. Measurable data
b. Objective data
c. Subjective data
d. Planning data

21. What is the first step in designing a community-level intervention?
    a. Touring the community's dining establishments
    b. Conducting a needs assessment for the community
    c. Holding a press conference with a community leader
    d. Working with policy-makers to create a new law for the community

22. The prefix *cardi-* generally indicates what?
    a. Skin
    b. Stomach
    c. Liver
    d. Heart

23. The prefix gastro- generally indicates what body area?
    a. Skin
    b. Stomach
    c. Liver
    d. Heart

24. Angina pectoris is marked by which of the following?
    a. Sharp chest pain
    b. Bone fractures
    c. Hair loss
    d. Allergies

25. Osteopenia is a disease marked by which of the following?
    a. Decline in cognitive function
    b. Decrease in bone density
    c. Decrease in red blood cells
    d. Decrease in liver function

26. Danny wakes up every morning and drinks three beers. Then he goes to work, where he's a senior manager. Lately, his subordinates have said that he never answers their emails or questions, and often they are unable to find him for important client meetings. Danny recently went to court for a driving under the influence charge, but he was released after paying a fine. Danny feels that because he's employed and isn't in jail, the charge isn't really a big deal. Before sleeping, he always drinks half a bottle of wine and two shots of whiskey. Danny is exhibiting signs of what?
    a. An eating disorder
    b. A liver disorder
    c. A gambling addiction
    d. Substance abuse

27. Approximately what percentage of Americans take at least one prescription medication?
    a. 90
    b. 80
    c. 70
    d. 60

28. Excessive sleepiness, untreated medical problems, excessive hunger, and reports that no one is around to provide care are indicators of what?
    a. Physical neglect
    b. Biological assessment flaws
    c. Sexual neglect
    d. Starvation

29. Interventions matched to client problems are based on _____ and empirical data gathered by the social worker.
    a. Biopsychosocial assessment information
    b. Behavioral approach
    c. Problem causation
    d. Solution identification

30. When does resistance from a client appear?
    a. Usually at the beginning of an intervention plan
    b. Usually at the end of an intervention plan
    c. At any time during the intervention
    d. Rarely; once a client has started seeing the practitioner, they are unlikely to resist

31. The terms Other Specified Disorder and Unspecified Disorder have been added to the DSM-5 to replace what?
    a. Not Otherwise Specified
    b. No Specification
    c. Always Specified
    d. These two terms are not in the DSM-5.

32. Prescriptions used to treat psychopathologies typically work best when paired with which of the following?
    a. Lifestyle modifications
    b. The Paleo diet
    c. Relocation
    d. Service pets

33. What is the most commonly prescribed drug in the United States and is used to treat thyroid problems?
    a. Synthyroid
    b. Lexapro
    c. Thryonate
    d. Lithium

34. When creating an intervention plan, who should be treated as the expert on the client's life?
    a. The practitioner
    b. The client
    c. The client's parents
    d. The client's primary care physician

35. What is the primary difference between atypical and typical antipsychotics?
    a. Atypical antipsychotics were developed decades after typical antipsychotics and generally have fewer side effects.
    b. Typical antipsychotics were developed decades after atypical antipsychotics and generally have fewer side effects.
    c. Atypical antipsychotics were developed decades after typical antipsychotics and generally have more side effects.
    d. Typical antipsychotics were developed decades after atypical antipsychotics and generally have more side effects.

36. The Bricklin Perceptual Scales are typically utilized in what type of cases?
    a. Custodial cases
    b. Homicide cases
    c. Suicide cases
    d. Substance abuse cases

Answer Explanations

1. B: Verifying payment is not a critical part of the client interview. Payment may occur before the interview process or may be pre-determined based on the work setting. Choice A, building rapport, happens at all stages of the client interview and is an important characteristic of interviews. Choice C, starting where the client is, is another important feature of the interview and is part of empowering the client by hearing things from his or her perspective. Choice D, the use of encouraging, neutral questions, is also part of empowering the client and moves the conversation forward, encouraging the client to share.

2. C: The DSM-5 has three sections—one that explains an overview of the changes, one that lists the classes of and criteria for disorders, and one that covers areas for future research.

3. A: Psychosocial stress. Gout is a kind of arthritis characterized by joint pain and inflammation. Alzheimer's disease is a neurological condition characterized by memory loss and confusion. Generalized anxiety disorder is characterized by persistent and excessive worrying and fear.

4. D: Abilify. Vyvanse and Ritalin are stimulants typically used to treat attention-deficit/hyperactivity disorders. Nexium is a proton-pump inhibitor used to treat reflux diseases. Abilify is an atypical anti-psychotic used to treat symptoms of schizophrenia.

5. B: Social interactions over a specific period of time. The other three answers do not fit the function or purpose of a genogram, which is used to show how a person's social (often familial) relationships affect attachment, behavioral patterns, and relationship dynamics.

6. C: An official medical report brought by the client to their first session. The other three examples show primary sources of information, as all of the information available is provided directly by the client. While the client is still the one physically giving the medical history report to the practitioner, it's considered a collateral source because it was officially documented and then obtained from a secondary source (the client's healthcare provider).

7. D: The Millers Analogy Test is a standardized test used for admissions in high IQ societies. The Myers-Briggs Type Indicator, the Beck Depression Inventory, and the Wechsler Adult Intelligence Scale are all commonly used psychometrics in social work.

8. B: Biopsychosocial. While social workers look at an individual's clinical, psychosomatic, and environmental history, these are small components that make up a full spectrum of influences in the individual's history. The biopsychosocial lens allows the social worker to look at biological, psychological, and social factors together to make reliable diagnoses and plan treatments.

9. D: Specific, Measurable, Achievable, Relevant, Time-Specific. SMART objectives should have specific features that can be measured, are achievable for the client's abilities and resources, are relevant to resolving the presenting problem, and have a time-frame for resolution in mind. Choice D is the only choice that includes all of these factors.

10. C: Culture is influenced by a person's race, ethnicity, immigration status, and traditions, to name a few. It can also include one's upbringing, class, and friendships, but these answers do not encompass *all* of the qualities listed in the question.

11. D: Low, high. Ella is not engaging productively with her social worker and doesn't seem to want to be in the session or pursue change, showing low motivation and high resistance to intervention.

12. C: Antidepressants. These medications are used to treat symptoms of depression. Atypical and typical antipsychotics are typically used to treat symptoms of schizophrenia or schizotypal behavior. Anti-inflammatory drugs are a type of pain reliever.

13. B: Neurodevelopmental Disorders. This class and chapter were not previously included in the DSM-IV.

14. A: I and II only. Internet Gaming Disorder and Caffeine Abuse Disorder have been listed in Section III of the DSM-5 as suggested topics for future research. Pica consumption is mentioned under Pica and Rumination Disorder, a subtopic of Feeding and Eating Disorders in Section II of the DSM-5.

15. A: A data-driven intervention plan supports reliable, measurable, unbiased outcomes. Intervention plans should generally be detailed, and details should be clearly documented, which eliminates Choice *B*. Intervention plans shouldn't be cumbersome to develop or implement, or the chances of producing successful outcomes diminishes, which eliminates Choice *C*. Observations are helpful parts of developing and implementing interventions, but they shouldn't provide most of the information, therefore eliminating Choice *D*.

16. B: A flexible intervention plan can be tailored to the client's needs, and can be updated as needs change. A tightly structured plan doesn't allow for this. An intervention plan certainly can be typed, but it's not necessary. The answer "five-dimensional" is not relevant to the question.

17. C: During a mental status exam (MSE), assessing how well the client pays attention is an example of cognition. Attention, level of concentration, memory, orientation, and judgment are examples of cognition during an MSE. Choice A, psychomotor behavior, involves eye contact, a handshake, posture, movement and coordination. Mood and affect (Choice B) involve cooperation, appropriateness, stability, and demeanor, while thought patterns (Choice D) include flow of thought and the ability to be present and engage in relevant conversation.

18. C: Securely. Choices *A* and *B* provide examples of how client information can be stored, and Choice *D* provides an example of when client information can be stored. These are all personal managing options for the practitioner, but regardless of the manner or time of storage, it's essential that client information is stored securely in order to maintain privacy and confidentiality.

19. B: Neurodevelopmental Disorders. Neurocognitive Disorders typically include cognition disorders that originate from physiological degeneration in the brain. Neurological Disorders aren't a classification in the DSM-5. Section III covers areas for future research, and attention-deficit/hyperactivity disorder has already been documented.

20. C: Subjective data is when the client provides his or her perspective on what happened and the correlated feelings and experiences felt. The social worker may use the information to tease out facts related to the client's situation, which is known as objective data, Choice B. Measurable data (Choice A) and planning data (Choice D) are not relevant to the context of the question.

21. B: Conducting a needs assessment for the community. This step allows the practitioner to see the current state of the community and determine if there are any areas for change. Choices A, C, and D may occur at a later stage, but they aren't the starting point for developing an intervention.

22. D: The prefix *cardi-* indicates *heart*. Skin is usually indicated by the prefix *cutaneo-* or *derm-*. Stomach is usually indicated by the prefix *gastro-*. Liver is usually indicated by the prefix *hep-*.

23. B: The prefix *gastro-* indicates the stomach. Skin is usually indicated by the prefix *cutaneo-* or *derm-*. Liver is usually indicated by the prefix *hep-*. Heart is usually indicated by the prefix *cardi-*.

24. A: Sharp chest pain. Angina pectoris can come on at any time and is a result of the heart not receiving enough oxygen. It's usually an indicator of heart disease.

25. B: Decrease in bone density. This is indicated by the prefix *osteo-*, meaning bone.

26. D: Substance abuse. Danny is showing signs of alcohol problems that include inappropriate consumption levels, interference with his work responsibilities, and legal troubles related to the substance.

27. C: Reports indicate that about 70 percent of Americans take at least one prescription medication.

28. A: These symptoms are indicators of physical neglect. Physical neglect can be the appearance of always being hungry, excessive sleepiness, or untreated medical problems. Other indicators of physical neglect are parents of caregivers demonstrating lack of interest or suffering from chronic illness. Usually, the home is an unsafe environment for victims who experience physical neglect.

29. A: The components of the biopsychosocial assessment drive the data pertinent to designing interventions that match the client's problems, such as client strengths and risk factors. In turn, these strengths and risk factors help guide the practitioner in the selection of a theoretical model to apply (in an effort to enhance client functioning and improve the client's overall well-being).

30. C: Resistance can appear any time during the intervention. Its presence is an important influence in how interventions are developed and managed.

31. A: Not Otherwise Specified. The terms Other Specified Disorder and Unspecified Disorder, respectively, describe disorders that do not fully meet the criteria for a DSM disorder or disorders that cannot be specified at all.

32. A: Lifestyle modifications. Prescription medications for mental disorders generally show the best results when paired with numerous, client-specific lifestyle modifications. These modifications may include changes to diet, a change of environment, or getting a service pet, but those examples on their own may not be the driving factor behind results.

33. A: Synthyroid. It's important to know commonly prescribed drugs, as many clients may take these medications. This is relevant intervention and treatment plan information. Lexapro and lithium are used to treat mental disorders and aren't more commonly prescribed drugs. Thryonate is not a real drug.

34. B: The client is the expert on his or her own life and should be treated as such. Doing so also helps the practitioner involve the client in care. The client's parents and clinicians are important in providing collateral sources of information, but shouldn't be viewed as the experts.

35. A: Atypical antipsychotics were developed decades after typical antipsychotics and generally have fewer side effects. Atypical antipsychotics were developed in the 1990s and have been shown to have less severe side effects. Typical antipsychotics were developed in the 1950s. They can be used if atypical antipsychotics don't work for the client, but they usually have severe side effects.

36. A: Custodial cases. The Bricklin Perceptual Scales are typically administered to children six years of age and older in custody cases to determine the child's perception of each caregiver.

Interventions with Clients/Client Systems

Intervention Processes and Techniques for Use Across Systems

Interviewing Techniques

Interviewing is common in social work. An interview should always be focused and have a purpose—this is often to gather data, diagnose, and provide therapy. An interview can be used to discuss behavior patterns, ensure the practitioner and the individual are discussing the same presenting issues, bring attention to presenting issues, or provide new perspectives on presenting issues. Interviews are generally verbal, although the practitioner should be mindful of observing non-verbal communication. While the questions of the interview should be planned, the practitioner should be able to tailor the questions based on the individual's needs.

There are several communication techniques beneficial to the social work practice other than the basic interview process used to gather general demographic and presenting problem information. Here are several:

Furthering
A technique that reinforces the idea that the worker is listening to the client and encourages further information to be gathered. This technique includes nodding of the head, facial expressions, or encouragement responses such as "yes" or "I understand." It also includes accent responses, whereby workers repeat or parrot back a few words of a client's last response.

Close/Open-Ended Questions
Depending on the timing or information the worker is seeking to elicit from the client, one of these types of questions may be used. Close-ended questions, such as "How old are you?" will typically elicit a short answer. Conversely, open-ended questions, such as "What are your feelings about school?" allow for longer, more-involved responses.

Clarifying and Paraphrasing
This is when social workers ask a client for clarification to ensure they understand the client's message. Clarifying also includes encouraging clients to speak more concretely and in less abstract terms to provide clearer messages. When paraphrasing, workers should convey a message back to the client to ensure an understanding of the client's meaning.

Summarizing
This is similar to paraphrasing, but summarizing includes more information. It's frequently used to help focus the session and allow the worker to summarize the overall messages, problems, or goals of the client.

Active Listening

Using facial expressions, body language, and postures to show the worker is engaged and listening to the client. Workers should display eye contact and natural but engaged body movements and gestures. An example would be sitting slightly forward with a non-rigid posture. As with all communication techniques, social workers should be aware of cultural differences in what is appropriate, especially related to direct eye contact and posturing.

Methods of Summarizing Communication

Social workers may paraphrase and echo clients' verbal statements to acknowledge their feelings. Summarizing may involve reflecting back the statements made by the client to clarify what the client has said. Social workers also must summarize communication in order to provide sufficient records of the session. Further, during the end of the session, the social worker may wish to clarify goals and homework assigned for the next week so that the client is clear on the changes that need to take place.

Methods of Facilitating Communication

Social workers may facilitate communication with the client by verbally encouraging communication or by addressing the client with constructive information concerning the case. Social workers need to recall information concerning the client from session to session in order to facilitate communication and move forward with the client. Clarifying what the client has said, and the client's feelings, helps not only to ensure the social worker clearly understands what is being communicated, but also lets the client know that the social worker is engaged and actively listening. Development of trust with the client may facilitate additional communication, and social workers should be sensitive to the trust-building process because it is the cornerstone of the helping relationship. Social workers may provide clients with homework outside of a session that facilitates communication during the next session.

Mandated clients, including court ordered clients or clients ordered to counseling from child protective services, may face challenges in communicating with the social worker because they do not choose to be in treatment. Developing trust with these clients to facilitate communication is especially important for progress to be made. It's helpful to acknowledge the client's feelings and possible frustration about the mandated treatment. Clients who require out-of-home placement need clear communication with the social worker to clarify what is happening and make appropriate psychological adjustments to their circumstances.

Using Bias-Free Language in Interviewing

When interviewing a client, a social worker must be careful to eliminate all personal bias from their language. This relates to all subtle negative phrasing related to race, ethnicity, socioeconomic status, gender, gender identity, life choices, disability, or psychological disorders. The job of the social worker is to support the client without bias, always promoting the client's self-identity. Phrases or expressions that demean or stereotype a particular group of people should never be used. Similarly, labeling someone can be hurtful, especially in cases where that label has a negative connotation or stigma attached to it. Sometimes it may even be appropriate for the social worker to ask the client how they wish to be identified or addressed. Inclusive and affirming language should be used when talking about all groups of people, and especially when talking to or about the client. Terms that are known to be offensive or degrading should always be avoided.

The Phases of Intervention and Treatment

The treatment intervention process consists of four stages. There is some crossover between stages, and the activities of each stage may occur at other times during the process. For instance, the assessment and evaluation phases of intervention are ongoing throughout treatment. Here are the four stages:

Engagement and Assessment

During this stage, the worker focuses on relationship and rapport building with the client. The worker gathers data, assesses the client's history and systems, and identifies problems and challenges.

Goal Identification and Intervention Planning

This stage consists of the client and worker collaborating to identify goals to be accomplished. Plan of care/treatment is developed and the contract is implemented.

Implementation

The caseworker implements selected interventions and tasks. The client works toward identified goals. During this stage, the plan is frequently reviewed by the worker in collaboration with the client to assess progress toward goals. Adjustments are made by either party if necessary.

Termination and Evaluation

The social worker should begin the termination phase at the onset of services, since the client may abruptly terminate services for various reasons. It is within best practice guidelines and the best interest of both social worker and client to be prepared for service termination. The social worker should inform the client about the termination guidelines once services begin. Moreover, goal attainment is assessed and evaluation of interventions occurs. The social worker should also review the plan for maintenance of acquired skills while follow-up procedures are discussed and implemented.

Problem-Solving Models and Approaches

When working with clients to develop problem-solving skills, workers must first engage and prepare clients by discussing the benefits of improving such skills and encouraging clients to commit to the problem-solving process during the goal setting/contracting phase.

Steps in the problem-solving process:

Assess, Define, and Clarify the Problem

As with goal setting, social workers should assist clients in clearly determining and defining the specific problem. Workers should focus on the current problem and ensure clients do not become distracted by other past or current difficulties. Examine specific aspects of the problem, including behaviors and the needs of those involved.

Determine Possible Solutions

Social workers should lead discussion among participants to determine possible solutions and encourage client(s) to refrain from limiting options at this point. The purpose is for clients to gain practice in solution development. In the case of family work, all capable members should be allowed to offer solutions and should feel safe to do so without fear or criticism from other members.

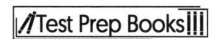

<u>Examine Options and Select/Implement a Solution</u>
Workers should assist clients in examining the benefits and drawbacks of each possible solution and choose an option that best meets the needs of those involved.

<u>Evaluate and Adjust</u>
Social workers should help clients to determine the success of the solution. Client(s) can use a practical form of tracking solution effectiveness (charts, logs, etc.). If it is determined the solution is not working, the client can return to the solution-generating stage.

Engaging and Motivating Clients/Client Systems

When determining a client's motivation, the engagement and assessment stage is crucial. When clients voluntarily seek services and/or are facing a crisis, the commitment and motivation will likely be high. Non-voluntary clients are identified as those who are seeking assistance based on pressure outside of the legal system (i.e., a woman gives her spouse an ultimatum to get help or she will leave). When working with non-voluntary or involuntary clients who are mandated legally to seek treatment, the social worker must help determine client-identified problems. This should be in addition or complementary to the presenting problem. The worker and client collaboratively should create a treatment plan that addresses both types of issues.

Additionally, the worker must help the client overcome any negative feelings of anger or mistrust about treatment. With all clients, appropriate relationship building between the worker and client is a necessary part of engagement and motivation. Clients must feel they are in a safe, empathetic environment. They also should experience a sufficient level of trust for the social worker in order for treatment to be effective. To create an effective treatment relationship, the social worker must project an attitude free of judgment, recognize the client's individual attributes, strengths, and abilities, and encourage the client's right to be an active participant in his or her own treatment.

Engaging and Working with Involuntary Clients/Client Systems

When working with involuntary clients, motivation levels can be improved by helping the client realize they have options. Even if services are mandated by a government agency, the client can choose to accept the consequences of not participating. Therefore, agreeing to adhere to the mandate is still a choice. When setting goals and treatment planning, ensure that the client's identified problems are included along with the mandated goals. Attempts to protect a client's right to self-determination should be practiced as much as possible (e.g., encouraging a client's participation in goal setting, problem identification, and priority setting, etc.).

Obtaining and Providing Feedback

There are several ways social workers can receive feedback. It can come in the form of evaluation by another social worker during supervision, or from a client during treatment. Obtaining feedback is an important means to improve a social worker's skill and ensure effective treatment for clients. Feedback from clients may be formal or informal. Clients may offer unsolicited feedback verbally or non-verbally during treatment, using words, body language, or tone of voice. Social workers must be sensitive to the messages clients are expressing to decipher how to interpret feedback that may not be clear.

When seeking feedback from a client, the social worker should ensure the method is appropriate to the skills, resources, and abilities of the client (i.e., in writing, by mail, text, in person, etc.)

Factors to consider when obtaining feedback from clients:

- Social workers may consider a client's progress toward a goal or lack thereof as a type of feedback. If treatment is not progressing as expected, the worker should evaluate and make adjustments as necessary.

- Always be clear why the information is needed and ensure client confidentiality to the fullest extent possible.

- Feedback can be sought at different times throughout the treatment process to ensure reliability and consistency.

- Workers should seek feedback regardless of whether it is expected to be negative or positive. All feedback should be viewed as a learning tool to enhance treatment and worker skill.

Factors to consider when receiving feedback during supervision/consultation:

- Social workers can benefit from feedback during supervision or consultation, especially with difficult clients/cases or at significant times in treatment, such as termination.

- When discussing cases, client confidentiality should be protected as much as possible, and client consent to release information should be acquired.

Active Listening and Observation

Active listening is crucial to the relationship and rapport building stage with clients. Social workers must be fully engaged in the listening process and not distracted by thoughts of what will come next or intervention planning. The worker must not only hear the audible language the client is offering but must also look at the non-verbal behaviors and the underlying meaning in the words and expressions of the client. Nonverbal behaviors include body language, facial expressions, voice quality, and physical reactions of the client. Other aspects of active listening include head nodding, eye contact, and using phrases of understanding and clarity such as, "What I hear you saying is . . ." and "You (may) wish to . . ." Workers may verify they understand the client's message by paraphrasing and asking for validation that it is correct (i.e., "What I hear you saying is . . .").

Verbal and Nonverbal Communication Techniques

Social workers use verbal and nonverbal communication techniques to engage clients in completing treatment goals. Verbal communication is vital to the social worker/client relationship, and social workers should be skilled at greetings, summarization, reflection, and the conveyance of new information to the client. The client may misconstrue a social worker's body language if it does not represent openness and trust. Likewise, the social worker needs to be adept at analyzing the client's body language in order to move forward. Clients use both verbal and nonverbal communication to convey their story to the social worker, and communication techniques used by the social worker can be modeled to teach the client improved communication. Clients should be instructed to recognize their own communication techniques in the context of the relationship with the social worker. Clients who are withdrawn or isolated may need especially sensitive communication with the social worker in order to better communicate verbally and nonverbally.

In order to build a strong helping relationship with the client, the worker must learn to use effective verbal and nonverbal techniques. These skills are necessary throughout the treatment process, but especially during assessment and engagement.

Congruence in Communication

Social workers need to be congruent—in agreement and harmony—with client feedback and encourage clients' self-direction. Social workers and clients begin treatment by enhancing congruence in communication so that mutually agreed upon goals may be developed for the client. The social worker should be invested in the therapeutic relationship and able to participate in a way that assists the client in becoming more self-aware. If a social worker is not congruent with the client, then treatment progress may be hindered and the client should be referred to another worker who is a more appropriate fit.

Limit-Setting Techniques

Although it may be difficult for social workers to develop the ability to set limits with clients, it is necessary for treatment to be effective. Many clients struggle with the ability to follow rules and maintain healthy boundaries. In addition to ensuring the treatment process progresses smoothly, when workers set limits, clients also learn to develop helpful life skills. This is especially important with involuntary clients receiving legally mandated services that cannot be modified or negotiated. Other reasons for limit setting are ensuring the maintenance of an appropriate client-worker relationship, refusing a client request to give misinformation to a legal institution/employer, and saying no if a client asks for monetary loans.

Role-Play Techniques

Role-play is a type of modeling, also called behavior reversal. This technique enables clients to view the different ways a person may handle a challenging situation. It also allows a client to view a non-tangible behavior in a more tangible way. When clients practice skills and develop new and more productive methods of coping, they are able to take an active role in treatment, increasing their sense of empowerment and self-determination.

Role Modeling Techniques

Role modeling, which offers the client a real life view of desired target behaviors, can be an important tool to learn new skills. The social worker can request that clients demonstrate the behavior before modeling it, thereby allowing the worker to assess a client's current skills and abilities. Social workers can demonstrate a coping model showing the skill or desired behaviors, including difficulties, anxieties, or challenges. The worker can also demonstrate a mastery model, which shows confidence and competence with the desired behaviors. Each method has benefits and drawbacks. In coping mode, the client and worker can process the interaction and identify improvements or changes that can be made to the desired behaviors or actions. There are several types of modeling:

- Symbolic Modeling: client watches a visual representation of the modeled behavior (i.e., video, TV, images)
- Live Modeling: client watches while a person performs the behavior

- Participant Modeling or Guided Participation: client observes model performing behavior and then performs the behavior and/or interacts with the model
- Covert Modeling: client visualizes the desired behavior

Harm Reduction for Self and Others

Clients who are in immediate danger of self-harm should be referred to a local emergency room or hospital immediately. Clients who are a danger for self-harm may develop a no-harm contract with the social worker, even though this may not be legally binding. Clients who engage in self-harm may find relief in applying ice to the area of harm, snapping a rubber band, or using colored markers instead of sharp objects. Social workers also need to engage clients in changing distorted thinking related to harm reduction. Clients who are at risk for harm to others may need to be hospitalized or placed in protective custody. Social workers who are aware that the client is at risk of harming a specific victim have a duty to warn the potential victim and report this threat to the appropriate authorities. This mandate originated with the Tarasoff case involving a client who was not reported to the prospective victim and then proceeded to kill her. This is a mandatory legal requirement when a client threatens a specific victim.

Teaching Coping and Other Self-Care Skills to Clients

Social workers may act in the role of teacher to instruct clients about coping and other skills. Coping skills may include relaxation techniques, deep breathing, time out, and improved communication skills. Common diagnoses that often require the instruction of coping skills include stress reduction, anxiety, and major depression. Clients may be able to utilize coping and acceptance skills for these diagnoses because they are frequently chronic, and clients will need to cope with them on an almost daily basis. Clients often need to learn a plethora of new skills to manage their issues and complex problems, and they and the social worker should collaborate on coping and other skills to manage these circumstances. Social workers can partialize and brainstorm with clients concerning coping and other treatment skills. Clients sometimes need detailed instructions in order to succeed with treatment goals. Clients need to be engaged in therapy outside of sessions and learn how to cope when the social worker is not present, so assigning clients homework between sessions is a method of skills building. While the social worker may offer suggestions to the client for coping and other skills, the client is ultimately the most effective arbiter of their own treatment.

Client Self-Monitoring Techniques

Client self-monitoring can be a useful technique for turning subjective qualitative information into more quantifiable data. Clients may engage in self-assessment techniques and practices that include journaling, questionnaires, and evaluations. Clients collect data about goals, objectives, and the targeted behavior. This technique collects important information about client progress, but it also adds to clients' feelings of empowerment and self-determination as they become collaborators in treatment. Clients can either track information related to thoughts or behaviors or can use more formal charting techniques. Social workers should assist clients with defining and identifying which type of information to track and then demonstrate how to use the selected tracking technique. Self-monitoring methods serve several purposes. As clients become more invested in treatment, their awareness of strengths and areas in need of improvement may also increase. This will enable the client to monitor behaviors as they occur, allowing for the development of insight related to behavioral change.

Methods of Conflict Resolution

Social workers may engage in conflict resolution with clients by acting as a mediator or advocate. Mediators work with clients to intervene in the conflict and develop helpful solutions that reflect all parties involved. For example, the social worker may act as a mediator in family or couples therapy conflicts. Social workers may also work with clients on developing their own conflict resolution skills through methods such as reflection, role-playing, and empty chair techniques. Social workers may also encourage clients to practice the use of *metacommunication*, which is communication about the behaviors and reactions of their regular and possibly dysfunctional method of interactions or communication. Sometimes the client is in conflict with the social worker and transference issues must be resolved before progress can be made. Social workers and clients need to be in collaboration concerning treatment goals and modalities so that conflict is reduced.

In some cases, agencies contract with mediation services outside the agency to assist clients in resolving conflicts. Professional mediators are trained in mediation techniques and are paid by the agency for their services. They can be the final step of resolution when the agency cannot resolve client conflict. Child protective services agencies sometimes use professional mediators to reduce or eliminate conflict in cases involving juveniles.

Crisis Intervention and Treatment Approaches

A crisis can occur whenever a client is in physical danger or extreme emotional need. For example, suicidal threats or ideation qualify as a crisis situation. When a crisis arises, the very first concern is always safety. It is important to get the client into a safe situation, protected from themselves or others. After safety is established, it is then possible to assess the level of need and what should happen next in order to best assist the client.

Another important strategy is de-escalation. When there is a crisis, extreme emotions are usually involved. If possible, a client should be guided through relaxation techniques to help calm them down. Oftentimes, a calm and neutral party who can facilitate a conversation or listen to the client empathetically, but without feeding the emotion, will automatically de-escalate the situation. Confrontation or matching the client's emotions will escalate the situation. Allowing the client to communicate the situation fully may help them to become less emotional and more focused on the facts. At this point the client may be able to focus on the next steps and specific tasks that need to be done. If possible, help the client to regain emotional control so that extreme options such as restraints are unnecessary.

In cases where a client is suicidal, it is important to establish if there is a suicide plan or means of committing suicide in place. These two things will determine the severity of suicidal ideation and how at-risk the client is. If it is determined that a client is at imminent risk of suicide, they should be admitted to the hospital or a mental health facility for their own protection.

Creating crisis plans ahead of time, in collaboration with clients, may assist them in preventing crisis situations or more quickly regaining control when the crisis arises. If clients have been part of the planning process, they may feel empowered, even when their emotions are overwhelming them. Part of the plan should be to identify the potential triggers or warning signs, and have immediate steps that can be taken to avoid a crisis. This could be engaging in relaxation strategies, or calling a supportive friend, family member, or clinician.

Trauma-Informed Care

Trauma-informed care systems ensure that trauma and its effects are understood by health services providers and that signs and symptoms of trauma are recognized even when not explicitly stated by the client. Trauma-informed care means that trauma-informed practices are integrated into all procedures of the care system. Incorporating these aspects into care involves ensuring a sense of safety and security for the client and the client's family. Trauma-informed care also ensures that the client feels they can trust the social worker and that all procedures are communicated and transparent. It provides a network of support, empowers the client to collaborate with their health care providers to develop a suitable intervention, and encourages the client to ask questions and voice concerns at any time. Trauma-informed care also accounts for each client's specific personal history, cultural and social norms, and other unique factors. Interventions encourage respect, self-efficacy, hope for future outcomes, and identify that various behaviors correlate as coping mechanisms to specific instances of trauma. Trauma-informed care is a model that is encouraged with any social services client, but it is especially beneficial for survivors of abuse, those experiencing eating disorders or addiction, or those who grew up in poverty or violence.

Anger Management Techniques

Anger management is a fairly common treatment goal for clients, so social workers need to be familiar with anger management techniques. Clients may manage anger by counting to ten before responding to a situation, taking a time out from the situation to reduce intensity, or practicing deep breathing techniques. Clients may also benefit from vigorous physical exercise to reduce anger. If clients are involved in vigorous exercise, they may need to consult with a physician for approval. Clients may also engage in thought stopping techniques to alleviate anger. Thought stopping sometimes involves the use of guided imagery, such as a stop sign, to reduce moments of intense emotion or thinking.

Stress Management Techniques

Social workers will often encounter clients with stress related problems and should be well versed in stress management techniques to offer clients suggestions for this issue. Social workers may engage clients to practice relaxation techniques in order to manage stressors. Clients may engage in physical exercise at their physician's discretion to relieve stress. Deep breathing exercises are also beneficial in relieving stress. Clients may work to change fallacious thinking patterns and distorted perceptions to reduce stress through treatment such as cognitive behavior therapy or rational emotive therapy. Clients may be stressed concerning basic living needs and social workers can link clients to services in the community to assist them with these issues. If clients are at the safety and physical stages of the hierarchy of needs, these stressors should be addressed before other issues are included in the therapeutic process.

Cognitive and Behavioral Interventions

Cognitive Approaches

Cognitive approaches to the social work process involve changing the way the client thinks in order to facilitate progress and problem solving skills. Cognitive approaches tend to be evidence based and favored by insurance carriers, as they are efficacious for a variety of client issues, including substance use and personality disorders. Cognitive approaches focus on changing maladaptive thinking and cognitive distortions, and thus may help clients engage in behavior change. Cognitive distortions involve fallacious thinking patterns engaged in by the client, such as black-and-white thinking. Types of cognitive

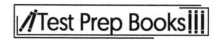

approaches may include cognitive behavior therapy, rational emotive behavior therapy, and solution focused brief therapy. There are many modalities of cognitive therapies and social workers should become familiar with—and implement—them when necessary.

Behavioral Approaches

Behavioral approaches, which originated with Skinner and Pavlov, include methods of changing and motivating client behaviors toward reaching constructive goals. The underlying concept is that if clients can change behavior, they may also alter the way they think. Skinner and Pavlov believed that all behavior is learned, and they believed in conditioning. Tokens may be awarded for positive behavioral changes in the client; this occurs in what is called a token economy. Cognitive behavioral therapies, which focus on both the cognition and the behavior of the client, are considered evidence based and are favored by managed care insurers.

Strengths-Based and Empowerment Strategies and Interventions

Empowerment is a strengths based modality, and the goal is that all clients should feel empowered based on their personal identities. Clients need to feel in control of most of their lives and circumstances, and this is what empowerment permits. Working from a strengths based perspective empowers clients to facilitate change in their own lives. Social workers may seek to empower clients by focusing on strengths and bolstering clients' social constructs. Clients may need to be empowered from a racial, ethnic, religious, gender, or age perspective because they have suffered discrimination in these areas. Social workers may act as political advocates in these realms to combat social oppression affecting clients. The social worker should take into account the differences each client possesses due to their personal race, religion or circumstance, and use these differences as strengths.

Client Contracting and Goal-Setting Techniques

Goal setting is a necessary factor in both the treatment and evaluation of direct practice. Social workers should work collaboratively with clients to determine goals. To be effective, goals need to be specific, measurable, achievable, realistic, and timely. They also should be directly related to the target problem. During the assessment process, begin identifying possible goals for treatment. Depending on the identified issues, goals may focus on desired behavioral, cognitive, or emotional changes.

Reciprocal goals are complimentary goals agreed upon by members of a system related to the same target problem (i.e., a father's goal is to offer more compliments to his son, while son agrees to increase verbal acknowledgement to father's positive feedback).

Shared goals are when members of a system choose the same goal that addresses an identified problem (i.e., spouses each agree to communicate needs more frequently).

Contracts

Once goals are determined, a contract is the next step to engage the client in services. Contracts can be formal or informal, and written or verbal depending on the policies of the agency and the nature of treatment. A contract between client and worker provides a set of expectations and guidelines for treatment. Clients should be made aware the contract is a commitment by both parties, but not a legal document. Components of the contract include goals, assignments of tasks, timeframes, frequency of sessions, methods for determining progress, and how updates or revisions of the contract can occur. Other items that can be included are lengths of sessions, financial arrangements, and procedures for cancelling appointments.

Partializing techniques

Partializing means to break down into smaller steps. Clients sometimes need partializing techniques to address complex problems, which may involve trauma, grief, or even personality disorders. A social worker can partialize with the client by encouraging the client's suggestions about solving the problem or making a written list. Partializing assists the client in reaching treatment goals in a more organized and efficient fashion. Case management of the client's goals may also include partializing techniques so that the client does not encounter stressors in addition to the problem solving process. Clients with complex cases may benefit from partializing techniques because they can focus on one step at a time and avoid becoming overwhelmed with treatment goals. Clients may learn partializing techniques from the social worker and then learn to implement them in their own lives so that they can partialize issues that they encounter at home.

Assertiveness Training

Assertiveness training is an intervention that can be used in multiple settings with an assortment of interpersonal difficulties. This type of training helps individuals learn to express their emotions, thoughts, and desires, even when difficult, while not infringing on the rights of others. There are ways in which individuals can assert themselves, including saying no to a request, having a difference of opinion with another person, asking others to change their behavior, and starting conversations. Social workers must respect cultural differences when working with clients to develop assertiveness skills. For example, some cultures feel it is inappropriate for women or children to assert themselves. Role-play is an effective technique to help clients develop assertiveness skills.

Task-Centered Approaches

Task Centered Practice is comprised of a practical, evidence-based intervention that lasts for six to twelve sessions (short term). Task Centered Practice can help resolve problems related to daily living tasks, i.e., lack of basic needs, interpersonal/social relationships, role performance, and decision-making skills. This method is client-driven, with the social worker as a guide or collaborator. A specific problem is identified with an associated goal to be accomplished. Afterward, the social worker assists the client in identifying and conquering smaller tasks to resolve the problem. Subsequently, the assessment phase is vital to this process as both client and social worker identify issues, strengths, and resources, and work together to define goals/tasks. The Task Centered Practice model also places emphasis on contracting, carefully planned task implementation, evaluation, and termination.

Psychoeducation Methods

Psychoeducation refers to any form of training or instruction that is provided to clients and the client system as a part of understanding mental health or psychological issues and treatments. Its goal is to support clients experiencing mental illnesses, their families, and their networks while eliminating the stigma that has been associated with mental health issues for decades. Psychoeducation methods include explaining potential causes for specific mental health issues, understanding the challenges of specific mental health issues, explaining how support systems can acknowledge and cope with not only a client's mental health condition but also their own caregiving stress, and teaching coping skills, building resiliency, and overcoming obstacles in ways that are accessible. This form of education can occur in group settings, seminars or webinars, and in individual or family sessions. It can also through newsletters, other media, and formal courses. It may be offered in-home, online, in hospitals or other healthcare facilities, in community centers, or at conference venues. It is not considered treatment, but

it is a beneficial complement to clinical care. It promotes positive and inclusive language, eliminates shame and fear around mental illnesses, creates educational value, fosters network support and understanding, and acknowledges a variety of feelings and responses to mental health conditions. Psychoeducation techniques are associated with reduced inpatient and hospitalization rates for clients with mental health conditions. Psychoeducation is correlated with clients' self-reported feelings of acceptance and increased family support. Family and friends self-report a better understanding of their loved one who may have a mental health condition, a better understanding of their role in providing positive support and care, the ability to draw healthy boundaries for themselves, and relief from learning and utilizing self-care techniques that reduce caregiver stress.

Group Work Techniques and Approaches

Group work can be defined as a goal-directed intervention with small groups of people. The intention of this work is to improve the socioemotional and psychoeducation needs of the individual members of the group through the group process. There are two types of groups in social work: therapeutic and task groups. Task groups are created to perform a specific task or purpose. These groups differ in the amount and type of self-disclosure, confidentiality, and communication patterns. There are several types of treatment groups, including support, educational, and therapy groups. Groups can also be long-term or short-term, depending on the type and purpose.

Groups can be open or closed. Open groups are ongoing and allow for new members to enter at any time. Open groups are typically used for support and life transitions. There are challenges to this type of group, since the members are at different stages in the group process. The frequently changing membership can be disruptive to the group process because members may not feel as emotionally safe to share with others. Closed groups are time-limited, and new members can only join during the beginning stage. The advantages to this type of group is more engagement and better trust by the members, since the group process is more stable. A disadvantage is that if several members leave the group, the group process may not be as effective. There are several variations by theorists that describe the stages of group development. A general method of categorizing the group process is the beginning, middle, and end stages. Each stage is classified by different activities, processes, and tasks:

Beginning Stage
Social workers determine the group's purpose, members, objectives, and other logistical tasks (time, location, etc.). Group formation occurs at this stage as new members come together. The social worker fosters a safe and trusting environment by establishing acceptable group norms. As group members become more comfortable, conflicts arise as power and control behaviors emerge. Group roles and alliances begin to form. The worker's role is to help guide the group through these challenges and process any conflicts that arise within the group.

Middle Stage
This stage is where most group work is done. Members share information, openly address issues, and work through conflicts. Some groups do not make it to this stage for several reasons, including member dynamics and a lack of investment of the group members. Group cohesion or the connectedness of the members is extremely important at this stage. The role of the worker is to help members focus on methods and the meaning of communication, working through group differences and confronting members when necessary. Workers should also help develop more intensive levels of cohesiveness while building on member individuality.

End Stage

Group members come to resolutions on the issues addressed during the group process. Members may have strong reactions to termination, especially if there was a high level of cohesion developed during the group process. The social worker should lead the group in discussing feelings about termination and be aware of negative reactions that may surface. When these types of emotions occur, social workers should address any challenges that arise with members. The social worker should also help group members identify and reflect on the skills learned in the group process and how those skills can benefit the members with future challenges.

Working with Individuals in the Group Context

It is the role of the social worker to encourage all members to participate in the group process. The worker can solicit feedback from each member of the group throughout the group process. Clients typically take on various roles during group treatment. Roles can be defined as functions the individual members of the group are fulfilling or performing that facilitate the group process. Some roles include that of a clown, scapegoat, mediator, etc. The worker must be aware of the roles of each individual and how those roles are affecting the group so interventions can be made when necessary.

Family Therapy Models, Interventions, and Approaches

One of the main goals of family therapy is to allow each family member to function at his or her best while maintaining the functionality of the family unit. When working with families, the social worker must do the following:

- Examine and consider all systems affecting a family and each individual member to determine problems, solutions, and strengths, and must also consider the functionality of the family subsystems.

- Respect cultural, socio-economic, and non-traditional family systems and not automatically define those systems as dysfunctional if they are not the norm. The overall and individual family functioning should be accounted for.

- Work to engage the family in the treatment, while considering the specific traits of the family (i.e., culture, history, family structure, race, dynamics, etc.).

- Assist in identifying and changing dysfunctional patterns, boundaries, and family problems.

Important Concepts

Boundaries: Healthy boundaries around and within the family must exist for families to function effectively. The boundaries must be clear and appropriate.

Emotional Proximity and Distance: the type of boundaries that exist within a family system

Enmeshed: Boundaries are unclear and pliable. Families that have very open boundaries within the family unit may have very fixed boundaries between outside forces and the family.

Disengaged: Boundaries are rigid with little interaction and emotional engagement. Families that are disengaged within the family system tend to have very open boundaries around the family unit.

Family Hierarchy: The power structure within the family. For families to function effectively, there must be a clear delineation of authority. There must be an individual or individuals who hold the power and

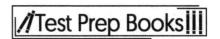

authority in a family system. In a traditional family, this should ideally be located within the parental system.

Homeostasis: Family systems should maintain homeostasis or remain regular and stable. When life events become too stressful and the family can no longer function as it normally would, the state of homeostasis is threatened. This is usually when many families seek help.

Alliances: Partnerships or collaborations between certain members of a family. When alliances exist between some members of a family, it can lead to dysfunction (i.e., parent and child have an alliance that undermines the parental subsystem).

Couples Interventions and Treatment Approaches

Many couples enter treatment after experiencing long-standing problems and may seek help because all other options have failed. One of the goals of couple's therapy is to help clients develop effective communication and problem-solving skills so they can solve problems throughout and after treatment. Other goals include helping the couple form a more objective view of their relationship, modifying dysfunctional behavior/patterns, increasing emotional expression, and recognizing strengths. Workers should create an environment to help the couple understand treatment goals, feel safe in expressing their feelings, and reconnect by developing trust in each other. Interventions for couples are often centered on goals geared toward preventing conflicting verbal communication and improving empathy, respect, and intimacy in a relationship. Therapeutic interventions, along with exercises, are designed to help couples learn to treat each other as partners and not rivals. Cognitive Behavioral Therapy is also used in working with couples. It uses cognitive restructuring techniques to help change distorted thinking and modify behavior.

Out-Of-Home Displacement

Out-of-home displacement is considered one of the most stressful adjustments a person can experience in their lifetime. It often leads to homelessness, an inability to work, and permanent loss of meaningful personal items. Out-of-home displacement also usually results from a distressing event to begin with (such as a natural disaster, a divorce, immigration from a poor situation in another country, flight from a war zone or other humanitarian crisis, job loss, and so on). Alongside the long-term consequences, individuals can face considerable internal and external struggle as a result of out-of-home displacement.

The intensity of struggle is correlated with four distinct factors: how far the individual is displaced, the type of housing (or lack thereof) to which they are displaced, how many times the individual has to move, and how long the individual has to stay in displacement housing. Another important variable is whether or not separation from family members, close friends, or other important community members occurs. Clients may deal with general psychological distress, post-traumatic stress disorder, acute or long-term poverty, adjustment stress disorder, and unhealthy coping mechanisms, such as substance abuse. Children are more profoundly affected and become vulnerable to future risks of obesity, substance abuse, and chronic disease. It is also important to note, however, that while many clients who experience home loss or displacement experience health and wellness issues that impact them in the long term, a fair number also self-report feeling an increased sense of resiliency and self-efficacy, a strong sense of community and gratitude for receiving aid from others, and hope for the future as their situation begins to improve.

Permanency Planning

Juvenile clients who are in danger within their families of origin and/or in foster care may benefit from permanency planning. Clients whose parents have terminated parental rights may be adopted into their foster home or put up for adoption by the state. While the first goal of social workers is to reunite juveniles with their family of origin, this is not always possible due to harmful circumstances in the home. Native American juvenile clients, for instance, are bound by the Indian Child Welfare Act (ICWA) when making considerations for permanency planning. ICWA regulations favor the placement of the child with Native families so that the child does not lose contact with their heritage.

Adults who are at risk of abuse and neglect may require permanency planning. Vulnerable adults may be reported to Adult Protective Services agencies. Adult foster care has become more popular in the last few decades and may be an option for at-risk adults. Group homes are another form of permanency planning for vulnerable adults, but the quality of these homes varies. The social worker should make careful screening of these facilities.

Mindfulness and Complementary Therapeutic Approaches

Complementary therapeutic approaches, such as mindfulness, meditation, yoga, exercise, spending time in nature, music therapy, and art therapy can provide emotional, physical, and mental relief for clients who are struggling to cope with adverse events. Mindfulness is the act of paying purposeful attention to specific or general events without attaching feelings, judgment, or reason to the events. It can be practiced during a specific time set aside for it, it can be incorporated in increments, or it can be an ongoing behavior throughout one's day. This practice allows clients a way of introspecting and reducing external stimuli, and it is an evidence-based method of stress reduction.

Meditation, another evidence-based method of stress reduction, can include mindfulness as a component. Meditation encourages the practitioner to focus on thoughts and repetitive mental patterns in order to clear them, relax the mind, and improve physiological indicators of stress (such as deeper and slower breathing rates, lowered heart rates, and reduced muscular tension).

Yoga incorporates meditation, focused breathing exercises, and movements to promote mental clarity and strength, improved circulation and respiration, reduce muscular tension, and connect with one's mind and body. Under the guidance of well-trained instructors or a certified yoga therapist, clients can take group or private sessions that are tailored to and address common counseling issues, such as trauma, grief, post-traumatic stress disorder, aging, physical changes, and so on.

Different forms of exercise can have a therapeutic effect, including strength and resiliency building (both mentally and physically), stress reduction, and the management of chronic disease indicators (such as excess weight or blood lipid levels). Group exercise can also be a way to build community and support through a shared, wellness-oriented interest. Finally, exercise programs often support clients in the practice of setting and achieving goals. While this may start off as a primarily physical practice, a number of mental and emotional benefits (such as improved moods and higher self-esteem), introspection, and behavior change often follow suit. Other types of recreational activity, such as creating art, listening to musical sounds and vibrations, and spending time in nature are associated with positive changes at the cellular level.

Case Management

Clients frequently experience difficulty navigating everyday life problems and systems. One of the roles of a social worker is to help link clients with needed services and resources. To perform this role effectively, social workers must have a thorough knowledge of available local resources to aid the client.

When acting in the case manager role, social workers help clients define, locate, and access needed services and resources. Additionally, social workers must often interact with other professionals, including external resources to ensure the client's needs are met. In the case management role, social workers also make referrals directing the client to the appropriate resource for needed services. The worker acts as a manager, following up with the client on a regular basis to ensure the client is following through with his or her case plan. Workers may also serve as an advocate in this role, working on behalf of the client if any barriers to resources are met.

Process of case management:

- Assessing needs and client engagement
- Creating an intervention plan of care that includes goals, needed services, and timelines
- Administering the plan
- Monitoring progress and reassessing the plan at fixed intervals
- Termination of services
- Evaluation and follow-up

Follow-Up Techniques

At the final session, the social worker and client can schedule a follow-up session at a predetermined time to evaluate the client's continued progress after termination. Another option is to propose a time to meet and alert the client that the worker will contact the client to schedule a follow up. The follow-up session enables the social worker the opportunity to determine how well the client has progressed and to determine the effectiveness of the intervention(s) used during sessions.

Case Presentation

Elements of a social work case presentation may include identifying data, the presenting problem, history of the presenting problem, medical/psychiatric information, significant personal and/or social information, impressions and summary, and recommendations. This format is only one model to choose from. There are many formats for a case presentation, and the social worker needs to make sure that they are following their agency's or organization's case presentation format.

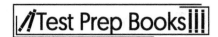

Measurable Objectives for Client System Intervention, Treatment, and Service Plans

Goals in intervention plans should be SMART—Specific, Measurable, Achievable, Relevant, and Time-specific. Devoting specific attention to the measurability of a goal requires mutual agreement between the client and practitioner.

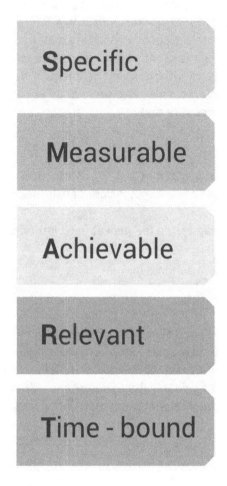

Key recommendations are noted, here:

- Measurable terms used in writing the goals should be based on the criteria of the type of desired behavior or action to be demonstrated (and how often), in order to achieve the proposed solution(s).

- Positive, action-oriented language should be utilized when describing the methods that an objective will be measured by. For example, the client should "plan" or "attend" a social gathering. Success of the stated objective will be "demonstrated" or "evidenced" by actually attending or planning a social gathering of some kind. The use of action-oriented language with specific targets assists the practitioner in more effective data collection.

- Objectives should be both short and long-term.

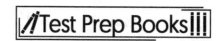

- Short-term objectives should only be a few weeks in length.

- Long-term objectives should be broken down into incremental, small chunks so as not to overwhelm the client and make progress towards success readily visible. The time-frame for completion should align with the nature of the objective. Often, many short-term objectives can make up one long-term objective or goal (for example, the short-term objective of developing a twice-weekly exercise habit leads to a long-term objective of losing five pounds).

Evaluating a Client's Progress

Treatment evaluation is a necessary part of direct practice. Social workers should strive to exercise best practice techniques by using evidence-based practice evaluation. It is beneficial for clients to see the progress they have made, while simultaneously providing information to funders and insurance companies that typically require documentation and outcome measures for reimbursement of services. Other benefits include providing indicators that interventions should be modified or that treatment is complete and termination is warranted. Several factors are important in the evaluation of a client's progress, including identifying specific issues to be addressed; creating appropriate goals, objectives, and tasks; using effective and relevant techniques and tools to measure success; and routinely documenting progress.

Client progress may be measured using a quantitative or qualitative approach used in research. Quantitative measures relate to the rate of occurrence or severity of a behavior or problem. When performing quantitative evaluation, first establish a baseline, which is a measurement of the target problem, prior to intervention. Qualitative measures are more subjective and reflective of the client's experience (information is gathered largely from observation and different forms of interviewing) and provide a view of whether progress is being made.

Primary, Secondary, and Tertiary Prevention Strategies

Emphasis on Prevention in Social Work

During the past few decades, the social work profession has increasingly moved toward a prevention-focused service distribution model. This movement has resulted in the development of a three-stage model of prevention in social work practice. These three stages are primary prevention, secondary prevention, and tertiary prevention. Each stage assesses the severity of the problem impacting individuals or groups and provides appropriate and evidence-based social work interventions.

Primary Prevention

The *primary prevention* stage includes actions that practitioners take before a problem occurs for the client to address the potential causes of the problem. These actions are specifically aimed at getting rid of a problem's root cause, such as advocating against unfair policies or laws before they are voted upon or take effect. This type of prevention focuses on meeting the needs of the population at an almost universal level.

Secondary Prevention

The *secondary prevention* stage occurs when a problem has already started to impact a person or group. Actions to be taken involve attempts to stop specific social problems before they spread and cause further harm. These actions are designed to help any individuals or groups that are beginning to show symptoms of increased problem severity.

Tertiary Prevention

The *tertiary prevention* stage occurs when both previous stages have failed to address the problem. These actions are designed to decrease a problem's severity through remedial service provision that will decrease its lasting effects and duration. This stage is more intense than the previous stages and focuses on individuals that are most impacted by the problem.

Visualizing the Three Stages of Prevention

These stages can be visualized as three parts of a pyramid. The wide base of the pyramid represents primary prevention, as these are more universal services that reach the broadest portion of the population. The middle of the pyramid represents secondary prevention, more prevention services applied to a smaller portion of the population. The top of the pyramid represents tertiary prevention, with the highest degree of prevention services for the smallest percentage of the population.

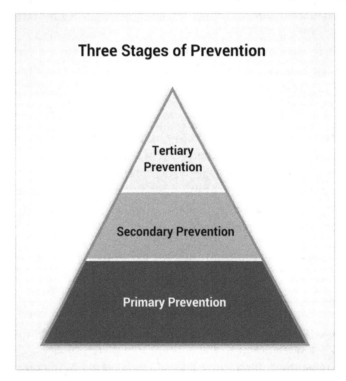

Client Readiness for Termination

When clients have made significant progress on the treatment plan, goals, and objectives, the worker can begin planning for termination. Depending on the identified goals and objectives, a standardized assessment can be used to determine how much progress has been made. Social worker practices vary depending on what level of goal attainment should be completed before termination (i.e., some, most, all). Other options can be offered to the client for continued work and learning such as groups, workshops, and reading materials. In many instances, services are terminated due to limitations by insurance or other funding sources. It is extremely important in these circumstances that the worker assists the client in locating additional resources that can be used following service termination.

When preparing clients for termination, workers should discuss the following topics with the client:

- Initial reasons for requesting help
- What skills the client initially lacked that led to initiating services
- Skills developed as a result of treatment and how those new skills will help the client with future challenges
- Ways the client will continue to build on new skills development
- Social worker and client feelings about termination

Methods, Techniques, and Instruments Used to Evaluate Social Work Practice

Evaluation is an important component of any field of study, as it allows practitioners to understand which processes are working well and providing results. Evaluation also allows one to identify areas of opportunity and areas for improvement. The process often utilizes data and consumer feedback, and it focuses on processes in place and specific desired outcomes of the practice.

Social workers should continuously evaluate their practice. This evaluation begins with what exactly they would like to evaluate. An evaluation typically focuses on processes (such as clinical intake, client satisfaction, time spent with clients, frequency of sessions, type of intervention) and outcomes (such as were specific goals met for a client, how many clients return after being discharged). Many health care organizations provide evaluation tools for social workers, such as benchmark reports that provide client satisfaction responses or practice outcomes. Additionally, social workers can employ pre-tests before an intervention to serve as a baseline data set, and they can employ a post-test to measure changes from the baseline. Social workers can also administer surveys, Likert scale questionnaires, or specific intervention evaluation assessments to the client or client system. These tools can measure quantitative results as well as provide an option for anecdotal or testimonial information. Entrance and exit interviews with the client or the client system can also provide a wealth of evaluation information. When evaluating clients face-to-face or through a survey, it's important to create an environment that fosters comfort, open dialogue, and honesty. Clients may feel pressured to provide positive evaluations if they are answering directly to the social worker, or if they feel as though a satisfaction survey they are completing can be traced back to them. This can bias the evaluation process and produce skewed results.

Evidence-Based Practice

Social workers can use Evidence-Based Practice methods to ensure effective treatment for clients. This type of practice uses both research and clinical knowledge. Social workers using evidence-based practice will choose interventions that have scientifically documented effectiveness. With this method, workers also evaluate chosen interventions throughout treatment to ensure a successful outcome.

Research Terms

Independent variable: a factor changed or controlled when conducting an experiment or research

Dependent variable: a factor dependent on the independent variable and is observed for changes as the independent variable is manipulated

Randomized controlled trial (RCT): a quantitative study that uses participants or subjects who are chosen randomly to participate

Reliability: the consistency of a measure, or the likelihood the same result will be achieved each time a measure is used

Validity: reflects whether a test, tool, or study is measuring what it intends to measure

External validity: the ability of a study to be generalized to other people or circumstances

Internal validity: refers to cause and effect; one question that can be posed: Are the effects of the study caused by the intervention?

Case Recording for Practice Evaluation or Supervision

Social workers must document their practice with the client. Social workers document sessions with clients as well as client legal mandates, such as visitation with minors in state custody. Documentation may be a combination of narrative and quantitative descriptions, depending on agency requirements. Records should be kept confidential either electronically or in a physical location. New laws require that all records be electronic, and they are called an electronic health records. These records must be confidential as stated in the Health Insurance Portability and Accountability Act of 1996 (HIPAA). It is crucial for the social worker to maintain accurate documentation.

Consultation Approaches

Although it may lead to possible conflict due to differing perspectives, opinions, and approaches to treatment, the use of consultation assistance from an expert in a related field can be extremely beneficial to an individual's treatment. The NASW Code of Ethics (2.05) specifically addresses consultation with other disciplines. Accordingly, workers should seek consultations with other areas when it benefits clients. When seeking consultation, social workers should maintain client confidentiality to the greatest extent possible, only releasing necessary information. When seeking consultation, the worker should seek competent colleagues and only consult with those who are appropriately qualified. Additionally, the worker should ensure the guidelines are clear for the consultation process by defining goals, the presenting problem, and the role of the consultant(s). In line with the code of ethics, social workers also may provide consultation or supervision. When providing consultation, workers must also be knowledgeable in the focus area and always maintain appropriate and culturally sensitive boundaries.

Interdisciplinary and Intradisciplinary Team Collaboration

Interdisciplinary collaboration is a frequent part of social work practice. This process can be beneficial to the client, offering the availability of different views and a varied knowledge base. While collaborations are advantageous, they may lead to conflicts due to differences in approaches, treatment preferences, and codes of ethics. The social worker should attempt to resolve these issues within the group, seeking alternative methods to address conflict when necessary. Collaborations can be completed by phone or in person, and can be ongoing or limited to a single occurrence. As with any group, the social worker should lead the effort to ensure all members' opinions and contributions are valued and validated. Social workers should identify and define roles and responsibilities for all members of the team, acknowledge the differences between disciplines and perspectives, and help to resolve any conflicts.

Basic Terminology of Other Professions

Social workers may need to work with professionals in a number of other fields to support their clients. Therefore, it is important to have a basic understanding of some of the terminology that is used in the professions with which social workers most commonly collaborate. These include the criminal and legal fields, since social workers may often support legal cases such as those of abuse, negligence, divorce, and child custody. Social workers should understand basic legal terms so that they can provide relevant support to the clients as well as to the other professionals involved in the case.

Socials workers often collaborate with educators in the school setting, and they work with children who may be in a vulnerable position. In these contexts, social workers should understand the values of the school system, the laws that school systems must follow when working with children, and ensure that social work does not detract from the child's educational experience.

Social workers may commonly collaborate with or refer patients to professionals in the medical field. They may need to understand basic medical and health terminology associated with their client's conditions. They may need to understand the impact that clinical issues may have on both the client's current behavior and desired outcomes. For example, a social worker may see a client who has severe depression linked with alcoholism. A physician may diagnose the client with stage 4 cirrhosis; the social worker will need to understand the severity of this diagnosis and how it will impact the client's depression and future sessions with the social worker. When in doubt, the social worker should ensure that their working relationships allow clarifying questions to be asked. Asking questions as needed will allow the social worker to fully understand any unfamiliar contexts and to serve the client.

Case Recording, Documentation, and Management of Practice Records

Accurate case recording is an integral part of social work practice. It is necessary to accurately document clients' information for effective treatment and protection of confidentiality. It is also required to protect the agency from possible legal ramifications and to ensure reimbursement from funders. Client records should be kept up-to-date, objective, and completed as soon as possible to ensure accuracy of information. Social workers should assume it is always possible that records may be requested as part of legal proceedings. Treatment notes should always be clearly written and only include information necessary to the client's treatment to protect confidentiality as much as possible. Social workers must also adhere to any state or federal legal requirements related to storage, disclosure of information, release of client records, and confidential information.

Intervention Processes and Techniques for Use with Larger Systems

Methods to Establish Program Objectives and Outcomes

When developing a social work program, objectives should be developed for each process that is used or evaluated and for each outcome that is desired or evaluated. Often, a funding source will require that certain process and outcome objectives are evaluated in order for the organization to receive funds; this often provides a practice with some objectives to manage. When objectives are not tied to a funding source, programs may decide to develop them based on a needs assessment, or the program's service interest and capacity. These may be inspired by evidence-based research, successful outcomes in other programs, from data collected from focus groups, or may be tailored to a specific case. A logic model is a useful tool to map out what the program hopes to achieve, the inputs it requires, and the expected outputs. It can also be used at the end of a program to map out the actual intervention, and analyze how it compared to the expected plan.

Process objectives set standards for procedures, activities, and other implementation constructs of the social work program. Outcome objectives set standards for what exactly the program hopes to achieve. All objectives should follow SMART criteria. This means that any objective that is set forth should be Specific (it is clear what the action will be taken and who will it), Measurable (changes can be measured and analyzed), Achievable (the objective is realistic for the client, the social worker, and the available resources), Relevant (the objective relates to the desired overall goal), and Time-bound (the objective can be achieved in a specified time period).

Availability of Community Resources

There is a wide range of community resources available, making it confusing for some clients to navigate the system and identify what would be most helpful for them. Therefore, a case manager plays a critical role in helping the client to find and utilize the community resources that would be most beneficial. When seeking resources, it is useful to look at the different domains of life—physical, psychological, emotional, spiritual, and educational—and then compile a collection of resources that may be useful for the client in each of these domains.

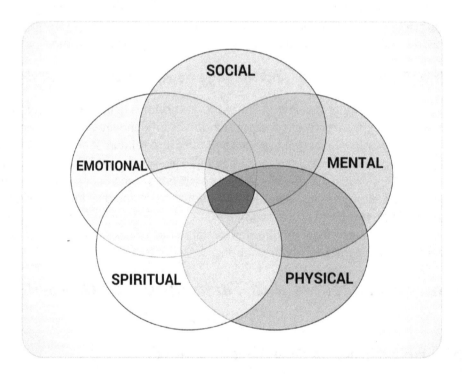

Physical needs can include food, shelter, clothing, or medical care, and there are many government programs available for these needs, such as free health care, affordable housing, and food stamps. For the elderly or disabled, their greatest need may be related to the accessibility of physical resources. In that case, the delivery of meals through Meals on Wheels or transportation services may be the most appropriate recommendation. Another help would be prescription assistance programs offered by some pharmaceutical companies to those with low income, which provide medications for free or at reduced

cost. Other resources for the elderly can be accessed through the Administration on Aging and other local departments for elder care.

Ensuring the provision of adequate emotional and psychological services would first involve making sure the client is receiving emotional support from family and friends, or getting involved in support groups with others who have similar struggles. For the elderly, there may be community centers with programs to help seniors connect with each other and stay active. When it comes to finding the right psychological resources, both therapeutic and psychiatric, there are many options, so the client must be involved in the process of deciding what type and format of therapy would be best.

An often overlooked area of whole-person care is the spiritual needs of the client. In addition to providing spiritual support, religious organizations are often nonprofits that can assist the client in physical or emotional ways as well. Fraternal organizations may provide similar benefits to a person, offering emotional, social, and spiritual components.

Educational resources should not be disregarded, especially in the case of someone who has mental or physical health needs. Whether formal training or informal learning through the library or online, there are many resources for gaining knowledge in almost any area. As discussed, education related to the individual's specific health needs is a crucial element of self-management care, client activation, and empowerment.

Calling United Way's helpline at 211, checking the U.S. government website, or conducting an internet search are easy and effective means of identifying the relevant community resources in the client's locality. Collaborating with other service providers can also make use of those who already know the client and can also prevent overlap in the provision of services. Finally, and perhaps most important, help the client to find resources through the people and organizations with whom they are already connected. Not only does this encourage self-determination and empowerment by helping the client see how many resources they already have in their life, but many clients will be most comfortable with places and people they already know.

Methods of Service Delivery

Social workers may be employed in a variety of agencies. Some organizations, such as hospitals or government entities, employ diverse professionals. Other types of organizations, such as direct service non-profits or private practice agencies, maintain predominantly social services staff. Agency policies directly and significantly impact the working environment, the services provided, and, as a result, the effectiveness of the care clients receive. All agencies should have a mission statement that gives the agency purpose and serves as an umbrella for the agency's smaller goals and objectives. Agency policies must be in the best interest of the client and must support the ethical guidelines to which social workers adhere. They must also be clearly written and available to workers and clients where appropriate. Social workers and all those providing care to clients should be able to help shape policy development to ensure consistency with client and worker needs and protection. Policies must address the following:

- Appropriate confidentiality, consent, and information protection
- Case management and supervision
- Cultural competency guidelines
- Professional development and ongoing trainings
- Anti-discriminatory/diversity practices

Methods of Advocacy for Policies, Services, and Resources to Meet Client Needs

Social workers must help clients understand their needs versus the services and resources available to them. Workers must be knowledgeable of the services available at their agency and in the communities in which their clients live. It is the role of the worker to assist clients in obtaining resources, but also to help clients understand their options and their right to choose or refuse which resources to access. Clients should receive assistance in identifying the pros and cons of each resource. They should also be involved in identifying and seeking resources as much as possible to foster the development of self-determination and empowerment.

Policies and Procedures that Minimize Risk for Individuals, Families, Groups, Organizations, and Communities

Often, the clients and client systems that require the services of a social worker are already in a vulnerable place. Therefore, minimizing additional risk to individuals, families, groups, and their associated organizations and communities (such as places of employment and recreation) is an important component of providing care. To ensure policies and procedures minimize additional stress, burden, discomfort, or suffering on the part of the client and client systems, practices should employ the constructs of the National Association of Social Work's Code of Ethics in their policies and procedures. Practices should utilize a sense of transparency, empowerment, and respect in all service procedures. These factors support clients and their systems in playing an active role, when possible, in the services they receive. Policies and procedure should ensure that all services offered have the overarching goal of benefiting clients or client systems, maintain the dignity and self-respect of the client and client systems, and emphasize the importance of cultivating healthy human relationships and the effects those have on recovery.

As social workers implement interventions and treatment, they should always keep lines of communication open with their clients, foster and nurture trust, and continue their educational efforts to ensure they are delivering the highest quality of care at each session. All client intake work should include an informed consent process, and it should engage the client in developing portions of the intervention plan. Social workers should treat all clients of all backgrounds with open-mindedness, without judgment, and with the client's desired intervention outcomes at the center of all interactions. Social workers may work with clients of different cultures, and social workers should respect the opinions and boundaries that these differences bring to treatment. If a social worker runs into a situation that falls outside the scope of the practice, such as the requirement of clinical intervention for a client, there should be policies in place to address such a situation, and social workers should feel comfortable referring to avenues of care outside of their scope.

Social Policy Development and Analysis

Social policy analysis is a process of systematically and strategically examining policies to determine overall effectiveness. When analyzing policies, social workers must determine both the intentional and unintentional effects of the policy, examine whether the policy is cost-effective and feasible, identify potential problems with the policy, determine how the policy is viewed by those affected, and identify possible policy alternatives.

Organizational and Social Policy

Social workers may act in a macro capacity for the common public good and serve as policy advocates, or provide leadership in the policy change process. There are many types of societal influences that can affect social policy.

Cultural

Societal perceptions or beliefs can shape policy. For instance, a general belief that children should have access to health care can aid in the development of child health care laws. Additionally, the media can bring problems/issues to the forefront and have a huge impact on public opinion, which can then influence policy development.

Economic

Lack of or an availability of resources has a significant impact on policy development. Additionally, those who control the resources also impact how policy is shaped.

Institutional

The capabilities, resources, and structure of government offices affect policy development. The institutions that create and implement policies have to be able to do so in an effective manner for those policies to be successful.

Social

The social environment, including events or situations such as recessions, wars, or poverty, all affect how policies are developed.

Legal

Existing laws and policies can influence future trends in policy development. New policies may or may not be adopted, depending on how they complement those already in existence and the current social climate. Legal events may also influence new policies.

Political

The political climate directly influences social policy, since the parties in control of governing bodies directly affect which policies and laws are implemented and repealed.

Formal Documents

Social workers may need to develop formal documents that are used for a broad range of functions; therefore, it is important to develop writing and communication skills that can be employed in a variety of professional contexts.

Social workers may be expected to write grant and research proposals, used for securing external funding for practical and applied work. They may need to write brochures or pamphlets that advertise their practice (especially if they are running their own business), explain types of interventions, or promote community initiatives. Social workers may need to communicate through letter or email correspondence regarding a client's progress. In these instances, they must be careful to explain clinical concepts in ways the client can understand from simply reading the correspondence without the social worker there to answer any potential questions. Additionally, written correspondence with the client must always remain appropriate and be mindful of HIPAA compliance and other privacy concerns. Social workers may be required to provide their superiors with weekly, monthly, or annual reports about the work they performed. They may also need to maintain regular reports of individual client progress updates or milestones. Social workers can be expected to provide evaluation reports on processes and outcomes utilized in their cases. Depending on the field of work (such as government agency, private institution, medical setting, et cetera), the requirements for reporting and evaluation may vary significantly.

Finally, today's social workers can expect to maintain some degree of technological capability and have the ability to leverage web platforms and social media. Web platforms can provide an avenue for blogging or other information sharing that makes people aware of the work of social institutions. Social media posts can provide this avenue as well, and they can also serve as another point of connection for clients and colleagues. Social media can be an important tool in business-building and networking. It is imperative that social workers maintain a respectful, professional online presence that maintains both the trust and privacy of their potential clients.

Service Networks or Community Resources

Due to limited funding and resources and a rapidly growing demand for services, establishing service networks to maximize community resources has become a necessary part of social work practice. Social workers and social service agencies frequently create partnerships, collaborations, or networks to bridge gaps in service and provide a comprehensive system of care for clients. These collaborations can be formal with the use of a comprehensive intake process and service or memorandums of agreements between programs. Partnerships can also be informal in which workers routinely refer clients to specific providers. When establishing new community resources, social workers must first perform a community assessment, which involves examining existing resources, community needs, and demographics.

Community Organizing and Social Planning Methods

The social change process is one in which interested groups (i.e., community members, lawmakers, businesses, government agencies, community organizations) can work together to create change or solve an identified community or societal problem. Collaborative social planning increases the chances of positive change and allows community members to take ownership of the change and resulting policies. It also encourages the community to become more energized and more likely to make positive changes in the future. The role of the social worker as a leader in this process includes the following:

- Community engagement
- Problem identification
- Organization and engagement of community members
- Identification of resources, challenges, and solutions
- Creation and implementation of a plan
- Evaluation and follow-up

Methods of Networking

Networking in social work can be defined in different ways. One type of networking occurs when social workers connect with colleagues and other professionals to improve services and skills. External collaboration with community resources and colleagues with similar goals enables social workers to learn about available resources and to provide opportunities for developing relationships with others who have a similar purpose.

Additionally, social workers may also help develop connections between clients, organizations, or other groups. This networking assists with the acquisition of support, skill development, and the facilitation of ongoing learning related to resources. Networks are typically more informal than official organizations and can therefore sometimes be more easily accessed by individuals.

Mobilizing Community Participation

Limited resources in communities make community member participation in social change movements vital to the success of the community. Mobilizing community members is an important part of creating macro-level change. The community develops a sense of self-determination when it takes an active role in removing barriers, creating needed services and resources and advocating for the rights of its members. Members are encouraged to participate in problem identification, goal setting, and resource mobilization to create change. When community members become engaged in the change process, the overall sense of community empowerment increases. There are some challenges with community participation in which social workers can assist. Community members may lack necessary skills, or there may be barriers created by institutions that operate in the community. Social workers can serve the role of educator to help community members develop needed social organizational skills. The worker may also serve as an advocate to overcome barriers created by larger systems and institutions. Workers must engage a community and mobilize its strengths, resources, and supports systems to create positive changes.

Governance Structures

The National Association of Social Workers (NASW) is considered the most reputable association for the field of social work. NASW sets the tone for the field's standards, competency requirements, and public and legislative initiatives. It also provides a resource for social workers to stay current on emerging research and news, and resources with which to continue their social work education.

Other important governance structures in the United States that social workers may deal with depend on their field of practice. Social workers who work in a small, private setting may only have a single office manager to whom they report. If a social worker owns their own practice, they may choose how they establish the organization's reporting hierarchy. Social workers who work as part of a large government agency, such as a case worker for a state's Department of Child and Family Services, may work with a more bureaucratic structure that involves a supervisor, manager, division director, agency director, and the state governor. Social workers who work as part of a national non-profit may have a large, hierarchical governing structure similar to that of a state or federal agency, whereas social workers who work in local non-profits may be part of a lateral leadership system.

Often, non-profit and government groups will collaborate with one another or with private companies to lead social work initiatives. Therefore, social workers may need to be flexible in how they adapt to the governance structures of the organization they are serving while still maintaining the standards established by the NASW.

Organizational Development and Structure

One aspect of mezzo-level social work is intervening with organizations. Social work organizations often begin with the admirable desire to help vulnerable populations. However, developing and sustaining such an organization can be an overwhelming challenge. Organizational policy development can improve the efficiency and effectiveness of the organization, by providing assessments and identifying the strengths and weaknesses. This type of policy development is also important to ensure that the goals and objectives of the organization are being met, and that they are in compliance with legal and ethical standards. Another aspect of organizational development has to do with the leadership hierarchy, or the formal power structure. This outlines the various positions of authority and leadership in relation to one another, and is necessary for the smooth functioning and decision-making of the organization. However, in addition to the formal power structure, there is also informal power, which has more to do with the influence of relationships and skills than with structured influence. Organizational intervention in this area may address issues of team building, skills enhancement, and interpersonal skills. Intervention and development in both informal and formal power structures are necessary for a successful and sustainable organization.

Impact of Agency Policy and Function on Service Delivery

Social workers may be employed in a variety of agencies. Some organizations, such as hospitals or government entities, employ diverse professionals. Other types of organizations, such as direct service non-profits or private practice agencies, maintain predominantly social services staff. Agency policies directly and significantly impact the working environment, the services provided, and as a result, the effectiveness of the care clients receive. All agencies should have a mission statement that gives the agency purpose and serves as an umbrella for the agency's smaller goals and objectives. Agency policies must be in the best interest of the client and must support the ethical guidelines to which social workers adhere. They must also be clearly written and available to workers and clients where appropriate. Social workers and all those providing care to clients should be able to help shape policy development to ensure consistency with client and worker needs and protection. Policies must address:

- Appropriate confidentiality, consent, and information protection.
- Case management and supervision.
- Cultural competency guidelines.
- Professional development and ongoing trainings.
- Anti-discriminatory/diversity practices

Policies, Procedures, Regulations, and Legislation on Social Work Practice and Service Delivery

Policies and procedures are typically established by an organization to define its operational standards. These are normally managed by the organization's human resource department. Regulations and legislation are typically established by external entities, such as independent or government-run regulatory agencies. Organizations should tailor their policies and procedure to ensure they align and comply with established regulations and standards.

Policies and procedures establish the flow of operations within an organization that provides social work services. They integrate business needs and employee need while also accounting for legal implications and risk mitigation. Policies and procedures related to service delivery often guide how clients should be treated, what (if any) conditions exclude a client from treatment, what to do in emergency cases or crises, payment and reimbursement requirements, privacy and security practices, hours of operation, and organizational map of staff members. Employee code of conduct and other information related to the workplace are often its own set of policies and procedures, normally part of an employee handbook or human resources manual. These documents often cover workplace culture, workplace expectations, leadership roles and responsibilities, employee benefits programs, payroll questions, examples of inappropriate workplace conduct, grounds for termination, an outline of required ethics, licensure

(when applicable), and other forms of workplace training, useful phone numbers and emails for employees, and other information that may be pertinent to a specific role.

Social work regulations and legislation set standards to which all social work organizations and employees should adhere. These may include documentation processes, licensure rules, payment rules, continuing education requirements, and patient privacy and security rules. Groups such as the NASW often compile research and promote initiatives to serve the field and its clients, for which they advocate to lawmakers.

Quality Assurance

In social work, quality assurance is the practice of ensuring that services rendered meet established criteria and deliver intended, beneficial outcomes. Quality assurance practices review procedures in place to ensure they lead to high caliber service delivery, to identify gaps that need to be addressed, and to prevent errors before they are made.

Methods of quality assurance include program assessments, benchmarking, social worker evaluations, and internal and external audits. Program assessments and social worker evaluations are often conducted off a list of standardized best practices; actual processes are compared to the standardized best practices to determine compliance. Benchmarks are clear, quantitative indicators of performance that serve as a standard for outcomes. Program evaluations may compare program outcomes to benchmark metrics to determine how well the program is performing. If there is a large gap, the program may undergo quality improvement procedures (such as a gap analysis r root cause analysis) to determine what is causing the discrepancy. Once this has been determined, a plan-do-study-act cycle (PDSA, a quality-oriented test of change) can be implemented to see whether benchmark indicators improve.

Auditing is a regular practice in the social work field. Auditing is conducted both on processes performed, as well as on the actions of the social worker to ensure ethical conduct and high levels of competence. For example, during licensure application and renewals, social workers' educational histories are audited to ensure they meet licensure and continuing education requirements. Audits may be conducted internally by the organization in which the social worker is employed; they will also be conducted by external regulatory bodies. The NASW performs comprehensive audits nationally, while state or local appointed boards and associations may audit for other requirements.

Impact of the Political Environment on Policy-Making

Social welfare legislation can have a dramatic effect on social work practice. Some legislation may help solve social problems that social workers encounter and other legislation may create more problems, challenges, and barriers through which social workers must help clients navigate. To be effective, social workers must be knowledgeable about legislative measures that affect clients. Another possible role of a social worker is that of legislative advocate, which is working to change, modify, or create legislation for the benefit of a group of people.

Significant Social Welfare Legislation:

- Civil Rights Act of 1964
- Older Americans Act of 1965
- The Child Abuse and Prevention Act of 1974
- Adoption Assistance and Child Welfare Act of 1980

- Americans with Disabilities Act of 1990
- The Family Medical Leave Act of 1993
- The Health Insurance Portability and Accountability Act of 1996 (HIPAA)
- The Patient Protection and Affordable Care Act of 2010

Leadership and Management Techniques

Leading and managing teams requires a range of organizational and interpersonal skills. An effective leader can clearly develop a vision for a preferred future state, as well as develop strategies to make the vision a reality. An effective leader must also be able to identify key stakeholders who are necessary to reach the vision, and be able to keep them actively engaged throughout the operational process. These tactics require that the leader is self-motivated, able to think uniquely to solve problems, and has a desire to develop and attain a feasible end result. However, a single leader cannot accomplish a vision alone. Therefore, leaders must be able to communicate the vision and motivate their team to take the actions that are necessary to reach the desired goal.

Leaders should be individuals who the team can trust and feel comfortable supporting. The most effective team will be one where leadership vision and team motivation align; however, this arrangement may not always be the case in a work setting. Therefore, a leader must know how to make projects seem of value to the employee, know which tasks are a good fit with an employee's personality type, and understand what motivates a team member's work. When managing a team, leaders may fall on a spectrum of laissez-faire (hands-off and relatively unstructured) to autocratic (which involves a high-level of micromanaging). Most successful leaders manage their teams by falling somewhere in the middle—establishing clearly defined goals and strategies and hand-selecting appropriate workers to execute tasks, but allowing their team members have to a sense of autonomy and creativity over their delegated responsibilities.

Fiscal Management Techniques

Social workers should be well-versed in basic fiscal management techniques for a number of reasons. First, they may be involved in running a practice or owning a practice, in which case they must have a foundational understanding of business finances. Next, social workers should have personal financial health and know how to manage their own money. As financial issues are considered one of the leading causes of stress, social workers who are dealing with these kinds of issues will be unable to fully serve their clients. Finally, since many clients who come through social work organizations are likely to be dealing directly or indirectly with financial issues, social workers must know how to serve clients in various situations (such as in poverty, having relationship issues due to money management, et cetera). A lack of money and resources, or improper management of money and resources, can lead to stress, anxiety, malnutrition, unmet basic needs, and other health issues. Fiscal management techniques that social workers may need to utilize in client sessions may include providing resources to earn more money or spend less, education focused on social support and benefit programs, debt counseling, practical and impractical methods of debt relief (such as credit counseling programs versus pawn shop schemes), working through emotional states related to money (such as feelings of lack, shame, or control), and teaching parents fiscal management skills to teach their children.

Educational Components, Techniques, and Methods of Supervision

Social workers should expect to continuously learn. Educational components include staying abreast of new and emerging research and methodology in the field, brushing up on less-used skills, learning from

mentors and more experienced social workers, and ensuring that one's practical expertise is up to the most recent standards. Supervisors or managers may choose to ensure that social workers who report to them have the time and resources to continuously learn, that they can learn materials for their needs, and that they feel comfortable addressing any gaps in their education with their superiors in order to resolve the discrepancies.

Techniques for learning may include visual techniques (such as books, videos, newspaper articles, and journal articles), listening techniques (such as lectures, seminars, podcasts, and audiobooks), or hands-on techniques (such as field work or practicums with a mentor). Some learning opportunities include tactics from all three learning techniques.

Supervisors may choose to be more involved in their approach to their team's education, or may be more distant and allow their team members to pursue their educational goals and requirements independently. An effective supervisor will allow their team members to introspect as to what may be the best educational route for them, and provide space coupled with guidance and support to support their team members in achieving their goals. Effective supervisors will also ensure that the professional goals individual team members are seeking serve the goals of the group, as well.

Learning Needs and Learning Objectives for Supervisees

Supervisors must ensure that their team members are competent and ethical, that they deliver service effectively, and that they are satisfied with their performance and work environment. Supervisors may audit or review performance with their team members to ensure standard competency and operational requirements are met. If gaps exist, supervisors may choose to develop trainings that address them. Speaking directly with team members individually or as a group can also help supervisors to find out where personal learning concerns or interests lie. In general, supervisors should ensure that their team is knowledgeable about current literature and able to deliver social service to the highest acceptable quality, that their team understands the legalities and risks of their work, and that all team members perform professional and ethically in any given situation.

When choosing to develop learning objectives that are not based on any existing gaps, supervisors may focus on new and emerging research, skillsets, or modalities that their team may want to use in their practical work. They may also choose to focus on improving current processes to enhance the client experience; often, this practice may focus on areas that are important but may not regularly get attention in the day-to-day routine tasks (such as writing competence, leadership skills, business skills, and so on). Supervisors may choose to teach learning objectives in a workshop or other interactive format, conduct online trainings, or engage in field work as a learning modality.

Effect of Program Evaluation Findings on Services

Often the urgency of immediate client services takes precedence over program evaluation, but evaluation is a necessary step in ensuring that an organization provides effective and affordable services for clients. Program evaluation can be conducted during the formative stage of a program, in order to establish the best objectives and methods, but it can also be summative, evaluating outcomes of the program at a later stage. Summative evaluations can be used to determine what changes should be made or even if the program should continue.

Needs assessments, which explore the needs of constituents or clients, play a pivotal role in developing programs. Needs assessments provide evidence for the necessity of a program trying to obtain funding and measure program usefulness. Cost-effectiveness looks at whether programs are being conducted in a way that makes the best use of the available money. Cost-benefit analysis is a process of comparing the beneficial outcomes of a program to the amount of money spent on them to see if the benefits are worth the cost. Both of these cost-related aspects of program evaluation are important, especially for grant proposals. Ultimately, program evaluation seeks to do outcomes assessments, something frequently requested by funding agencies. Outcomes assessments look at the program's effectiveness at meeting its objectives and in making the expected changes.

Techniques Used to Evaluate a Client's Progress

There are several techniques to evaluate client progress, including self-reporting by the client, quantitative measures that are collaboratively discussed by the social worker and the client, and narrative approaches that utilize a textual basis for describing progress. Social workers may ask client scaling questions to measure client mood and/or progress. Client progress should be measured at regular intervals in order to assist with treatment planning and intervention efficacy. Clients should be informed of progress, and social workers should develop progress notes to reflect client progress. Social workers need to be aware of client progress and compliance in order to accurately measure the steps the client is taking to move forward.

Practice Questions

1. Which BEST describes a definition of client advocacy?
    a. Helping clients recognize and then use their strengths, resources, and systems to obtain goals
    b. Working on behalf of clients to remove barriers and obtain needed resources and/or services
    c. A short-term treatment usually lasting four to six weeks and is implemented when a client enters treatment following some type of traumatic event that causes significant distress
    d. Helping to link clients with needed services and resources

2. Which is NOT a method of working with involuntary clients?
    a. Helping clients to recognize participation is still a choice
    b. Including a client's goals in a service plan along with mandated goals
    c. Protecting a client's right to self-determination
    d. Refraining from getting a client's consent in treatment, since participation is mandatory

3. Which of the following is an aspect of the psychosocial approach to treatment?
    a. Unique to the field of social work and allows it to stand out from other professions
    b. Used when clients experience a state of disequilibrium, are out of balance, and can no longer function effectively
    c. Emphasizes the concept of problems of living
    d. Short-term, practical, and evidence-based intervention

4. Which component of the problem-solving process is left out of these steps?

    1. Assess, define, and clarify the problem
    2. Examine options and select/implement a solution
    3. Evaluate and adjust

    a. Emphasize contracting and carefully planned task implementation.
    b. Determine possible solutions.
    c. Social worker functions as a collaborator to assist the client in identifying smaller tasks.
    d. Social worker identifies issues, strengths, and resources.

5. Due to the brief nature of short-term therapy, what should begin early in the treatment process?
    a. Assessment
    b. Termination
    c. Educational services
    d. Metacommunication

6. What is NOT a typical role of a social worker?
    a. Advocate
    b. Case manager
    c. Educator
    d. Scapegoat

7. Which is NOT associated with the provision of educational services to clients?
    a. It may be done in individual, family, small group, classes, or large group forums.
    b. Workers may recommend resources such as books, articles, or websites.
    c. Workers must have a thorough knowledge of available local resources.
    d. The social worker must determine what skills, information, or knowledge needs to be acquired by clients.

8. Which factor is NOT part of evaluating a client's progress?
    a. Identifying specific issues to be addressed
    b. Creating appropriate goals, objectives, and tasks
    c. Administering the intervention plan
    d. Using effective and relevant techniques and tools to measure success

9. What is the definition of reciprocal goals?
    a. Complementary goals agreed upon by members of a system and related to the same target problem
    b. When members of a system choose the same goal that addresses an identified problem
    c. Social worker's goals related to ending treatment
    d. The plan to rate the occurrence or severity of a behavior or problem

10. Which choice is NOT a frequently used term in family therapy?
    a. Disengaged
    b. Boundaries
    c. Alliances
    d. Cohesion

11. Which choice is NOT a stage of the group process?
    a. Pre-beginning
    b. Beginning
    c. Middle
    d. End

12. Which of the following is NOT a type of coordination that social workers can provide?
    a. Case management
    b. Wraparound services
    c. Service integration
    d. Prescribing medication

13. Which choice is NOT a reason to accurately record case information?
    a. Contribute to effective treatment
    b. Protect the agency from possible legal ramifications
    c. Protect confidentiality
    d. Engage clients in the treatment process

14. What are two components of emphatic communication?
    a. Social worker perceives client's feelings and communicates understanding of those emotions back to client.
    b. Social worker nods and displays genuineness.
    c. Social worker engages client in treatment and creates an environment of trust.
    d. Social worker shares common feelings with the client and is affected by those feelings in the same way.

15. What is the goal of cognitive restructuring?
    a. Use of self-monitoring to keep track of situations that occur and accompanying thoughts or feelings
    b. To help clients change irrational or unrealistic thoughts that result in a change in behaviors
    c. Identify situations that evoke reoccurring themes in dysfunctional thoughts and beliefs
    d. Rewarding oneself for using functional coping skills

16. Which of the following is NOT a way that social workers receive feedback from clients?
    a. Verbally or non-verbally
    b. Intentionally or unintentionally
    c. By the amount of progress toward goals
    d. The client's expression of negative feelings about termination

17. What is the first stage a client experiences after a crisis event?
    a. Higher levels of stress as the usual coping mechanisms fail. Client may employ higher-level coping skills to alleviate the increasing stress levels.
    b. Increase in feelings of stress. Client may experience denial and typically tries to resolve the stressful reactions using past problem-solving and coping skills.
    c. Client experiences complete psychological and emotional collapse, or the individual finds a method to resolve the situation; however, there may be remaining emotional and psychological problems.
    d. Client experiences major emotional turmoil, possible feelings of hopelessness, depression, and anxiety.

18. What factor influences the crisis intervention approach?
    a. The situation itself
    b. Homeostasis
    c. Environmental balance and social circumstances
    d. Client reaction to the situation

19. What is the furthering communication technique?
    a. Allows clients to know that the worker is listening and encourages more information
    b. Using questions that elicit short answers
    c. Using facial expressions, body language, and postures to show that the worker is engaged and listening
    d. When the social worker asks for clarification to ensure the client's message is understood

20. Which is NOT a factor in policy and procedure development?
    a. Front line workers should be involved in policy and procedure development, since they are in the best position to determine and evaluate how clients are affected.
    b. Policies should be clearly written and communicated to clients/workers, with copies available for distribution.
    c. Polices should be in the best interest of clients, but also protect the agency and staff.
    d. The origins of the policy and/or procedure, including values and the related ideology.

21. What is the definition of external validity?
    a. Uses participants or subjects chosen randomly to participate
    b. The consistency of a measure. The likelihood the same result will be achieved each time it's used.
    c. The ability of a study to be generalized to other people or circumstances
    d. Refers to cause and effect

22. Which significant social welfare legislation was enacted first?
    a. The Child Abuse and Prevention Act
    b. The Family Medical Leave Act
    c. Civil Rights Act
    d. The Patient Protection and Affordable Care Act

23. All of these are factors that must be considered in client empowerment with the exception of which choice?
    a. Self-perception, including strengths and knowledge
    b. Interactions and experiences with others that affect the client's present situation
    c. Interactions with relevant institutions or groups
    d. A client's feelings of anger or mistrust about treatment

24. Which item is NOT something social workers should discuss with clients when preparing for termination?
    a. What skills the client initially lacked that led to initiating services
    b. Initial reasons for requesting help
    c. Assisting the client in identifying and changing dysfunctional patterns
    d. Ways the client will continue to build on new skill development

25. What is the second phase of treatment intervention?
    a. Termination and Evaluation
    b. Engagement and Assessment
    c. Implementation
    d. Goal Identification and Intervention Planning

26. Which choice is NOT an advantage of single subject designs?
    a. Cost-effective
    b. Easy to use, efficient
    c. Results can easily be generalized to other clients
    d. Provides immediate data

27. Which criteria is NOT outlined in the NASW Code of Ethics in regards to evaluation?
    a. Social workers should be knowledgeable and use evaluation procedures responsibly.
    b. Social workers should report findings accurately using institutional review boards when appropriate.
    c. Clients must consent to evaluation.
    d. Single subject designs should be used to provide individualized evaluation.

28. Which is a type of evaluation tool?
    a. Independent variable
    b. Dependent variable
    c. Validity
    d. Target problem scaling

29. Which is NOT an activity performed by a social worker when referring clients for services?
    a. Rewarding clients for using functional coping skills
    b. Making contact with other providers through phone calls, meetings, letters, etc.
    c. Assisting clients with the completion of paperwork and ensuring clients qualify for the referred services
    d. Monitoring clients' progress to ensure services are effective

30. According to the NASW Code of Ethics, social workers must do which of the following related to culturally competent practice?
    a. Identify which thoughts and belief patterns or self-statements lead to the target problems.
    b. Use self-monitoring techniques.
    c. Emphasize strong boundaries.
    d. Be aware of their own biases and prejudices.

31. Which organizational theory is NOT considered a classical theory?
    a. Human Relations Theory
    b. Scientific Management Theory
    c. Administrative Theory
    d. Bureaucracy Theory

32. What is the definition of Contingency Theory?
    a. Based on the notion that systems within an organization are dependent on each other
    b. Emphasizes the protection of women from gender-based discrimination
    c. Places emphasis on organizations and employees obtaining maximum profits
    d. Describes organizations in terms of the complexity of all the forces affecting them and their ability to function

33. Which role of a social worker can be defined as working to change, modify, or create legislation for the benefit of a group of people?
    a. Legislative advocate
    b. Broker
    c. Case manager
    d. Cause advocate

34. What is a task performed by community members during the mobilization process?
    a. Participating in problem identification and goal-setting
    b. Creating comprehensive intake processes
    c. Performing a community assessment
    d. Establishing service networks

35. Which choice is NOT a benefit of collaborative social planning?
    a. Changes are more likely to occur
    b. It is cost-effective, easy to use, and efficient
    c. Community members take ownership of the change and related policies
    d. Participants become energized and more likely to continue to make positive changes in the future

36. Which choice is NOT a topic that should be addressed by agency policies?
    a. Professional development
    b. Inducements
    c. Case management
    d. Cultural competency

Answer Explanations

1. B: Client advocacy is working on behalf of a client to remove barriers and obtain needed resources and/or services. Choice A, client empowerment, is helping clients to recognize and then use their strengths, resources, and systems to obtain goals. Choice C, crisis-intervention approach, is a short-term treatment usually lasting four to six weeks and is implemented when a client enters treatment following some type of traumatic event that causes significant distress. Choice D, case management, is helping to link clients with needed services and resources.

2. D: It is important that social workers always acquire client consent, even when working with involuntary clients. Guidelines about client consent are mentioned throughout the NASW Code of Ethics. When working with involuntary clients, social workers should help clients to recognize participation is still a choice, include a client's goals in a service plan along with mandated goals, and protect a client's right to self-determination.

3. A: The psychosocial approach is unique to the field of social work and allows it to stand out from other professions. Choice B is related to the crisis intervention theory, whereby clients experience a state of disequilibrium and are out of balance. Choices C and D are related to Task Centered Practice, which emphasizes concepts of living and is a short term, practical, and evidence-based intervention.

4. B: Determining possible solutions is the second step in the problem-solving process. Choices B, C and D are components of Task Centered Practice, which includes: contracting and carefully planning task implementation, along with the social worker functioning as a collaborator to help client identify issues, strengths, resources, and smaller tasks.

5. B: Short-term therapies typically only last six to twelve sessions. To ensure a client is prepared for closure of services, the social worker should start termination planning as soon as possible. Choice A, assessment, typically begins early in all interventions and not just specifically in short-term therapy. Choice C, educational services, can be included at any time, depending on the type of intervention. Choice D, metacommunication, is frequently addressed during conflict resolution.

6. D: The scapegoat role is typically used to define a role filled by a participant in group or family treatment. Social workers can fulfill many types of roles in practice. Choice A, the advocate role, can be defined as working on behalf of a client to remove barriers and obtain needed resources and/or services. Choice B, case management, is helping to link clients with needed services and resources. Social workers can also function as educators (Choice C) and frequently provide educational services to improve skills and increase knowledge.

7. C: Having thorough knowledge of local resources is better suited to the definition of case management. Choices A, B, and C are all related to providing educational services that can be performed in individual, family, small group, classes, or large group forums. Also, when providing these services, social workers determine skills, information, or knowledge that needs to be acquired by clients and also recommend resources such as books, articles, or websites.

8. C: Administering the intervention plan is part of the overall treatment process, not specifically evaluation. Identifying specific issues to be addressed; creating appropriate goals, objectives, and tasks; and using effective and relevant techniques and tools to measure success are all aspects of effective treatment evaluation.

9. A: Complementary goals benefit each other and are agreed upon by members of a system related to the same target problem. Choice *B* is the definition of shared goals, which are when members of a system choose the same goal that addresses an identified problem. Choice *C* refers to social worker's goals and ending treatment. Choice *D* refers to quantitative measures or the rate or occurrence of a behavior or problem.

10. D: Cohesion refers to an important function of group work, whereby members connect. The term is not necessarily a term used in family work. The other terms are all related to family therapy. When families are disengaged (Choice *A*), boundaries are rigid with little interaction and emotional engagement. Healthy boundaries (Choice *B*) around and within the family must exist for families to function effectively. Alliances (Choice *C*) are partnerships or collaborations between certain members of a family.

11. A: Pre-beginning is not a stage in group treatment. During the beginning stage (Choice *B*), social workers determine the group's purpose, members, objectives, and other logistical tasks, and then group formation occurs. During the middle stage (Choice *C*), most of the group work is done. During the end stage (Choice *D*), group members come to resolutions on the issues addressed during the group process.

12. D: Social workers may not prescribe medication. Social worker coordination can be provided during case management (Choice *A*), including linking clients with resources. Other types of coordination include wraparound services (Choice *B*), which are inter-organizational collaborations where agencies form shared goals for client(s). Service integration (Choice *C*) refers to different types of services provided simultaneously.

13. D: Engaging clients in treatment is a way to facilitate communication during treatment. Accurately recording case information contributes to effective treatment (Choice *A*), protects the agency from possible legal ramifications (Choice *B*), and protects patient confidentially (Choice *D*), since only information necessary to the purpose of the documentation should be recorded.

14. A: A social worker's ability to perceive a client's feelings and communicate an understanding of those emotions back to the client are concepts of emphatic communication. If a social worker shares common feelings with a client and is affected by those feelings in the same way (Choice *D*), it is a sympathetic response and not a desirable method of displaying empathy in treatment. A social worker nodding, displaying genuineness, and engaging clients are ways to display emphatic communication, but Choice *A* shows the main concepts.

15. B: The goal of cognitive restructuring is to help clients change irrational or unrealistic thoughts that result in a change in behaviors. Using self-monitoring to track situations, identifying situations that evoke dysfunctional thoughts and beliefs, and rewarding oneself for using functional coping skills are steps in the restructuring process, but not the ultimate goal.

16. D: It is normal for clients to have difficult feelings as termination approaches. This is not necessarily feedback toward the treatment process. Social workers can receive feedback from clients verbally/non-verbally, intentionally/unintentionally, or by the amount of progress toward goals.

17. B: In the first stage following a crisis event, clients experience an increase in feelings of stress and denial. They typically try to resolve the stressful reactions using past problem-solving and coping skills.

Second stage: Clients continue to experience higher levels of stress as the usual coping mechanisms fail. Clients may employ higher-level coping skills to alleviate the increasing stress levels. (Choice *A*)

Third stage: Clients experience major emotional turmoil and possible feelings of hopelessness, depression, and anxiety. (Choice *D*)

Fourth stage: Clients experience complete psychological and emotional collapse, or the individual finds a method to resolve the situation; however, there may be remaining emotional and psychological problems. (Choice *C*)

18. D: The crisis is caused by the individual's reaction to the situation, not by the actual incident. Caplan theorized that individuals need to maintain homeostasis or remain in balance with their environment.

19. A: The furthering communication technique allows clients to know that the worker is listening and encourages more information. Questions that elicit short answers are called closed-ended questions (Choice *B*). Using facial expressions, body language, and postures to show that the worker is engaged and listening is called active listening (Choice *C*), and clarifying is when the social worker asks for clarification to ensure the client's message is understood (Choice *D*). All techniques are methods of facilitating communication with clients.

20. D: Examining the origins of the policies and procedures, including values and the related ideology, is an important step in the policy evaluation, not necessarily in the development process. When developing policies and procedures, front line workers should be involved because they are in the best position to determine how clients are affected. Additionally, policies should be clearly written and communicated and should be in the best interest of clients while still protecting agency and staff.

21. C: The definition of external validity is the ability of a study to be generalized to other people or circumstances. The other choices are all general research terms. Choice *A* is randomized controlled trials, which uses participants or subjects who are chosen randomly to participate. Choice *B* is reliability, the consistency of a measure, or the likelihood the same result will be achieved each time it's used. Choice *D* is internal validity, which refers to cause and effect (i.e., are the effects of the study caused by the intervention?).

22. C: The Civil Rights Act was the earliest, enacted in 1964. The Child Abuse and Prevention Act was enacted in 1974 (Choice *A*), the Family Medical Leave Act in 1993 (Choice *B*), and the Patient Protection and Affordable Care Act (Choice *D*) in 2010. All of these acts were significant social welfare legislations.

23. D: Social workers must overcome clients' feelings of anger or mistrust about treatment when motivating clients for participation in treatment, especially in the case of involuntary or non-voluntary clients. The other choices centered on clients' self-perceptions, interactions, and experiences with others, including institutions or groups, which are all factors to consider when empowering clients.

24. C: Social workers should assist clients in identifying and changing dysfunctional patterns when working with families. When preparing for termination, a social worker should help a client identify which skills the client lacked and other reasons that led to initiating services to help determine progress. The worker should also help the client find ways to continue building skills following the termination of services.

25. D: Goal Identification and Intervention Planning is the second phase of treatment. This is when goals, the treatment plan, and the contract are developed. During the first phase, Engagement and Assessment, the social worker focuses on rapport building and data gathering. The third phase, Implementation, is when interventions and tasks are implemented. During the last phase, Termination and Evaluation, the client and worker assess goal attainment and evaluation.

26. C: Single subject designs typically cannot be generalized to other clients or problems. The advantages of single subject designs include cost-effectiveness, ease of use, and immediacy of data.

27. D: The NASW Code of Ethics does not indicate the use of singe subject designs for evaluation. The code requires social workers to be knowledgeable about evaluation procedures, report findings accurately, use review boards when appropriate, and acquire client consent to participation in evaluation measures.

28. D: Target problem scaling is an evaluation tool that can be used when identified problems are difficult to quantify. The other terms are general research terms. Choice *A*, independent variable, is the variable changed or controlled when conducting an experiment or research. Choice *B*, dependent variable, is the variable dependent on the independent variable and observed for changes as the independent variable is manipulated. Choice *C*, validity, reflects whether a test, tool, or study is measuring what it intends to measure.

29. A: Rewarding clients for using functional coping skills is a step in cognitive restructuring, not an activity performed when referring clients for services. When referring clients, social workers must contact other providers through phone calls, meetings, or letters; assist clients with completion of paperwork; and monitor client progress to ensure services are effective and accessible.

30. D: According to the NASW Code of Ethics, social workers must be aware of their own biases and prejudices to successfully offer culturally competent practice. Choices *A* and *B* are steps in cognitive restructuring, including identifying which thoughts and belief patterns or self-statements lead to the target problems and using self-monitoring techniques. Choice *C* is a component of Scientific Management Theory, which emphasizes strong boundaries between the management who delegates tasks and the workers who perform the tasks.

31. A: Human Relations Theory is a neoclassical theory. It has roots in psychology and theorizes that higher levels of an employee's job satisfaction and morale lead to better performance and more loyalty to an organization. All other choices are classical theories. Scientific Management Theory emphasizes strong boundaries between the management who delegates the tasks and the workers who perform the tasks. Administrative Theory is a hierarchical system that uses five basic functions to be administered by management that relate to planning, coordination, and control. Bureaucracy Theory places emphasis on specialized areas with well-defined duties and uses a hierarchical, impersonal structure with heavy reliance on rules and procedures with the goal of maintaining control.

32. A: Contingency Theory is based on the notion that systems within an organization are dependent on each other. Feminist Theory emphasizes the protection of women from gender-based discrimination. Economics Theory places emphasis on organizations and employees obtaining maximum profits. Chaos Theory describes organizations in terms of the complexity of all the forces affecting them and their ability to function.

33. A: A social worker working to change, modify, or create legislation for the benefit of a group of people is fulfilling the role of a legislative advocate. The broker role is a part of case management that includes identifying and linking clients to resources. Case management also includes service planning and managing client care throughout the service process. Cause advocacy is working to assist individuals or groups and to affect change on a larger level to allow significant systemic shifts.

34. A: During the community mobilization process, community members participate in problem identification, goal setting, and resource mobilization to create change. The other choices include creating comprehensive intake processes, performing a community assessment, and establishing service networks – all roles of the social worker in establishing service networks or community resources.

35. B: The benefits of collaborative social planning are increased chances of change, community members taking ownership of the process, and members becoming more energized to create change in the future. Cost-effectiveness, ease of use, and efficiency are advantages of single subject designs.

36. B: Agency policies should address a social worker's professional development, cultural competency, and case management and treatment guidelines. Inducements mean salary and benefits and is a term introduced by neoclassical theories.

Professional Relationships, Values, and Ethics

Professional Values and Ethical Issues

Professional relationships with clients develop in six stages. In the first stage, social workers focus their efforts on building rapport and trust with clients. This involves the development of a comfortable and trusting working relationship using listening skills, empathic understanding, cultural sensitivity, and good social skills. In the second stage, the practitioner identifies the problem(s) that led the client to seek the assistance of a social worker. Together, the practitioner and client identify the initial problems that will be addressed, check the understanding of each issue through a conversation, and make appropriate changes as necessary. The third stage involves the social worker using skills that allow him or her to understand the client in deeper ways. The practitioner begins to make inferences based on his or her theoretical orientation about the underlying themes in the client's history. Once these inferences are made, then goals can be established based on these overarching themes.

The fourth stage of professional relationship development involves working on the issues that were identified and agreed upon between the practitioner and client. The client takes responsibility for and actively works on the identified issues and themes during and between sessions. As the client successfully works through issues, it becomes increasingly clear that there is little reason for the meetings to continue. Therefore, in stage five, the end of sessions is discussed, and both the client and the social worker work through feelings of loss. The sixth stage occurs after the relationship has ended if clients return with new issues, if they want to revisit old ones, or if they want to delve deeper into their self-understanding. This stage is the post-interview stage and occurs with many—but not all—clients.

Legal and Ethical Issues Related to the Practice of Social Work

Social workers are, by nature, helping professionals. In theory, they are much like other helping professionals such as counselors or family therapists. The goal of the field of social work is not only social justice, however, but improving the lives of individuals through empowerment and advocacy. Social work maintains a person-focused perspective that stipulates that the profession strives to "meet people where they are," not forcing ideals and decisions onto those in need, but instead using their own values to empower them to make changes.

The social work profession has a set of values that governs how social workers do their jobs. These values are the root of the social work profession and lay the groundwork for everything that social workers do. These six values are: service, social justice, dignity and worth of the person, importance of human relationships, integrity, and competence.

In order to meet the needs of the various populations served by social workers, there are certain rules and regulations regarding ethics that social workers must follow. The National Association of Social Workers (NASW) has a Code of Ethics that serves to educate social workers on how they should conduct themselves.

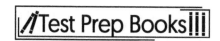

The NASW Code of Ethics has six core purposes. These purposes are:

- To establish the core values on which the mission of social work is based

- To provide a set of ethical standards for social workers, as well as specific information regarding different ethical dilemmas

- To help identify information that social workers should take under advisement when ethical conflicts may exist or when an ethical dilemma presents itself

- To provide standards that can be used by others to ensure accountability and responsibility by those in the profession

- To inform new social workers about core issues relating to the mission of social work and to the ethical standards of the field

- To provide the rules and standards that social workers can use to evaluate the conduct of others in the profession

Professional Values and Principles

Values are ideas or beliefs that guide an individual's thoughts and actions. The values that a person holds have their basis in the moral foundation to which they were exposed in childhood and adolescence. Moral foundations can include anything from family-specific beliefs and religious moral codes to the ethics and laws of society. As an individual gets older, they are increasingly exposed to new value systems that coincide or challenge their existing values. When someone must consider adopting one value system over another, this is called a *value conflict*. Value conflicts may occur when someone makes new friends, engages in romantic relationships, joins a new community, attends a new school, and accepts a new job.

The process of acquiring values is important for social workers to keep in mind when working to understand where their own values and their clients' values originated. Social workers should be aware of their own moral codes, values, biases, and prejudices to avoid conflict with the treatment they are providing to clients. The process of acknowledging and controlling personal values in social work practice is called *value suspension*. Self-awareness is a vital part of ensuring that one's personal values and beliefs do not intrude on the social worker/client relationship. It may be necessary to seek consultation from a supervisor or colleague in situations where one's personal values or beliefs conflict with those of the client and when those feelings cannot be resolved. In extreme cases where consultation and self-reflection cannot remedy the conflict, termination of the social worker/client relationship and referral to another therapist may be necessary.

All professions are built upon a foundation of values and guided by ethical codes. At times, these values trump that profession's empirical knowledge base. The focus of the social work profession is providing care and improving society rather than simply defining and explaining existing problems. To these ends, social workers must apply the knowledge and skills in other fields, including sociology, philosophy, law, and psychology.

Social workers must distinguish between and cater to social and individual morality. Individual morality describes the behavior of one person in private or specific people in public roles. Social morality is the wide range of behaviors that create and contribute to public life and impact greater society. Social workers must recognize the interplay between these types of morality and advocate when their absence creates social injustice.

Below are the three main values in social work.

Preserving Human Rights

Social workers are charged with preserving the rights of all people. This means taking a compassionate, holistic view of the individuals that social workers serve and advocating for them when society cannot meet their needs. Still, it's important that clients retain the power to make decisions about the direction their lives will take. The social worker can guide clients, but the clients maintain the ultimate decision. Only when clients pose a risk to the well-being of others should social workers intervene on their behalf. Social workers should take a strengths-based approach in their practice and help their clients develop and use their personal strengths to achieve their goals and compensate for weaknesses. The ultimate goal of social work is to provide clients with the tools they need to empower themselves to make their own decisions and enhance their personal health and the well-being of their family, community, and the greater society.

Advocating for Social Justice

Social workers advocate for justice and fair treatment for those they serve. Practitioners should challenge prejudice and discrimination against their clients to model good moral judgment and to uphold anti-discrimination laws. Practitioners must also inform those in power when they become aware of policies that violate anti-discrimination laws or unethical practices. In this role, social workers are agents of social change who help improve society for future citizens.

Social workers should celebrate the diversity of their clients and the communities where they work. This includes identifying differences and similarities between cultures and maintaining an "open door" policy to all individuals in need of assistance. These practices are intended to promote a society inclusive to all individuals and groups, regardless of their personal characteristics, values, or beliefs. Practitioners must identify resources in their community and their own organization to best serve their clients. Social workers should use good moral judgment to make sure that these resources are given equally to their clients and are tailored to the specific needs of those they serve.

Following the Ethics and Morality of the Profession

Practitioners must follow the profession's code of ethics and act with honesty, compassion, and dignity. Social workers should be familiar with the most recent version of the social work code of ethics, which contains the values and principles endorsed by the practitioners and researchers in the field. They should apply these principles in practice and evaluate how they can be tailored to their specific communities. Practitioners should also be respectful of clients and colleagues by acting with sincerity and good moral judgment. This includes setting and following professional boundaries with clients and coworkers, following the profession's ethical code, and taking responsibility for their actions.

Ethical Dilemmas

Ethical dilemmas occur when three different conditions are met in a situation. The first is that the practitioner must make a decision. If the situation does not require that a decision be made, then there isn't an ethical dilemma. The second is that there are different decisions that could be made or different actions one could take. The third condition is that an ethical ideal will be conceded no matter what decision is made.

One type of ethical dilemma occurs when you have a situation in which two ethical principles are conflicting. This is a pure ethical dilemma because either choice of action involves conceding one of these principles, and there is no way to keep both principles intact. Another type of ethical dilemma occurs when ethical principles conflict with values and/or laws. In these types of situations, a social worker's values may conflict with an ethical principle, and a decision must be made.

Once you have determined which kind of ethical dilemma you are facing, there are steps to take in order to reach a conclusion and, ultimately, the resolution of the dilemma. The NASW lays out steps that should be taken when attempting to resolve an ethical dilemma.

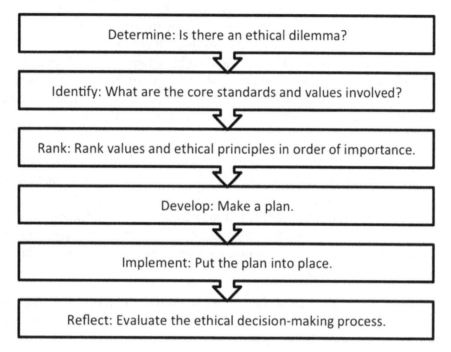

Determine: Is there an ethical dilemma?

Identify: What are the core standards and values involved?

Rank: Rank values and ethical principles in order of importance.

Develop: Make a plan.

Implement: Put the plan into place.

Reflect: Evaluate the ethical decision-making process.

Client Competence and Self-Determination

Social workers realize that clients have a right to lead their lives as they see fit, making their own decisions based on their values. Issues may arise when the values of clients do not align with how others believe clients should behave or live. Social workers must advocate on the behalf of clients with other professionals to ensure that their values are at the core of any plan. It is the job of the social worker to work with the client to aid in goal creation and identification that is congruent to the client's values.

There are situations where promoting client self-determination may cause conflict between the client, social worker, and other professionals. For example, if a client has entered a hospital due to medical issues arising from alcohol abuse, healthcare professionals may recommend that the client attend an alcohol and drug rehabilitation facility for treatment. However, if the client does not wish to seek treatment, then the social worker should advocate on their behalf and help to devise a plan that honors the client's wishes. Exceptions to this value would be when a client needs protection from self-harm or harming or others. In this situation, the social worker must act in accordance with legal and ethical standards to do no harm versus promoting the self-determination of the client.

Protecting and Enhancing Client Self-Determination

Social workers realize that clients have a right to lead their lives as they see fit, making their own decisions based on their values. Issues may arise when the values of clients do not align with how others believe clients should behave or live. Social workers must advocate on the behalf of clients with other professionals to ensure that their values are at the core of any plan. It is the job of the social worker to work with the client to aid in goal creation and identification that is congruent to the client's values.

There are situations where promoting client self-determination may cause conflict between the client, social worker, and other professionals. For example, if a client has entered a hospital due to medical issues arising from alcohol abuse, healthcare professionals may recommend that the client attend an alcohol and drug rehabilitation facility for treatment. However, if the client does not wish to seek treatment, then the social worker should advocate on their behalf and help to devise a plan that honors the client's wishes. Exceptions to this value would be when a client needs protection from self-harm or harming others. In this situation, the social worker must act in accordance with legal and ethical standards to do no harm versus promoting the self-determination of the client.

Client's Right to Refuse Services

As per the NASW Code of Ethics, the client has the right to refuse all or a portion social work services and utilize self-direction at any point. Social workers should address this possibility with the client during the intake process, as well as inform the client fully about the possible ramifications of refusing services. Clients may need outside service linkages from the social worker during the termination process; they may also choose to continue service but decide to work with a different social worker or in an entirely different social or health field.

Social workers should be respectful of clients who terminate services before completing the problem-solving process, and they should remain detached and objective during the termination without taking any critical feedback too personally. Rather, this can be viewed as a learning opportunity to understand different types of clients better. It is important to note that not all clients can voluntarily cease services. For example, court-appointed social work sessions often cannot be terminated by the client. In these cases, the social worker may have difficult interactions with the client and face resistance, especially if the client truly does not want to be in the session. Additionally, clients who are unable to make decisions due to a medical reason (such as a mental condition that inhibits decision-making) may voice opposition to the treatment, but they cannot be the actual person who terminates treatment. This is usually left to a proxy, such as a legal representative or family member.

Professional Boundaries

Difficulties in Setting and Maintaining Professional Boundaries in Social Work

Professional boundaries in social work are clearly defined limits on the practitioner-client relationship that provide a space for the creation of safe connections. Some helpful things to keep in mind include: the line between being friendly and being friends; being with the client versus becoming the client; and understanding the limits and responsibilities of the social worker role.

Conflicting values occur when the social worker's values and knowledge about best practices are at odds with the client's values, history, relationships, or lifestyle. *Vicarious trauma* may happen when a social worker experiences symptoms of trauma after listening to a client's experience. These symptoms may arise due to the practitioner sharing a similar history of trauma. Boundaries may be difficult to maintain

if the social worker feels that they need to rescue the client due to an unhealthy attachment to positive results in practice. This is termed the *rescuer role*. Professional boundaries may also be difficult to set and maintain if there is poor teamwork between colleagues in the social work organization. This is evident when social workers assume the roles of other team members because they believe they are not fulfilling their responsibilities to the client.

Professional boundary issues occur when social workers have multiple types of relationships with a client. This may include a professional, business, or personal relationship. For example, it is permissible to see a client out in public at a restaurant, but not to invite a client to dinner for business or personal reasons. When encountering a client in public, the relationship with the client must be kept confidential. However, if the client chooses to say hello, saying hello in return and quickly ending the encounter would be acceptable.

There are several boundary issues that come with working with clients. These issues are:

- Intimate contact: This refers to things such as hugging a client at the end of a working relationship, or patting a client on the hand during a crying session. Sexual contact also falls into this category.

- Personal gain: This refers to instances in which a social worker engages in activity with a client that results in a monetary (or otherwise valuable) benefit to the social worker. This could involve situations such as referring a client to a business owned by the social worker or a friend/family member of the social worker, selling something to a client, or even asking a client for professional suggestions.

- Emotional and dependency issues: This refers to instances in which a social worker's own personal issues cause the social worker to have impaired judgment, possibly resulting in other boundary issues, such as a dual relationship with the client.

- Altruistic instincts: In some instances, a social worker's own good intentions and concerns for a client can result in boundary violations and confusion about the relationship between the social worker and the client. An example of this would be going to a client's bridal shower or retirement party.

Strategies for Setting and Maintaining Professional Boundaries in Social Work

Despite these difficulties, social workers must set and maintain boundaries with their clients and colleagues to ensure an effective practice. Practitioners should consistently monitor how their professional boundaries enhance or harm relationships with clients, colleagues, supervisors and administrators. They must also gauge the impact of their boundaries on the amount of time they devote to work, their ability to cope with stress at work, and the amount of time and energy that they spend on extraneous activities and relationships.

There are several strategies for building and maintaining appropriate professional boundaries and relationships. First, practitioners should examine their motivations for giving extra time and attention to a client. If a social worker treats one client differently, this indicates that the boundary may be overextended. Social workers can manage this situation by determining whether the services provided are in line with the client's care plan, the organization's mission, the job description, and scope of practice.

Social workers should also avoid encouraging clients to contact them through personal channels. Clients should use the channels of communication set in place by the organization, such as work email, voicemail, cell phones, pagers, receptionists, on-call staff, and procedures for after-hours referrals to 911, emergency rooms, or mental health crisis centers. Extending the professional boundaries of the social worker role puts colleagues and the organization at risk for failure. It also sets an unfair expectation that other colleagues will extend their professional boundaries. If boundaries are inconsistent between colleagues and within the organization, then clients may become confused and distrust the entire organization.

A third strategy for building appropriate professional boundaries is establishing clear agreements with clients during the initial sessions about the role of a social worker and the dynamics of a client-practitioner relationship. When warning signs indicate that healthy boundaries may be in jeopardy, social workers must address the issues with the client clearly, quickly, and sensitively. This involves clarifying the roles and boundaries with the client and asking the client to restate these boundaries to ensure understanding.

A fourth strategy is limiting self-disclosure about the social worker's personal life to information directly related to the client's goals. If there is a dual relationship between the social worker and client, the practitioner must preserve the client's confidentiality, physical security, and emotional well-being in social situations.

A fifth strategy is avoiding social media within professional practice. Practitioners should not connect with clients on social media. This includes adding clients as friends on Facebook or following clients on Twitter. Social workers should use discretion and limit the amount of online information that is made available to the public or social network connections to prevent conflicts of interest. Social workers also shouldn't attempt to access online information about clients without prior informed consent. Finally, practitioners shouldn't post negative information about colleagues or the organization online.

A sixth strategy is for social workers to foster strong work relationships with their colleagues at the organization. These connections will help practitioners cope with stresses, think through questions of ethics and professional relationships, and help maintain a sense of humor. Practitioners should be sensitive to signs of bullying in the workplace, as each practitioner deserves respect and dignity to ensure social justice for others. It's important that social workers use appropriate channels of supervision and consultation to determine appropriate boundaries in difficult situations. Supervision can also be useful when trying to remedy concerns with existing organization procedures that address or inhibit client needs.

A final strategy for maintaining professional boundaries is ensuring appropriate self-care. This includes taking time for nurturing oneself throughout the workday, maintaining a regular work schedule, and taking time away from the office each day to refocus. Practitioners should limit communication when they are away from work to ensure time for rejuvenation, especially during vacations or personal time. They must also be aware of how they handle work stress and monitor how often they take work home. This includes physical work, emotional strain, or hyper-vigilance about work situations. If a practitioner consistently struggles to maintain professional relationships and work boundaries, they should seek supervision or outside mental health counseling.

Self-Disclosure Principles and Applications

To build professional boundaries, it is recommended that social workers limit self-disclosure about their personal lives to information directly related to the client's goals. If there is a dual relationship between the social worker and client, the practitioner must preserve the client's confidentiality, physical security, and emotional well-being in social situations.

Documentation

Keeping accurate client records has many purposes, such as documenting the history and treatment of a client, getting insurance reimbursement, and providing social workers a historical account of client sessions. The information contained in a client record can also be used to evaluate the effectiveness of services. Client records, when combined with other evaluation tools (e.g., client satisfaction surveys, reactions to treatments, accomplishments of goals), can be an effective method of evaluating treatment progress. Supervisors may review client records to evaluate the effectiveness of the treatment process, social worker performance, and client progress, or to ensure documentation is being completed accurately and on time. When reviewing client records for evaluation, ethical standards must always be upheld.

The NASW Code of Ethics specifically addresses guidelines for using client information for evaluation, including:

- Protecting confidentially to the fullest extent possible
- Accurately reporting information
- Protecting clients from harm
- Obtaining required client consent for all uses of their information (e.g., supervisory review, reimbursement)
- Making clients aware that the consent can be withdrawn without punishment

Termination

Termination of the relationship occurs when the client and the social worker have reached treatment goals. Even though the relationship is terminated, the client may feel warmly toward the social worker, and congruence and empathy may still be part of the relationship. Some clients may require maintenance sessions to continue stability, but when termination is the next clear stage in the relationship, psychotherapy sessions should end.

In the case of a client choosing to prematurely terminate services, the social worker should clearly explain the risks to the client and also carefully document all meetings and interactions to protect against legal ramifications. Abandonment, which refers to the social worker terminating services prematurely without adequate reason or in an improper manner, is considered malpractice and can lead to lawsuits. When the social worker decides to end the working relationship, they must ensure that the client is adequately prepared and warned about the end of services, and that the client is emotionally equipped to deal with the termination. Social workers can refer clients to other types of providers, who can continue working with the client after their own services have ceased. If a social worker needs to terminate services early, such as in the case of leaving a job, they should connect the client to a new social worker who can continue to provide the same level of services.

Death and Dying

Some clients have documented clear wishes about their death and dying (advance directives), while others do not. In these cases, social workers may be called upon to provide information and counsel to the client and client system. This can be an emotional process, and social workers should show compassion, sympathy, and respect as the client and the client system adjust to the news. Terminal clients are allowed to take comfort measures, such as hospice services, but are not allowed to take any external measures that would intensify or speed up the dying process (such as requesting a lethal medication dose). Terminal clients may choose to refuse treatment and pass away naturally; while this process may hasten death, it is considered a natural and acceptable alternative to prolonging the dying experience with intervention, and it is also considered the client's choice. Terminal clients may choose this route if they have made peace with the decision and with their family and friends, if they want to remove a physical and financial burden from loved ones, and if they are ready for the process. Still, in such a case a social worker could provide guidance to ensure the client truly understands the process and consequences of their decision. With a do not resuscitate (DNR) order, a client chooses to refuse services if their cardiopulmonary system ceases to work.

In clients who are unable to make decisions (such as those who are in a permanent vegetative state), the next of kin or a legal appointee may make medical decisions on the client's behalf. This may include taking the client off life support, if applicable. This can be a highly contentious situation if family members or legal proxies do not agree on the best course of action. This situation can be avoided by preparing advanced directives, which document the client's wishes in such contexts.

Research Ethics

Research performed on living creatures, especially humans, is always scrutinized for ethical concerns. Such research often uses experiments for which the outcomes are unknown. Therefore, it is possible that any research performed on a person may have unintended, unwanted, or otherwise harmful psychological, physiological, emotional, or social effects. Research ethics are intended to protect participants, ensure that research is being conducted for some public benefits, and ensure that participants who are involved have been provided with informed consent. Informed consent involves explaining to an individual, in as much detail possible, the processes of the experiment or study, all potential side effects or outcomes, and the opportunity to make an educated decision independently about participation in such a study. Informed consent also documents the fact that the participant may leave the study at any time. Informed consent paperwork is usually signed by the participants, the researcher, and an independent third party. Some controversy still exists over research that affects vulnerable populations, such as those with psychological disorders, the elderly, children, the poor, and others who cannot easily make objective decisions or could be persuaded by experiment incentives (such as gift cards or the like).

An Institutional Review Board (IRB) is any independent group that reviews research and clinical trial designs that have human participants to ensure there are no potential ethical violations. IRBs are accredited by the US Food and Drug Administration. These groups can request changes, additions, and eliminations to any study proposal; they can also completely deny a proposal for approval. Without IRB approval, research designs cannot come to the experiment phase. While research is in session, IRB committees conduct regular audits to ensure compliance is still intact. Noncompliance can result in heavy fines, penalties, criminal investigation, and termination of a study.

Supervision and Consultation

In social work, supervision takes place when a more experienced professional mentors or coaches an emerging professional in fieldwork, practical application, or other service delivery setting. This requires strong interpersonal skills, a sense of respect, and open communication between both parties. The supervisor should be able to provide supportive instruction and guidance without arrogance and condescension; the supervisee should be receptive to instruction and have an honest desire for professional growth and learning. Some commonly used models of supervision in the social work setting include individual-oriented types of supervision, in which the supervisor may ask the supervisee to reflect upon their interactions with different clients or their personal judgments and biases that may have arisen during a session. The supervisor may also present the supervisee with different forms of research and data, and ask the supervisee to utilize the evidence to structure interventions. Finally, the supervisor may provide coaching related to the supervisee's development, by establishing small objectives that lead to larger professional goals.

In peer-oriented and group-oriented approaches, lateral-level colleagues (perhaps with the aid of one or two supervisors) learn from one another by sharing clinical experiences and lessons, new research and literature, or other professional development opportunities. This may take the form of team meetings at the beginning or end of the day, social events where work can be discussed, or conference settings. In some workplaces, individual, peer, and group models may be integrated to provide a more holistic sense of supervision.

Consultation can take place in any interaction that a social worker has with a client, regardless of setting or context. Consultation can primarily be divided into organizational, program, educational, mental health, and clinical cases. These can take place one-one-one with an individual or in group therapy settings.

Supervision and Management

Supervisors and managers should always be aware of the hierarchical power they wield over subordinates, and they should ensure that their leadership does not take advantage of this dynamic. Behaviors that would be unsuitable in a lateral colleague may be ignored in a supervisor if a subordinate feels their job or work environment would be in jeopardy should a complaint be filed.

Interpersonal work dynamics between supervisors and subordinates should ensure that the supervisor treats subordinates with professional respect and support, even when they are challenging them to grow professionally or learn more. It is critical to not become domineering in this regard. Additionally, if a supervisor needs to coach a subordinate on performance, this should be done privately rather than in front of other colleagues. On the other hand, supervisors also need to make sure that their relationships with subordinates do not become overly friendly or intimate. Supervisors should avoid confiding overly personal details to subordinates or pursuing romantic relationships in the workplace. Not only could this cause extreme discomfort for colleagues, it could also be reported for harassment. When in doubt, supervisors can refer to the NASW Code of Ethics to drive not only their service delivery, but also their interactions in the workplace.

Social Worker Safety

Social workers are often in high-risk situations, working with high-risk populations. The threat of violence or other personal safety issues is relatively high compared to other fields of work.

Implementing policies and procedures that help protect social workers during their workday can help mitigate some of this risk. This includes the provision of an avenue to report unsafe settings or clients, and if necessary, to terminate working relationships in which the social worker does not feel safe without fear of workplace reprisal. Reviewing the daily processes of service delivery can help identify areas where risk management techniques may be necessary.

Since social workers work in a number of different places—office settings, jails, courtrooms, family homes, community centers, hospitals, and so on—they should treat each session individually and assess safety risks each time. This assessment may include an overview of the location, the ability to receive emergency services quickly, other available workers who may be able to help in an emergency, and the state of the client at each visit (even if it is someone the social worker has treated for some time). Social workers should also protect their personal boundaries, such as not allowing clients to call or visit them at home, not sharing personal information in person or online, and maintaining protocols to address client emotions that could lead to violence. (Examples include shouting at or threatening the social worker. While these are not physical assaults, they are still verbal and emotional violence toward the social worker, and they could escalate.)

The Supervisee's Role in Supervision

Although the focus is often on the supervisor's role of ensuring that clients are provided with ethical services by training and evaluating the supervisee, the supervisee's role in supervision is not passive. The social worker should fully engage in the process of supervision and use this relationship to grow and improve. In order to do that, the supervisee must be willing to discuss areas of ethical or legal concern that have arisen in their interactions with clients. They must also be ready to honestly address their own struggles and identify their learning needs, and seek the help and advice of the supervisor. This can only happen effectively through genuine self-assessment, which flows from a real desire to become a better social worker. The process of self-assessment in supervision can help them see any biases or weaknesses that may be holding them back from fully meeting their clients' needs. If the social worker is defensive or resistant to the supervisory relationship, then they will make little progress.

Factors to consider when receiving feedback during supervision/consultation:

- Social workers can benefit from feedback during supervision or consultation, especially with difficult clients/cases or at significant times in treatment, such as termination.

- When discussing cases, client confidentiality should be protected as much as possible, and client consent to release information should be acquired.

Accreditation and Licensing Requirements

In the United States, social work accreditation and licensure requirements vary by state. Therefore, aspiring social workers should ensure they follow standards set forth in the state in which they hope to practice.

The Council on Social Work Education (CSWE) is the main accrediting body for higher education programs in social work, and the majority of states require that social workers receive undergraduate or graduate degrees from universities whose social work curriculum is CSWE-accredited in order to become a licensed professional. CSWE-accredited programs ensure that coursework includes not only informational related to competencies established by the NASW, but that an emphasis is placed on

ethics, professionalism, and practical application. Most states do not allow aspiring social workers to take board examinations without proof of a CSWE-accredited degree.

Other licensing information pertains to the type of social work a person hopes to do and the education they have received. Clinical social workers have different licensing requirements. Some states require post-graduate education in social work before licensure can be obtained. Other levels of licensure require practical and field work for a designated period of time. While board scores may be transferred across state lines, licensure is a separate process in each state that reviews both the worker's education and working experience comprehensively.

Professional Development Activities

Professional development activities are a vital component of continuing education and ensuring social workers remain competent over the course of their careers, especially as public needs and norms shift. Social workers can find a plethora of continuing education courses, seminars, and trainings at the college or university from which they received their degree. Often, these are free or discounted for alumni. The NASW provides various free to for-cost opportunities on their website, including a portal which allows the user to filter opportunities by date, topic, location, and cost. The web site also provides online courses that can be done at home, free teleconferences in which to learn from peers, online articles, and links to new scholarly literature. The NASW also invites professionals to write and advocate for issues on behalf of the organization, which allows social workers to hone research and writing skills while also promoting themselves professionally and serving causes about which they are personally passionate. Networking and conferences are another way to meet and learn from peers and develop professionally. Additionally, employers may provide free or discounted opportunities for social workers to pursue professional development activities. This may include activities such as in-house workshops or sponsoring employees to attend conferences or trainings.

In order to maintain licensure, social workers must pursue a certain number of continuing education hours per designated time cycle. Therefore, all social workers can inherently expect to continuously develop as professionals as long as they are continuing to renew their licenses. The specifics of continuing education are determined by the state issuing the license and the type of license that is held. Certain licenses may also require that all or a portion of the continuing education credits cover specific topics.

Confidentiality

Elements of Client Reports

Elements of client reports may include developmental history, family history, substance use information, medical history, presenting problem, and recommendations. There are a variety of elements of client reports that may be required by the agency. With the advent of electronic records, client reports are often built into the software that the agency uses. Client reports may also be in DAP (data, assessment, plan) format or in the model of SOAP notes (subjective, objective, assessment, and plan). Reports are at the agency's discretion and the social worker should use the format that is required by the agency to develop client reports.

Obtaining Informed Consent

When disclosing information due to legal requirements, it is always important to discuss the situation with the client. It should be noted that the social worker should evaluate their own safety when discussing disclosure of confidential information with the client. If the social worker believes the situation to be unsafe if/when the client learns of the disclosure, then it is not necessary to alert the client prior to disclosing the confidential information. This is something that should be discussed in detail with clients during the informed consent process and throughout the relationship.

One of the difficulties associated with breaking confidentiality to protect a third party is that the threat isn't always clearly established. If a client discloses during treatment that he is going to go home and stab his neighbor, this is clearly a plan of intended harm. However, what about an HIV-positive client who fails to warn sexual partners of her HIV status? What if the client fully understands the risk to her partners and has no intention of disclosing her status? This is a situation that would require thorough documentation, thoughtful debate, and possibly conferencing with colleagues to decide upon the best course of action.

Confidentiality also becomes more complicated when a social worker is working with two or more people, either in a family or group session. All participants must agree that any information shared within the context of treatment will be kept confidential and not shared with others. However, the social worker should stress with clients that they cannot force other members to abide by the confidentiality agreement and that breach of confidentiality is a risk.

Client Records

Issues relating to confidentiality include the storage and maintenance of records and charts. All confidential material should be kept in a secure location and locked at all times. For example, if a social worker takes a clipboard into client rooms to make notes for later documentation, that clipboard should be locked in a drawer when not in use so that no one can turn it over and see confidential information when the social worker is away from their desk. With the use of electronics and computers, there should be policies in place to lock computers when away to avoid anyone seeing notes or other confidential information. Collaboration between colleagues in which clients may be discussed should be done behind closed doors to avoid anyone else hearing the conversation.

Social workers are to provide clients with reasonable access to records. Social workers are permitted, however, by the Code of Ethics to withhold all or part of the client record from the client if the social worker determines there is a great risk of harm in releasing the information. In these cases, it is important to fully document the request, whether the records were released, and the rationale for either releasing or not releasing them.

There may be instances in which a social worker is sued for malpractice. In these cases, the Code of Ethics states that it is permissible for the social worker to share confidential client information to aid in self-defense, but only so far as is necessary to adequately defend oneself.

Throughout the development of a professional relationship in social work, it is important to keep case notes and records for several reasons. Case notes are important in the process of conceptualizing the case and the client's needs. They can help the practitioner pull together his or her thoughts when making a diagnosis. Case records also serve as a measure of the standard of care and subsequently can be used in court to show adequate client care. They help social workers determine whether clients have

made progress, remember what the client said from visit to visit, and can be used when a practitioner seeks supervision about the case. In addition, case notes are needed by insurance companies, agencies, and schools to support the treatment that is provided to clients.

Legal and Ethical Issues Regarding Confidentiality

Social workers have a duty to protect confidential information of clients. Ethically, client information should not be discussed with anyone other than the client. Legally, a client has a right to keep their medical and therapeutic information confidential. The Health Insurance Portability and Accountability Act of 1996 (HIPAA) requires that medical information (including therapeutic and mental health information) be protected and kept confidential. However, there are certain limitations to confidentiality. These generally involve risk of harm to the individual being served, as well as others.

Social workers are not as protected as some other professionals when it comes to confidentiality and often find themselves being called to testify in court cases related to their clients. There are also certain situations in which social workers may have to release confidential information to protect the client or satisfy the duty to warn.

Providing services to minors can be challenging when it comes to confidentiality issues, especially since the legal rules and regulations vary from state to state. At times, there can be a conflict between the social worker's feeling of ethical responsibility to maintain the privacy of the minor and the legal right of parents to be informed of issues discussed. Adolescents in particular may discuss concerns with a social worker that they do not want their parents to be aware of, and it can be a violation of trust if these issues are subsequently revealed to parents. It is imperative that at the start of treatment, the expectations of the social worker's relationship with each person are discussed with the parents and minors, as well as the benefits and limits of confidentiality. Minors should never be promised confidentiality when the social worker cannot keep that promise, but the privacy and individuality of the minor should be maintained as much as possible. In cases where private information about the minor is going to be revealed, social workers should always inform the minor. This holds true regardless as to whether it is with the client's consent, mandated reporting, or due to the parent utilizing their right to information.

With technology being utilized extensively by helping professionals, confidentiality of electronic information is another important issue. Counseling sessions are now being provided by telephone, video chat, and online simulation, and these media open new possibilities for information abuse. If a practitioner provides a video therapy session, they should be aware that it is possible for the client to have someone else in the room, off-camera, without informing the clinician or other participants. The same could be true with electronic communication such as texting or email. There is no way to know if a client is forwarding electronic information to third parties without the clinician's knowledge.

Mandatory Reporting

Some clients may disclose intent to harm themselves. It is necessary in these situations to fully assess suicidal intent and determine if the client is serious about carrying out a plan for self-harm. It might be sufficient, in cases where a client has considered self-harm but has no clear plan, to complete a safety plan with the client. The safety plan will outline what the client agrees to do should they begin to experience the desire to engage in self-harm. However, if the client has a clear plan of action and access to items necessary to carry out the plan, then confidentiality should be broken to protect the client. This would involve notifying police and having the client committed for observation for their own protection.

In addition to protecting clients from themselves, social workers also have a duty to warn third-party individuals if there is threat of harm. Duty to warn was established by the 1976 case Tarasoff vs. Regents of the University of California. In this case, a graduate student at the University of California-Berkley had become obsessed with Tatiana Tarasoff. After significant distress, he sought psychological treatment and disclosed to his therapist that he had a plan to kill Tarasoff. Although the psychologist did have the student temporarily committed, he was ultimately released. He eventually stopped seeking treatment and attacked and killed Tarasoff. Tarasoff's family sued the psychologist and various other individuals involved with the university. This case evolved into the duty to warn third parties of potential risk of harm. Satisfying the duty to warn can be done by notifying police or the individual who is the intended victim.

Because ethical dilemmas can involve legal situations, they may also have legal consequences for a social worker or necessitate involving the legal system. For example, a client may disclose that he frequently drinks large amounts of alcohol and then drives his children to school. Ethically, there is an obligation to keep what the client has said in confidence. However, the client's children are being placed in a situation in which they are in great danger of being injured or harmed. Due to laws protecting the welfare of children, the social worker would need to make a report to Child Protective Services. In some states, if someone has a good faith reason to believe that a child is being neglected or abused, and does not report the situation, that person may face a civil lawsuit and even criminal charges.

It's important to note as well that social workers are considered mandated reporters in all states. This means there is a legal and ethical obligation to break confidentiality to report any signs and symptoms of child and elder abuse. In some cases, it will be impossible to know for sure if abuse or neglect is happening. Often the social worker will have only a small amount of information that may raise concerns, but must make a report so that an investigation can occur. A social worker cannot be held liable for reports made in good faith to Child Protective Services or Adult Protective Services.

Liability is another legal issue that social workers may sometimes face. Clients can sue a social worker for malpractice. When a social worker is sued, the liability does not stop with the social worker. In lawsuits, a social worker's supervisor can be named as a defendant, and liability can extend as far as the head of the agency that employs the social worker. Agencies that provide social services carry malpractice insurance for this very reason. It is good practice, however, for individual social workers to also carry malpractice insurance for extra protection.

Ethical and Legal Issues Regarding Mandatory Reporting of Abuse

Mandatory reporting laws require social workers, and other professionals, to report any suspected abuse or neglect. This means that any professional who has a suspicion of abuse or neglect of a child or a vulnerable adult must legally make a report to either Child Protective Services or Adult Protective Services. Note that some states, such as Tennessee, have laws that require all citizens to report suspected abuse or neglect, making everyone a mandated reporter.

Often when abuse or neglect is suspected, the concern about breaking confidentiality is at the forefront of the mind of the social worker. During informed consent, this requirement to report any signs of abuse or neglect should have been disclosed to the client. When such breaks in confidentiality occur, they can damage the relationship. In some cases, it may be necessary or appropriate to disclose to the client that a report is being made. For example, if a new mother has tested positive for cocaine and the infant has tested positive for cocaine while in the hospital, the infant will remain in the Neonatal Intensive Care Unit due to withdrawal. Disclosing to the mother that a report is being made, and why it's being made, could prepare her and create an opportunity to speak further with her about treatment options and

other important considerations. It's important to note that social workers who fail to report suspected abuse or neglect can be subject to civil penalties and/or prosecution.

Professional Development and Use of Self

Components of the Social Worker-Client Relationship

The relationship between the social worker and the client or client system is influenced by a number of components. These include the type of emotion that is shown by the parties during sessions, the general attitude toward the working relationship (e.g., positive, supportive), and the value each party places on the working relationship. The social worker should ensure that empathy, sympathy, and acceptance of the client and client system are shown during sessions to help foster a positive relationship. These aspects can be further supported by the social worker's initiative to build rapport with the client, such as through allowing the client to openly express feelings, work at a pace that feels comfortable, and encouraging them to shape and make decisions related to the intervention.

Additionally, a number of external tools may be a vital part of the social worker/client relationship. These include tools and documents that provide information related to the client's personality and behavior, and can help the social worker shape the intervention for the client. These might include items such as assessments, medical history, family history, current living situation, socioeconomic situation, and personal goals for the intervention.

Client's Role in the Problem-Solving Process

Whenever possible, social workers should invite their clients to take a collaborative perspective in designing interventions, establishing objectives, and developing program goals. This allows the client to feel empowered and engaged as an active member of the problem-solving process. These factors are associated with higher incidences of positive outcomes, as they encourage clients to feel accountable for their behaviors, actions, and personal changes.

Collaboration should begin at the intake process. This is a period in which the social worker can make assessments, but they can also get information directly from clients about why they are in the session and what they hope to achieve. The social worker can also ask clients the steps they believe they need to take to reach their desired outcomes. While clients may or may not provide useful or feasible answers, this process still sets the tone that allows clients to feel acknowledged and involved in their own care.

In the intake session or in the sessions that immediately follow, the social worker can invite the client to develop SMART objectives to reach their goals. This may also include establishing accountability tools, documenting plans of action to address potential barriers and how to overcome them, and any other support protocols that clients may need for their individual situations. Depending on the client's specific case, this process may take one session or may take much longer. Social workers should continuously show patience, compassion, and a welcoming desire to engage the client in the process.

Social Worker's Role in the Problem-Solving Process

The problem solving therapeutic model serves to teach clients how to manage stressors that come in life. Often clients do not possess skills that allow them to effectively navigate negative events or emotions without increasing personal harm. The goal of the problem-solving model is to teach clients the skills necessary to deal with negative life events, negative emotions, and stressful situations. In particular, goals of this model should be to assist clients in identifying which particular situations may trigger unpleasant emotions, understanding the range of emotions one might feel, planning how to effectively deal with situations when they arise, and even recognizing and accepting that some situations are not able to be solved.

The social worker, however, may be an instructional guide to facilitate problem solving for the client. Because problem-solving skills are one of the primary methods of resolving issues, and often are skills that clients lack, the social worker may need to model them for the client so that the client can then develop their own skills. Social workers need to maintain empathy and congruence with the client during the problem solving process, and even though they may have verbally instructed or modeled problem-solving methods, they need to maintain rapport in the relationship.

Roles and Responsibilities of the Social Worker and Client in the Intervention Process

Clarifying the roles and responsibilities of the social worker, the client, and the client system in the intervention process can reduce the chance of miscommunication, misunderstanding, and interventions not working as intended. This clarification process can be developed during the intake process and initial sessions by actively listening to what the client hopes to achieve, and working together to develop a step-by-step intervention methodology. When possible, the stages, objectives, and milestones of the intervention should be documented in order to have an available reference point, drive accountability, and reduce any confusion around the expectations of all involved parties.

The problem-solving approach to interventions is a commonly used framework to cover these points. This is a seven-stage model that encourages active listening and engagement techniques (such as eye contact and other receptive body language); fostering trust and collaboration with the client (such as by showing genuine interest in the client as a person, rather than just in the context of the issues at hand); working together to identify the problem to be addressed and possible solutions, introducing allies in the resolution processes (such as clinical providers, a yoga or meditation teacher, or other experts that could help the client); developing a documented resolution plan and actively engaging all parties to follow it (such as through accountability cues, positive reinforcement, and celebrating small victories); and support for sustaining the desired behaviors until the client is capable of terminating the intervention. While one can be hopeful that the client and client systems will be cooperative and willing in this framework, that is not always the case. Clients may show distrust, anxiety, fear, or apathy, especially in the beginning. Often, the most important role of the social worker is building trust with the client and the client system. The social worker should continue to encourage a trusting, collaborative relationship until the time of service termination.

Building and Maintaining a Helping Relationship

As the principal conduit for client change and acceptance, the social worker/client relationship is primary to the problem solving and therapy process. If the social worker cannot develop a positive relationship with the client, the change process is hindered. The worker/client relationship should be based on trust, empathy, and acceptance by both parties in order to facilitate growth. Some clients may have difficulty building trust with the social worker, and the social worker may need to be patient with the client in order to make treatment goal progress. If the social worker cannot develop an appropriate trusting, empathetic, and accepting relationship with the client, the social worker should seek supervision. In some cases, the social worker will need to transfer the client because it will be very

challenging for the client to make progress if trust does not exist. Social workers should be alert for countertransference issues in the relationship with the client and address these issues promptly if they occur.

Principles of Relationship Building

Rapport building begins during the initial contact the social worker has with the client, a crucial time for establishing trust and harmony. After building rapport, the client and the social worker can begin working on client issues and continue developing the relationship on deeper levels. The relationship that the client has with the social worker is representative of the relationships the client has in other areas of life; the social worker needs to engage with the client within this framework to effect the greatest change.

Termination of the relationship occurs when the client and the social worker have reached treatment goals. Even though the relationship is terminated, the client may feel warmly toward the social worker, and congruence and empathy may still be part of the relationship. Some clients may require maintenance sessions to continue stability, but when termination is the next clear stage in the relationship, psychotherapy sessions should end.

Acceptance and Empathy in the Social Worker-Client Relationship

Empathy is being able to relate to client circumstances and direction without the social worker actually experiencing it themselves. Sympathy differs from empathy in that sympathy is compassion for the client without having experienced the client's state of being. Empathy involves "being with" the client in their time and frame of mind. It involves connecting to the client on a visceral level while still maintaining some objectivity. Because empathy is the framework on which social work practice is built, it is imperative that social workers be empathetic with their clients. Those who cannot be empathetic should seek additional supervision or counsel in order to do their work effectively, or refer the client to another worker.

Power and Transparency in the Social Worker-Client Relationship

Throughout their careers and in specific interventions, social workers should always remain aware of the power differential that is likely to exist between themselves and their clients. As the main person guiding the intervention, social workers inherently have more power in the relationship. Additionally, social workers may have more education, more independence, a clean legal record, better finances, or some other privilege that may make the client feel uncomfortable, ashamed, or defensive (especially when the client is involuntarily in the session, such as court-ordered cases). Awareness is one fundamental component of ensuring that this power dynamic doesn't have a negative effect. Transparency is another fundamental component, as it allows the client to feel like an equal who is involved in the problem-solving process. Social workers can foster transparency in the working relationship by openly discussing areas of privilege they may have, sharing as much information as they can about the problem-solving process and how it may be of benefit to the client, and empowering the client to take as much of the process as possible into their own control (such as through independent decision making). When possible, the social worker should avoid hiding information or being unclear about why certain processed of interventions are being pursued.

Dual Relationships

Dual relationships are clearly outlined in the NASW Code of Ethics. The Code of Ethics states that social workers should not engage in dual relationships with clients or former clients in which exploitation of the client may occur. The Code of Ethics does recognize that there might be situations where dual relationships are unavoidable. For example, a social worker might have two jobs, one of which involves providing group therapy to survivors of sexual abuse. It is possible that a member of the aforementioned therapy group could become an employee or client at the social worker's second place of work. In these types of situations, the Code of Ethics suggests that the social worker establish clear boundaries that are sensitive to the client/former client.

Under no circumstances should a social worker ever become involved in a sexual relationship with a client. In addition, the Code of Ethics establishes that social workers must avoid sexual relationships with anyone who is related to or has a close personal relationship with a client or former client. The Code of Ethics also states that social workers should not become involved in sexual relationships with former clients because of the high risk of harm that may occur with such relationships. If, however, a social worker does become involved in a sexual relationship with a former client, the social worker is responsible for demonstrating that the former client entered into the relationship without manipulation or exploitation. The Code of Ethics also specifies that, due to the obvious risk of harm, a social worker should not provide professional services to anyone with whom the social worker has had a previous sexual relationship.

Situations called "boundary crossings" are when a social worker does not intend to create a dual relationship but inadvertently does so, as would be the case were a clinician to self-disclose personal information during a therapy session. This is distinguished from a boundary *violation*, which occurs when a dual relationship is established that is inherently coercive or manipulative and therefore harmful to the client. What are some clues about whether a boundary crossing is unethical?

- It hinders the social worker's care
- It prevents the social worker from being impartial
- It exploits or manipulates the client or another person
- It harms clients or colleagues

Dual relationships are sometimes unavoidable in practice, particularly in small communities. However, it is possible to avoid dual relationships that involve boundary violations and ethical violations.

Transference and Countertransference in the Social Worker-Client Relationship

Transference occurs when the client consciously or unconsciously relates to the social worker because the social worker reminds the client, in some way, of a person from a past relationship. Transference by clients toward the social worker often occurs during the course of treatment and the client needs to be made aware of transference issues and how to reduce them. If clients are experiencing transference with the social worker, they may also be experiencing transference in other relationships in their lives, and this needs to be addressed. Transference is a common occurrence for many clients and can be a useful tool in therapeutic treatment to develop both healthier relationships and a productive relationship with the social worker.

Countertransference occurs when the social worker identifies the client with someone from the social worker's past. Social workers must work through countertransference issues while assisting the client in

recognizing and coping with transference situations. If social workers recognize countertransference, they may want to seek the assistance of a supervisor to work through countertransference issues. Transference and countertransference may be useful for the social worker and client to experience because they may impact other areas in the relationships of both.

Domestic, Intimate Partner, and Other Violence on the Helping Relationship

Any type of abuse in a client's life can impart symptoms of trauma to the client. These symptoms may be subtle in nature, or they may be relatively obvious to the social worker. Obvious indicators of abuse include physical marks, chronic muscular or stomach pain (as a result of trauma or stress), consistently dressing in high-coverage clothing, even in cases where it seems abnormal (such as a hot day), or particular body language when the abuser is in the room or attending a session. Most abusive relationships occur as a manifestation of dysfunctional power and control tactics. If the client is an abuser, it may be difficult for him or her to be guided by a social worker, as there may be an experience of a loss of control or power. Abuse victims may feel distrustful or fearful of the social worker and the helping relationship; they also may be uncomfortable discussing their abuser in a negative light. This can be a setback to the intervention process, and social workers may need to spend extra time fostering rapport and building a trusting relationship with these types of clients.

Diversity in the Social Worker-Client Relationship

Attitudes and Beliefs
Social workers should be culturally aware in their attitudes and beliefs. This requires a keen awareness of their own cultural background and gaining awareness of any personal biases, stereotypes, and values that they hold. Practitioners should also accept different worldviews, be sensitive to differences, and refer minority clients to a practitioner from the client's culture when it would benefit the client.

Knowledge
Practitioners should have the appropriate knowledge of different cultures. Specifically, practitioners must understand the client's culture and should not jump to conclusions about the client's way of being. Throughout their careers, social workers should be willing to gain a greater depth of knowledge of various cultural groups and update this knowledge as necessary. This includes understanding how issues like racism, sexism, and homophobia can negatively affect minority clients. Practitioners should understand how different therapeutic theories carry values that may be detrimental for some clients. Social workers should also understand how institutional barriers can affect the willingness of minority clients to use mental health services.

Cultural Skills
Social workers should be well-versed in cultural skills. They must be able to apply interviewing and counseling techniques with clients and should be able to employ specialized skills and interventions that might be effective with specific minority populations. Practitioners should be able to communicate effectively and understand the verbal and nonverbal language of a client. They also should take a systematic perspective in their practice, work collaboratively with community leaders, and advocate for clients when it's in their best interests.

When working with clients from diverse backgrounds, practitioners should be able to shift their professional strategies. Below are techniques and strategies social workers should keep in mind when working with clients of different cultures.

183

<u>Various Cultural and Racial Backgrounds</u>

- Have appropriate attitudes and beliefs, gain knowledge about the client's background, and learn new skills as needed.

- Encourage the client to speak in his or her native language and arrange for an interpreter when necessary.

- Assess the client's cultural identity and how important it is to the client.

- Check accuracy of any interpretations of the client's nonverbal cues.

- Make use of alternate modes of communication, such as writing, typing, translation services, and the use of art.

- Assess the impact of sociopolitical issues on the client.

- Encourage the client to bring culturally significant and personally relevant items.

- Vary the helping environment to make it conducive to effective work with the client.

<u>Various Religious Backgrounds</u>

- Determine the client's religious background in the beginning sessions.
- Check personal biases and gain information about the client's religion.
- Ask the client how important religion is in his or her life.
- Assess the client's level of faith development.
- Avoid making assumptions about the religion.
- Become familiar with the client's religious beliefs, important holidays, and faith traditions.
- Understand that religion can deeply affect the client unconsciously.

Client's Developmental Level on the Social Worker-Client Relationship

A client's development level will vary from client to client, and it may even vary for the same client over the full course of an intervention. Therefore, the social worker should make no assumptions about the client's ability to cope, the way the intervention will be accepted and utilized, or any other aspect of the working relationship. These factors should be assessed upon intake and at regular intervals thereafter, the frequency of which may vary on a case-by-case basis. Assessments should holistically take into account the client development, including age, psychological factors, emotional factors, social factors, acute personal conditions (such as an impending divorce or recent refugee status) that may temporarily impact the client's functioning, and any other scope of development that may be appropriate for the client's need. For example, a client who has a history of violent behavior and a history of playing physical sports with extreme contact may find it beneficial to undergo neurological development assessments. By viewing the client through a holistic perspective, social workers can ensure interventions are appropriate across all domains of development; if so, the interventions are more likely to be effective and received positively by the client.

Social Worker Self-Care Principles and Techniques

Due to the highly emotional, interpersonal, and empathic demands of the social work field, social workers must employ and sustain self-care practices to protect their personal health. Without self-care,

social workers are highly susceptible to burnout and compassion fatigue, two risks that occur when working in a field that often provides exposure to disheartening humanitarian situations, abusive intrapersonal relationships, and cases that, for bureaucratic or personal reasons, take a long time to resolve. Unchecked, these experiences can lead the social worker to feel detached from work and hopeless toward cases, or to consistently experience the ill effects of chronic stress. Self-care practices may include establishing boundaries between one's work and personal life, having a regular meditation practice or other mental exercises that are shown to soothe the nervous system, eating a healthy diet and engaging in regular physical exercise (as these behaviors decrease inflammation in the body and reduce stress hormones), and having a trustworthy support system of friends and colleagues. Introspective exercises, such as daily journaling, can provide the social worker with a better understanding of which activities bring stress to their lives and which activities bring peace. By knowing these, the social worker can bridge the gap to reduce stress in areas they can control (such as setting a clear cut-off time for answering emails, or scheduling personal activities that bring them joy). They can adopt healthy coping mechanisms for the areas in which they are unable to control factors that might contribute to their stress (such as an emotional case or external funding issues).

Burnout, Secondary Trauma, and Compassion Fatigue

Sometimes it may be necessary to seek supervision if the social worker experiences burnout, secondary trauma, compassion fatigue, countertransference or the inability to develop a trusting relationship with the client. Although the focus is often on the supervisor's role of ensuring that clients are provided with ethical services by training and evaluating the supervisee, the supervisee's role in supervision is not passive. The social worker should fully engage in the process of supervision and use this relationship to grow and improve. In order to do that, the supervisee must be willing to discuss areas of ethical or legal concern that have arisen in their interactions with clients. They must also be ready to honestly address their own struggles and identify their learning needs, and seek the help and advice of the supervisor. This can only happen effectively through genuine self-assessment, which flows from a real desire to become a better social worker. The process of self-assessment in supervision can help them see any biases or weaknesses that may be holding them back from fully meeting their clients' needs. If the social worker is defensive or resistant to the supervisory relationship, then they will make little progress.

Factors to consider when receiving feedback during supervision/consultation:

- Social workers can benefit from feedback during supervision or consultation, especially with difficult clients/cases or at significant times in treatment, such as termination.

- When discussing cases, client confidentiality should be protected as much as possible, and client consent to release information should be acquired.

Impairment is a professional issue that should be addressed swiftly. Impairment occurs when a social worker's personal problems (e.g., mental health conditions, difficult life circumstances, or alcohol/drug use) have an impact upon their practice. The Code of Ethics states that social workers should seek to rectify their impairment by consulting with colleagues or supervisors, seeking their own treatment, limiting work, and/or terminating client relationships until the impairment has been fully addressed. In the event that a colleague is suffering from some sort of impairment, a social worker should address the concern with the colleague and encourage the colleague to rectify the issue. If the issue continues without proper attention, the social worker should go through appropriate channels to seek additional help for the colleague and to prevent consequences to clients. The same is true if the social worker feels there has been unethical behavior by a colleague. The social worker should discuss the behavior with the colleague and possibly with a supervisor. If a colleague is unfairly accused of unethical behavior, assisting the colleague in rectifying the situation is the best course of action.

Safe and Positive Work Environment

Social workers have an emotionally and physically taxing job; therefore, a safe and positive work environment is crucial in supporting social workers in their jobs and in doing their best work. A safe and positive work environment is characterized by processes that foster work-life balance, good boundaries between work and personal life, a culture of respect and ethical behavior toward colleagues and subordinates, just compensation for tasks performed, support for the social worker's personal and professional development, and a zero-tolerance policy for threats, violence, harassment, or bullying in the workplace. Additionally, a documented process that allows social workers to express when they feel unsafe (whether with coworkers or with clients) and established avenues for resolution are other ways to ensure a positive and safe work environment. Social workers should feel comfortable employing these avenues without fear of consequences from colleagues or supervisors. Finally, leadership should ensure their workers feel comfortable communicating their professional goals, successes, and obstacles; leadership should also provide opportunities that support professional goal achievement or resolution to overcome obstacles.

Professional Objectivity in the Social Worker-Client Relationship

While social workers should show empathy toward a client, it is also important that they remain objective and do not become enmeshed in the social worker/client relationship. Enmeshment occurs when the social worker is overly involved with the client's emotional life, and it may harm the client. Social workers must demonstrate professional objectivity with the client to avoid countertransference, which occurs when a social worker redirects their emotions onto the client. In addition, social workers can engage in professional objectivity by recognizing that the client is the party who needs to do the majority of the work in the relationship. It is difficult to maintain professional objectivity when enmeshment occurs, and social workers should seek supervision if they cannot maintain professional objectivity with the client.

Social workers must also ensure that they're competent to fulfill any job that they are assigned before practicing with clients. This includes being a life-long learner and reviewing relevant research literature related to their therapeutic approaches and the clients they serve. Practitioners should also use evidence-based practices in their work with clients whenever possible. Practitioners should behave in morally responsible ways, advocate for their clients when they are faced with discriminatory practices or policies, practice self-care to ensure that they are effective in their work, and should only work within the scope of their practice.

The Social Worker's Own Values and Beliefs on the Social Worker-Client Relationship

Social work as a profession prides itself on practitioners putting personal values aside, even when those values conflict with client values. Social workers must not engage in discriminatory practices or condone the discriminatory practices of others. For example, if a social worker is personally uncomfortable with same-sex relationships, but has a gay or lesbia client, the social worker will need to take steps to evaluate their own values and beliefs. The social worker must ensure that personal feelings are put aside in order to appropriately meet the client's needs. Self-awareness is a vital part of ensuring that one's personal values and beliefs do not intrude on the social worker/client relationship. It may be necessary

to seek consultation from a supervisor or colleague in situations where one's personal values or beliefs are in conflict with the client and when those feelings cannot be resolved. In extreme cases where consultation and self-reflection cannot remedy the conflict, termination of the social worker/client relationship and referral to another therapist may be necessary.

Time Management Approaches

Social workers can effectively manage their time through a number of organizational methods. These may include daily prioritization of tasks for the day (such as urgent tasks versus tasks that can wait until the next day), ensuring that all meeting and phone calls with colleagues are scheduled with objectives in mind (such as with the use of a meeting agenda), breaking more tedious tasks into chunks, and planning in a way that works best for one's personality. For example, one person may enjoy making weekly color-coded schedules of tasks with gaps available throughout the week for unexpected assignments that come up; another may prefer to manage tasks daily in a simple list style, with flexible room built in per day. While no schedule can be absolutely rigid, as unforeseen circumstances are guaranteed to arise from time to time, a schedule that is guarded and respected by the social worker fosters effective time management. It is important to decline non-urgent tasks or responsibilities if one's schedule is booked, while ensuring there is space in one's schedule to assist with unanticipated emergencies.

Transference and Countertransference Within Supervisory Relationships

Transference and countertransference are used to describe how projections occur in an interactive relationship. Transference occurs when supervisees project certain attitudes, values, beliefs, or feelings onto their supervisors; countertransference occurs when supervisors project certain attitudes, values, beliefs, or feelings onto their supervisees. Depending on the intensity or type of projections that take place, transference and countertransference experiences may impact the boundaries, mentoring relationship, or professional collaboration that takes place between supervisors and supervisees. Transference and countertransference experiences may also occur as a result of temporary situations the supervisor or supervisee find themselves in, and interactions that occur afterward may have a long-lasting impact. For example, a supervisee may have heard from a colleague a long, emotional story about harassment from another supervisor. Upon meeting with their personal supervisor, the supervisee may project irrational feelings of anger, fear, or resentment on the supervisor for the rest of their working relationship. Additionally, supervisors must take care to examine supervisees when they are working with clients. Transference and countertransference can take place unexpectedly between social workers and their clients, and it can have similar impacts on the intervention process. Finally, overly positive transference and countertransference experiences can be somewhat problematic as well. They may unwittingly place one person on a pedestal, result in an insincere mentoring relationship, or cause feelings of disillusionment in supervisees when they see their supervisors make an error.

Transference and countertransference experiences can be minimized by openly discussing their potential in the beginning of a professional relationship. By discussing the fact that both parties are vulnerable to this experience, both parties can become more self-aware and reflective about occurrences and how to handle them. This sets the stage for professional and collaborative growth, transparency, and effective communication.

Social Worker's Own Values and Beliefs on Interdisciplinary Collaboration

Reflecting on one's personal values and beliefs in order to maintain objectivity and reduce biases when providing treatment for clients is a fundamental component of the NASW's Code of Ethics. Providing treatment as part of an interdisciplinary collaboration (such as part of a team consisting of medical professionals, allied health workers, financial experts, legal experts, and other professionals that support a client) is becoming more common in the field of social work. It can be difficult to manage all competing interests, as each professional on a collaborative team will bring a different perspective with different ideas for the most effective treatment. While a social worker may focus primarily on psychosocial factors that influence a client's life, a doctor may focus more on the client's physical health, and a financial expert may focus on providing the client with better financial resources. Therefore, working in collaborative groups requires keeping the client's desired outcomes for the intervention as the primary goal of the interdisciplinary team. Documenting the client's goals and mapping out each professional's objectives can help mitigate the effects of professional and personal biases. Additionally, a documented plan can help establish clear job roles for each professional so that a single set of values does not take over the full scope of the intervention. When interdisciplinary collaboration accounts for these factors, the benefits of providing the client with multiple skillsets and perspectives can be tremendous.

Practice Questions

1. The NASW Code of Ethics has six core purposes. Which of the following choices are included in those core purposes?

   I. To provide the rules and standards that social workers can use to evaluate the conduct of others in the profession

   II. To help identify information that social workers should take under advisement when ethical conflicts may exist or when an ethical dilemma presents itself

   III. To inform new social workers about core issues relating to the mission of social work and to the ethical standards of the field

   IV. To relate the vision of social work in a standard way throughout the profession

   V. To establish the consequences of violating the ethical standards of social work

   VI. To ensure that collaborating professions are aware of the expectations to which social workers are held

   a. I, II, and III only
   b. I, IV, and V only
   c. II, III, and VI only
   d. III, IV, and VI only

2. Claudia is coming to therapy for the first time. She meets her therapist, Susan, a licensed clinical social worker, and Susan tells her what she can expect from treatment. Claudia says that she understands the process of therapy, as well as the risks, and that she is excited to begin. Susan makes a note of their discussion and begins her assessment. Has Susan satisfied the informed consent requirement, and why or why not?
   a. Yes. Susan discussed the process and risks of therapy, and the client agreed.
   b. No. Susan didn't ask Claudia if she understood everything fully.
   c. No. Susan did not have Claudia sign a consent form.
   d. Yes. Susan made a note that Claudia agreed as part of her documentation.

3. Susan's husband is employed in the IT sector and is looking for a new job. Susan's client, Claudia, mentions during their therapy session that her husband is an IT recruiter. At the end of their session, Susan asks Claudia for her husband's contact information. She says she would like her husband to reach out to Claudia's husband to find a better IT job. What boundary issue does this represent?
   a. Dependency
   b. Personal gain
   c. Dual relationship
   d. Altruism

4. Which of the following statements regarding the three stages of the prevention-focused service distribution model of social work is incorrect?
   a. The primary prevention stage involves addressing potential causes and getting rid of the problem's root cause.
   b. The problem occurs prior to the primary prevention stage.
   c. The secondary prevention stage involves actions that attempt to stop the problem before they spread and cause further harm.
   d. Actions in the tertiary stage are designed to decrease the problem's severity through remedial service provisions, which decrease the problem's lasting effects and duration.

5. What are the components of an ethical dilemma?
   a. Conflicting values; the social worker must decide between different courses of action; the social worker may have to terminate with the client.
   b. Ethical principles are at odds; the social worker can either make a decision or not; the situation is troubling to the social worker.
   c. Different courses of action exist; ethical principles are at odds; the social worker can either make a decision or not.
   d. The social worker must make a decision; different courses of action exist; no matter what choice of action is made, an ethical ideal will be compromised.

6. There are steps to resolving an ethical dilemma that have been outlined by the NASW Code of Ethics. What is the correct order of these steps?
   a. Consider, Specify, Rank, Establish, Implement, and Enforce
   b. Consider, Specify, Rank, Establish, Implement, and Reflect
   c. Determine, Identify, Rank, Develop, Implement, and Reflect
   d. Determine, Identify, Rank, Develop, Implement, and Enforce

7. Which of the following statements regarding the focus of the social work profession is false?
   a. It is to provide care and improve society.
   b. It is to define and explain existing problems in individuals and society at large.
   c. It involves incorporating knowledge and skills in other fields such as sociology, philosophy, law, and psychology.
   d. It involves distinguishing between and catering to social and individual morality and advocating when the absence of morality creates social injustice.

8. Janelle is a therapist at a nonprofit agency, and she is supervised by Susan, who meets with the executive director each month to alert her of any issues. Janelle has been seeing Brad for over a year for individual therapy. Brad wanted to focus on marital issues, but his wife refused to join him, telling him the issues in their marriage were because of his own personal problems. Brad told Janelle he wanted to improve himself to be a better husband. Last week, Brad's wife moved out and filed for divorce. She told him he had not improved himself during the last year of therapy. Brad believes this is Janelle's fault and has filed a malpractice lawsuit against Janelle. Legally, could Brad do anything else regarding malpractice?
   a. No. You can't sue someone because your wife left you.
   b. Yes. Brad could also file suit against Janelle's supervisor and go up the chain of command, naming even the executive director in the lawsuit.
   c. Yes. Brad can also file suit against Janelle's direct supervisor.
   d. No. Brad can only sue Janelle, because she was his therapist.

9. Brad has filed his malpractice lawsuit against his therapist, Janelle. The agency for which Janelle works has liability insurance. What options are available to social workers like Janelle, to protect them from malpractice lawsuits such as this one?

    a. If a social worker's agency has liability insurance, the social worker is covered by the agency insurance.

    b. A social worker needs their own liability insurance, because the agency insurance will only cover supervisors and the director.

    c. If the informed consent document states that the client holds the therapist harmless, then the therapist is protected from claims of malpractice.

    d. It is good practice to have personal liability insurance even if the agency one works for also has liability insurance.

10. Professional values for social workers focus on all but which of the following main values?

    a. Employing a scientifically sound solution-based model for clients' problems

    b. Preserving the general human rights of those they serve

    c. Preserving and advocating for social justice

    d. Maintaining the strong moral base of the profession

11. Client information is protected by confidentiality. However, in the instance where a client makes a threat against another individual during treatment, the social worker is required to warn the individual, thus breaking confidentiality. What court case established the duty to warn?

    a. Tarasoff vs. Regents of University of California

    b. Regents of University of California vs. Bakke

    c. Blonder-Tongue vs. University of Illinois

    d. Fisher vs. University of Texas

12. When required by law to disclose confidential information about a client, the social worker should always discuss the disclosure with the client before the disclosure occurs. Is this true or false? Why?

    a. False. At the time of the informed consent, the client should have been told about legal requirements that cause the social worker to break confidentiality, and therefore, the social worker never needs to discuss a specific disclosure with the client.

    b. True. The social worker must get the client to sign a new informed consent form stating that the client understands the disclosure will be made.

    c. False. The social worker should assess any threat to their personal safety, or the safety of others, and should only discuss the disclosure with the client if no one appears to be at risk of harm.

    d. True. The social worker has a duty to tell the client that a disclosure is being made and that confidentiality is being broken.

13. Which of the following is true regarding the difference between the Ethical Theory and Decision Making Period and the Ethical Standards and Risk Management Period of the social work ethics evolution?

a. The Ethical Standards and Risk Management Period preceded the Ethical Theory and Decision Making Period.

b. The Ethical Standards and Risk Management Period focused on the potential for abuse in the profession and how to avoid such abuse, malpractice, and litigation issues.

c. The Ethical Theory and Decision Making Period focused on the relationship between applying the Code of Ethics and managing the risk of malpractice and legal liability.

d. During the Ethical Standards and Risk Management Period, the National Association of Social Workers updated the Code of Ethics to include a summary of the core values and mission of social work.

14. Jane works in an agency providing individual therapy. She has an office that she shares with another social worker. Their office door has a lock on it, and they both have a key to the office. Jane keeps her records in a filing cabinet under her desk and does not lock it because her office door is always locked, even if she is in the building. Is Jane providing enough security for her records?

a. No. Even though Jane keeps her office locked, she should still lock her filing cabinet.

b. Yes. If Jane's office is locked, she is doing her part to keep her records secure.

c. Yes. Because Jane and her office mate work for the same agency, the office mate is not a risk.

d. No. Jane should advocate for records to be kept in a single location in the agency with a separate locked door.

15. Due to legal requirements, which of the following is the most important element when a social worker is dealing with record requests and disclosures of confidential information?

a. Follow through

b. Documentation

c. Consultation with colleagues and supervisors

d. Informed consent

16. Thomas is a social worker that has been working with client Karen for the past year. He has been implementing strengths-based assessments, life and vocational skills coaching, and connecting Karen with various community social groups such as the adult local softball team. The strategies that Tom is employing relate to which of the following core values of the social work field?

a. Competence

b. Service

c. Human dignity

d. Human relationships

17. Amy is a social worker for a home health company. She has been visiting her seventy-five-year-old client, Sofia, for about six months. Lately, Sofia's daughter has seemed on edge when Amy is visiting. As Amy approached the house for her most recent visit, she could hear Sofia's daughter yelling at her, along with what she believed to be sounds of Sofia being hit. Amy then observed Sofia holding her arm and saw red marks when Sofia moved her hand. Amy attempted to speak to Sofia about her home life, but Sofia simply shook her head "no." Amy also noticed that Sofia has lost some weight over the last couple of months. Amy has concerns about Sofia's well-being. What should Amy's course of action be?
   a. Amy should continue to observe Sofia and make notes regarding what she sees.
   b. Amy should make a report to Adult Protective Services.
   c. Amy should look at the nursing notes to find out what other health care professionals have observed.
   d. Amy should drop in more often to see if she can catch Sofia's daughter in the act.

18. Which of the following is NOT one of the five core values of the social work profession?
   a. Independence
   b. Dignity and worth of the person
   c. Importance of human relationships
   d. Competence

19. Ethically, social workers are required to maintain confidentiality when working with clients. Legally, HIPAA requires that social workers keep psychotherapy notes confidential. What does HIPAA stand for?
   a. Health Information Personal Acceptability Act
   b. Health Insurance Personal Acceptability Act
   c. Health Information Perpetuating Accountability Act
   d. Health Insurance Portability and Accountability Act

20. Due to mandated reporting laws, social workers must report any suspected abuse or neglect. Those who fail to report can be held to both civil and criminal lawsuits. Social workers cannot be held responsible for reports made in which of the following?
   a. Earnest
   b. Good faith
   c. Concern
   d. Private

21. Jane is working with a client whose goals are based on his personal values. Jane finds her own values in direct conflict with the client's values. Jane has tried to self-reflect and work through this issue, but she finds herself having a harder time putting her own values aside each session. What should Jane's next step be?
   a. Termination
   b. Consultation
   c. Speaking to the client about the conflict she is having
   d. Personal exploration

22. Social workers strive to consider cultural impact on individual values. How should cultural differences and values be addressed?
    a. Cultural values and differences should be pointed out so that the client knows the social worker is aware of them.
    b. Cultural values and differences should be learned by the social worker and worked around when issues arise.
    c. Cultural values and differences should be learned by the social worker and used as strengths and to empower change.
    d. Cultural values and differences should be compared to the greater society to find similarities.

23. Social workers have a set of core values that shape the profession. One of these values is service. What does this mean for a social worker?
    a. Service means that the social worker will address social problems and help those in need. Service also means that social workers will provide pro bono or volunteer work when not at a paid position.
    b. Service means that the social worker will provide the best client service possible and always look for ways to improve.
    c. Service means that the social worker will try to help as many people as possible, often working in more than one position.
    d. Service means having pride in how social workers serve their clientele.

24. The field of social work has a set of core goals for the profession. What are these core goals?
    I. Improve social function
    II. Consult with colleagues
    III. Resolve problems
    IV. Put the client first
    V. Achieve desired change
    VI. Meet self-defined goals
    VII. Challenge wrongs
    VIII. Make a difference

    a. II, IV, VII, and VIII only
    b. I, II, IV, and VII only
    c. III, IV, VI, and VII only
    d. I, III, V, and VI only

25. What is it called when a social worker's own mental health issues, such as anxiety or depression, begin to interfere with their ability to serve their clients?
    a. Self-awareness
    b. Interference
    c. Impairment
    d. Transference

26. A client's right to live life per their own values and beliefs is supported by social workers in a way that it is not by other professions. What is this right called?
    a. Personal responsibility
    b. Self-determination
    c. Self-guided
    d. Self-rule

27. Which of the following is true regarding sexual relationships between social workers and colleagues or co-workers?

    a. They are not permissible under any circumstance.
    b. They are permissible if the colleague is not at the same agency.
    c. They are not permissible unless the social worker was in the relationship prior to employment.
    d. They are permissible except when one person is in position of authority over the other.

28. Which of the following statements are true regarding the morality period of social work?

    I. It occurred during the late 19th to early 20th century.
    II. It focused on the morality of clients rather than the ethics of social workers.
    III. The goal was to build the ethics of individuals in poverty.
    IV. Controversial issues like economic hardship, substance abuse, and race relations were at the forefront.

    a. I, II, III
    b. I, II, IV
    c. I, III, IV
    d. II, III, IV

29. At every level of professional development, it is important to continually participate in education opportunities. Why is this important to the values of social work?

    a. Continuing education is necessary to maintain a level of competence in expertise that the social worker practices.
    b. Continuing education is required to maintain licensure, and licensure ensures that the social worker is regarded as a capable professional.
    c. Conferences and learning situations provide networking opportunities that can aid in interdisciplinary collaboration.
    d. Education is an ongoing personal journey.

30. Alex is a social worker in the Emergency Room where Lucas, who is homeless, frequently visits for ailments of varying severity. The Emergency Room staff advises Alex that he must find somewhere for Lucas to go. Alex speaks at length with Lucas, who states that he has no friends or family with whom he is in contact. Lucas tells Alex that he has lived at shelters before and that he doesn't like the rules that must be followed. Lucas declines a bed at the local shelter. Alex discusses this with Lucas' doctor and nurse and both become adamant that Lucas must go to a shelter; sleeping on the street is not acceptable. Alex facilitates a discussion between medical personnel and Lucas in which Lucas maintains that he does not intend to go to a shelter. Eventually, Alex asks to speak privately with the medical personnel, and he advocates strongly on Lucas' behalf, stating that Lucas has made his decision. Was Alex's course of action correct?

    a. No. If the doctor felt that a shelter was necessary, then Alex's responsibility was to listen to the doctor and to convince Lucas to go to the shelter.
    b. Yes. Having a private conversation with the medical staff was the best solution, so that Lucas didn't hear the discussion.
    c. Yes. By advocating on Lucas' behalf, Alex was protecting his right to self-determination.
    d. No. Alex should have asked to call Lucas' relatives on his behalf to convince them to take him in.

31. All but which of the following are suggested industry strategies for setting and maintaining professional boundaries in social work?
    a. Limiting self-disclosure about personal life unless it directly relates to the client's goals
    b. Establishing clear agreements with clients during the initial sessions about the dynamics of the client-practitioner relationship
    c. Fostering positive dual relationships with clients to further support their emotional needs
    d. Exercising caution regarding the use of social media within the professional practice

32. Which of the following best describes what is meant by value suspension?
    a. The social worker acknowledging and controlling for his or her personal values in social work practice.
    b. The client evaluating and choosing to adopt one value system over another.
    c. The client increasing his or her exposure to different values, beliefs, and morals as he or she gets older.
    d. The client challenging someone else's existing values when engaging in a new relationship with that person.

33. What is the purpose of the emphasis on understanding systems within the field of social work?
    a. To help increase the amount of field experience that a social work student participates in because only so much can be learned in the classroom.
    b. To better understand a client's place in society so that the social worker can help increase social understanding and make connections.
    c. To learn about diversity within family and social systems so that all clients receive unbiased and respectful care.
    d. To help the social worker advocate for clients on the local, state, and national levels by understanding the programs available.

34. Which of the following terms is used to describe the way in which a client aligns his or her ego for the therapeutic relationship and how much the ego is or is not joined with the social worker's ego?
    a. Empathy
    b. Cognitive complexity
    c. Psychological adjustment
    d. Therapeutic alliance

35. Which of the following are factors in the RESPECTFUL Counseling Model?
    I. Family history
    II. Sexual orientation and identity
    III. Career or vocation
    IV. Ethnic and racial identity

    a. I, II, III
    b. I, II, IV
    c. II, IV
    d. I, II, III, IV

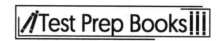

36. Bioethical issues in social work practice may include all but which of the following?
    a. Sustainable farming and recycling practices
    b. Pregnancy and fetal rights
    c. Juvenile rights to medical treatment
    d. End-of-life issues

37. When working in an interdisciplinary collaboration, what should be kept in mind to ensure a seamless working relationship?
    a. Educate, Communicate, Experience, Skill levels, Conflict
    b. Advocate, Understanding, Common Ground, Differences, Conflict
    c. Advocate, Communicate, Experience, Skill levels, Closure
    d. Educate, Understanding, Common Ground, Differences, Closure

38. Interdisciplinary collaboration is commonplace in social work. To avoid conflict, there are steps that can be taken to promote a smooth working relationship. The first step is to advocate. What does this mean within the context of interdisciplinary collaboration?
    a. Educating team members about the role of the social worker
    b. Standing up for the social workers when other team members try to keep them from being heard
    c. Making sure everyone on the team hears what the social workers have to say
    d. Asking team members to remember that everyone has strengths they bring to the table

Answer Explanations

1. A: The six core purposes of the NASW Code of Ethics are:

- To establish the core values on which the mission of social work is based

- To provide a set of ethical standards for social workers, as well as specific information regarding different ethical dilemmas

- To help identify information that social workers should take under advisement when ethical conflicts may exist or when an ethical dilemma presents itself

- To provide standards that can be used by others to ensure accountability and responsibility by those in the profession

- To inform new social workers about core issues relating to the mission of social work and to the ethical standards of the field

- To provide the rules and standards that social workers can use to evaluate the conduct of others in the profession

2. C: No, informed consent has not been satisfied. Susan did not have a document outlining what therapy would entail, including the risks and limitations. She also did not have Claudia sign such a document to become part of the chart. Documentation of informed consent protects both the client and the social worker.

3. B: Personal gain refers to instances where a social worker engages in activity with a client that results in a monetary (or otherwise valuable) benefit to the social worker. This could involve situations such as referring a client to a business owned by the social worker or a friend/family member of the social worker, selling something to a client, or even asking a client for professional suggestions.

4. B: Typically, the problem has not actually started to impact a person or group until the secondary prevention stage. In the primary prevention stage, the practitioner helps the client identify potential causes for a problem and get rid of the problem's root cause. While actions aiming to stop specific social problems before they spread and cause further harm occur in the secondary prevention stage, the tertiary prevention stage involves actions that try to decrease the problem's severity, lasting effects, and duration through remedial service provisions.

5. D: To have an ethical dilemma, three conditions must be met. The first is that the practitioner must make a decision. If the situation does not require that a decision be made, then there isn't an ethical dilemma. The second is that there are different decisions that could be made or different actions one could take. The third condition is that an ethical ideal will be conceded no matter what decision is made.

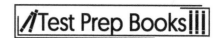

6. C: The steps to resolving an ethical dilemma are as follows:

- Determine: Is there an ethical conflict or dilemma?
- Identify: What are the core standards and values involved in the situation?
- Rank: Take the values and ethical principles and rank them in order of importance regarding the situation.
- Develop: Make a plan that correlates with the values and principles that were previously ranked as important to this situation. This may involve collaborating with colleagues or supervisors. When outlining the plan, identify any potential risks or adverse effects.
- Implement: Put the plan into motion taking care to use social work practice skills that allow for ultimate sensitivity.
- Reflect: Evaluate the ethical decision making process. How did all involved agencies and individuals fare? It is not uncommon for social workers to make use of ethical review committees or ethical consultations when facing dilemmas to gain assistance and perspective.

7. B: All professions, including social work, are built upon a foundation of values and guided by ethical codes. Rather than simply defining and explaining existing problems, the focus of the social work profession is providing care and improving society. As such, social workers must use and apply knowledge and skills from other fields, including sociology, philosophy, law, and psychology. Social workers should also distinguish between and cater to social and individual morality, recognize the interplay between these types of morality, and advocate when their absence creates social injustice.

8. B: During malpractice suits, the liability goes all the way up the chain of command. This means that not only the social worker at the heart of the lawsuit, but also any supervisors or persons above them, can be held liable and named in the lawsuit.

9. D: Although the agency has liability insurance, it's always best practice for a social worker to carry their own liability insurance. The liability insurance of the agency is going to protect the agency first and foremost. The social worker should always look out for their best interest in cases involving questions of malpractice or the risk of lawsuit.

10. A: Professional values for social workers focus on the general rights of those they serve, preserving and building social justice, and maintaining the strong moral base of the profession. While social workers should use scientifically sound practice and stay current with the latest in best practices through continuing education, a "solution-based" model, per se, is not necessarily appropriate in all situations for each client.

11. A: Tarasoff vs. Regents of University of California is the correct answer. In this 1976 case, the therapist failed to notify the intended victim of the threat of harm. After the client had stopped seeking treatment, he then attacked and killed Tarasoff, prompting her family to sue the University and therefore establishing the duty to warn. None of the other cases directly relate to duty to warn.

12. C: False. A social worker should always assess their own personal safety, as well as the safety of others, when deciding if a confidential disclosure should be discussed with the client. For example, a social worker is working with someone who has a history of violence toward women, and he discloses that he has been contemplating harming his neighbor who has turned down his advances. In this instance, it would be safer if the social worker didn't discuss the disclosure with the client. Given his history of violence, discussing the disclosure might put both the therapist and the neighbor at risk.

13. D: The Ethical Theory and Decision Making Period occurred in the 1970s and 1980s, preceding the Ethical Standards and Risk Management Period of the 1990s. Choices *B* and *C* reversed the focus of each period, but it is true as stated in Choice *D* that the national Association of Social Workers updated the Code of Ethics during the Ethical Standards and Risk Management Period. Also during this time, there was a focus on the development of risk management strategies to protect clients and social workers from ethical violations within the field.

14. A: Records must be kept in a secure and locked environment. Even though the office is always locked, a second form of security would be best. It is important to remember that cleaning staff or other individuals might have access to the office when neither social worker is there.

15. B: Documentation. Documentation is the social worker's best friend. If it isn't documented, it didn't happen. Social workers deal with very sensitive situations, some of which end up in a court of law. If there is no documentation that something happened, there is no proof. Documenting any requests from clients—as well as whether those were honored and why or why not—is just as important as what happens during sessions.

16. C: Human dignity relates to an awareness of the value of each client and the intention to help each client improve their well-being and effectiveness at interacting with society. The strategies that Tom is using with Karen will help her assess her current strengths and weaknesses and community involvement and improve upon these so that she can become a healthier, more integrated member of society. Human relationship work strives to help clients understand and remove barriers in their current relationships to better meet personal goals. The core value of service centers around providing services to disadvantaged individuals and working to solve the causes of such disadvantage. Tom is acting with competence, performing duties that correspond to his training and experience, but this is not the specific value addressed with Karen's treatment.

17. B: Amy should make a report to Adult Protective Services. Amy's job is not to prove or disprove that abuse or neglect is occurring; that is the job of Adult Protective Services. Amy has enough information to be concerned that something is not right about the situation and that Sofia may not be safe. A report should be made. Recall that mandatory reporting laws require social workers, and other professionals, to report any suspected abuse or neglect. This means that any professional who has a suspicion of abuse or neglect of a child or a vulnerable adult must legally make a report to either Child Protective Services or Adult Protective Services.

18. A: The five core values are: service, dignity and worth of the person, importance of human relationships, integrity, and competence.

19. D: HIPAA refers to the Health Insurance Portability and Accountability Act of 1996. HIPAA establishes that psychotherapy notes must be kept confidential by mental health professionals. This includes notes made during individual or group sessions, notes regarding conversations, notes pertaining to disclosures, and even notes that analyze situations involving the client.

20. B: Good faith means that the social worker has a reasonable suspicion and has no alternative reasons for reporting other than concern.

21. B: If Jane has been unable to rectify the situation through self-assessment, she should then turn to consultation with colleagues regarding her values conflict. If the consultation proves ineffective, she may ultimately need to consider termination and referring the client to another social worker. Social work as a profession prides itself on practitioners putting personal values aside, even when those values conflict with client values. Social workers must not engage in discriminatory practices or condone the discriminatory practices of others.

22. C: Cultural values and beliefs should be researched and learned when working with clients from a different culture. These values should then be used as strengths during goal development to aid the client in making the changes they desire.

23. A: Service means addressing social problems. This refers both to individual problems and problems in the broader society. Social workers are encouraged to provide some services pro bono to give back to society and to help those who otherwise could not afford services. It also means that social workers should volunteer in some aspect outside of their paying positions.

24. D: Social workers operate from the values and goals that have been established for the profession. The core goals of social work are to improve social function, to resolve problems, to achieve desired change, and to meet self-defined goals. While some of these goals regard clients, they also apply to social workers themselves.

25. C: Issues involving a social worker's personal mental health are considered a form of impairment. Alcohol and drug addiction also fall into this category. With any issues regarding professional impairment, the social worker should seek consultation from colleagues and supervisors. It may be necessary to lessen the workload, and possibly to terminate some client relationships and make referrals.

26. B: Self-determination refers to everyone's right to live the life they choose. This doesn't mean that the choices made and life lived will be relatable or understood by others. Social workers strive to preserve self-determination, to allow clients to decide their own goals, and to assist clients in achieving those goals.

27. D: Sexual relationships between colleagues are permitted by the Code of Ethics. The only exception is that a sexual relationship between a supervisor and supervisee is not permissible because of the obvious authority and power that one individual has over the other.

28. A: Over time, social work values and ethics have evolved in five broad stages: the Morality Period, the Values Period, the Ethical Theory and Decision Making Period, the Ethical Standards and Risk Management Period, and the Digital Period. The Morality Period occurred during the late nineteenth to early twentieth century. During this time, practitioners were concerned with the morality of clients, not the ethics of social workers. The goal of the field at the time was to build the ethics of individuals in poverty so they could get their lives on the right track. As the period progressed, the focus shifted to the need for significant social reforms to reduce the impact of social problems such as poverty, unemployment, and inadequate housing, health care, sanitation, and education. It was during the Values Period that discussion covered controversial issues like economic hardship, substance use, and race relations.

29. A: Competence is the reason that social workers need to be continually educated. This is important so that the social worker can provide the services in which they are trained and remain up-to-date on research and practice. While the other answers may be true, they are not the strategy specifically implicated for being an effective social worker.

30. C: Alex was correct in protecting Lucas' right to self-determination. Lucas had made it clear several times that he had tried going to a shelter in the past and did not like the restrictions. He preferred a freer life that allowed him permission to do as he pleased. If Lucas had been suffering from some sort of medical issue that would make him unsafe, then Alex would have needed to explain all the information to him so that he understood his choices. If Lucas still decided to avoid the shelter, then that would have been his right. Social workers should remember that clients have a right to lead their lives as they see fit, making their own decisions based on their values. Issues may arise when the values of clients do not align with how others believe clients should behave or live. Social workers must advocate on the behalf of clients with other professionals to ensure that their values are at the core of any plan. It is the job of the social worker to work with the client to aid in goal creation and identification that is congruent to the client's values.

31. C: Dual relationships are clearly outlined in the NASW Code of Ethics. The Code of Ethics states that social workers should not engage in dual relationships with clients or former clients in which exploitation of the client may occur. The Code of Ethics does recognize that there might be situations where dual relationships are unavoidable. For example, a social worker might have two jobs, one of which involves providing group therapy to survivors of sexual abuse. It is possible that a member of the aforementioned therapy group could become an employee or client at the social worker's second place of work. In these types of situations, the Code of Ethics suggests that the social worker establish clear boundaries that are sensitive to the client/former client. The other options listed are suggested strategies for maintaining professional boundaries, among others.

32. A: Value suspension is the process of the social worker acknowledging and controlling for his or her personal values in his or her social work practice, particularly in instances where their own moral codes, values, biases, and prejudices may differ from those of the client. To avoid conflict with the treatment he or she is providing to clients, the social worker should employ value suspension. Choice *B* describes a value conflict for the client, and can occur as a result of Choice *C*. Value conflicts may occur when someone makes new friends, engages in romantic relationships, joins a new community, attends a new school, or accepts a new job.

33. B: The field of social work places an emphasis on understanding systems because once the practitioner understands a client's place in society, then he or she can help increase the client's social understanding and make connections to help meet treatment goals. Understanding the client from an individual, family, and social system perspective sets the foundation for an understanding systems. The other choices describe other emphases in the field of social work, such as the emphasis on field experience, the emphasis on advocacy at the local, state, and national levels, and the emphasis on maintaining effectiveness in practice.

34. D: The therapeutic alliance, like the other choices listed, are strategies that social workers can employ to maintain effectiveness in practice. Therapeutic alliance refers to how the client aligns his or her ego for the therapeutic relationship and the degree to which his or her ego is—or is not—joined with social worker's ego or self. Choice *A*, empathy, refers to the therapist's ability to sense the client's feelings and communicate acceptance and understanding to the client. Choice *B*, cognitive complexity, refers to the social worker's ability to view an individual within both an individualistic and systemic

framework, to understand that knowledge is not fixed, and to remain open to feedback and different points of view. Psychological adjustment enables the social worker to identify and empathize with the client's own experience.

35. B: The RESPECTFUL Counseling Model suggests that practitioners pay careful attention to the following aspects of their clients because they may affect the client personally and the approach to working with the client: Religious and spiritual identity, Economic background, Sexual orientation and identity, Psychological development, Ethnic and racial identity, Chronological disposition, Trauma and other threats to personal well-being, Family history, Unique physical characteristics, and Language and location of residence. Career and vocation are not explicitly mentioned, although they can be factors that social workers should consider for certain clients. The "C" stands for chronological disposition or development.

36. A: Bioethical issues relate to areas regarding the society's responsibility for protecting the rights and values of human health and life. Social worker should familiarize themselves with bioethical issues through continuing education practices and reviewing relevant literature. Issues of sustainability, conservation, and the environment are not bioethical issues but those regarding prenatal and fetal rights, juvenile rights to healthcare, and end-of-life rights are some of the important topics that social workers may encounter.

37. B: The things to remember when working with an interdisciplinary collaboration are Advocate (educating team members about the role of the social worker), Understanding (striving to understand the other disciplines by asking questions about their roles, functions, and goals), Common Ground (attempting to find things in common that would contribute to better collaboration), Differences (recognizing that differences exist between disciplines and their goals and approaches), and Conflict (striving to approach conflict directly and with sensitivity and respect).

38. A: In this context, *advocate* means that the social worker will educate the rest of the team about the role of the social worker. Often the professional goals and vision of social work differs from that of other disciplines. The social worker should educate team members about this and attempt to gain understanding.

Dear ASWB Masters Test Taker,

We would like to start by thanking you for purchasing this study guide for your ASWB Masters exam. We hope that we exceeded your expectations.

Our goal in creating this study guide was to cover all of the topics that you will see on the test. We also strove to make our practice questions as similar as possible to what you will encounter on test day. With that being said, if you found something that you feel was not up to your standards, please send us an email and let us know.

We would also like to let you know about another book in our catalog that may interest you.

ASWB Clinical

This can be found on Amazon: amazon.com/dp/1628458208

ASWB Bachelors

This can be found on Amazon: amazon.com/dp/1628459336

We have study guides in a wide variety of fields. If the one you are looking for isn't listed above, then try searching for it on Amazon or send us an email.

Thanks Again and Happy Testing!
Product Development Team
info@studyguideteam.com

FREE Test Taking Tips DVD Offer

To help us better serve you, we have developed a Test Taking Tips DVD that we would like to give you for FREE. **This DVD covers world-class test taking tips that you can use to be even more successful when you are taking your test.**

All that we ask is that you email us your feedback about your study guide. Please let us know what you thought about it – whether that is good, bad or indifferent.

To get your **FREE Test Taking Tips DVD**, email freedvd@studyguideteam.com with "FREE DVD" in the subject line and the following information in the body of the email:

   a. The title of your study guide.

   b. Your product rating on a scale of 1-5, with 5 being the highest rating.

   c. Your feedback about the study guide. What did you think of it?

   d. Your full name and shipping address to send your free DVD.

If you have any questions or concerns, please don't hesitate to contact us at freedvd@studyguideteam.com.

Thanks again!

CPSIA information can be obtained
at www.ICGtesting.com
Printed in the USA
BVHW011543061220
595043BV00021B/1100